LEGEND
OF THE
WILDLINGS

BRITTNEY BREWER

To my mom, for pushing me to climb mountains, and catching me every time I fell.

To Miss. Reagan, for making me fall in love with writing.

To my husband, for believing in me when I didn't believe in myself, and listening to my incoherent rants.

To Ellie, my sunshine in the middle of a hurricane.

To my Papi, I will always be your Starshine.

To all of the children that left their windows open for
Peter Pan,
Waited for their letter to Hogwarts,
Searched for a closet to Narnia,
And waited for a satyr to take them to Camp Half-Blood…

Welcome to Ellesmere.

PLAYLIST

🟢 ⏸⏸⏸⏸⏸⏸⏸

Ireland- *Ellie Banke* ♥
Welcome to the Moors-*James Howard* ♥
Soldier, Poet, King-*The Oh Hellos* ♥
Love Grows- *Edison Lighthouse* ♥
Brother-*Kodaline* ♥
Mo Chroí-*Ajeet* ♥
Right Where You Left Me-*Taylor Swift* ♥
Monsters-*Ruelle* ♥
The Joker and the Queen-*Ed Sheeran* ♥
Ship in a Bottle-*Fin* ♥
Freedom Inside-*Christy Altomare* ♥
Welcome to Wonderland-*Anson Seabra* ♥
Till Forever Falls Apart- *Ashe, Finneas* ♥
Warriors- *Imagine Dragons* ♥
I Was An Island-*John-Allison Weiss* ♥
As the World Caves In-*Sarah Cothran* ♥
You Are Enough- *Sleeping At Last* ♥
Home- *Edward Sharpe and the Magnetic Zeros* ♥
Runaway- *Aurora* ♥
Lyfjaberg- *Wardruna* ♥

CONTENTS

PROLOGUE

The little girl giggled as her father spun her through the air and onto his shoulder, wisps of red hair flying across her face. The evening breeze enveloped them, and waves beat against the cliffs at their feet, melding with their laughter that echoed through the air and bounced off the stars burning brightly in the heavens.

"Again, Papa, again!" she squealed, clapping her tiny hands as she bounced on his shoulders and tugged at the collar of his coat.

"One more time." He laughed. "But the stars are getting tired, little love, and your mum will be wondering where we've gone."

The little girl giggled again, reaching up to the heavens and grasping at the air above her head. "Why do they twinkle like that?" she asked with a squint and a wrinkle of her nose.

"Old stories say that the stars are magic," he whispered, shifting his grip on her ankles, tracing his fingers against the night sky. "Some believe that there are people who can hear them talk—a special group of people that get their magic directly from the heavens."

More giggles erupted from the girl as she watched stars fall from the heavens, shooting back and forth like they were playing a game of tag. "You mean witches?" the little girl gasped, eyes wide as she stiffened.

"Aye." He nodded with a grin. "Special witches who can speak to the stars, who speak languages and stories long lost to humans."

The little girl hunched her back as she wrapped her tiny arms around her father's head, effectively blocking his eyes with her hands. "That sounds scary," she whispered. He pried her hands away from his face, and she wrapped her arms around his neck. "That doesn't sound like normal magic. I like the kind where funny animals talk." She rubbed her eyes with a yawn. "Especially the one about the big bear with the monocle."

Her father laughed gruffly as he held one of her tiny hands, reaching up to the sky again with his other. The stars twinkled and danced, creating pictures that glowed against the cloudless depths above them. "Sometimes the unknown is scary"—he nodded—"but we shouldn't fear the things we don't understand just because we don't understand them."

"You're not afraid of anything, Papa." She grinned as she squeezed his neck tighter.

"Everyone is afraid of something," he replied with a half smile, "but you have nothing to fear as long as I'm alive." He quickly pulled a small gold ring off his right hand and dug in his pocket, pulling a chain out and slipping it through the ring. He pulled the little girl off his shoulders, setting her gently on the ground, and slipped the chain over her head. "If there ever comes a day that I'm not here," he whispered, as tears pricked the corners of his eyes, "this will keep you close to me. This will keep you safe."

The little girl laughed as she held the ring in her hand, spinning it around one of her petite fingers. Her father lifted her into the air again, pressing her against his chest as they rocked back and forth with the sounds of the waves beating against the rocks.

"Promise you'll always be here?" she asked, as her eyes grew heavier, nestling her head under his chin.

"Of course, little love." He smiled, though it didn't quite reach his eyes.

"Forever?" the tiny girl asked, fingers clinging to the fabric of her father's coat as her eyes began to flutter closed.

"And always, Starshine," he whispered back, eyes twinkling along with the constellations reflecting off the inky water below the cliff.

CHAPTER I

HOME AGAIN

E mber's fingers twirled the end of her fiery red braid as she leaned her head against the fogged window. Her bedroom felt colder than normal as the rain clouds rolled closer in the distance, even with the sound of laughter echoing from the floor below her. She closed her eyes as she took a breath and clung to the memory. The older she got, the less she seemed to remember of her parents, but this singular memory seemed to play on a loop on the days she had to pack.

A worn suitcase lay open in the middle of the small room, still as empty as the night before when she had defeatedly pulled it out of the closet. Packing was fairly routine these days, but it certainly didn't make it any easier.

"I hope we can both see eye to eye on this," Mrs. Holloway had said to the agency through a forced smile that drifted through her cracked bedroom door last night after dinner. The fear on her foster mom's face was audible as she paced the length of the living room.

Foster *guardian*. Moms wouldn't give up on their little girls so easily and return them like a shirt that didn't fit.

Ember had wished she could hear the on-call receptionist

on the other end, but she at least knew what they must've been thinking.

That girl? Again?

She sat back against the cold wall without moving a muscle when Mrs. Holloway marched into her room and asked her, for the last time, if she had broken a marker or smuggled some paints from her neatly organized art drawer. For the tenth time since last night, her answer was no, showing her again how her palms and nails were clean.

Her guess was as good as Mrs. Holloway's as to why their award-winning schnauzer was purple from head to toe and on their way to a dog shampooer or the local parish, maybe both.

Ember had known it was coming, but no amount of trying to lose herself in her books or guesswork ever cushioned the blow. She surveyed the shadows of the barren bedroom she'd barely moved into, allowing the grief to wash over her before quickly wiping away the silent tears.

Crying never changed much of anything.

It started the same way every time—the family she was placed with would take to her immediately. They spent this weekend at parks and that weekend at zoos. Some took her to the theater to see the latest community play or on picnics to fly kites and play hide and seek. She ate warm dinners around tables filled with laughter. There was a faint prickle of hope, every time, that maybe this one would stick—that this family would see her for who she truly was. A lost girl in need of a home.

It didn't, of course. No matter how desperately she tried to wish it into existence, it never stuck. *She* never stuck.

These short-lived fairytales always ended the same, too. Locked doors. Hushed voices. Her first placement set the tone for the rest. She was six years old and had struggled to settle into her new life. Why was she sitting at a table of strangers when all she could think about was her parents? A flare of emotions had struck in the middle of dinner. All it took was one glance at the disgusting platter of peas being served, and Ember wailed until she thought she might pass out.

Her parents never would've served them to her, but her parents weren't here.

It wasn't until drops of water began hitting her already wet cheeks that she opened her eyes. The family's gazes flitted from her to the water pouring from the ceiling, all of their jaws collectively dropping, and Ember furrowed her brow as she looked up.

A rain cloud hovered above the table.

For the first time of dozens, she was gone the very next day, shuffled off to the group home that her puzzled first social worker dealt with, and a week later, she went to the next family who welcomed her with open arms. That one lasted two months.

Every home ended the same—rainstorms indoors, exploding vases every time her emotions warred inside her, family cats suddenly had three tails, and curious outdoor animals found their way into her bedroom window. She inevitably ended up banned from the rest of the home until the social worker could come to collect her, though there were a few times she was quietly placed in a shed or garage for a couple of nights, sworn to secrecy by the fear in the current family's eyes.

Over the years, she learned to keep her distance from the families who claimed to want her and kept her mouth shut, counting down the days until she never had to step foot in any place she was unwanted ever again.

She gripped the pendant swinging from her neck, clinging to the memories that accompanied it like a bottle of water in the middle of a drought. Doing her best to block out the Holloways' already improved tones and chipper voices floating up through the living room below, she gathered what few belongings she had and tossed them into the open suitcase. A few pairs of pants, a couple of decent looking shirts, her contacts, and all of the books she could squeeze in.

She wandered over to the other side of the room and leaned against the dresser pressed against the wall. She stared at herself in the mirror and grimaced, lavender eyes flecked with bright blue and ash staring back at her. Those were the icing on the disaster of the cake that was her life and gave every family she was with one more reason to fear her. The first family she had been placed with couldn't look her in the eye, forcing her to wear sunglasses when they left the house and always looking just past her head when they talked to her. Lavender eyes were strange, and strange felt wrong.

After she turned ten, she saved up all of her pocket change, took herself to the optometrist, and bought herself a pair of green contacts. It wasn't a permanent fix, but it kept the questions and fearful looks at bay, so she would deal with the dry eyes as long as she needed to.

She shook her head and quickly slipped the contacts in, letting out a breath as mossy green stared back.

Running her fingers along the etched lines in the cold metal of the disk-shaped necklace, Ember glanced around the room in bitter reflection, twirling her father's old ring around her finger, before her eyes landed on the old backpack she had laying on the bed. Content that she had everything, she zipped the suitcase closed and grabbed the backpack, slinging it over her small shoulders.

Closing the door behind her, Ember gritted her teeth. She hated goodbyes—especially these goodbyes, the ones she'd seen coming from a mile away. They were unnecessary, and she had no words for the parents who were so eager to rid their home of her. Blinking back angry tears, she made her way down the carpeted steps toward the front entryway. A few steps away from the landing, she watched as Mrs. Holloway came into view around the corner, busying herself with tidying the living room. Their two small girls played with dolls

6

in the center of the room, giggling back and forth like they were sharing a secret. The last step creaked under Ember's foot, giving her away.

Mrs. Holloway's head swung up and she stiffened, sucking in a breath and pursing her lips as she nodded. Ember's eyes widened as the family backed up slowly against the couch, like her mere presence was a threat to their lives, the peace of their home. All she'd ever wanted was to be part of that peace. Instead, the air in the home felt like a dense fog after a rainstorm—thick and impossible to navigate. Ember hung her head and made her way to a bench in the foyer. She shrunk into the seat and made herself as small as possible, just as she had so many times before.

Mr. Holloway entered the room and kissed his wife on the cheek before he noticed her on the bench. He narrowed his eyes at her, screwing his face into an ugly mask before placing himself between his wife and children, creating the physical barrier that she had been feeling for the last month.

A light knock on the door cut through the tension in the room. With a bob of his head, Mr. Holloway plastered a fake smile on before swinging open the door. Standing on the front stoop was a tall woman with a friendly smile, who could've given Freyja herself a run for her money. Her long coffee-colored hair was half secured by a gold clip, the rest of it falling to her bronze shoulders in a loose braid, framing eyes like honey and the warmest smile Ember had ever seen. She furrowed her brow as she eyed the unfamiliar woman. Over the last six years, the strict Miss Gardner had been the only person to facilitate her placement changes, the only person who had ever picked her up from her guardians' homes to move her to the next. She narrowed her eyes at the smiling woman, noting the stark difference between her and her normal caseworker.

This woman was bright and warm where Miss Gardner was cold and collected, reducing Ember to just another diffi-

7

cult case number with the way she checked off her list in her drafty office. This woman radiated kindness, along with a feeling Ember couldn't quite place—a feeling that made Ember's stomach coil into tight knots of apprehension. For a split second, she could've sworn she saw the woman's eyes sparkle.

"Hello there! You must be Ember," she sang, her voice enveloping Ember like a hug. "My name is Thea. I have taken over your case for Miss Gardner." She smiled down at Ember as she chewed on the inside of her cheek and gave her a curt nod. "I am here," she continued sweetly, "because—"

"Because the Holloways have decided that their family isn't the right *fit* for me," Ember interjected coldly. "I would be better off with a family that has the ability to see to my *specific needs*," she spat, as she crossed her arms tightly over her chest. She recited the words that she had heard time and time again, in some fashion, from every family she had been with. The words may have been different each time, but the sentiment was still the same. Ember was different, and different scared them. It scared her for the longest time, all of the strange things that happened around her, but at this point, it felt less like fear and more like a dull ache behind her eyes, like a constant headache beginning to form.

Thea's soft smile never wavered as she met the girl's eyes. "Have you had a chance to say your goodbyes, or do you need a moment?"

Ember turned briefly to the Holloways, hoping to catch some glimpse of remorse on their faces. The two little girls quickly ducked behind their parents, who each gave Ember a forced smile before she focused her eyes on the ground and turned back to Thea, taking in a deep breath.

"No, I'm fine," she whispered. Goodbyes were fairly routine at this point. She was glad to leave without them if it meant not feeling unwanted.

With a nod, Thea swiftly picked up the tattered suitcase by

the door, waved goodbye to the Holloways, and guided Ember to the green sedan parked on the side of the street. Ember dragged her feet even as rain drops started to fall on her freckled nose.

"I hear your fifteenth birthday is coming soon!" Thea chirped, as she buckled her seatbelt and swiftly put the car in drive. "And starting your first year of secondary school in just a few weeks? What a perfect time for a fresh start."

Ember nodded as she leaned her head against the cool window in the back seat, willing the tiny droplets of water to race down the foggy glass. Every school she had ever been to always had the same cold and lonely environments, a not so gentle reminder that she would always be on the outside looking in, and she wasn't expecting this fresh start to be anything different. She dragged her finger back and forth, one droplet mirroring her every move, as if its sole purpose was to follow the winding path her finger created along the glass. She had grown accustomed to the odd things that happened around her, this game being one of the more common occurrences. She made a quiet noise to agree with whatever Thea was saying before realizing what she'd been doing—how she'd manipulated the droplets on the glass. Her eyes met the bright emeralds staring expectantly back at her from the rearview mirror.

Quickly pulling her hands into her lap and sitting up a little taller, Ember held her breath. Fear settled into a tiny ball in the pit of her stomach as she grabbed the metal pendant around her neck. It was one thing for her foster families to see the odd things that happened around her, but a social worker? What would they do if they found out just how strange she actually was?

Thea only smiled knowingly back at her from the rearview, eyes sparkling as the sun tried to peek out from behind the clouds.

"That happen often?" she asked, as she winked in Ember's direction.

"Sometimes I like to watch the raindrops race," she whispered, hoping to play it off. "It's just a silly game I used to play with my da—" She stopped herself short. No one needed details. Those memories were hers, and she had every intention of keeping them locked away in her brain for the rest of her life. They were for her and her only.

"Ah, how interesting." Thea nodded with a grin. "My papa taught me a similar game when I was small. His version was with shooting stars, though." She pointed at the cloudy afternoon sky, swishing her finger back and forth. "A lot harder than it sounds, especially when Orion's Belt knocks you off-course."

Ember's cheeks turned hot as she nodded slowly, unsure exactly who this strange woman with emerald eyes was. She wondered why she was talking about her papa swiping constellations around like they were droplets of water, and whether or not she would've been better off at the Holloways', locking herself in her room until she was eighteen.

Nothing more was said, and Thea didn't pry.

Galway was never particularly sunny, but the weather couldn't seem to make up its mind. After what seemed like ages, the car rolled, in full sunlight, to a stop in front of the three-story social services building where Ember had spent most of her childhood—or so it seemed. Between this office and the large group home down the road, she really couldn't tell. She stepped out of the back seat and onto the cobblestone sidewalk, straightening her spine and setting her shoulders to look more sure of herself than she felt.

"My gaff is right above the office; it makes the commute a breeze every morning." Thea grinned as she led Ember to the front of the building. "I have a few things to finish up for the evening, and I think I have some food at my desk. Are you hungry?"

Ember hummed a distant response as she followed Thea inside. The office felt cold and empty as she followed Thea toward a door tucked away in the back, bumping a few of the desk corners with her hip as she numbly wandered through the maze of uncertainty in front of her, wondering where she would end up next.

Not that it mattered. Every house was the same. Every family was the same. Every tiny bedroom and fogged up window, every inevitable downward spiral. It all ended the same.

The only thing different today was this strange woman—this Thea.

Thea flipped the light switch on the wall and motioned Ember into the bright room where bookshelves overflowed with colors that gave rainbows a run for their money. She couldn't remember ever going into this office, almost like the woman had conjured it out of thin air. A big, comfy chair sat directly in front of the desk, and right behind it was a giant window, curtains flung open, bathing her in warm sunlight. With a growing grin she couldn't quite help, Ember made her way to the oak bookshelf along the back wall and ran her fingers across the spines. Littering the shelves were tomes of all shapes and sizes. Some were dusty and worn, while others looked like the spine had never even been cracked. Books that spoke tales of faraway places and magical creatures, of worlds where she wasn't just an orphan… she was magical.

Books had always been an escape. No matter where she found herself or how alone and scared she might be, the worlds of Odin and Freyja and magical talking animals always felt like home. She squinted her eyes curiously at the authors' names and the book titles, wondering why they seemed so familiar. Out of nowhere, small waves of electricity ran through her arm and into her fingertips, and she watched as tiny sparks briefly connected with the book in front of her hand. The novel shot a few inches away from the rest and landed with a *thud* in her palm.

Ember jumped back in shock. Her breath caught in her throat, barely holding back a scream as she turned to Thea. A small smile crept across the tall woman's face as she raised her eyebrow and nodded toward the worn tome still in Ember's hand.

"Does *that* happen often?" Thea laughed as she pulled a file from the drawer in her desk.

Ember couldn't form thoughts, much less actual words, to give her an answer. It absolutely did *not* happen often. She stared at the inky black book in her hand, twirling it around a few times to see if anything else happened. Convinced she had imagined it, she slowly placed the book back on the shelf and made her way to the comfy chair in front of the large desk.

"Who is 'T. L.?'" she asked, as she glanced over her shoulder at the shelves, the name that had stuck out to her.

Thea looked up from the paper she was signing and grinned toward the stack of books.

"Ah, he is one of my favorites." She smirked. "Wrote several of the school books you'll be using this year at Heksheim. I'm sure you'll become very well acquainted with his work. He has a way of… making his writing come to life." Her eyes sparkled a little as she spoke, hinting there was a riddle somewhere in her explanation.

Ember hated riddles.

She furrowed her brow and glanced down at the desk in front of her. Peeking out from underneath a pile of papers, she noticed a small metal disk lying on the desk that looked eerily similar to the one hanging around her own neck.

Holding the trinket near her collar bone, she tried to brush away her curiosity.

"Heksheim? Is that a school?" She frowned. "I've never heard of it before. Am I not attending Coláiste?" Relief flooded her at the realization that she wouldn't be going to the school she had been dreading starting at, but that feeling was quickly replaced with a dull panic. It wasn't a school in Galway that she had ever heard of, which meant she would be leaving, and something about that realization made her stomach sour.

Ignoring her question entirely, Thea looked back toward the bookshelf behind them, a wry smile creeping across her perfectly symmetrical face.

"How much do you remember about your parents?" she questioned, briefly eyeing the necklace Ember had her fingers tightened around.

Ember swallowed, shocked at the directness of her inquiry. "My father was a fisherman. He worked at the docks in Galway. My mother owned an apothecary in town." She took a shaky breath and fidgeted in her seat. "Other than that, not a lot. They died before I turned seven," she lied, fingers gripping a little tighter to the small pendant.

She remembered what her father's eyes looked like while he read her magical stories of talking bears and kind werewolves and spun tales of ancient goddesses and the magic they possessed. She remembered the way the air felt, like it had an electric current running through it, when he roared with laughter in front of the fire at night. She remembered the way her mother sang while she made stew and soda bread and how her voice sounded like a thousand bells chiming through their cottage, the melodies bouncing off the beads of dew that had settled on the open windowsill. Other memories blurred in and out of focus, sometimes stopping altogether or jumping ahead like a scratched CD. She tried desperately to mend it so she could listen to all of her favorite songs. Her parents were like a puzzle she couldn't quite finish, filling the gaps from the missing pieces with colorful paper and wishful thinking.

She remembered enough, but those memories were *hers*.

Thea opened the mini fridge behind her, grabbing two crisp sandwiches, and handed one to Ember.

"Give it a lash, you must be starving." She smiled. "Today is bound to be a long one. Eat, and we'll talk before we have to go and catch the ferry."

Ember twirled the sandwich in her hands, furrowing her brow as her chest tightened, chills running down her arms. Something in her gut told her today was different; something was changing.

"You're not answering my questions," Ember said sternly, as she set the sandwich down and crossed her arms tightly across her chest. "What is Heksheim? Why am I taking a ferry?" She narrowed her eyes as she took a shaky breath. "And what do you know about my parents?" She glanced a few times at the necklace on the desk, trying to shake off the anxiety building in her chest.

"Eat, and I'll answer," Thea replied, as she arched her brow and pushed the sandwich closer.

Ember huffed as she nodded, picking defiantly at the sandwich.

"I know that they were lovely people." Thea smiled reassuringly. "And that they would be overwhelmed with joy that you're finally going where you belong."

Ember swallowed dryly. "Is my next family not in Galway? Where am I going?" The thought of leaving the only home she had ever known unnerved her. These were the streets she rode bikes on with her parents, the parks they had picnics at, the museums where they would spend rainy weekends.

This was home. This was where she lost them.

Thea's eyes twinkled as she lent a sympathetic smile, almost as if she had access to the memories that were running through Ember's head.

"No, no, they aren't in Galway. I know it will be a bit of a change for you, but I think you'll enjoy the new scenery. The island is just *bubbling* with magic." She smirked.

Great. More riddles.

"An island? Which island?" She briefly ran through the

names of the small islands that dotted the coast. Was it Clare Island? Or Rutland? "What is *Heksheim*? Why can't I go to school with my friends?" Ember asked pleadingly.

That last part was a lie; she didn't really have friends. With the number of families she was placed with every school year, most children thought something had to be wrong with her, so they did their best to stay out of her way. She set her jaw as she crossed her arms tighter. She didn't need anyone's pity regarding the matter, so she kept it to herself. Nothing good ever came from friends anyway, but Thea didn't need to know that. The strange woman seemed to see right through Ember's meek facade.

"Your parents had a gift," Thea began. "A gift that they passed down to you. My job is to place children like you with the same types of families that share that gift."

Fear settled in Ember's chest, and she struggled to breathe. "What gift? I don't have any gifts," she replied with a shake of her head.

"The gift of *Seiðr*," Thea whispered, effervescent eyes sparkling as she pointed to the metal pendant on Ember's neck. "The gift of *magic*."

Ember's throat ran dry, and she swallowed. She wasn't special, and she certainly wasn't magic.

"Why now?" Ember whispered. "Why not when I was eight? Or ten? Or twelve? Why now?" What she really wanted to know was, *'Why was I left alone for so long?'*

"I've been tracking your bursts of accidental magic for some time now," she replied, as she leaned forward. "But every time I got close, I lost you again. Your file was sealed, even from me, and I was never assigned your case to be able to locate you. Luckily, Miss Gardner had a *pressing* family matter to take care of right after she received the call for your transfer, so your case was reassigned to me." She smiled sweetly, leaning closer still. "I found you as quickly as I could, and now, I'm taking you home."

Home?

Ember's head spun as a weight settled on her chest. Every strange occurrence from her childhood came barreling back into the forefront of her mind, and she began to slowly piece together the puzzle she had been handed. Every instance where something strange happened and she was forced out of another home, every time she was hidden away. She took a shaky breath. Realization sped straight toward her like a runaway train—maybe there was a reason she never fit anywhere else.

"Your parents shared this gift," Thea continued, either ignoring or completely unaware of the turmoil waging battle in Ember's mind. "There's a reason strange things always seem to happen around you. There's a reason you've always felt so different. You're a Vala, Ember."

The room was spinning again, and hot tears had formed behind her eyes, though she wasn't sure why. "A what?"

"A witch."

There it was.

This has to be a joke, she thought, as she shook her head, but the serious expression on Thea's face quickly told her otherwise. *A lonely orphan raised in solitude finds out she's a witch and is whisked away to a school where she'll learn how to do magic.* She scoffed as she sank back in her chair. It felt like every book she had read as a child, and somehow, she still didn't know how she was supposed to feel.

What shocked her most was that she wasn't surprised. Why should she be, after all? Was she not prone to oddities? To strange animals following her, to a disruption in the elements whenever she was excited or upset?

Ember's chest tightened, excitement and terror bubbling inside her while she mentally searched for the questions she had been longing to ask her whole childhood.

"And my parents?" She hesitated and bit her bottom lip. "My parents were witches... erm... Vala?"

"They were." Thea chuckled as she leaned back in her chair and laid her hands in her lap. "And very powerful ones, if I remember correctly."

"You knew them?" Ember perked up, straightening her back and scooting to the edge of her seat. She didn't have anything concrete about them other than the things her father had written in the journal he left behind. Everything else was just memories, and memories were finicky at best.

Thea offered a sympathetic smile as she shook her head. "I never had the pleasure," she replied softly, "but I've heard lovely things. Your family's reputation precedes you."

Ember's heart sank as she slumped in her chair and nodded. "And that's where they're from? This island..."

"Ellesmere." Thea nodded with a smile. "I can't give you much in the way of information about them, but I'm hoping you'll meet people who knew the parents you never got to get to know, as well as the magic that lives inside of you. There's something special about returning to where you come from and finding parts of yourself that you didn't even know were missing."

Ember took a shuddering breath and leaned back in her chair. She recalled the stories her father used to read to her at night, the stories filled with magic and wonder. Were they real? Was there something she missed? Were there traces of magic entwined in her memories that she had tucked away or lost completely? She thought back to the Holloways and how quickly they had called social services after their family dog had mysteriously turned a striking shade of purple. Magic or not, nothing good ever happened to Ember Lothbrok, and she couldn't see that changing any time soon.

"What is Ellesmere?" Ember asked, as she furrowed her brow. "Why is it any different than here?"

Thea glanced at the gold watch on her wrist before quickly jumping up and snapping her fingers. All of the papers that littered her desk flew into a neat pile in the open drawer before it closed and locked. Ember's eyes felt like they might pop out of her head as she stiffened and sucked in a breath.

"Best be going. We don't want to miss the ferry!" she chirped, ushering Ember out of the room, back out through the hallway, past the file-littered desks, and out to the car.

Her head waged war with her heart as she buckled into the backseat. Suddenly, everything she thought she knew about her parents felt wrong, and everything she thought she knew about herself felt like a lie. *What was this strange woman implying?*

Ember spent the long car ride to the ferry deep in thought, answering small talk with *mm-hmm*'s and nods. She had more questions about her parents now than ever before. So many more empty spaces in the puzzle she was trying to put together.

After half an hour, the car slowed to a stop in front of the Port of Galway, and Ember absentmindedly climbed out, clutching the strap of her backpack. The area was familiar, but only in the way recurrent dreams were. She'd never been here before and had only driven past. A light breeze came in from the loch, and Ember closed her eyes as the salty air filled her lungs. The pair headed toward a ticket booth to the far left, several feet away from all the others, where Thea greeted the man at the front with a smile. Every other terminal had a line stretching a dozen people deep, but no one seemed to notice the man at the ticket booth with the empty line. Ember titled her head in confusion as she followed behind Thea.

"Two tickets to the island please, one return," Thea said, as she briefly rolled up the sleeve on her left arm, exposing shapes that looked strikingly similar to the one carved into the metal necklace Ember was currently twirling through her fingers.

The man's eye twinkled as he nodded and handed Thea two tickets that read "Ellesmere Island" in small print. Thea guided Ember toward the door on their right, just as empty of people milling about as the ticket booth had been, and briefly lifted her sleeve again as she smiled at the man standing in front of it.

"*Sæll og blessaður*," she said with a smile. The man nodded and opened the door, ushering them in. Inside the terminal was much bigger than it looked from the outside. The place was packed with people, and Ember could feel the magic electrifying the air around her—something familiar she hadn't felt in a very long time.

Young children ran around squealing, sparks flying from their fingertips, hitting the others in the ankles as their mothers scolded them from their seats. A tall man in the corner twirled a small blue flame between his fingers as he spoke in a hushed tone on the phone, the ball of fire flickering to orange when his voice grew louder.

"Isn't this dangerous?" Ember asked, wide-eyed as she looked around the room. "What if someone comes in and sees all of this…"

"Magic?" Thea smirked. "This terminal is heavily warded. No one can enter unless they are Vala and can give the blessing like you heard back there." She nodded toward the door they had just entered through. "To anyone who passes by, this just looks like a terminal that is under construction."

Thea led Ember to the ferry waiting for them outside where she took a seat near the rail. The small boat departed from the dock as Ember took a shaky breath, watching the only home she had ever known slowly fade out of sight.

Resting her arms on the railing, Ember stared into Loch Lurgan and let her mind wander to the new foster family that was waiting for her. How long would it take for them to realize she was too much and send her back like all the others? As desperately as she wanted to look forward to the home that waited for her, she knew better than to get her hopes up. Every placement always ended the same way. This would be no different.

Out of the corner of her eye, the water next to the boat splashed briefly, interrupting Ember's train of thought. She spun her head toward the disturbance and could've sworn she saw lavender eyes staring back at her. But as quickly as it was there, it was gone again, leaving a flurry of bubbles in its wake. Ember squinted toward the water, hoping to catch a glimpse of whatever was watching her beneath the waves. She almost jumped out of her skin when Thea put a hand on her shoulder, like the creature had somehow boarded the boat and snuck up behind her.

Taking in a slow breath, she looked up at the woman, noticing the magic whirling like specks of gold and silver behind the emerald in her eyes. She smiled back at the girl, squeezing her shoulder in reassurance.

After an hour or so, the island finally came into view. Rocky beaches lined the shore around the town that looked like a small rainbow in the distance. Giant cliffs jutted off to the far left where Ember could see a waterfall coming off the side, crashing into the waves below it. Large rock formations loomed off the coast, and fishing boats could be seen sprinkled amongst them, the sound of the men shouting muffled by the waves breaking against the jagged rocks. Even from a distance, the magic around the island was almost palpable. Ember could feel a tug at her chest that almost took her breath away, like an invisible cord was running from the ethereal mass of land directly to her sternum.

"Hundreds of years ago, our ancestors landed their long-ships on the shores of Ellesmere Island and brought their magic with them." Thea smiled as she stared out toward the mass of land growing closer. "They warded the island against invaders and built a town where they could raise their families in peace, teaching them their ancient craft while keeping them out of harm's way."

Longships… but then that means they were…

"Vikings?" Ember squeaked with wide eyes. "I'm a Viking

and a witch?" Her eyes narrowed again as she digested the words. It couldn't be this simple—that the answer to all of her problems was waiting on an island not even one-hundred miles from her home. Nothing was ever that simple.

And happiness always came with a price.

"Something like that," Thea replied, a playful smile climbing the edge of her lips. "Our people are the Lochlannaich—people from the land of lakes—or Northmen, but most were Vikings by trade. Northmen and Vala are quite the powerful combination of genetics, so I think you'll fit in just fine."

"This feels so familiar," Ember whispered, staring toward the mass of land growing closer in the distance. Her breath shook as she bit the inside of her lip, forcing herself to take slow, deep breaths.

"Home always feels that way," Thea replied, elbows leaned against the metal railing. "Sometimes it's painful, and sometimes it's wonderful. But most of the time, it's both."

Home?

The island drew closer, and a smile began to spread across Thea's face.

"Those who are meant to end up here always do eventually."

CHAPTER 2
AN ELIXIR CALLED LOVE

E mber stepped off the ferry and onto the wet dock, breathing in the salty air that clung to every surface around her. People milled about, greeting family and friends as they exited the boat. Dock workers flung fish between them, and Ember craned her neck to look past them. A small town stood in the distance, buildings painted in reds and greens and purples, like a small rainbow hugging the coast. Children played on the beach to her left, stuffing their pockets full of stones and shells that weighed them down as they stumbled through the sand.

Ember fixed her eyes back on the dock and quickened her pace to catch up with Thea, who was now at the end of the dock smiling back at her. She followed her down the cobblestone road toward a small yellow building on the edge of the water that read "Seacrest Bed and Breakfast." The sun peeked through the clouds, making it appear as if beads of water danced in the light. Outside of the building, an older man in a brimmed hat leaned up against a horse-drawn covered cart, using a small pocketknife to cut up an apple, feeding some of it to his dog resting in the seat above him. The chestnut mare attached to the cart gave a light snort and stamped its foot before the man laughed and cut off a piece for her as well. Ember tightened her grip on the strap of her backpack as she positioned herself behind Thea.

"Howeyah, Thea!" The older man beamed, waving the small knife over his head. The dog raised his head and barked as his tail began to wag, almost like they were one brain inside two beings.

"Good afternoon, Thomas," Thea replied, reaching up to pat the dog on his head. "How's the missus?"

"Oh, she's grand." He grinned as he cut off another piece of the apple. "Haven't seen ya in donkey's years, workin' on the mainland keepin' ya busy?"

"Busy as ever." Thea laughed, eyes twinkling against the sun. "Think you have time to give us a lift to the Kitts'?"

"Of course, hop in." Thomas smiled as he threw the apple core over his shoulder and gave a hand to Thea, helping her into the cart.

Thea looked over her shoulder and nodded to Ember. "Ember, this is Thomas Faherty; he and his wife run the bed and breakfast in town."

"Nice to meet you, sir," Ember whispered quietly.

"A pleasure to meet you as well," he said, as he held out his hand to help her into the cart. "Miss...?"

Ember squinted at the man as she took in his disheveled clothes and crooked smile. He wasn't wealthy, that much was obvious, but something about the way he seemed to radiate happiness was comforting. She scuffed her shoes against the pebbles at her feet, looking down. "Lothbrok," she whispered, eyes glued to her shoelaces. "Ember Lothbrok." Ember looked up curiously at the man as he sucked in a breath, eyes misty as he smiled toward her.

"Lothbrok, of course, ya are," he whispered. "You look just like him, freckles and all."

Ember gave a slow nod, knitting her brows in confusion.

"You knew my father?" she asked quietly, tightening her grip around the strap of her bag.

"Aye." He nodded with a smile. "He liked to come down and feed the horses on the weekends in exchange for some apple cake. He was a good man."

Ember's heart fluttered as she thought about her father as boy, running around this island without a care in the world, spending his weekends with friends and eating apple cake.

Apple was his favorite.

She took a breath as she shook the thought away and hoisted herself up into the cart. She hugged her backpack against her chest, eyes fixed on her worn out sneakers dangling above the dusty floor.

The ride was bumpy, but Ember didn't mind. She let the cobblestone road under the wheels rock her back and forth while she took in the scenery around her. Lush hills rolled to her left, and rolling waves crashed on the shore as they raced to meet the horizon to her right. Wild thyme and honeysuckle danced across the grass, their scent triggering memories of long summer nights wedged somewhere in the back of her mind, buried beneath layers of loss and hopelessness. Ember breathed in the faint smell of copper mixed with salt in the air and let herself sink into the seat beneath her. Her thoughts drifted back to Galway as she swayed with the cart, and she couldn't help but think about how being with the Holloways already felt like a million years ago. It was like she had been teleported through time and space to another life completely. Thea chattered along with Thomas Faherty, most of their conversation muffled by the sound of the cart rolling over the dirt road, and every once in a while, she would glance back at Ember with a smile. Ember forced a smile back and almost choked on it as Thea conjured a small ball of light in her hand, whispered to it, and then sent it flying away.

What the bloody hell?

"Had to phone home." She smiled. "The missus hates when I forget to check in."

The cart slowed as they approached a large stone wall and an old-looking gate. Mr. Faherty hopped off and rolled the gate open, as Ember craned her neck toward the top of the drive. Mr. Faherty hopped back in and clicked at the mare, and the cart rolled on, passing donkeys and goats grazing in the fields to their left and right, briefly acknowledging the presence of the strangers before going back to the wildflowers in front of them. Dread began to settle in as they rolled closer, and the heavy realization that she was seconds away from her new foster family began to settle in her stomach. Would this be a fresh start, or would they have her on the first ferry back to Galway as soon as possible? The long path was lined with trees, ripe pears hanging low, begging to be snatched up and snacked on. Ember's mouth watered as she thought back to the crisp sandwich she had picked at during lunch, and her growling stomach reminded her that not eating it had been a poor decision.

A beautiful farmhouse became visible over the hill, the mahogany soaking up the deep reds and pinks of the sun beginning to set on the horizon. The house stood several stories tall, a large porch wrapping around the front and sides with floor to ceiling windows looking out toward them. It was reminiscent of the Viking homes Ember had only read about in books—dark wood and beautiful carvings at the curved pitch. It looked homey, somewhere she could almost imagine herself running through the pastures, getting lost in the wild-flowers sprouting below the summer sun. The windows were swung open, and Ember was greeted with the sweet smell of homemade apple cake as it wafted across the lawn toward her. Her heart ached as she thought back to her childhood home and the treats her mother would bake for her.

"Am I not going to Heksheim today?" Ember asked, as her eyes darted around the property in front of her.

"Heksheim isn't a boarding school," Thea replied, as she shook her head. "The Kitts are your new foster family. You'll be staying with them and going to school during the day."

Ember's chest tightened at the mention of yet another foster family, anxiety bubbling in her stomach. It was stunning, but would this farmhouse ever feel like home? Or would it just be another building she passed through like a ghost in her own personal purgatory?

Ember hopped off the cart and made her way toward the large front door as Thea waved goodbye to Mr. Faherty.

"I'll be seein' ya, Miss Lothbrok." He waved with a warm smile before turning his horse and buggy around and trotting down the drive. Ember followed Thea quickly onto the porch. The second their feet touched the top step, the door swung open and out stepped a short brunette woman with bright blue eyes smiling widely, what was left of the sun making the small specks of green in them sparkle. She cleaned her hands on the apron tied around her waist and blew soft ringlets out of her eyes. She was motherly and warm, like coming home and sitting in front of the fire after trekking through a monsoon. The kindness that radiated off her was something Ember hadn't felt in a very long time.

"Thea, love, welcome home." She beamed before turning to the girl beside her. "And you must be Ember." She smiled warmly. "We are so excited to meet you. My name is Eira Kitt, please come inside. I just put the kettle on."

Ember looked back at Thea, who gave her a bright smile before she slowly made her way through the oak door and into the entryway of the large home. The smell of apple cake and tea overwhelmed her senses as she looked around the foyer, feeling the evening breeze from the open window brush against her skin. She let out a small yelp as she instinctively ran her fingers along the etching in the disc hanging from her neck and felt tiny sparks leaving them as they met the cold

26

metal. Thea raised an eyebrow with a smile and gave her shoulder a gentle squeeze.

They made their way into the kitchen, passing by a simple dining room to her left, and sat around a small wooden table tucked in the corner past the back door. Eira pulled the kettle off the stove and poured the molten amber into their mugs, placing a slice of cake in front of both Ember and Thea.

"Did Thomas chatter your ear off again?" Eira chirped as she set the plates down.

"Couldn't stop him if I tried," Thea laughed in reply.

The sunset shone through the window, bathing them in pinks and purples. Beautiful wooden countertops lined the room, and she watched as Eira walked back and forth between the ivory fridge, the stove, and the sink with a window that looked out to the yard. Watching Mrs. Kitt float around the kitchen sent a swell of emotion shooting through her chest. She reminded her so much of her mother. The way she hummed to herself as she worked, the smile that never seemed to leave her mouth—it was all so reminiscent of a life she was trying desperately to remember. For just a moment, she felt hope trying to settle in her chest. As quickly as it settled, she brushed it away. This wouldn't last long.

Ember knew better.

"Otto should be home soon," Eira directed to Thea. "He got caught up at the docks and is running a little late. But please enjoy the cake and tea. I'm going to grab the children. Maevie has been in bits all day; she's so excited." And with a small smile, she disappeared through the door.

Ember held her mug a little tighter, forcing herself to sip the tea and eat small bites of cake, her hunger all but gone as anxiety built in her chest.

Great. Kids, she thought, as if it was the nail in the metaphorical coffin. Families with kids never lasted long.

Laughter and squeals filled the hallway outside the kitchen as a small girl burst through the doorway and into the nook, wild strawberry blonde ringlets framing her dirt-covered face. Her sun-yellow dress, equally as dirty as her arms, whipped around her knees as she ran into the kitchen. She barreled her way around the table to Ember and wrapped her tiny arms around her neck, standing on her tiptoes to reach.

Ember stiffened. "Um... Hello there," she said quietly, unsure what to do with the sudden affection. She wasn't much of a hugger on a good day, and definitely not with complete strangers.

"Maeve Kitt!" Eira said sternly from the doorway. "Try not to overwhelm the girl before she's even seen her room."

Maeve released Ember from her grasp and took a few steps back, still smiling like she was looking at the best present she had ever received.

"Calm down, Maevie. She's not going to disappear if you take your eyes off her," another voice joined in, as a tall boy with shaggy brown hair and the same bright blue eyes appeared in the kitchen. His hair was messy, like he had just stepped out of a wind tunnel, and a pair of rectangular glasses sat on the bridge of his freckled nose. He ran a tan hand through his hair, further mussing it as he took a seat beside Ember and nodded toward the little girl, now looking cross at her brother. "Maevie gets excited over guests; sometimes forgets most people don't react to her hugs like the animals do." He folded his arms loosely over his chest as he further antagonized his sister, pushing his glasses back up his nose after dodging a tiny hand that flew his way.

Eira stood behind the boy and popped him on the back of the head gently while she laughed. "Maeve just turned six. I sent her outside to run off some energy before you got here, but I don't know that it did a whole lot of good." She smiled at her daughter, who was bouncing on the balls of her feet, trying to unsuccessfully reign in her excitement. "And this is Fenrir. He'll be starting first year with you next week."

The boy glared at his mother as he pulled his cell phone

from his pocket. "I'm Fen. Please don't call me 'Fenrir.' I'm not *ancient*," he quipped as he rolled his eyes, seemingly annoyed with his mother's choice in name.

Eira swatted him on the head again, Maeve giggling behind them.

Thea laughed as she stood up, looking down at Ember with a smile. "I have to catch the last ferry back to Galway tonight, but I'll be checking in with you after you start school," she said gently. Setting the worn suitcase by Ember's chair, she put a hand on her shoulder and squeezed it. "Have a little faith, love. Don't take life too seriously, you might miss something."

Ember caught a small wink before Thea waved goodbye to Eira and walked out of the room toward the foyer. The door opened and closed in the other room, and boots could be heard thudding against the hardwood floor, sending Maeve rushing to the entryway, screaming "Papa!" as she ran.

A tall, tan man walked into the kitchen smiling, little Maeve hanging from his leg as he set his lunchbox on the counter by the sink. His clothes were dirty and smelled like saltwater and dead fish, hands calloused from manual labor. His eyes sparkled the familiar shade of blue that he shared with the rest of his family as he kissed his wife on the cheek. Fen groaned from embarrassment, and Ember uncomfortably averted her eyes to look anywhere other than at the happy couple.

"Welcome to Ellesmere, Ember. I'm Otto," the man said warmly.

Ember nodded her thanks with a smile as she shifted uncomfortably in her seat. Eira flicked her wrist toward the stove, and Ember's eyes grew wide as she watched the spoon in the pot begin to stir the contents on its own. With another flick, Ember's suitcase was lifted from the ground and sent soaring toward the entryway and up the stairs. No sooner than she blinked, cabinets were opening, and bowls, cups, spoons, and napkins were flying from their shelves, landing gently in front of the five seats at the table.

Well, this is different, Ember thought as she settled into the chair, smelling the stew that was being poured into her bowl by what seemed to be an invisible hand.

"Is it okay if I sit here?" she asked sheepishly, shifting nervously in her chair.

Fen's eyebrow arched as he shoveled a spoonful of stew in his mouth.

Eira tilted her head as she smiled. "You can sit there or pick another seat." She pointed at the other chairs around the table. "Wherever you feel most comfortable." She turned back to the kitchen but stopped in her tracks when Ember cleared her throat.

"No, I'm sorry," Ember said quietly. "I mean, would you prefer if I eat in another room?"

Eira's hand flew to her chest as she sucked in a breath and furrowed her brow. Otto raised an eyebrow, and Fen choked on a too-large bite of bread he had just popped in his mouth.

"Do you normally eat somewhere other than a kitchen?" Fen laughed after clearing his airway.

"Yes." Ember nodded quietly. "My room mostly, or outside if the weather permits."

Fen's jaw hung slack, and Eira shot him a warning glance, prompting him to snap his mouth shut. He had the sense to look properly abashed.

"You will eat your meals here or in the dining room," Eira said gently. "Whatever seat you choose, however, is entirely up to you."

Ember nodded as she bit the inside of her cheek, and Eira turned back into the kitchen to grab the second loaf of bread.

"You can sit by me." Maeve grinned as she bounced on the balls of her feet and then quickly hopped away when her mother called her name.

"Maeve, will you grab a few bottles of cider from the

fridge?" Eira asked over her shoulder, as she pulled the bread from the oven. "And wash up before you sit down!"

The small girl skipped to the other side of the room, giggling as she tried to balance four bottles of the sparkling cider in her arms. One tumbled from her grip, and right before it shattered on the hardwood floor, Otto waved his hand and guided it toward the table. Maeve gave a sheepish grin to her father and handed one to Ember before setting the other two on the table. Otto ruffled her hair affectionately before she took off at a run down the hall to wash the dirt off her hands and arms. Ember twirled the bottle around in her hand, the amber and gold spinning together inside the bottle as she squinted.

"Moon Cider," Fen said, grinning, head buried in his phone like he was doing something very important. "Much better than that nasty orange soda you drink on the mainland. It won't bite."

"Phone away at the dinner table, Fenrir," Otto said with a gruff laugh, as he poured himself a drink. "You can finish what you're working on after we eat. The internet will still be waiting when you're done."

Fen stuffed his phone in his pocket and gave his mom a sheepish smile as she glared at him from across the kitchen, hand on her hip while a knife behind her cut into the piping hot loaf of bread. Ember made a mental note to never get on the woman's bad side.

Eira made her way to the table, slices of bread zipping through the air around her and landing on each of the plates. Ember's eyes widened, and her jaw hung slack as she watched the magic happening around her, one hand in her lap and the other firmly gripping the pendant around her neck, as if it was the lifeline she was clinging to for survival.

Eira's gaze softened as she looked over at her and motioned to the bowl in front of her. "Eat up. Warm stew does wonders for a tired soul," she said with a smile, taking her seat next to her husband.

"Thank you," she whispered with a smile. Ember quietly ate her beef stew, listening to the laughter fill the room as she watched the family talk and joke and share stories about their day. Otto's laughter boomed as Maeve recounted her run in with the rooster that morning, and Eira shook her head with a grin as Fen and his father went on about a game they had watched the night before. They pulled her into the conversation with ease, smiling as she quietly answered questions about her life in Galway and respecting the unanswered questions about her childhood and life in the city with understanding smiles. Fen shoveled food quickly into his mouth as he changed the subject and quizzed her about pop culture, and she let out a small laugh as he choked on a bite of bread again.

Ember relaxed in her chair as she pulled her legs up and crossed them both underneath her. She felt her breathing even out as she savored the feeling that she wasn't sure she would ever experience again. They made her feel like she had always been a part of their home, like she belonged here. Ember's heart sank, even amidst all of the love she could feel in the air. She knew better than to get too comfortable.

Nothing this good ever lasted very long.

"Maeve, it's your turn to do the dishes," Eira said, flipping her hand as she sent the empty dishes flying from the table and into the sink that was already filling with water and bubbles. The young girl let out a dramatic sigh as she reluctantly made her way across the kitchen. "Tomorrow, we have to go into town to get your things for school," Eira said, glancing at Fen and Ember as she cleared away the empty bottles of cider, "so I think that calls for an early night. Fen, help your father get the animals settled. Ember, I'll show you where your room is."

Fen followed Otto out the back door while Ember watched

them through the window, briefly letting her mind wander back to her own father and what he would've been like if time hadn't stolen him from her. All of a sudden, a loud crash sounded from the sink, followed by a yelp from Maeve and a deep sigh from Eira.

"If you want to head up stairs, your room is the last door on the left." The woman smiled as she turned to clean up the broken plate. "I'll be up in a few minutes."

Ember nodded and made her way into the hall and up the winding steps. The top of the staircase opened into a wide hallway lined with beautiful wooden doors and pictures along the walls. Making her way to the end of the hall, she glanced into each room, constructing a mental map of where everything was. A bathroom on the right, Otto and Eira's room on the left, next door was Maeve's bedroom, complete with a bunk bed and beautiful shades of pink and purple all over the walls. Between several spare rooms and another staircase a little further down was Fen's room—a typical teenage boy's room with a computer desk and numerous electronics scattered all over the messy bed. Posters hung all over the walls with what looked like men riding dragons.

Ember reached the end of the hall, the last door on the left, and began to make her way into the room when she glanced over her shoulder, and the room behind her caught her eye. The door was cracked slightly, and Ember's curiosity got the better of her. Checking over her shoulder, she gently pushed the door open and let out a small gasp as she quietly stepped inside.

The floor was bathed in what was left of the sunlight that was quickly sinking over the horizon outside the giant window. The walls were lined from floor to ceiling with hundreds upon hundreds of books of all colors and sizes. A ladder leaned against one side, wheels on the top and bottom so it could glide across the bookshelf with ease. A white spiral staircase sat in the corner, traveling up to what Ember could assume was even more books on the third floor. In front of the window was a large comfy chair with a blanket draped over the top. Plants of various sizes filled the room and hung from the ceiling, turning the library into what resembled the most magical forest Ember had ever seen.

Ember walked to the bookshelf, breathing in the smell of the aged paper as she read the titles on the tomes. She thought back to supper and how *right* everything had felt, how this place felt more like home than anywhere she had ever been. Hope fluttered inside of her for a brief moment. Maybe this one would stick. Maybe this was going to be okay.

"I see you found my favorite room," a voice rang from behind her.

Ember spun around, dropping the book that she had been holding on the ground. She quickly picked it back up, brushing off the cover and placing it back in its home on the shelf. "I'm sorry, I didn't mean to intrude," she said quietly, glancing down at the ground.

Eira smiled gently, wiping her hands on the apron tied around her waist. "This is your home now, Ember. You're more than welcome to explore wherever you would like."

Ember smiled softly as she watched the woman make her way across the room to the bookshelf, an odd sense of peace washing over her.

"Books are the greatest kind of magic, if you ask me," she said as she ran her fingers down the spines thoughtfully. "And despite what some believe, magic is meant to be shared. Knowledge is power, but it is a dangerous kind of power when it is hoarded and hidden."

"I don't know much about magic, honestly." Ember shrugged, hands stuffed in her pockets. "I didn't even know it was real until this morning. I can't remember my parents ever using it before they…" Her voice trailed off as she cleared her throat.

"I am more than happy to share the library with you."

Eira smiled gently, taking the hint that the conversation needed to be redirected. "Odin knows none of my other children want anything to do with books. Maeve very rarely comes inside, and Fen would much rather work on his computer. Having a daughter to read alongside on a rainy day sounds lovely."

Ember stiffened, hope tugging at her chest.

Daughter?

"Now, let's go get you settled. It's been a long day," Eira breathed and quickly made her way out the door.

Ember sighed happily as she followed Eira out of the library and across the hall to her room. They walked into a huge bedroom, a large four-poster bed nestled into the corner, surrounded by sage green walls and a large window to the left. Ember grinned as she looked around, and a feeling of warmth began to wash over her. The love that had been put into making sure everything was perfect was obvious, and it sent a swell of emotions shooting through her chest. She couldn't remember a time when she felt this safe, like the missing piece of herself that she was looking for had been here waiting for her.

"We left everything fairly plain, so you can decorate however you like," Eira said as Ember walked around the room, running her hands along the bed and walls, checking to make sure everything was real. "I have to go get Maevie ready for bed," she said, walking toward the door, "but make yourself at home. I'm right down the hall if you need anything." And with a gentle wink, she closed the door behind her.

Ember sat on the edge of the bed and twirled the sheets through her fingers, silently absorbing the reality that had finally hit her. The adrenaline had worn off, and she could feel a familiar emotion trying to nudge its way into her chest—a feeling she had learned not to trust on the first night in a new home, but this time, she couldn't quite shake it.

Hope. Hope that maybe this time was different. This time felt different.

She brushed the feeling away and began to unpack her suitcase, piling the few pieces of clothing away in the dresser opposite her bed. On the bottom of the bag, she pulled out an old leather journal and smiled as she ran her hand over the cover.

"I'm going to be okay, Papa," she whispered as she hugged the book to her chest.

"Talking to yourself is a clear sign of insanity, Em," a voice said from the door.

Ember spun around to see Fen leaning against the frame, dirt covering his hands and t-shirt. "I hate nicknames," she mumbled, stuffing the book in the drawer of her bedside table.

"Fair enough." Fen shrugged. "Am I your first brother?"

"I don't have any brothers," she replied, her patience growing thinner.

"You sort of do now."

"*Foster* brother," she huffed, rearranging the clothes in the drawers of the large dresser.

"Same difference." He shrugged. "Family is family."

Ember rolled her eyes as she walked to the door. "Good-night, *Fenrir*," she replied sarcastically, promptly slamming the door in his face. She took a shaky breath as she looked around the room again. Family wasn't that simple. Her family was dead, and nothing was changing that now.

After hearing his defeated footsteps echo down the hall, Ember threw on the pajamas she had packed and grabbed her toiletries and contacts case. She quietly made her way down the hall to the bathroom, careful not to make much noise. From the other side of the hall, she could hear Eira tucking Maeve in for bed.

"Oh, Mama, just one story, please!" she begged from the

other side of the door. "Just one, and I promise I'll go straight to sleep!"

"One story," Eira laughed. "But only one, then you have to get some rest. No playing with the stars tonight."

Ember grinned as she leaned against the wall, listening quietly to the giggles coming from the other room.

"Once upon a time," Eira began, "in a faraway, blithe land, Odin created an elixir and called it Love. Loki couldn't put up with all the joy and happiness, so he created a poison and called it Love too. And now, nobody seems to know which one is which…"

Ember made her way into the bathroom, quietly closing the door behind her as the story she had heard time and time again from her father trailed off. Familiar pangs of grief threatened to force their way to the surface before she quickly pushed them back down. She went through the motions of brushing her teeth and washing her face before opening her contacts case and setting it on the counter. She gently took both contacts out of her eyes, blinking a few times to adjust her sight.

She let out a sigh as lavender stared back at her. She thought back to the bright blue that the rest of the Kitt family shared and the soothing green in Thea's, and she knew this was a trait that was still best hidden away. Something this different, even in a magical community, could never be a good thing. She quickly brushed her teeth and washed her face before slipping out the door and into the dark hallway.

Ember made her way quietly back to her bedroom, rolling her eyes at the loud snores already coming from behind Fen's closed door. Climbing into bed, she rubbed her eyes and yawned, trying to force the adrenaline from the day to wear off. The canopy above her swayed with the breeze coming through the open window, and it hit her just how different this place actually was. The home almost vibrated with love, something so palpable it rattled her bones. The first night in a new home was always a scary one, but this time, the fear was speckled with hope, a hope that made her chest shake and lip tremble. Gone were the days of silent meals and locked doors. She knew this place was special. Something was changing.

She closed her eyes and listened to the sounds of her new home, allowing it to lull her to sleep.

Maybe this one will be different, she thought. *Maybe this one will stick.*

CHAPTER 3

CHILDREN OF THE GODS

Ember's eyes fluttered open as she took in her surroundings, debating rolling over to sleep for a few more minutes, sinking into the cloud of blankets and pillows that threatened to envelop her body. The early morning sun broke through the bedroom window and bathed the room in warm light. Staring toward the window, still drifting between sleep and awake, she tried to decide whether the day before had been a dream or not.

At that moment, a small ball of bright blue light whizzed under the crack of her door and landed on her bedside table. It floated ominously for a few moments before Eira's calm voice came out of it, making Ember scoot back a few inches.

"Breakfast is ready!" it sang loudly and then vanished in a puff of mist.

Nope. Not a dream.

She heaved her legs over the edge of the four-poster bed, rubbing out the knot in her left shoulder. Eying her old backpack in the corner, she made a mental note to mend the straps before term started. Backpacks weren't cheap, and she had been patching and sewing the same one that she received from Social Services when she was six years old.

After throwing on some of her nicer clothes and tiptoeing to the bathroom to put her contacts back in and brush her hair, Ember made her way down the long steps toward the kitchen. The floorboards creaked with each step, causing Maeve to squeal in excitement from the breakfast table.

"Ember! Ember! Come sit by me!" she squeaked as she barreled toward her, almost knocking her off her feet. Ember smiled as she let the little girl lead her to the table. She had come to terms with the fact that there was probably no fighting that affection from her, so instead, she focused on not flinching every time she ran in her direction.

Maeve led her through the kitchen and over to the small table, passing by Eira cooking breakfast and making tea. For a brief moment, she let her mind wander back to memories of her own mother dancing through the kitchen every morning, singing along with the tea kettle as her father kissed her cheek. Maeve yanked her back to reality as she pulled her to her seat and the sudden realization of how hungry she was began to set in.

"Good morning, love," Eira said with a smile, as she brought over a cup of tea and the sugar bowl. "How did you sleep?"

"Just fine, thank you, Mrs. Kitt," she whispered, as she began to spoon the sugar into the steaming cup.

Eira was sending plates and cutlery gently toward the table as the back door swung open, a cool morning breeze following Fen inside as he tracked dirt on the floor.

"Mornin', Em!" he said brightly from the doorway, wiping dirt all over his shirt and jeans.

"Shoes, Fenrir!" Eira scolded, as a plate of sausage and bacon whizzed past his head and to the table.

Rolling his eyes, he kicked his shoes off into the mudroom behind him and made his way to the table.

Ember sipped on her tea as he sat down and began to fill

his plate. "I don't like nicknames, *Fenrir*," she hissed, eyes locked on the spoon she was twirling around in her cup.

"Touché." He smirked as he began to shovel food into his mouth.

Ember rolled her eyes and began to fill her plate with sausage, bacon, potato farls, mushrooms, baked beans, tomatoes, and all of the black pudding she could fit. She couldn't remember the last time she had anything for breakfast other than toast and some beans. It was absolute heaven.

She watched Maeve bounce on her knees as she ate while simultaneously coloring on a stray napkin with crayons she had pulled from her pocket, humming along to whatever song was playing in her head. She looked across the table and watched Fen as he absentmindedly typed something on his phone and then quickly pulled out a notebook to scribble in, stuffing a piece of bacon in his mouth every now and then as he chewed thoughtfully. Eira sang to herself in the kitchen while waving her hand at the stack of dishes in the sink that began to bob in and out of the water, dancing along between the suds.

"How do you do that?" Ember directed at Eira as she sipped the warm tea. "My magic feels more… destructive."

Eira smiled back at her as she wiped her hands on her apron. "With lots of practice." She winked. "It won't always feel that way."

Ember watched the scene play out in front of her. What was probably an average Saturday morning for them was something of an enigma to her, and not even because of the magic. She could count on one hand the number of family breakfasts she had sat down to since she had entered the system, and almost none of them felt this…

Happy?

There was no fear in the air. No silence hanging between all of them, mingling with the pudding at the breakfast table. No watching from the shadows as parents did their best to shelter their children from the horrors that they had come to expect from her. What other reason was there for her to constantly be bouncing from home to home? This was different, somehow. She could feel it in her bones. She took another sip of her tea as she closed her eyes, allowing herself to breathe for the first time in what felt like years. A tiny glimmer of hope fluttered in her chest.

Maybe this one will stick.

Ember was quickly jolted back to reality as Eira entered the breakfast nook, wiping her hands on the apron that hung around her waist.

"Fenrir, I won't say it again—phone away at the table," she barked from the doorway, sending a tiny green spark from her fingertip straight to the phone in his hands, shorting it out immediately. Fen jumped, dropping the phone onto his plate as he huffed dramatically.

Ember laughed quietly as he did his best to clean his phone off and stick it back in his pocket and begrudgingly inhaled the last of the tomatoes on his plate.

"Go upstairs and get changed," she said to Fen as she cleared the table. "Shops are already open, and I can't take you into town looking like you just spent the morning rolling in the mud with the draic."

"Will I get a wand today?" Ember blurted out after slurping the last of her now cold tea. That was what witches used, wasn't it?

Eira smiled at her gently. "No dear, no wands. Our magic works a little differently." Her eyes quickly flitted between Ember's and the piece of metal hanging around her neck as she nodded her head.

"What about robes? Will we be sorted into houses during school?"

"You read too much," Fen laughed. "No fancy castles or flying brooms, either, before you ask. You've got a lot to learn!" And then he was gone, running up the steps at full speed before his mother could swat at him, Maeve giggling behind him.

Ember's face screwed up in confusion as she chewed at her bottom lip. "What do you mean, different?"

"Our magic is ancient," Eira began, as she sat in the chair opposite the girl. "It doesn't follow the laws of the magic that most witches and wizards use. It isn't something that can be earned or created, only inherited."

Ember bit the inside of her cheek. "There are others?"

"Oh, yes," Eira nodded. "Scotland has a very prestigious boarding school for most of the witches and wizards in Britain. I have a few friends who have children starting there this year." Eira gave her a small smile as she took a sip of her tea. "You'll find that magic doesn't start and end on this island, almost every country and community around the world has it in one form or another. It is so much bigger than just us."

"What makes our magic so different then? Where did it come from?" Something about this woman felt comfortable. Every question she couldn't find the words for suddenly spilled out in front of her, and the realization of that vulnerability was jarring.

"Thousands of years ago," Eira continued, "the Old Gods came down and mingled with the Northmen, conquering new lands and falling in love on their shores. The gods brought their magic with them and passed it down to their children. Each child was given a necklace with runes carved into them by the gods— runes that gave them the ability to focus their magic and control it, like a wand." She pointed to the pendant that dangled around Ember's neck. "They formed a Clann, a community of families, and vowed to protect each other as long as the magic flowed through their veins. When they found that the safety of their secret was in danger, they left Norway and made their way toward Ireland, settling on this island and calling it Ellesmere. Wards were placed for protection so no outside forces could ever threaten their peace again. Heksheim was founded by the First Families, so the Children of the Gods had somewhere safe to learn and grow. This island, and all of its magic, is your birthright."

Ember clutched the pendant around her neck, suddenly hyperaware of the warmth of the magic flowing from the cold metal and into her fingertips. "I didn't know," she whispered, feeling a lump grow steadily in her throat. "My mum and dad never..." Her voice trailed off as she stared at the grains of wood weaving through the table. There was so much she didn't know about them, so many stories they never got to tell her, and she would never get to hear it from them. They would always come through other people, and the realization that so many people knew them longer than she ever would made her chest ache.

"You were too young to remember anything, even if they had told you everything," Eira said softly. "I'm sure they were doing what they thought was best."

Ember nodded numbly and tried to offer a small smile to no avail.

"Well, that's enough history for today," Eira said lightly, brushing the stray hairs from Ember's eyes. "Run upstairs and get ready, and we'll head to town in fifteen minutes." She turned around, busying herself in the kitchen again.

Grief settled like a stone in Ember's chest, forcing her to focus on her breathing as she walked upstairs and into her room, mindlessly twisting her long hair in a messy braid. She always expected that learning about where she came from would make her feel whole again. She never expected that it could make her feel this utterly lonely. With a deep sigh, she tucked her necklace in her shirt, slipped her father's ring on her finger, and tied the laces on her worn-out sneakers. Everything she owned was second hand, and she was already nervous about the Kitts seeing her hand-me-downs in all their glory.

"Children of the Gods," she huffed. "I don't remember ever reading about any Children of Gods growing up in foster care." A loud knock brought her back to reality as she heard Fen's voice from the other side.

"We're leaving, Em!"

Ember rolled her eyes as she brushed the braid off of her shoulder and made her way out the door. Maeve was standing at the bottom of the stairs bouncing on the balls of her feet, her mother's hand on her shoulder, trying unsuccessfully to rein in her excitement.

"We only have a few minutes before the station opens. Does everyone have their things?"

Ember nodded her head along with the other children and instinctively turned to head toward the front door, only to turn around and notice she was the only one doing so. The rest of the small family was standing oddly in front of a closet door at the back of the stairs, Eira checking her watch and looking up at the threshold above the door.

Fen laughed and walked over to Ember, grabbing her hand and dragging her back to the group. "This will be a little bit faster than walkin'," he chuckled.

Ember stood in front of the door, and her eyes were immediately drawn to the beautiful tree carved into the threshold above it. Its roots fanned out above the door, limbs reaching toward the ceiling. Maeve clung to her mother's hand and giggled as the tree started to glow, a bright green radiating from it, illuminating the dark wood above the door. A soft light began to shine behind it, and Eira reached for the handle, swinging it open. Ember's breath hitched in her chest, making Fen snicker beside her.

"All right, in you all go," Eira prodded, as she ushered the children through the closet door. Ember's feet felt cemented to the floor until she felt Eira's gentle hand on her shoulder, wordlessly assuring her that she was safe, and this was completely normal. But normal was beginning to have a new meaning.

After stepping through the closet and out the other side, Ember glanced around at what could only resemble a train station of sorts. Dozens of doors lined the walls of the large room as people of all ages walked in and out of them, while others stood in lines checking their watches, children darting between their legs. The building was filled with conversation and laughter and a warmth Ember couldn't quite place.

"Yggdrasil Terminal," Fen whispered, as he walked up behind her, "Much faster than walking."

Ember nodded her head as she shuffled behind Eira toward the door. She stepped through the exit and outside, the warmth of the sun beating down on her face and the sound of laughter and conversation hitting her ears the second her feet touched the cobblestone. Magic coursed through the air like electricity, making the hairs on the back of her neck stand up. It mixed with the smell of fresh baked bread and wild lavender, leaving the slight taste of iron lingering in her mouth. Her necklace vibrated against her chest, like it was connecting with the force it had been separated from for so long.

"Welcome to Sigurvik," Fen nudged, as he nodded toward the bustling town, "the heart of Ellesmere.

Instead of feeling afraid and out of place, she felt a strange sense of peace ripple through her chest. Maeve reached up to grab her hand, giving her a bright, toothy grin. She let out a shaky breath as she smiled back down and squeezed Maeve's hand in return.

Here we go.

CHAPTER 4

CAMPFIRE SMOKE AND
DYING STARS

W alking down Waterware Street, the main street in Sigurvik was like stepping into a story book. Ember felt like her head could spin off at any moment, and she wondered briefly if magic could fix that. She stuck close to Fen, Eira, and Maeve as her eyes traveled across the shops of all shapes, sizes, and colors lining the streets. It looked like a rainbow sat on top of the worn cobblestone. People milled about, laughing and catching up with friends while they ran their morning errands. Children played at the park that sat on the beach while their mothers sipped tea and allowed the salty air to wake them up. The town square was alive in a way that Ember had never seen on the mainland. Shop doors jingled in the distance as laughter danced across the breeze, and she silently breathed it all in.

Tall beings with sage skin and branches that resembled antlers protruding from the tops of their heads trimmed the fruit trees surrounding the fountain in the middle of the town square, chattering along as they spoke to the leaves. Their eyes were narrow slits, and Ember could see pointed ears sticking out from their raven hair. Moss, clover, and leaves covered their bodies, whipping along with the breeze as they moved.

Every now and then, she would watch them pluck an apple from the branches and float it toward the children giggling beneath them.

Ember sucked in a breath as her eyes widened. Magic itself was something that would take some getting used to, but part of it was familiar—it had lived in a cage inside her for so long, it almost felt natural to not have to hide certain parts of herself now.

The magical creatures were another story, and seeing them out and about in the open was something she wasn't sure she would ever get used to.

"Dryads." Fen pointed. "They protect our groves and trees. Not big on talking, though, unless you happen to be a birch."

Ember's eyes flitted back and forth across the square, watching the sun dance across the cobblestones. She let out a small gasp as a large, winged horse walked by and snorted, pulling a buggy filled with fish behind it.

She leaned into Fen and whispered, "Was that a—"

"A Pegasus." He smirked, finishing the sentence for her. "A few hundred years ago, a group of witches immigrated from Greece and brought a small herd with them. They're mostly used to help with work and labor. They're a lot stronger than mortal horses and can travel further distances on the island. Not to mention they're much less intimidating than a draic."

"A what?" she asked, but before Fen could answer, he yelped and lunged for his sister.

Maeve broke away from him and ran toward a bright red shop across the street, dodging another Pegasus and buggy in the process. She pressed her face against the window, eyes flitting back and forth between all of the toys flying around inside. Tiny plastic dragons with men on their backs soared around the window, making loops around the lights hanging from the ceiling. A toy train drove around the top of the vaulted ceiling, plumes of smoke billowing around it while the muffled sound of its whistle rang out. A small princess doll, perched on a tall tower, brushed her long blonde hair as she watched the plastic men soar past her before waving briefly at Maeve.

Ember's jaw hung slack as she watched the toys fly back and forth, mesmerized by the colors and lights in the little shop. Maeve's eyes sparkled as the flying figurines reflected against the bright blue. She squealed, jumping up and down, and spun around expectantly to her mother, bright puppy dog eyes already in full effect.

"Not today, Maevie," Eira responded to the silent question. "We're already running behind."

Maeve's brow squeezed together, her lips pressed tightly and turned down at the edges. She crossed her arms defiantly and walked toward her mother, eyes set to the ground in front of her. Ember's widened as she saw the fiery footsteps Maeve left in her wake.

"We also don't have time for pouting," Eira scolded, as she waved her hand at the ground, dousing the flames left by the angry little girl. "Now in you go."

Ember briefly glanced up at the sign hanging over the door before following the family inside The Lucky Scroll and was immediately hit with the scent of fresh parchment and leather. The room was bathed in the afternoon sun shining through the giant windows, bouncing off the shelves that lined the floor.

"Good morning, Eira," the shopkeeper said from behind the counter. "And how are you, little one?" she directed at Maeve. The little girl shrugged her shoulders and kicked the floor with the toe of her shoe, arms crossed tightly against her chest.

"Fine, miss," she answered quietly after Fen gave her a nudge.

"We're running behind this morning, and Maevie is a little upset that we couldn't stop and look around Tinker's," Eira said sweetly, putting her hand on Maeve's shoulder and squeezing gently.

"I think I have just the thing to cheer you up," the shopkeeper said with a grin. She pulled a paper stick from behind her back and handed it to Maeve. She whispered something against her palm, then slowly twirled her fingers around it. Wisps of pink and purple starlight bent around the stick, and Ember rubbed her eyes a few times as she watched a lollipop appear on top of it. Maeve giggled as she grinned her thanks to the woman and quickly grabbed her mother's hand again, lost in the candy hanging from her mouth.

"Fenrir, please take Ember and grab your school supplies. I need to have a word with Miss Browne," Eira said as she shooed the children away, turning back toward the shopkeeper.

The Lucky Scroll was a small shop filled with paper, pens, pencils, parchment, and quills. Ember couldn't imagine what use anyone would have for quills and ink when pens were so much easier to carry and use, but she did love how elegant they looked. She ran her hands along the leather journals and aged parchment. One specific journal caught her eye, beautiful leather, hand bound, and thoughtfully crafted. Her heart ached as she thought about the one her father used to write in, the one he carried with him everywhere. She pulled her hand away and refocused her attention to the task at hand, quickly realizing she had no idea where Fen had gone. She spun around to see him struggling behind her, stacks of pens and notebooks threatening to fall out of his arms and onto the floor.

"Refillable pens and standard notebooks, I think that's all we need from here." He strained, right as a case of pens fell from his arms onto his foot.

Ember gave a small smile as she picked up the fallen box and helped him carry everything to the front, only to find Eira and Maeve waiting for them with an excited grin on their faces.

"Mr. Kitt and I talked last night," Eira began with a nod at Ember as she took the notebooks and pens from the children's arms, "and we both agreed that there was no better time than now for a fresh start."

Ember's face quickly shifted from confused to surprised as Eira pulled a beautiful leather satchel from behind her back and handed it to the stunned girl. She opened and closed her mouth a few times in shock as she ran her fingers along the buckles of the bag.

"I noticed your bag looked a little worse for wear. I hope this is alright," Eira said gently.

"I can't accept this," Ember whispered as she ran her fingers across the new leather and gold buckles. "It's too much. My backpack will be fine, really."

Eira shook her head and tutted. "No daughter of mine will start her first day at Heksheim with a backpack not even fit for a common house boggart to carry." And with that, she turned to Miss Browne and set several coins on the counter.

Daughter?

"Thank you," she whispered with a smile, as she carefully draped it cross-body over her shoulder. She had never received anything new from a foster family, and the physical representation of their acceptance of her already was almost overwhelming. Eira paid for the rest of their school supplies before ushering them out the door and back into the street. The sun was directly overhead, and the street was even busier than it had been before. Children zipped by on boards hovering above the cobblestones, weaving in and out of the adults lost in conversation with their friends.

"Alright, I have to run a few errands," Eira said, as she dug in her bag before handing each child a small satchel of coins and a folded list. "Go grab your schoolbooks, and try not to get into too much trouble, *Fenrir*. And stay together. I'll meet

51

you both at Florin's in an hour." And with that, she was off, Maeve trailing behind her.

Ember followed Fen down the street, glancing at window displays as she went. She stopped in front of a green and orange shop, Beasts of Burden, and gently pressed her hand up against the large glass window. Small creatures ran around the cage behind the glass, animals she had only ever read about in books and then some she couldn't have thought up if she tried. A small bird with hot pink feathers and a bright blue beak that was far too large for its body sat sweetly on a perch cleaning its feathers while what looked like a baby griffin wrestled across the floor with a small chimera, barely the size of a puppy. Ember grinned as she watched them roll around, but her breath caught in her throat when she glanced over to the small bed in the corner, where little eyes locked with hers.

Lavender eyes.

She squinted, pressing her hands and face up against the glass to get a better look, but whatever the tiny creature was, it was hidden under piles of blankets, only its eyes visible. She was quickly brought back to reality when she felt a hand grip her shoulder.

"Come on, Em," Fen said as he tugged her away from the window, pulling her back into the crowd and down the cobblestone road. She shook her head as she sucked in a breath. She must have been seeing things. She plastered on a smile and let Fen lead her through the town, listening to him chatter her ear off about how excited he was to finally start school.

The street was bustling with people with overflowing shopping bags enjoying the last few days of summer. The conversations were light and happy, and all of the magic mingling together felt like electricity in the air. She was so busy people-watching that she almost missed it—a small bookstore, barely noticeable, tucked between the wall of shops that lined the street.

Fen walked quickly past it, eyes set on a sweets shop a few doors down.

"We're supposed to be getting our schoolbooks," she sighed as he hurried past her. "I don't think we'll find"—she quickly pulled out the list Eira had handed her and squinted as she read—"*First Year Sigils and Runes* under all that chocolate."

"I'll meet you there in a few minutes," Fen replied, as he licked his lips and heaved the door open, disappearing inside. Ember sighed as she rolled her eyes and turned back toward the red door, quickly making her way into the tiny bookshop.

The store was dimly lit by candles hovering in the air against the walls, casting dancing shadows onto the tall book-shelves and old tomes. Ember ran her fingers across the spines, reading the odd titles. She ran through the list of books she needed for school—*A First Year's Guide to Galdr, Sigils and Runes, History of the Gods*—plucking two of each off the shelves and piling them into her arms, one for her and one for Fen. She was so busy double-checking that she was in the right section that she almost jumped out of her skin when a small voice rang from the front of the store.

"Welcome to The Bookwyrm, miss," the voice said. It almost sounded like bells, barely above a whisper. "Most schoolbooks are in the second row, but I've had this one waiting at the front for you for ages."

Ember raised a brow and turned to see a small woman with white hair staring back at her. Her skin almost glowed, a golden hue radiating off her. She held a forest green book in her hand with gold trim and motioned for her to come closer. Ember hesitated briefly before walking to the front of the shop and taking the book.

"Waiting for me?" Ember asked. "You must have me confused with someone else. I only just arrived yesterday."

"I don't think I do." The young woman smirked.

Ember spun the book in her hand, feeling the weight of it

sink into her fingers. It was her First Year *Zoomancy* textbook, whatever that was. Upon further inspection, she recognized the author as the one from Thea's library a few days prior. *T.L.*

"We've been waiting for you to come home for a long time, Miss Lothbrok," the woman answered.

Ember's chest tightened as a pit settled in her stomach. Who was this golden woman, and why on Earth does she already know her name? Suddenly, all of the peace she was feeling felt like it had been sucked out of her chest. "Um, right," she mumbled, ringing her sweaty hands together as she set the rest of the books on the counter. "How much do I owe you?"

The young woman shook her head and waved her hand. "It's been taken care of," she said sweetly.

Ember nodded her thanks as she bit the inside of her cheek. The confusion was written plainly on her face, and she didn't bother trying to hide it. She told the woman goodbye and loaded all of her books in arms and began to turn toward the door. The woman smiled, making her eyes twinkle, and as she tilted her head in curiosity, Ember barely noticed two pointed ears peeking out from her white hair.

Letting the door close behind her, she walked forward, trying to stick her books in the new leather satchel that hung over her shoulder. Lost in the myriad of questions running through her mind, she didn't notice that she was in the middle of the street or that there was a tall boy flying toward her. She tried to catch herself as he barreled into her, but she was caught off guard. Her knees hit the cobblestones with a *thud*, and she winced as she felt her palms sting against the sand-stone, books toppling forward in front of her. The boy stumbled back off the hovering board he had been riding, catching himself quickly before he hit the ground.

"Do you need a hand?"

Ember turned her head to look at him, sun beating down

around his head and into her eyes. She squinted at him as he held a hand out to help her off the ground. "Does it look like I need your help?" she hissed, wiping the bits of dirt from her now bleeding palm. The very last thing she needed was help from the absentminded stranger who had thrown her into the ground. Honestly, who did he think he was, riding around the streets like he owned the place, without a care in the world for the people around him? She heaved herself onto her feet and quickly wiped the dust off her pants.

"Do you really want me to answer that, or would you like to maintain plausible deniability for later?" He smirked, picking up the books that had scattered across the cobblestones. "You can't just walk into the street without looking. You're lucky it was just me you ran into and not a fish cart. You'd smell like cod for a week."

Ember squinted back at him as she snatched the books from him and stuffed them in her bag, mildly insulted that he thought this was her fault, considering he was the one who ran directly into her. Before she could voice her annoyance, Fen's voice sounded behind her.

"Em! Are you okay?" He puffed as he ran up beside her. "Killian, is this really how you're going to introduce yourself to my sister?" He barked a laugh as Killian puffed out his chest and straightened his spine, like a peacock ready to strut.

"*Foster* sister," she corrected him under her breath.

"Where are my manners?" The boy grinned. "I'm Killian Vargr, pleased to make your acquaintance." He bowed dramatically as he held his hand out to her, and she rolled her eyes at his dramatics.

Ember got a good look at him for the first time since he had absentmindedly shoved her to the ground. He was tall— taller than her and probably Fen, and his slate gray eyes sparkled in the sunlight, emitting a warmth like campfire smoke. He swept his pale blond hair out of his eyes as he smirked at her, a lopsided grin dancing across his mouth. She took note of the freckles that traveled over the bridge of his nose, across his alabaster skin. The sun beat down around him, forming a halo around his body, outlining his wide shoulders as he held his hand toward her.

Ember reached out and shook it, rolling her eyes as he winked back at her. She could've sworn she saw his eyes flash amber for a brief second before quickly shifting back to gray as he grinned. When their hands connected, Ember felt her necklace tingle and something tug at her chest, like a cord attached to her sternum was yanking her forward.

"Ember Lothbrok." She squinted, shaking his hand quickly before pulling it back down to her side and squeezing her palms together. "And if you can't stop for pedestrians, maybe you shouldn't be riding that thing in public." She pointed to the board in his hands.

"Well, aren't you just a little ray of sunshine." He smirked at her, and Ember shot him a rude gesture, the grin on his face growing as he narrowed his eyes at her. "No... more like the remnants of a dying star."

Ember narrowed her eyes and squeezed her hands together harder. She winced as she felt blood run down her fingers, quickly bringing attention to the shallow cut on her palm.

"Em, you're bleeding..." Fen pointed out, grabbing her wrist to examine it closer.

"I'm fine," she insisted. "It's just a cut. I'll bandage it later." She pulled her wrist out of Fen's hand and firmly held it in hers.

"I've seen Mum do loads of healing spells. I can give it a try! Can't be that hard," Fen said confidently, as he clutched the pendant around his neck. Ember was taken aback for a moment. It was the first time she had seen the disc around his neck, a near perfect match to the one around hers.

"Don't you remember what happened last time you tried a

healing spell?" Killian retorted as he crossed his arms and arched a brow.

"That fire had nothing to do with me," Fen glared.

"Right, of course. Spontaneous combustion is perfectly normal in the middle of a thunderstorm."

"You're bleedin' hilarious," Fen huffed, as he narrowed his eyes. He dropped his hand from his necklace and crossed his arms as Killian cocked his head and grinned.

"Killian, is everything alright?" a soft voice rang from behind the group of children.

Ember spun around to see where the voice was coming from, and her breath hitched in her chest when she saw a tall woman, maybe in her early twenties, with beautiful pale skin that almost glowed with a greenish hue, standing behind her. Her seafoam hair hung below her shoulders in waves, blowing gently with the wind. But this wasn't what caused Ember's breath to catch in her chest—it was the eyes that were staring back at her.

Lavender eyes.

"Maren, can you fix her hand?" Killian asked the woman, immediately breaking the trance-like state Ember had found herself in.

Before she had a chance to argue, Maren had Ember's hand in her own, smiling softly down at Ember, whose stomach was already doing flips. Her touch was soft, and her skin felt like satin. Her fingers were stitched together with a translucent webbing that blended seamlessly with the green hue in her slim fingers.

"This is a nasty cut, Miss Lothbrok, do you mind?" she said gently, almost singing.

Ember nodded, ignoring the fact that she hadn't told the woman her name, as Maren held her hand up higher, hovering her fingers over the gash in her palm.

"*Aguacura,*" she whispered, as her fingers made small circles in the air. Before Ember had the chance to ask what it meant, drops of water started falling from the woman's fingertips, enveloping her hand and the wound in small streams of glowing water. Just as quickly as it appeared, it was gone, leaving her hand blemish free, without even a scar.

"Thank you," Ember whispered as she flexed her hand, looking it over several times.

Maren nodded with a smile as she turned toward Killian. "Your mum doesn't like to be kept waiting, Killian. I have your school things, it's time we head back home."

Killian huffed in acceptance, hopping back on his board before waving his goodbyes.

"See ya at school, *Starshine*." He grinned.

Ember sucked in a breath and straightened her spine. Her chest ached as the nickname washed over her, the name only her father had ever called her. As a baby, like most, she had gotten her days and nights mixed up. Her father had stayed up with her most nights, content to read her stories and sit under the stars, and had affectionately bestowed her the nickname he used for the rest of her childhood, for the rest of his life. Ember furrowed her brow and called out to Killian, bewildered at his choice of words, but he was already gone, flying away, weaving in and out of the crowds of people. Ember rubbed the bridge of her nose, the same way she did when she felt a headache coming on.

"Is he always so..." she started.

"Charming?" Fen laughed in reply.

"I was going to say irritating," she scoffed as she rolled her eyes.

"Yeah... yeah, he's definitely that too." Fen shrugged in reply. "He means well, though."

Ember breathed a heavy sigh. "Meaning well isn't an excuse for boys to act like *eejits*," she scolded, almost startling herself with how forward she was being with the boy who was a complete stranger a few days prior. Was Killian being an idiot? Maybe not, but he was incredibly annoying.

Fen shrugged as the two made their way down the street, pulling a candy bar out of his trouser pocket.

"How's your hand?" he mumbled, his mouth full of chocolate.

"Like nothing ever happened," she replied, turning her hand over again to check her palm. "Who was that, anyway? Why does she look so…"

"Different?" Fen said, quickly finishing her sentence. "She's a Merrow. She works for the Vargrs."

"A… what?" Ember asked, as her face screwed up in confusion.

"A Merrow," he replied. "They're Fair Folk. They mostly work for descendants of the First Families, doing stuff like cooking, cleaning, and raising kids. Mum never wanted one, said she didn't need help raisin' us up. Didn't like the idea of having a maid, either. Killian's family has had Maren as long as I can remember."

Ember slowed her gait as she nodded, then she screwed up her face in confusion. "What's a First Family?"

"The direct descendant of the families that settled the island." Fen shrugged, as if it should be common knowledge.

"There are people on the island who aren't descendants?" Ember questioned, as she slowed her stride.

"Some, yeah." Fen nodded. "Some people from other magical communities have moved and started families here or married into families on the island."

"And the Vargrs haven't?" she questioned, stealing a bite of chocolate out of the boy's hand.

Fen pulled his hand away and guarded his sweets like it was a pot of gold. "Married someone who is not from here?" He scoffed. "Absolutely not. Luckily, Ellesmere is pretty big, but *eventually*, they'll run out of options. I'd imagine Killian will be the first to break away from tradition."

Ember sighed as she rubbed her temple. "Will we learn that spell? Can your mum heal like that?" she asked, trying to change the subject. The last thing she wanted to continue to talk about was the cocky boy with irritatingly beautiful eyes. Her question was cut short as they stepped through the crowd and saw Eira waving them toward her. Ember was confused by the peace settling in her stomach at the sight of the cheery woman. It was comforting to see that someone else, an *adult*, was happy to see her. That her presence wasn't insulting.

"Dad will be late tonight, so we're grabbing takeaway for dinner," she chimed as the teenagers made their way toward her. "I hope you don't mind curry chips, love," she directed at Ember. "Florin's is famous for them around here."

Ember gave her a polite nod and smiled. Those were actually her favorite. Most of the time, when her previous families got takeaway, she made herself a sandwich or found leftovers in the fridge. No one ever explicitly told her she wasn't welcome to eat, but they made it very plain that there wasn't enough to go around. The few times she had money of her own that she had scrounged up from mowing lawns or raking leaves, she would go straight into the city and grab a bag of curry chips all for herself.

"That sounds lovely, thank you, Mrs. Kitt," was all she could muster.

"I also took the liberty of grabbing you new clothes and shoes. I hope that wasn't too forward of me. Every girl deserves a new wardrobe before she starts school."

Ember felt her eyes grow misty as she bit her bottom lip. "Thank you, Mrs. Kitt," she whispered. "I really appreciate that." She appreciated it more than anyone would ever know.

THE FAMILY MADE their way back home, Fen talking loudly the whole way about the new AirWave that had just been released. Ember quickly figured out that that was the board Killian and a bunch of other kids had been riding and that it was involved in some sort of sport Fen was obsessed with. She laughed quietly to herself as she watched him plead with Eira for the new toy, only to be shot down with, "The one you got last year will work perfectly fine for Rukr tryouts."

Dinner that evening was a laidback affair. After finishing their curry chips, the family made their way into the den where Otto lit the fireplace and Eira settled into her chair to patch a dress that Maeve had torn a hole in. Ember was confused by the fire, considering it was only the end of August and hadn't even begun to get cold yet, until she sat in one of the chairs in front of it. Instead of heat radiating from the flames, it was a soft, cool breeze. Ember furrowed her brow as she gazed into them, tempted to reach and touch them.

"Seasonal fireplace," Fen said frankly. "Though, I think mum just likes lighting it for aesthetic purposes." Otto thumped the back of his head as he took his seat opposite of Eira, newspaper in hand. Ember sat cross-legged in her chair, watching Fen and Maeve play a card game on the floor. She shook her head when Fen asked if she wanted to play and sunk back into the oversized armchair. She let out a breath and smiled as she allowed herself to relax into the cushion and open the book she pulled from a shelf in the library.

She had lived in so many homes since she woke up in the hospital at six years old, becoming an orphan overnight. She had sat in front of numerous fireplaces, slept in countless bedrooms, and held on to hope as long as she could. Everywhere she lived felt like she was just floating between lives, never settling down to live in it. Nothing ever felt like home.

Sitting in front of this fireplace with these people felt different. Ember sunk further into the chair, a tiny flutter settling in her chest.

"Relaxing, isn't it?" Fen asked, as he leaned back on one elbow on the floor and stared at the fire.

"I can't believe it took me so long to get here," she whispered in reply, mostly to herself. She wasn't talking about the farm, but Fen smiled like he followed her train of thought exactly, nudging her leg playfully from his seat on the floor.

"Ellesmere isn't a secret if you know where to look." He grinned.

Ember smiled as she hugged her book to her chest, closing her eyes with a sigh.

Maybe this one will stick.

CHAPTER 5

A FUN SURPRISE

W aves crashed against the side of the small boat and rocked them violently across the black water.

"Papa, I'm scared," Ember whimpered, cheeks soaked with salt from the storm and the tears streaming down her freckled cheeks.

Her father held her against his chest as another wave beat against the side of the boat, spraying water on their already drenched life vests. "Fear is only the absence of hope, Starshine," he whispered in her ear, "and even in the darkest of storms, we will always have hope."

"Em, wake up! We're losing daylight!"

Ember blinked her eyes as she listened to Fen bang on the other side of her closed door. She squinted as she rolled over and pushed herself up on her elbow, grief washing over her as the dream—memory—slipped away. Looking out her bedroom window, she noticed the morning light was barely beginning to break over the horizon, bathing the room in warm pinks and purples. Ember rubbed her eyes a few times, willing the sleepiness to leave as she sunk back into her pillow.

"What daylight?" She yawned. "What time is it?" Sitting up slowly, she stretched her arms over her head and rubbed the sleep from her eyes. As comfortable as her new bed was, she still tossed and turned throughout the night, fighting dreams that tried to inch their way into her head. Some nights, she dreamed of her parents and woke up feeling refreshed, like she had just visited them for afternoon tea. Those mornings, before night had fully washed away and reality taken over, she felt like they could be right downstairs, waiting for her at the breakfast table. Other nights, like the one she had just had, were harder. Memories of a summer storm, waves twenty feet high, and small fingers wrapped around her father's arm. She wasn't sure she would ever escape those.

"Nearly half six," he shouted. "Mum won't have breakfast ready for another hour, but it'll take that long to finish chores, up and at 'em!"

She heard his heavy footsteps fade down the hall and slowly climbed out of bed to rub the same knot from yesterday out of her shoulder. She dug her palm into her eye, rubbing away the last of the sleep from the night before. She slipped into an old pair of jeans and a worn-out t-shirt, saving her new clothes for when term started on the first of September so they didn't get messed up. Walking over to her dresser, she began to throw her hair into a braid when she looked in the mirror and grimaced at the view.

Lavender eyes with flecks of ash stared back at her.

She grabbed the case sitting on top of the dresser and carefully placed the contacts in her eyes before someone could barge into the room. She sighed as she leaned against the dresser, green eyes now staring back at her. She twirled the ring around her finger and shook away the grief that was welling in her chest. She quickly pulled on her sneakers and made her way out of her room, down the creaking step.

Fen was leaning against the mudroom door when Ember entered the kitchen. Eira was so busy preparing breakfast that she didn't hear the quiet footsteps as she entered the room. Fen took his chance and snuck behind his mother, grabbing a piece of bacon and quickly sticking it in his mouth. Ember giggled involuntarily at the scene, causing Eira to jump as she turned around to examine the noise. Her surprise quickly turned to a smile as she greeted the giggling girl.

"Oh, good morning, love. I didn't hear you come in," she chirped, as she wiped her hand on her apron. She turned her head toward Fen and his mouth full of bacon and quickly swatted her towel at him as he ran to the door. "Breakfast will be ready after you both finish your chores. Fenrir will show you where everything is." She smiled as she turned back to the stove.

Ember followed Fen through the mudroom and out the back door. The summer morning was warm, but a cool breeze gently blew through the air.

"Grab this, and we'll start with the chickens," Fen said as he shoved a woven basket in her hands. She followed him toward the coop and watched as dozens of hens made their way out of the door in a single file line, clucking happily as they pecked at the ground. As she walked into the coop behind Fen, she heard a scream erupt from across the yard. She poked her head out of the coop door to see Maeve running across the yard, boots in hand and wild curls bouncing on her shoulders.

"Fen! Mum said eggs are *my* job!" she screeched angrily as she hopped on one foot across the wet grass. As she tried to pull a boot on, her foot quickly slipped out from under her, resulting in her landing face-first in the morning dew that had settled on the yard.

"I'm trying to give Em an easy job, Maevie." He laughed as he walked toward his little sister, quickly pulling her up from the ground. Ember furrowed her brow at his insinuation that she needed something easy. "Besides, you wouldn't wake up this morning when Mum sent up the Helio."

Maeve crossed her arms as she narrowed her eyes at her older brother, lightly tapping her foot on the ground below her feet. "Well, I'm awake now, and Mum said eggs were my job," she replied crossly.

"Here, Maeve," Ember said with a smile as she handed the girl the basket. "I think the job is better suited for you anyway. I wouldn't want to break any."

Maeve smiled as she took the basket from Ember and hurried toward the open coop. The hens clucked as she ran past them, quickly trying to get out of the way of the clumsy girl in her pink rain boots. Ember smiled as she heard her talking animatedly with the hens, dropping each of the eggs into her basket.

"I am perfectly capable of doing whatever chores you do, you know," Ember huffed, as she followed Fen toward the barn. "You don't have to give me your sister's jobs just because I'm a girl."

Fen let out a barking laugh as he opened a door on the side of the barn, leading them into a room filled with buckets and feed scattered on the floor.

"It's not because you're a girl," he chuckled. "You two get worked up so easily."

Ember rolled her eyes as she adjusted the pendant around her neck. The sibling rivalry was nothing new. She had watched it play out with dozens of other brothers and sisters before, but she had never been thrust in the middle of it or felt hope that maybe she would one day be part of the rivalry, having someone who loved her enough to fight with her. Fighting with siblings seemed better than all the times she'd been completely ignored.

She grabbed a bucket of chicken scratch and helped Fen mix the feed in with it. She made her way back outside and started scattering the feed across the ground for the eager hens as Fen filled their water dish. Maeve ran across the grass, chasing the clucking chickens to try and snatch one up in her already dirt covered arms. Ember laughed as she eyed the egg basket that lay forgotten by the door of the coop, as catching the hens became top priority that morning.

As Ember followed Fen toward the pasture, she felt fur brush up against the side of her leg and jumped back, looking down to see a large black cat, almost the size of a dog, with a white spot on its chest purring as it rubbed its head on her calf. She reached down to pet the animal as Maeve ran up beside her.

"Della!" she screeched as she wrapped her arms around the cat's neck. The cat purred its approval, nuzzling its face into the little girl's. "Ember, this is Della. She loves to snuggle with me on the grass."

"Well, hello, Della, it's very nice to meet you," Ember said, as she ran her hand along the cat's head. "Why is she so big?"

Della looked toward Ember, amber eyes meeting hers, and nodded her head as if to say hello. Ember's brow furrowed as Fen walked up behind them.

"Della is a Cat Sidhe," he answered, but Ember's face remained puzzled as she exchanged glances with the animal. "They're Fae animals… Honestly, did they teach you anything on the mainland?"

Ember rolled her eyes as she walked toward the pasture to put her feed bucket in its place, the cat's yellow eyes following her quizzically as she moved across the grass. Della lazily turned around and began following Maeve around the yard, now stuck to her like glue. The feline did her best to keep Maeve out of trouble, gently steering her away from mud puddles, water troughs, or unsuspecting chickens. It was endearing, the way she had such patience with the wild-haired girl, the way she purred and mewed and didn't show any signs of annoyance that she was in charge of this small child's safety. Ember grinned as she watched them run through the yard and felt her heart flutter as she turned back to Fen.

"Okay, what's next?" Ember asked, as she brushed away the

sweat that was quickly building on her brow. She was already exhausted, but at the same time, she felt oddly satisfied with the way the morning was going. The sun was beginning to warm her up, and manual labor tended to have that effect anyway.

"We check the rest of the animals' feed and water," Fen began, "and then we can head back into the barn. I've got something to show you." A mischievous grin creeped across his face, lighting up his eyes as the different hues of blue mixed together in the early morning light.

Ember grimaced. She didn't enjoy surprises. She walked the fence line, filling water troughs for the donkeys and goats. She stopped every so often to gently pat them on the head, not eager to finish quickly. There was something relaxing about the Kitts' farm compared to the bustle of the city she was used to. Time almost seemed to stand still here, and she was savoring every second of it.

Fen bounced around the pasture with buckets of feed, a small army of hungry goats voicing their disdain for his lack of speed behind him. Ember laughed as she watched him carelessly swing the feed bucket, brushing his messy brown hair out of his eyes. Ember felt her chest grow heavy as she leaned against the fence post. She couldn't remember a time in her life where she felt as carefree as Maeve and Fen seemed to be. The childhood she could remember was riddled with loneliness. Memories of closed doors, silent meals, and days spent with only her books for company.

"Alright, that's the last of 'em," Fen said as he wiped his hands on his jeans, turning on the balls of his feet to head toward the barn. "You comin'?" he asked as he briefly turned to Ember and nodded in the direction of the door.

Ember's feet felt like lead as she made her way toward Fen, knowing good and well that her fears were misplaced. She bit the inside of her cheeks and forced herself to take slow steps behind him, just to be on the safe side. Fen wouldn't knowingly put her in danger just for a laugh…

Right?

He quickly swung the barn door open and made his way down the center aisle. Empty stalls filled each side, some stacked with extra hay and broken farm equipment. Fen stopped at the end of the aisle in front of a stall, where he reached his hand up to pet the waiting animal.

Ember breathed a sigh of relief as she picked up her pace, relief washing over her as she made her way to the waiting boy, who had a huge grin plastered across his face.

"Honestly, Fen, do you really think I've never seen a horse before?" She stopped abruptly as she walked up beside him, a small gasp leaving her mouth as she stumbled back into the stall behind her. She could feel her heart beating violently in her throat as she gripped the stall door, knuckles turning white against the weathered wood. Her feet were rooted to the floor, completely frozen in fear. Everything in her told her to run back to the safety of the house, but she couldn't move. Couldn't breathe. Fen broke the silence as he turned to her, grinning from ear to ear.

Standing directly behind the smiling boy was a dragon.

Deep black and blue scales ran down its neck, meeting with the wings that lay against his back. Two beautiful ivory horns lay against its head by its ears, its head tilted up as it looked impassively at the trembling girl.

"Ember, I'd like you to meet Arlo."

Ember stood straight and tried to wrap her mind around her foster brother running his hand carelessly down the snout of the animal.

"A DRAGON?" she screeched, finding her voice again. "You have a pet DRAGON?"

Fen doubled over in a fit of giggles as he wrapped his arms around his waist. The animal above him snorted his disapproval before he turned to ignore the two, causing Ember to jump at the sudden movement.

"Arlo is a draic," he said between wheezes.

"What's the difference?" she asked crossly, arms pressed tight across her chest as she shot daggers at him with her eyes.

"Dragons and draics are very different," Fen replied like it was common knowledge, laughter beginning to die down as he straightened himself back up. "Arlo will never get any bigger than this, about the size of a horse. They don't breathe fire, and they're very calm, loyal animals. They bond for life." As he said this, the creature leaned its head over the stall door, nuzzling its snout in the boy's neck.

"Does he bite?" Ember asked cautiously. Just because the creature was loyal to Fen didn't mean he wouldn't snap her fingers off if she got too close.

"Even a field mouse will bite if it feels threatened." Fen smiled as he motioned for Ember to come toward him. Ember slowly shuffled her feet forward, careful not to make any sudden movements that might spook the majestic creature. Fire or not, she could still see the sharp teeth peeking out of its mouth, and that was threatening enough to warrant a silent approach.

"Lower your head before you pet him," Fen said, as he held his hand on Ember's wrist, "Let him make the first move. Draics are gentle creatures, but they require respect."

Ember lowered her head as she approached the creature, eyes glued to the dusty floor. She waited for what felt like an eternity, heart threatening to beat out of her chest before she felt Arlo's hot breath above her head. Her heart rate quickened as he gently brushed his snout against her, moving her head to look up at him. She was met with red eyes staring back at her, but not a red that evoked any sort of fear. It was warm and inviting, deep gold swirling through the crimson, creating a hurricane of fire.

"He's beautiful," she whispered, mostly to herself, as she ran her fingers along his head and down his elongated snout. The warmth radiating from his scales surprised her—she assumed he would feel like a big, scaly lizard. Instead, his scales were soft and sleek, like velvet against her fingertips. Arlo snorted as if to say thank you, right before he turned his head to continue eating the berries in his feeder.

"Does he stay in here all the time?" Ember asked, as she leaned against the stall door.

"He can leave whenever he wants." Fen shrugged as he motioned to a door at the back of the stall. "He prefers to spend his mornings here, though. Most afternoons, I'll take him flying if the weather's nice."

Ember coughed as she choked on her own spit. "Fly?" she whispered. "You ride on him while he flies?"

"Of course, I do," Fen said with a grin. "I don't just sit on the ground and watch him." He pulled his phone out of his pocket to check it before quickly putting it away and nodding in the direction of the house. "Breakfast should be ready, so we better get going." He stopped halfway down the aisle before he turned back around, a wicked grin lighting up his face. "Unless..." he drawled out, tapping his finger lightly against his chin.

Ember stiffened as she gripped stall door beside her. "Unless what?" she asked warily, though she felt like she might know the answer.

"Unless you would like a tour of the island?" He grinned, stuffing his hands in his pockets as he headed toward an interior door at the front of the barn.

"A tour?" she questioned, furrowing her brow. "How do you intend to give me a tour of the entire island before breakfast?" She almost laughed—she wanted to laugh—but she was afraid of his answer.

Fen waltzed out of the room with a saddle draped over his arms and a halter over his shoulder, that stupid grin still lighting up his entire face.

"Arlo is a very fast flier," he quipped as he laid the saddle on the side of the stall and went to open the wooden door.

"You're not doing a great job at convincing me," Ember

replied, trying—and failing—to disguise the fear that was bubbling in the pit of her stomach.

"It's not that bad." Fen laughed as he rolled his eyes. "It's just like riding a bike or a horse… but in the air. Otherwise, there's very little difference."

Ember pinched the bridge of her nose as she let out a sigh. There really was no point in telling him no, was there? And he looked so excited… The thought of disappointing him left Ember with a hollow feeling in her chest.

"One ride," she said as she jabbed her finger in his chest. "One *quick, slow* ride, and that's it." She crossed her arms tightly over her chest as she watched him warily. Somehow, he seemed to smile even brighter as he reached his hand out to shake hers.

"Deal," he grinned, and then turned quickly to finish putting Arlo's tack on. Ember stayed close behind as he led the draic out of the barn and into the pasture at the back. She took a shaky breath as she looked up toward the sky and suddenly realized just how small she actually was. Her thoughts were quickly interrupted by a snort from Arlo and Fen's hand on her shoulder.

"Ready?" He smiled as he nodded toward the saddle on the draic's back.

"As I'll ever be," she breathed. Fen put his foot in the stirrup and gracefully hoisted himself onto the saddle, then extended his hand toward Ember. She took a shaky breath before grabbing his hand and clamped her eyes closed as he pulled her up, wrapping her arms tightly around his waist.

"Just breathe, Em." Fen laughed as he snapped the reins, and before Ember could answer, she felt all of the breath get sucked from her lungs as her stomach dropped. She opened her eyes warily as she felt them climb into the sky, and by the time she felt comfortable enough to look around, the Kitts' farm looked like a tiny dollhouse nestled in an emerald rug. Ember sucked in a breath as she looked around, watching the green below them bend and sway in the morning breeze. Fen snapped the reins gently and leaned to his right, and Arlo turned with him in one fluid movement, the trust they seemed to have in each other remarkable.

"You live by the ocean?" Ember yelled as they made their way toward the turquoise water that lapped gently below them.

Fen nodded as he pointed back toward the house. "We have about twenty acres. Me and Killian like to come out here during the summer. Ready to see more?"

Ember nodded as she tightened her grip around his waist and braced herself as Arlo made a sharp turn, heading back past the house and over the greenest pastures Ember had ever seen. They traveled over fields of wildflowers the made the rolling hills look like a quilt sewn by the gods themselves. Ember's smile widened as they flew over the town, watching the people mill about like little dolls. They sped further inland, stopping abruptly over a wide tree line, the tops of the trees covered by a dense fog. Arlo flapped gently, seeming to hover eerily in one place as Fen caught his breath.

"Heksheim is through there." He pointed toward the forest.

Ember squinted in the direction of his fingers but couldn't see anything. "Can we go closer?" she asked, as she shifted in the saddle, feeling oddly comfortable now despite being hundreds of feet up in the air.

Fen shook his hand as he wiped a hand across his brow. "It's warded," he replied. "We won't be able to get in 'til the start of term."

Ember huffed as she chewed on her lip. "What about over those trees," she asked as she pointed toward the fog, feeling very bold all of a sudden. "Can we go see what's past the trees?"

Fen stiffened as he shook his head. "That's the Dark

Forest. We cannot, for any reason, go there, not over or through it."

Ember nodded silently and sank back in the saddle, suddenly feeling like a five-year-old who had been caught with their hand stuck in the cookie jar.

Fen turned and smiled at her, brightening her mood a bit, before he nodded behind them. "Best get back before Mum notices we're missing. Hold on tight, yeah?"

Ember nodded as they turned and sped away, back in the direction of the little farm she had quickly grown so fond of. Just as they were in view of the barn, Fen leaned forward on Arlo and tightened his grip around the draic's ribs.

"*Casadh!*" he yelled, and before Ember could register what he had said, Arlo was suddenly doing barrel rolls in midair, flipping around like a siren in the sea. Ember clamped her eyes closed and squeezed Fen's waist so hard she was sure she would crack one of his ribs. She gritted her teeth and held her breath, determined not to scream no matter how desperately she wanted to. Arlo finally stopped spinning, landing gracefully in the pasture by the barn, and Ember couldn't get off his back fast enough. Fen dropped to the ground, patting the animal on his snout, and Ember quickly smacked him on the arm.

"Ow!" he yelled, as he rubbed the spot her hand had connected with on his bicep. "What was that for?"

"I said no funny business!" she all but screeched as she gasped for air.

Fen barked a laugh as he untacked Arlo, quickly walking into the barn to put everything away. Ember followed him angrily inside, stomping her feet like a child.

"I'm sorry," he said sincerely through a laugh. "I thought it would be a fun surprise."

"Well, you thought wrong," Ember replied, but she couldn't control the smile that was beginning to take over.

CHAPTER 6
HEKSHEIM ACADEMY OF MYTH AND MAGIC

E mber fidgeted with the strap on her leather satchel and twirled her father's ring around her finger while she stared at herself in the mirror above her dresser. The first day of school always made her nervous, and her stomach was still doing somersaults after choking down her breakfast that morning. Not only was it the nervousness of making friends, something she had failed at spectacularly before, but the thought of learning magic and failing at that as well nearly sent her in a downward spiral. She adjusted the straps of her green dress and straightened out the yellow shirt underneath to make sure no wrinkles were present. First impressions were impossible to recover from, she learned, and she was determined to do everything possible to blend in flawlessly.

She took a deep breath with one last look in the mirror and swallowed back the breakfast that threatened at her lips before making her way downstairs. Fen was waiting by the front door, casually leaning against the frame as he scrolled mindlessly through his phone. His obvious comfort did absolutely nothing to calm her nerves. If anything, it set her off even more. How could he be so calm? Why was he not as stressed as she was? It was borderline infuriating. As her feet hit the bottom step, Fen's head popped up, and he hastily stuffed his phone in his pocket, picking up the backpack that lay by his feet.

"I thought I was going to have to come find you," he joked as he reached for the door and ushered her toward it.

Eira popped out of the kitchen and kissed both of them on the head. "Have a lovely first day!" She smiled at Ember as she rubbed her cheek. "And be on your best behavior," she said in Fen's direction as he blushed.

"We will, Mum," he groaned and pulled Ember toward the open door.

Ember smiled as she waved goodbye and felt a small pang of sadness as the door shut behind her. She would be back that evening, but she had begun to find comfort in the chipper woman's presence, and the idea of spending her day without her sing-song voice echoing through the house made her heart sink.

Ember followed Fen down the long dirt driveway toward the gate, hesitating briefly as she wondered why they didn't just go through the closet again. She inhaled the fresh morning air, the cool breeze filling her lungs as she worked to slow her breathing. Fen walked ahead of her, happily humming to himself as he worked to swing open the gate. After crossing the boundary of the Kitts' property, he stopped for a moment to look around before heading toward a small tree on their right.

"Oh, good," he breathed as he walked up to the tree. "We're right on time. Here, come grab the trunk."

Ember raised her eyebrows as she walked toward Fen and touched the trunk of the tree, noting the jagged lines of the rune, almost resembling the letter *R*, that was carved into the bark. "What's that?" she asked, pointing at the rune on the tree.

"*Raihdo*," Fen responded, as he rolled up his sleeves. "It's the rune for travel. Now, grab on. We don't want to be late."

Ember quickly grabbed a low hanging branch and held her breath. One second, they were standing at the edge of the property, and before she knew it, she felt a tug, and she was spinning through starlight. The taste of copper hit her tongue as she squeezed her eyes closed and spun through the cold air. A starlight-filled mist whipped around her and gave her the oddest sensation that she was flying through the cosmos. Just when she was certain she couldn't take it anymore, the spinning stopped, and she landed with a thud on the side of a dirt road. Fen landed beside her, gracefully on his feet, laughing as he extended his hand to help Ember back to hers.

"What... in the world... was that?" she asked through gasps. She stumbled back a few steps, her head still spinning. Green pastures surrounded them on either side of the road, and Ember could just barely make out a tree line in the distance.

"That," Fen said as he brushed lingering dust off his shirt, "was an Echopoint. It would've been too far to walk, and going through the Yggdrasil Terminal only takes you into Sigurvik."

Ember furrowed her brow and nodded. She felt like she had whiplash. She wasn't sure how many more surprises she could handle today, and they hadn't even made it to the school yet. A thud sounded behind them, and Ember let out a yelp.

"Howeyah, Fen!" a voice echoed behind her.

Ember groaned at the familiar voice as she quickened her pace to catch up with Fen, who had already started down the road.

"What is he doing here?" Ember mumbled to Fen as she adjusted the bag on her shoulder.

"Now, Starshine..." Killian grinned. "Don't act like you aren't excited to see me."

Ember sneered at him as she narrowed her eyes. She was in no mood for him today.

Killian threw his arm over her shoulder with a grin, completely oblivious to the annoyed look plastered all over her face.

She shoved his arm away and distanced herself from the boys as they greeted one another. "I don't like nicknames," she hissed. "Maybe you should go back over there." She pointed toward the tree they had walked away from. "And then come back. You seem to have missed running me over this time."

Killian ignored her quip entirely, and instead turned to Fen. "Did you introduce her to Arlo yet?" He grinned, stuffing a hand in one of his pockets.

"I thought she was going to pass out from shock," Fen laughed. "Almost broke my ribs when he rolled. You should've heard her scream!"

Ember glared at both boys as they flung their heads back and laughed.

"I didn't scream," she spat, "and you should've warned me before you did something like that!"

"Now, where's the fun in that, Starshine?" Killian grinned.

Ember rolled her eyes, but what she really wanted to do was slap the smug grin off his face. He had an air about him that grated on her every nerve, and she had a feeling these boys were going to be a handful this year.

She kicked up dust as the boys talked animatedly in front of her. They passed green pastures with cows grazing as they continued down the dirt path, and Ember let out a sigh as she was met with the salt blowing through the air. She closed her eyes. The longer she walked, the more her anxiety seemed to ease, and she could finally feel her breathing begin to return to normal. Fen shoved Killian as he laughed about some joke the boy had made, and Ember watched as he stumbled back, catching himself before he hit the dirt. He shot her a smile and a wink before turning back toward Fen and returning the shove.

Killian looked every bit of what Ember assumed a descendant of magical gods would look like. He brushed his bright blond hair from in front of his eyes as the sun cast shadows on his perfectly chiseled face, a lopsided grin sliding across his mouth. His eyes sparkled in the sun as mischief played across them. He wore a freshly pressed white button up shirt, sleeves rolled to his elbows, with black slacks and shoes that looked like they had never seen the outdoors. Ember looked at him like he was the sun, in the sense that she only ever looked at him in frustration, squinting in annoyance at how brightly he shined.

"It's the first day of the rest of our lives, mate!" Killian said as he slung his arm over Fen's shoulder, ignoring the annoyance that radiated from the girl next to them.

It was going to be a long day.

The two continued to chatter as they walked down the winding road. Several other children popped in on the sides of the path, hurrying forward as they chattered excitedly with each other. Ember clutched the pendant around her neck as she chewed on her bottom lip. The butterflies in her stomach seemed to whirl and grow, and she had to consciously make her feet move, one in front of the other. After a few minutes, a tree line came into view, the road leading straight into what looked like a very deep forest. Ember felt her heart jump as they edged closer. They followed the other children into the tree line, and she felt the metal disc around her neck vibrate as they stepped through what seemed to be a barrier of some sort. The green energy shifted to let them pass, and the sight that greeted them made Ember stop in her tracks, sucking in a deep breath as her eyes widened.

Right in front of them was a large clearing, greenery on either side of the path being bathed in warm sunlight. Children stood on the clover-filled lawn talking excitedly with each other while the majority continued toward the end of the road. Parents kissed their children goodbye, spouting off checklists and well wishes, and their children quickly shooed them away and ran down the path. At the end, in the middle of the large clearing, stood the largest tree Ember had ever seen.

Or at least, she thought it was a tree. The trunk was easily the size of a castle, grooves of the bark running from the roots to the very top. Branches reached to the sky, filtering the bright sun through their leaves. Large windows jutted out from the sides of the trunk, spiraling their way up to the top of the tree. Ember let her eyes fall from the top of the tree, down to the base of the trunk where a large door stood open, children slowly making their way inside. All the magical knowledge in the world could never have prepared her for the magnitude of what was standing in front of her.

Ember felt a gentle tug on her wrist as she looked up at a smiling Fen. Her heart rate slowed a bit, and she forced herself to walk toward the towering doors, up the rocky front steps, and into the giant entryway. The walls on the inside were a beautiful, deep oak that looked like they had been there for hundreds of years. They were rounded, just like the outside of the tree, and Ember suddenly wondered if this was how squirrels felt when they settled down in their homes for winter. There was a warmth surrounding her that was almost palpable—the magic in the air tasting like copper and lavender and laughter reverberating off the stained glass that dotted the high walls.

Ember looked at the pictures hanging around her, pictures she assumed were of the original families that settled the islands. Majestic longboats sailed across choppy waters, and Ember was taken aback by how *alive* they looked. Above a large doorway, sculptures of gods and goddesses were carved into the ancient wood, gleaming in the sunlight that was pouring through the hundreds of windows. Loki and Odin next to Freyja and Hel—they looked exactly like the pictures in the books Ember spent her childhood reading, adorned with small jewels that sparkled against the morning sun.

"What is this?" Ember mumbled as she waded through the sea of students, sticking closely to both boys as Killian led that way.

"It's our school." Fen shrugged. "I told you it wasn't a castle."

Ember took in a deep breath as her head spun, trying to soak in all of the details carved into the walls. "Right, but you also failed to mention that the school was inside of a giant tree."

"Details." Fen shrugged again.

"Bit of a shock to the system the first time." Killian smirked. "You get used to it."

"You've been here before?" Ember asked as she furrowed her brow.

"A few times." Killian nodded. "My dad is on the school board. I've had to come with him a handful of times."

Ember noted the few parents seeing their children off, first years like them to their first day of school. Other children wandered around alone through the wide entry way, chattering animatedly together, but Ember was still puzzled.

"Why didn't your mum drop us off?" she questioned, as she turned to look at Fen, who was very busy with his nose buried in his phone. Worry suddenly filled her chest. Had she done something wrong?

"Your first day at Heksheim is like your first step into adulthood," he replied as he stuffed his phone in his pocket. "Mum and Dad wanted to let us do this on our own. It's sort of a rite of passage."

Ember nodded as she took another shaky breath and adjusted the strap of her bag. Standing in this sea of students, on an island she had barely lived on for three days, she felt like anything but an adult.

"Plus," Fen continued, "I've been here loads of times when they came with Siris. Between me and Killian, we'll take care of you."

As much as she didn't want to admit it, that was begrudgingly comforting. She narrowed her eyes as she tilted her head. Instead of the eye roll she wanted to give, she sighed. "Who is Siris?" she asked.

"Osiris," Fen replied. "My older brother."

"*Brother?*" Ember gasped, as her eyes widened. "You have a *brother?* Why haven't I met him?"

He looked at her in confusion, like *she* had been the one to give him totally new information just now. Fen shrugged. "He's older, so we don't see him much." He pushed his hair out of his eyes as he huffed, "I honestly didn't think to mention him."

Ember studied the crease above his brow, and the way the corners of his mouth tightened as his eyes narrowed at nothing in particular in front of him, lost in whatever memory was consuming him.

Huh, maybe the Kitts aren't so perfect after all.

The trio followed the group of chattering children into a large room that reminded Ember of a cathedral. The ceilings were tall and arched, but instead of solid timber, the only thing in between them and the sky outside were several hundred branches, all woven together into a canopy. Large round tables were lined up in rows throughout the room, children already sitting in their seats, talking excitedly amongst themselves.

Ember followed the talkative boys to a table in the middle of the room and took a seat. She fidgeted nervously with her necklace as the room began to fill, and more people sat at their table, but her thoughts were drowned out by the excited chatter of students.

"Please settle down and find a seat," a loud voice boomed from the front of the room.

Ember craned her neck to look for the source. Standing on a large stage was a young woman, tight, dark brown curls framing her bronze skin. She cleared her throat as she brushed the wrinkles out of her gray pencil skirt and matching vest, then straightened the sleeves of the white, long sleeve button up underneath it. She smiled and adjusted the glasses on her nose, as the room fell silent.

"Good morning, students," she announced loudly. "For those who are new, I am Professor Moran, your Dean of Magic. In front of you, you will find your class syllabus, along with teacher names and the required books you will need to have with you for each of their classes. Please make it a point to be respectful of the time they put into each and every one of your lessons and do your best to be punctual. First years"— her eyes met Ember's table, as well as several others toward the front—"you have been broken into two groups. You will be in these groups for the remainder of your time at Heksheim, attending classes with the same students during each period." Professor Moran's eyes roamed across the room as they met with each of the students', keeping her posture perfect and her hands folded in front of her. "You should all be aware by now that the Dark Forest is off limits. Not only is the entrance to the Fae territory inside of it, but there are many creatures that would take pleasure in doing you harm."

Ember felt a chill run down her spine as she stiffened.

"You are safe inside our wards, but I cannot protect you if you willingly seek danger."

Ember dropped her gaze to the formerly empty table, a perfectly penned piece of parchment now lying in front of her. As she picked it up, her mind wandered to what could be living beyond the wards. Danger on the island was something that hadn't occurred to her. She shivered at the thought of a hairy beast with razor sharp teeth lurking in the shadow, howling at the moon. Ember's heart began to thud against her ribs. She quickly leaned over and checked both Fen and

Killian's schedules, breathing a sigh of relief as she saw they were the same as her own.

"Your professors are all looking forward to another year and kindly request that you keep extracurriculars outside of the classroom." Her gaze dropped as she looked toward Killian and Fen, right at a balled up piece of paper in the former's hand that he was just about to hurl toward Ember's head. It burst into flames and smoke. The blond had the sense to look properly abashed. "For those of you who are beginning your first year with us, welcome to Heksheim. And to those of you who are returning, welcome home."

The large room began to empty out as students chatted excitedly about their upcoming day and made their way to their classes, some whispering quietly about Professor Moran's warning. Ember slung her bag over her shoulder and followed Killian and Fen into the entryway, nose buried in the syllabus in her hands. Killian led the way, falling naturally into the perfect tour guide as he glided through the halls, shoulders back and chin raised in aristocratic grace.

"The steps are this way," he said over his shoulder, as he nodded to his left. Ember adjusted the strap on her shoulder as she nodded, but she couldn't see through the sea of students around her. She looked up and felt her breath hitch in her chest as she saw just how high the ceiling was above her. The walls were solid wood, stairs hugging the wall and wrapping all the way up to the top, and she quietly wondered where the windows were that she had seen outside, as well as all of the classrooms. It took her breath away, how majestic it looked, and she couldn't believe everyone else wasn't just as in awe as she was. Just as she thought it, she wondered again if she would every truly feel like she belonged here, like Killian and Fen seemed to. She shook her head as she picked up her pace, following Killian through the sea of students.

The boys talked in front of her, and she did her best to tune them out as she focused on the day before her. She read the class names, along with room numbers and the floors they were located on, over and over to try to commit everything to memory, as if the paper itself would spontaneously combust at any moment. She flipped the paper over to see a map had appeared on the back side of the syllabus, smiling as she saw small red dots scattered across the parchment, blinking like tiny lighthouses on the coast. She saw the names of all of her classes on the second floor under each dot, along with the time the class began and the room number. When she touched the corner to see if there was a second page, the image changed and showed her a zoomed image of the second floor, with the same red dots where her classes were located.

All of a sudden, the floor jerked underneath her, and she felt her heart leap into her throat. Her head whipped up, and her stomach dropped as she saw she was moving *up*. She gripped the rail next to her and spun her head around. Students were in front of and behind her, and she realized she was on the staircase. It was spiraling up, lining the round walls on the inside of the tree, and the steps were moving on their own. There was a banister to her right, as well as one on her left that seemed to split the staircase in half, the other half spiraling back down to the first floor.

She gripped the railing beside her until her knuckles turned white, her heart still thumping steadily in her throat. When her feet hit the landing, she turned behind her and let out a breath.

"A little warning would have been nice," she scolded, but no one was there. "Fen? Killian?" she called out as other students passed by her, but they had disappeared. She huffed as she pinched the bridge of her nose, annoyance and nerves bubbling in her stomach. "Absolutely useless boys," she mumbled as she walked through the door to her right and into the corridor. She walked swiftly as she glanced down at the paper in her hands, now seeing a little green dot that represented her, moving toward her first class. She smiled as she watched the magical GPS tracking her every move, but she was quickly jolted back to reality as she crashed into something in front of her, causing the contents of her bag—as well as her head—to hit the stone floor as she fell back.

"Watch it!" a shrill voice shrieked from above her.

Ember rubbed the knot that was already forming on the back of her head as she tried to focus on where the voice was coming from. Standing above her was a tall girl with jet black hair and the most striking blue eyes she had ever seen. Beside her was a boy with the same raven hair and blue eyes, both of them glaring at her on the floor. Ember picked herself up off the ground and brushed her dress off as she turned to face them.

"Didn't your mother teach you any manners?" the girl said with a growl.

"I-I'm sorry," Ember stuttered. "I think I might be lost. I didn't even see you there." When she didn't get a reply from the raven-haired girl, she stuck out her hand in an attempt to make amends. "I'm Ember. Ember Lothbrok," she said, faking every ounce of confidence she could muster.

The girl cocked an eyebrow and rolled her eyes as she laughed with the boy next to her.

"Of course, you are," he said arrogantly before they turned together and walked away.

Ember let out a heavy sigh as she bent back down to pick up her belongings from the floor.

"Already had a run in with the Ellingboe twins?" another voice rang from above her. "Not a brilliant way to start the year."

Ember lifted her head to see a girl kneeling in front of her, picking up the books and pens that had scattered across the corridor. Brown curls hung around her tan face and glasses as she offered a warm smile. She handed Ember her things and then offered her hand to shake, which she graciously accepted.

"The who?" Ember asked, smoothing out her, now trampled, syllabus.

"Veda and Oryn Ellingboe," she replied. "Best to just stay out of their way. They're not the type you wanted to be acquainted with. I'm Rowan."

Of course she would have a run in with snotty twins on her first day at a magical school. That had to be something that could only ever happen to her. Her thoughts wandered back to every unfortunate instance that ended with her being removed from her foster homes, and she felt her heart sink. She straightened her back and took a deep breath. This time it would be different. It had to be.

"Well, thank you," she replied quietly. "I'm Ember."

Rowan snatched the parchment from Ember's hand faster than she could blink and quickly compared it to her own. Before Ember had a chance to process that it had left her hand, Rowan thrust it back toward her.

"Looks like we have the same schedule!" Rowan exclaimed, far too chipper for Ember's taste. "I've had the school layout memorized for as long as I can remember. Come on, we'll walk together!" And before Ember could ask her *how* she already knew the layout so well, Rowan grabbed her by the wrist and began quickly dragging her down the hall.

Well, that's one way to make friends, I guess.

The girls weaved in and out of the crowd of students chatting in the halls until they made their way to a small door. Ember bent over, bracing her hands on her knees as she tried to catch her breath.

"Getting around is a lot easier if you run, in my opinion," Rowan said with a confident smile. "People tend to move out of your way a lot faster if they think you're going to mow them over."

Ember looked up at the girl in shock as she took in deep breaths. She wasn't entirely sure what she was getting herself into, but she guessed one nice friend who might talk her ear off was better than no friends at all. "Um, I suppose so," she replied, as she lifted herself upright and adjusted the strap of her bag.

Ember audibly gasped as the door swung open, and she stepped across the threshold. Instead of the hard stone floor in the corridor behind her, her shoes met lush, green grass. The walls, or lack thereof, were lined with trees, their branches jutting out across the high ceiling. Odd colored fruit hung low on the branches, and an odd breeze blew through Ember's hair. She took a seat next to Rowan in a chair that resembled an old tree trunk, but when she sat down, it felt like there was a pillow underneath her.

"Thought you got lost, Starshine."

Ember turned around to see a smug grin plastered across Killian's face as he leaned back in his seat, arms crossed over his chest.

"Sorry 'bout that, Em," Fen mumbled with an apologetic smile. "We thought you were behind us."

Ember glared at both of the boys before turning back around, giving up on fighting the nickname for now. She busied herself with pulling out her Zoomancy book, along with a new pen and notebook, as she heard a door at the front of the classroom close.

"Good morning, young Vala," a voice boomed from the top of a spiral staircase. "Welcome to your first year of Zoomancy. I am Professor Bjorn."

Ember looked up from her book and felt like her eyes were going to bulge from her head. Standing in front of her, with a gold monocle covering one of his eyes, was a giant grizzly bear. A green robe hung over his burly frame, and a tan shirt was showing underneath it with what looked like leaves hanging off his sleeves. Odd-shaped bottles hung from a leather belt around his waist, along with a small notebook. Both his arms bore bandages wrapped up halfway under the sleeve of his robe, and his bare paws left deep prints in the grass as he walked. A small gasp left Ember's lips before she quickly covered her mouth. Killian snickered behind her as Rowan placed her hand gently on her forearm.

"He's a Transmutant," she whispered quietly. "You know… like a shapeshifter. You're not from around here, are you?"

Ember shook her head slowly, not daring to take her eyes off the man—or animal—in front of her.

"He won't bite or anything," Rowan laughed under her breath. "Professor Bjorn taught my brother, said he was one of the nicest teachers at Heksheim."

"Alright, class, open your books to chapter five," Professor Bjorn boomed.

"But, sir, aren't you going to take the roll?" a chipper voice asked from the front of the room.

"Now, what makes you think I don't already know exactly who is sitting in my classroom, Miss Hawthorne?" he asked playfully, looking over the top of his monocle. His eyes flitted about the room for a moment, until they landed firmly on Ember. "You've all had your names written down since the day you were born," he replied, onyx eyes never leaving her, "and we have been waiting a very long time for you."

Ember's throat went dry as she looked down at her hands on the desk, breaking their involuntary staring contest. The center of attention was not somewhere she liked to stay for very long.

"Now that that's sorted," the professor announced gruffly, "please continue to open your books to chapter five."

With a flick of his wrist, every textbook in the room flew open, pages fluttering gently as they all landed in the correct spot. Ember jumped as the book settled in front of her and began admiring the beautiful illustrations on the page, each one hugging the words below and beside them.

"If you will," the professor continued, "place your dominant hand on the text in front of you, anywhere will do."

Ember furrowed her brow as she hovered her hand over the book. She felt silly at best and wasn't sure how she was supposed to read if her hand was hiding all of the words. Her heart skipped a beat when she placed her hand on the text and a green light began to shine behind each of the words. There was a collective gasp that sounded around the classroom as the books roared to life and projections rose from each of the parchments. Sitting directly on top of each open book, was a small black cat with a large white spot on its chest, cleaning its paws.

"This semester, we will be learning about familiars, something I know several of you are already familiar with." He chuckled to himself at his own joke before clearing his throat and addressing the silent classroom again. "We will dive deep into several different types of familiars and their background. As easy as you think studying Zoomancy might be, I urge you not to shrug it off. I have no intention of going easy on you during your final exams."

The classroom nodded silently as Professor Bjorn shuffled his giant paws toward the class.

"Now, who can tell me about the Cat Sidhe?"

A hand shot up in the air, directly in front of Ember. Mr. Bjorn nodded his head in her direction as he leaned back on his desk to listen.

"The Cat Sidhe," the girl said whimsically, "is a fairy creature. They are large black cats with a white spot on their chest. Oftentimes, they imprint on children as young as three years old, and they bond for life. They are very protective of their Vala and guard them with their life."

"Very good, Miss Quinn," the professor replied. "And who can tell me what they do for their Vala?"

Ember was shocked when she heard Fen's voice behind her.

"They're companions and protectors, mostly, but they also predict the weather and sometimes tell the future. My sister has a Cat Sidhe, and she gets real finicky when she knows rain is comin'."

Ember smiled as she thought about Maeve and how attentive Della was with the girl.

The professor chuckled as he nodded. "Ah, yes, they tend to do that," he laughed. "Legend also says that a powerful Vala can look into their Cat Sidhe's eyes and see the Otherworld. But that has never been proven, of course. The Cat Sidhe demands justice and harmony. They represent virtue and honor. They imbue with good intentions and well-meaning actions. Not to mention, they are one of the most wise, intuitive, and intelligent magical creatures that exist. When picking a Vala, they look for one who is pure and seeks the things that they are embodiments of."

The voices around Ember drowned out as she watched the image dance in front of her. It was like books she had read about the future and holograms. A video being projected from the pages and into the air, it was almost so real she could touch it. Her heart fluttered as the cat pranced around the page chasing a butterfly, and she felt the hairs on her arm stand up as the projection rubbed its head on her. No amount of previous schooling could ever have prepared her for any of this.

She spent the rest of the class with eyes and ears glued to the professor in front of her. She had a sudden thirst for knowledge that she hadn't felt in years, and she was afraid if she took her eyes off him even for a moment, she would miss something. Her pen scratched furiously across her paper, and her thoughts were only disrupted as a bird in one of the trees above her, that she had somehow missed until then, tweeted loudly.

"Ah, well, that seems to be all the time we have for today," Professor Bjorn announced. "I will expect a two-page paper on the Cat Sidhe and its history on my desk by Friday. You're dismissed."

Textbooks were flung closed all across the classroom as everyone hurried to their next class. Ember begrudgingly said goodbye to the cat, who was chasing another butterfly across the pages, as she closed the tome. The classroom emptied as Ember slung her bag over her shoulder, turning to follow Rowan out the door.

"One moment, Miss Lothbrok," the professor's voice said from behind her.

Ember stiffened as she turned toward the desk at the front of the room.

"I'll wait for you," Rowan said with a small wave.

Ember nodded her thanks, and her stomach did somersaults as she walked up to the large bear—she would never get past that—at the front of the room.

"Yes, sir?" she said, as she gripped the strap of her bag a little too tightly.

"I just wanted to take a moment and welcome you to Ellesmere personally," he said softly. "Your father was a good friend of mine, and I was very sad to hear of him and your mum's passing. I know he would be proud to see you here."

Ember's heart fluttered at the mention of her parents and she felt her breath catch in her throat.

"I must say," he continued, "I hope you have the same talent with Zoomancy that Torin once did." His eyes twinkled as he briefly glanced down at the textbook lying in front of him.

Just like that, puzzle pieces began to shift into place. Her father's name was Torin. They were just always Mum and Dad, but of course, they had regular names. Of course, they did.

Torin. Torin Lothbrok.

She turned her book over a few times in her hand, landing on the writing on the spine.

T.L.

"Did… Did my father write these books?" she stuttered as she motioned to the name on the back.

"Aye," he said with a smile. "This one and many more. I'm excited to introduce you to a part of him you never got to meet."

Ember remembered the way her father's hands and clothes smelled of fish and saltwater when he walked in the door, his day at the docks clinging to his auburn beard and button-up shirt. His hands were rough and calloused, and the thought that he ever used them to write a book was baffling and awe inspiring. She smiled as she held a part of him in her hands, almost like she would be learning directly from him, like the stories he used to tell under the moon when she couldn't sleep.

"What was he like?" Ember asked cautiously. It was almost a relief to meet someone who knew her parents. She was beginning to think maybe she had just made everything up.

"Oh, he was a mischievous one." He laughed gruffly. "Always dragging me into one scheme or another. Though, I suppose he would probably say the same thing about me if given the chance." He leaned back in his chair and crossed his giant paws over his chest. "We made quite the pair during our school days. He always had something up his sleeve. Would've eaten adrenaline for lunch every day if it was on the menu."

Ember laughed at the thought of her father running around the school with his friends, a boy without a care in the world. The memory made her swell with pride and ache at the same time. What she would give to hear these stories from him.

"Best be goin' now," he said with a wave toward the door. "Wouldn't want to be late for class on your first day. Off you get."

Ember choked down the lump building in her throat as she nodded and walked toward the door. Rowan stood patiently on the other side, along with Killian and Fen.

"I definitely didn't peg you as the trouble makin' type, Starshine," Killian said with a laugh.

Ember rolled her eyes, fighting back tears as she walked past the boys, both of them bickering back and forth as to who would be the first to receive detention.

"You okay?" Rowan asked quietly, as they walked to their next class.

Ember's heart leaped as she listened to the boys roughhouse behind her. She sank into a comfort she hadn't felt in years as she noticed the way Rowan's smile seemed to light up every dark corner in her chest. It was like all of the loneliness was building up to this very moment, and she felt like her chest might explode with the peace that she was finally feeling.

"Yeah..." Ember smiled at her new friend. "Yeah, I think I will be."

CHAPTER 7

YOU CAN'T ESCAPE FATE

E mber walked down the winding corridors, nose
buried in her syllabus, making mental notes about
each class. Rowan walked in front of her chatting
animatedly, acting as her eyes so she didn't wind up lost or
under the boot of another Ellingboe twin again. The two had
only known each other for a few hours, but it already felt like
an eternity.

"I was born and raised on Ellesmere," Rowan chirped as
they walked down the hall. "My brother attended Heksheim
before me, so if there's anything you don't understand, I'm
your girl!"

Ember found herself doubled over in a fit of giggles more
often than not. The girl's laughter was contagious. Her nose
scrunched beneath her glasses as her curls bounced across her
olive cheeks. Ember had never had a friend before, just
another thing that death had stolen from her when it took her
parents. She began to watch the semblance of a normal life
form in the image of the friendly, brown haired girl in front
of her.

Killian and Fen stayed closely behind as they walked the
corridor to their next class. They walked around with their

heads held high, her two knights in shining armor, no matter how much she protested.

"Em, we just don't want you to get hurt!" Fen said with concern. "You never know what dangers could be lurking around the corners."

And right on cue, Killian jumped out from an alcove around the corner in front of them. Ember instinctively punched him in the arm, and he winced dramatically, smacking against the wall behind him with a thud.

"It was only a joke, Starshine." He grinned as he rubbed his bicep.

Ember glared at both the boys and prepared to retaliate before Rowan gently grabbed her arm and tugged her away. She huffed as she shot both of them a rude gesture and pushed open the large wooden doors in front of them.

The room was huge and had a wooden stage directly in the middle. Desks were formed in a U shape around the circular stage, giving every student the perfect seat. Ember and Rowan made their way to two empty desks on the side, as Killian and Fen hurried behind them.

"I am perfectly capable of surviving class without you breathing down my neck the whole time," she hissed at the blond boy behind her. Killian kicked his feet up on the desk and leaned back in his chair, a smug grin plastered on his face.

"I'd rather not take any chances, Starshine."

A loud *crack* sounded through the room as a jet of purple light flew through the air, smacking Killian in the foot and sending him crashing to the ground with a yelp. Ember burst into a fit of giggles as she turned to look for the source of her joy.

"Feet off the desk, Mr. Vargr," a voice sounded from the back of the classroom. The slender, onyx-haired woman walked to the middle of the stage, her long skirt flowing just above her feet. "'I don't quite care how you treat your things at home, but in my classroom, you will respect this school's possessions, as well as my time."

The room bubbled with laughter as Killian pulled himself back into his chair and folded his hands on top of his desk. The smirk that was painted across his face had now been replaced with a deep flush as he nodded his head silently. Ember turned back to face the woman on the stage, in complete awe of someone who could put Killian in his place the way she had.

The professor cleared her throat and turned her attention back to the rest of the class, who all fell silent as her gaze fell on each of them. "For the next four years while I teach you Galdr in this classroom, you will learn incantations, charms, chants, hexes, and jinxes. While some lessons might feel frivolous to you, it would behoove you to take your education seriously. Galdr is a class that will require immense dedication to be successful in. A dedication I know each of you possess." Her eyes fell briefly back to Killian before turning her head. "While magic is a gift that was bestowed upon you at birth, it also comes with great responsibility. The responsibility to use it wisely, as well as respecting those around you whose abilities might differ from your own."

A hand shot up in the crowd, and the brunette boy didn't hesitate to speak before the professor had a chance to call his name. "But miss, I don't understand. Do each of us have different magical abilities?"

"It is Professor Walsh, Mr. Flannery," she scolded. "And no. Each of you possess the same magical abilities. What you do with those abilities and how you apply yourselves, however, is completely up to you."

"Then, who are we supposed to be respecting? If we all have the same magic, doesn't that make us all equal?" the boy asked nonchalantly, face screwed up in a question.

Professor Walsh smiled softly as she addressed the class. "It would be arrogant to believe that magic begins and ends with us," she replied as she adjusted the sleeves on her blouse. "We are surrounded by it every day. From the Merrow that raise the next generation of Vala, to the dryads that work on the grounds to keep you fed and safe." Professor Walsh made a displeased face as she sighed and shook her head. "Even the creatures and beings that live in the forest outside our wards. Their magic is different and unlike anything you or I would ever be able to achieve." Her eyes traveled across the room, meeting each and every one of them. "Different doesn't always mean evil, though, and it's important that you remember that. There are some people that believe other magical creatures and beings are below us, that they should remain in servitude to us instead of living alongside us in harmony. Despite what those in power may think, these beings still deserve respect, the same respect that is demanded from them."

An arrogant laugh sounded from the back of the class-room, cutting through the silence like a freshly sharpened knife. "I hardly think the creatures who changed our nappies are equal to us in any way," Oryn spat.

"The idea that we are anything other than equals to those we share life with is a very dangerous belief to have, Mr. Ellingboe."

Oryn and Veda rolled their eyes and began to speak at a whisper, heads pressed closely together.

"But our magic came from the gods," another voice said. "Surely, that makes us more powerful."

Professor Walsh gave a small smirk as she shook her head. "Different, yes" —she nodded—"but not more. Never more."

"For now." Veda smirked. Her grin sent shivers down Ember's spine as she sank further into her chair.

"Do you have something you would like to add, Miss Ellingboe?" the professor asked, as she turned toward the smug looking twins.

"Well, if the legend is correct, eventually, we won't have

any competition." Veda smirked in Killian's direction, who looked like he wanted to be anywhere other than that very room as he avoided the girl's gaze.

"What legend?" Fen asked loudly, hand waving above his head.

The rest of the class began chattering loudly as Professor Walsh pinched the bridge of her nose. "There is a legend," she began, raising a hand in the air to quiet the room, "that has been passed down for generations about our magical abilities."

Each student clamped their mouths shut and seemed to hold their breath while they waited for her to continue, hanging on every syllable that fell off her tongue.

"But it is only a legend, and I urge you to keep that in mind." She paused briefly as students nodded their heads before she took a deep breath and continued. "There is a prophecy that a descendant of the First Families, a Vala born of both dark and light, will rise to power, developing the ability to have dominion over all magical beings. They will take control of our ancient magic, as well as all other magic on the island Seiðr, the magical abilities that other creatures and beings possess. They will be the downfall of the rest of magical civilizations. Should this legend become true in any capacity, it will devastate and destroy entire races."

Professor Walsh's words hung in the air, thick like fog. Ember felt her throat run dry, and she spun the ring around her finger.

"Like, they'll rule over all the creatures on the island? Like a king?" a small girl asked, breaking the silence.

Before the professor could answer, Veda's voice cut through the air. "They won't rule over them, you eejit," she spat. "They'll exterminate them." The grin that danced across her mouth was reminiscent of the way Ember was sure a fox looked at a rabbit. She sunk further into her seat.

"That will be enough of that, Miss Ellingboe," Professor Walsh scolded.

"Exterminate?" Fen asked quietly. "Why would they want to do that?"

"Their magic is their lifeline, just like it is yours," the professor said softly, eyes floating around the room. "The legend states that the Vala will take their magic, depleting their magical core and harnessing it as their own. If you take away another being's magic, you take away their essence. The magic that runs through your veins does much more than give you the ability to curse or heal. It is the very thing that keeps you alive. As different as we might look, that is true for every creature with magic in their blood."

"So, if we kill a magic creature," another boy asked, as he scrunched his nose, "we can gain their magic?"

Professor Walsh shook her head as she rubbed her hands together. "No," she replied seriously. "Killing another magical being doesn't take away their magic. But depleting their magical core while they're still alive, siphoning out the essence of who they are, will not only take their magic, but their life as well. Our magic is tied to our life force. Without your magical core, you would cease to exist." A hush fell over the room as Professor Walsh walked back to the center of the stage. "Now, please take out your textbooks and turn to page forty-five."

The rest of their time in class was almost completely silent, even Fen and Killian kept their whispers to a minimum. Before she knew it, Ember was packing her things and heading out the door. As she shoved the large doors open, she was stopped in her tracks as a chipper voice sounded behind her.

"Hello, Ember," the melodic voice said. "I was wondering when I would meet you."

Ember turned around to see a small girl staring in her direction. Her white hair and sapphire eyes looked striking against her bronze skin. Her voice sounded more like a song than words, and her eyes looked like she was still stuck some-where between sleep and awake, like she was stuck in some perpetual dream state. She never made eye contact, not with any of them. It was almost as if she couldn't see the red head, almost as if she was…

"Erm, I'm sorry… have we met?" Ember asked cautiously.

"No, I'm afraid not in this life," she said dreamily with her eyes focused right above Ember's head. "But there have been whispers of your return since the Summer Solstice."

"Whispers? From who?" Ember squinted.

"From the Fae, of course. Quite talkative when they want to be," the girl answered, a wistful smile still plastered across her face. "I'm very happy to finally make your acquaintance, Ember Lothbrok." And with a bob of her head, she walked past the group and toward the classroom, bells chiming as they bounced around on her boots. Ember's face screwed up in confusion as she turned to the group standing behind her.

"Odette Quinn," Rowan answered before Ember could even ask. "She's a bit…"

"She's bleedin' crazy is what she is," Killian interjected as he adjusted his backpack on his shoulder. "Thinks the Fair Folk speak to her, the loon."

"She wouldn't look at me," Ember contemplated, more a question than a statement.

"She's blind," Rowan said quietly. "I think she sees a lot more than she lets on, though, just maybe not with her eyes."

"Don't know how anyone could ever take her seriously," Killian continued, oblivious to the girl's conversation. "And do ya see the way she dresses? Their whole family oughta be locked up."

Rowan rolled her eyes as she hooked her arm in the crook of Ember's elbow and continued down the hall, "She's an odd one, but she doesn't mean any harm. Not like those two," she said, as she motioned to the boys.

The boys walked ahead of them, cutting their eyes at Rowan as they went.

"I don't think I've heard Killian that quiet at all today." Rowan laughed as they walked through the corridor.

"Quiet? He barely stopped talking to Fen during the whole lecture. I could hardly hear anything," Ember replied, as she rolled her eyes.

"I meant before that," Rowan replied. "When Walsh was talking about the legend."

"Everyone was quiet." Ember shrugged.

"It's different with Killian, though," she replied. "Surely, your brother has told you about the Vargrs."

Ember looked at her with a raised brow, oblivious to whatever previous information Rowan had about the family.

"Right, you're not from around here," she stated as she grabbed Ember's wrist and pulled her closer, lowering her voice to a whisper. "The Vargrs are one of the First Families. Notoriously dark Vala have come from their bloodline, and it wouldn't shock me if it continued to trickle down. Mum and Dad have always said how shocked they were that Mrs. Vargr married into the family. She's sweet as pie, so they never understood what she saw in him. Killian probably grew up hearing about the legend, and knowing them, they probably teach about it alongside history and science. I wouldn't be shocked if it was about him."

She said it like she was talking about weather or what she had for breakfast, not like she had just announced that she thought her foster brother's best friend was a dark Vala that was destined to exterminate entire races of magical creatures. Ember scrunched her eyebrows together as she looked toward the two boys who were standing at the end of the hall, laughing together.

"That's a bit of a stretch, don't you think?" Ember whispered, her voice barely audible. "I mean he's a right eejit, don't get me wrong, but he hardly seems dark to me. Maybe a little dense, but not dark."

Rowan shrugged her shoulders as they walked down the corridor past the boys. "All I'm saying is, it's in his blood. It's only a matter of time before he turns out like the rest of them. You can't escape fate."

THE WALK back to the Echopoint that afternoon felt even longer than it had that morning. Fen said his goodbyes to Killian as the group was pulled back to their homes. Ember felt her stomach drop as her feet hit the dirt road outside the homestead. She took a few seconds to orient herself before starting the walk up the long driveway toward the house. They could see Eira waiting on the front porch for them, as Maeve ran down the dirt drive to meet them.

"Ember! Ember! Look what I made!" she squealed, as she hopped up and down, tiny hands clutching a large piece of paper that had drawings all over it.

"That's so great, Maeve," Ember said, forcing a smile. "I wish my homework was that fun."

Fen ruffled the small girl's curls as he ran past them and up the steps to the front porch.

"Tea is on. I can't wait to hear all about your first day!" Eira fluttered as she ushered them inside and kissed her son on the cheek.

"Mum, I have to practice!" he whined, furiously scrubbing at his wet cheek. "Tryouts are in a week." His mother gave him a stern look as he smiled apologetically before bolting up to his bedroom, taking the steps two at a time.

"I could go for a cup while I start on my homework." Ember smiled at the disgruntled woman. Eira's frustration faded, and she led her into the kitchen, cups already on the table and filled. The woman's excitement to spend time with her left her feeling warm and fuzzy inside, a comfort she hadn't felt from an adult in a very long time.

"Homework on your first day?" Eira said as she took a seat, flicking her wrist toward the kitchen. A small plate of biscuits floated to the center of the table, filling the room with a sweet aroma that made Ember's stomach growl. Her mouth watered as Eira flicked her wrist gently to set one on the empty plate in front of her.

"Our Zoomancy paper isn't due until Friday, technically. I just like to get a jump on homework when I can."

Eira held her cup with both hands as she stared up at the ceiling wistfully.

"Zoomancy was my favorite class during my time at Heksheim," she said thoughtfully. "Of course, we didn't have a teacher quite like Professor Bjorn, but the magical creatures that lived on the island were something that always fascinated me as a child. And with the classmates I had, your professor included, the lessons were never dull."

Her eyes twinkled as she sipped her tea, taking a moment to slip into the past and reminisce. Ember thought back to her professor and the startling fact that he knew her parents. If he knew them, did that mean the Kitts did too? She had a sudden hunger to learn everything she could about the family she had lost. Her stomach felt lodged in her throat as she took a breath and took another sip of her tea.

"Mrs. Kitt…" Ember said hesitantly, as she chewed her bottom lip. "Did you… did you know my parents?"

"I did." She smiled gently as she set her cup back on the table. "They were in my year at Heksheim. Your father was quite the prankster, always cooking up schemes and jokes and causing disruptions." She looked wistfully out the small window, allowing the memory to play out in the front of her mind. "Our professors had a right difficult time keeping him and our friends in line." She laughed as she took another sip of tea, shaking her head at the memory.

Ember's stomach was doing flips. "You were close with him then? My dad?" she asked, as she leaned forward.

"I was." Eira nodded. "Him and Professor Bjorn were like brothers to me. They practically lived at my house during the summer holidays."

Ember felt her heart flutter as she grinned. The thought of her father as a teenager running around the island, much like she imagined Fen and Killian did, wasn't something she had ever stopped to think about. She would give up all the money in the world just to hear these stories from him, but she would have to settle with hearing them from the people he shared his adolescent years with.

"And my mum?" Ember asked, as she twirled the pen in her fingers.

"Your mum liked to keep to herself," Eira said. "She was kind but very quiet and didn't let many people in. We were all quite shocked when she took to your dad the way she did. She kept herself quite guarded most of the time."

Ember bobbed her head as she listened, focusing her eyes on the grains of wood weaving their way through the tabletop. Learning about her father would be easy—he was an outgoing man who wore his heart on his sleeve. Ember was certain she would hear tales about his misadventures from his childhood friends for the rest of her life, but her mother was another story.

The truth was, she knew more about her father than she probably ever would her mother. He left her with a journal filled with notes and thoughts and stories from her childhood and before. She had memories of his jokes and the way he had different voices for all of the characters in his stories— stories she was beginning to think were not quite fiction.

Her mother, though, was something of an enigma. She could remember her smile and her laugh, the way she danced with her father under the moonlight, barefoot in the kitchen. She loved with her entire being and was fiercely protective of what was hers, but she kept the important things close, some things she didn't ever share. Even years after she married and they had Ember, she was still very guarded. She kept her secrets close to her chest. She was strong and fearless, things Ember tried to mirror most of her childhood. She wasn't sure what parts of her came from her parents and what parts came from living in survival mode most of her life, but she knew with every fiber of her being that her grit and determination came from her mum.

"You remind me a lot of her, your mum," Eira said quietly, pulling Ember from the memories she was falling through. "You have her smile."

Ember rubbed at her eyes as she blinked away the quickly forming tears. Everyone always said she looked like her dad, but she knew deep down she favored her mum in more ways than one.

"Did they have any other friends before they moved?" Ember asked eagerly. "Who did they spend time with? Do you know why they left the island?" The questions seemed to tumble out of her mouth one after the other before she even realized what she was saying. She ached to know more, to beg for every morsel Eira had. She wanted to relive every moment of their lives possible through her memories.

Eira let out a gentle laugh. "After you were born, they spent most of their time with each other, but we did our best to have dinner together with Professor Bjorn when we could all make the time." Her eyes flitted to the table in the dining room as she smiled, her eyes glistening with unshed tears. "Lots of memories were made at that table. I just wish we knew what little time we had left with each other."

Ember sucked in a breath as her heart leaped into her throat. Her chest began to ache as she bit the inside of her cheek. She was quite intimate with that feeling of craving time that had been ripped away from her. Her heart sank as she looked around the room, suddenly craving the memories she could have accumulated as a child inside of these walls.

"So... I've been here before?" she asked quietly. "Why didn't you say anything sooner?" Her heart began to race. Did Eira know about her eyes, about how different she truly was?

If she did, she never let on.

"We didn't want to overwhelm you too early on," Eira replied as she reached across the table and squeezed her hand. "But you were so young, we barely got to know you. You were only a few months old when they left."

"Why did they leave?" Ember's throat was dry at this point, a lump steadily growing in her as she intentionally took slow breaths.

"Now that, I don't know," Eira said as she shook her head. "I don't think anyone does, I'm afraid. They gave little to no warning, just disappeared with you in the middle of the night. Professor Bjorn came around and told me a few days later you all had moved to the mainland, but he didn't know why."

Ember nodded as she tapped a finger on the table. More questions she would likely never have an answer to, it appeared. She let out a sharp breath and choked back the lump in her throat; dwelling on the 'why' wouldn't change anything. "Did they have any other friends? Anyone else they might have confided in?" she asked hesitantly.

"I'm not sure," Eira breathed as she shook her head. "They had drifted away toward the end. I can't be certain who they were close to and who they weren't."

"What about the Vargrs?" Ember knew that was a long shot—she couldn't imagine why her parents would be involved with a family like them, but it was worth a shot. She had to know.

Eira raised her brow as she lifted her cup to her lips. "Absolutely not." She shook her head. "That I know for certain. Your father would have rather died than be involved with them."

Ember spun the ring on her finger and sucked in a breath. "How much do you know about the Vargrs?" she asked carefully, thinking back to the conversation she had with Rowan earlier that day.

"They are an odd bunch at best. Why the sudden curiosity?"

"Just some stuff we talked about in Galdr today, and things that older families believe."

Eira nodded her head. "They're one of the First Families, just like us, and they hold tight to the ideals of our ancestors. Some of us believe these ideals are outdated, but many of the families, like the Vargrs, believe we should cling to the beliefs of our fathers."

"Mum!" Maeve yelled, as she barreled into the room. "I need a bandage!"

Eira sighed. "I told you to leave that old rooster alone, Maeve Kitt," she scolded as she excused herself from the table and walked to the cabinet, rummaging through it until she found the bandage Maeve needed, wrapping it around her scraped arm.

"What kind of beliefs?" Ember asked as she took a sip of her drink.

"Many of them believe that all magical beings who are not Vala should be in servitude to those who are. The Merrow haven't always raised their young or worked in their kitchens, that was an ideal the First Families brought with them to the island." She sighed as she smoothed Maeve's unruly curls and shooed her out of the room. "Some believe that any magic that isn't Vala isn't pure; they believe it to be dirty and less than. The Fae rarely set foot outside of their gates anymore because of the way they're treated. Most of us have grown out of those beliefs and moved forward, but there are still families who are determined to remain stuck in the past."

Ember let her mind wander back to the things Rowan told her about Killian and his family. Was it possible? Was the cocky blond boy really going to be the downfall of their magical civilization?

"Why would anyone believe things like that?"

"Evil is a weed," Eira breathed, as she looked out the kitchen window toward the garden. "It grows in cracked roads, crumbling houses, and forgotten corners, rooted in indifference and watered by suffering. Until we demand the broken things be mended and the suffering people be made well, evil will continue to grow among us. We must starve it to death."

Ember let out a breath as she sipped the last of her tea. "Is it possible, though?" she asked, as she ran her fingers along the rim of the mug. "When so many people believe one thing to be right, even if it isn't, is it possible to change things for the better?"

Eira gave her a smile as she flicked her wrist and sent both empty mugs floating to the sink. "It isn't our job to change everything, but it is our job to change the things we can, to be a light to those that are searching for a way out of the darkness."

Ember gave her a small smile as she mulled over her words. Was it truly that simple? It seemed cliché at best. It was an easy enough thing to think to just be *'a light'* and things will get better, but that wasn't how the world worked. Not the world Ember had ever experienced, at least. Her entire life had been spent in darkness, and no one had ever saved her from it. No one saw her while she was drowning and reached in to pull her out of the churning waves. Eira gave her a knowing look and squeezed her hand. No one had ever bothered to notice her.

Not until now.

Eira stood up from the table and glanced at the clock on the wall. "I best be getting dinner ready," she said softly, as she headed into the kitchen and began pulling pots and pans from the cupboards.

"Thank you for the tea, Mrs. Kitt." Ember smiled as she pushed away from the table. "I think I'm going to go up to the library and do some research for my paper."

"Of course, love." Eira smiled back. "I'm here if you need anything."

Ember gathered her things and headed up the steps and toward the library. At the end of the hall, she quickly ran into her room and grabbed her father's journal off her nightstand before heading back to the cozy room across the hall. Curled up into the oversized chair, she gently opened the old leather journal, hoping to find some interesting information her father had recorded that she could use for her paper. Her fingers flitted between the pages, smiling as she ran them along the worn handwriting that had given her so much comfort as a scared child.

She quietly laughed to herself as she skimmed over the drawings that were scattered across the pages, pictures of poorly drawn creatures with X's through them, like he couldn't quite get them right and had to start over. She read through his notes about the Pegasus's on the island and their strict diet of fruit and honeysuckle until she landed on a page with strange inscriptions and a drawing of a very old book. Her eyes scanned the pages, reading the notes her father had put in, and they grew wider as her jaw hung slack. She closed the book quickly and ran down the hall toward the stairs, taking two at a time.

"Mrs. Kitt!" she called from the foyer.

The woman poked her head out of the kitchen with a worried look on her face. "Everything alright, love?" she asked with a raised eyebrow.

"Oh, yes, um…" Ember stuttered, now realizing just how loud she had been. "Do you have a phone I could borrow?"

Eira chuckled to herself. "I don't, but you can Helio call anyone you like."

Ember bit her lip. "I'm sorry I don't…"

"Oh, no, of course not, love," Eira said with a smile. "Here, let me get it for you." Eira laid her hand flat in between the two and quietly mumbled, *"Avisodor,"* hovering two fingers above her palm. A bluish white stream of light appeared from her fingertips, swirling around and forming a small ball of glowing light in her hand. Eira motioned for Ember to lay out her hand and dropped the ball of light in it.

Ember blinked at it, letting it hover right above her palm while she stared in wonder.

"Say your message, then close your hand and tell it who the message is for," Eira said to the girl. "I'll leave you to it." She stepped back into the other room, closing the door behind her, leaving Ember alone in the foyer, magic humming against her fingers.

She took a breath and began to speak. "Rowan I need some help," she whispered into the glowing orb. "Meet me in town before school tomorrow."

And the orb was whisked away.

CHAPTER 8

TEA WITH A SIDE OF MISCHIEF

E mber rubbed her hands together in front of Hidden Moon Teas and Tonics early the next morning. The morning air was cooler than normal, a sure sign that autumn was on its way. She took a shaky breath as she pulled her sweater tighter around her torso, wrapping her arms together in an attempt to create more warmth. Her chest felt lighter as she saw Rowan appear down the street in the distance. Her friend waved wildly with a grin as she tore down the street toward her.

"So, why the early morning meeting?" she asked excitedly, bouncing on the balls of her feet. Just being in her presence made Ember feel warmer; she was sunshine manifested.

"Can we grab some breakfast first?" Ember laughed, still shivering slightly from the brisk wind that was coming in off the water. "I'm dying for something warm."

Rowan chuckled as they headed into the shop, the door chiming as it opened. The room they walked into was like stepping into an enchanted forest. The ceiling was covered with dark green moss, the walls crawling with vines and flowers that seemed to sprout from nowhere and everywhere at the same time. The girls made their way to the oak counter where a young woman busied herself with preparing tea, her back turned to them.

"Mornin', Asteria," Rowan chimed. "Can we have two Red Rivers with a shot of Invigoration?"

The young woman turned toward them with a grin. Her hair was long, the moss green waves flowing down over her mahogany shoulders. Ember blinked a few times as she noticed delicate wings folded behind her back and dropping almost to the floor, colors matching the shades of green and yellow that weaved in and out of her hair. She was like a walking flower, with her pink top flowing freely around her waist.

"Mornin', loves," she chirped, the lyrical words bouncing off the leaves around them. "Busy day at school ahead of ya?" She handed each girl a cup, pulling a small vial out from behind the counter and pouring two drops of the shimmering gold liquid in each cup. Ember took the cup in her hand, watching the red and gold swirl together, small bubbles popping on the surfaces as they mixed. She was certain it wasn't dangerous, but she kept it at a distance just in case.

"We've got some research to go over before class. Professor Bjorn likes to keep us on our toes." Rowan laughed as she grabbed two muffins from a shelf with odd looking berries coming out of the top of them. She laid down a handful of coins on the counter.

The girls nodded in thanks and made their way to a table in the back corner of the tea room. Ember sipped the tea cautiously and immediately felt what was left of her sleepiness fade away. All of a sudden, she was completely alert and aware of everything around her, like she had drunk three cups of coffee in a matter of seconds. She looked over to Rowan, who was eating her muffin and chuckling slightly.

"The invigorating draught takes some getting used to." She laughed. "It's perfect when you've had to stay up all night cramming for finals, though. My brother used to stop by and get a giant mug of it before school when he had a big exam coming up."

Ember sat her cup down and reached for the bag hanging over her chair, her sudden burst of energy reminding her why she had asked Rowan to meet in the first place. She took a breath as she fumbled with the straps. She had to be careful—too much information right now seemed like the wrong idea, and she needed to know more about the prophecy first.

"So, I was thinking we could go ahead and start Professor Bjorn's paper today," she said, digging through the contents of the leather satchel. After finding what she was looking for, she pulled her Zoomancy book from the bag and flipped it open on the table. "We can see what's in here, and maybe stop in the library later for some more sources."

Rowan scrunched her nose. "You really just want to study?"

"Of course," Ember replied, shifting uncomfortably in her seat. "What else?"

Rowan shrugged. "Just thought you maybe had some juicy gossip you wanted to share over tea."

Ember rolled her eyes. "Nope, just wanted some help with this paper."

Rowan nodded thoughtfully as she narrowed her eyes. "If you say so," she hummed. "Let's get to work then."

The girls worked diligently for around ten minutes, reading through their textbooks and taking notes as they went.

"I hate cats," Rowan mumbled, as they went through a section about the Cat Sidhe's diet.

"Really?" Ember laughed as she flipped the page, quickly jotting down her notes as she went. "They're so smart, though. They're really interesting animals."

"I suppose." Rowan shrugged. "They're just annoying, almost as annoying as Vargr and your brother."

"Foster brother," Ember said as her pen scratched across her notebook, "and I don't know that that's possible." She swallowed as her eyes flitted to Rowan, who was currently reading about the mating rituals for the Cat Sidhe. "Speaking of Killian..." She bit her lip as she flipped another page, trying to seem casual. "Do you know anything else about that prophecy we talked about in class yesterday?"

Rowan tilted her head as she arched her brow. "Like what?"

Ember shrugged as she spun her pen through her fingers. "I don't know, like where did it come from? Are there pieces that are missing?"

"Slow down, Lothbrok." Rowan laughed. "I don't know any more than you do at this point."

Ember nodded as she hummed, "Right, of course."

Rowan tilted her head as she leaned back in her chair, crossing her arms over her chest. "Why do you ask?"

Ember swallowed dryly. "No reason, just curious," she replied with a shrug, trying to act more nonchalant than she felt.

Rowan narrowed her eyes playfully. "I don't believe you," she prodded as she snapped her book shut.

"Really," Ember stuttered, "I... I'm just curious. A lifelong learner, what can I say."

"You know something." Rowan grinned. "You *found* something. What is it? Where did you find it?"

"I don't know what you're talking about," Ember replied as she started flipping through her textbook, not even registering that she was in the section about unicorns now. "We have a paper to write."

Rowan grabbed the textbook in front of Ember and quickly snapped it shut, pushing it out of the way. "Spill, I won't give the book back until you do."

Ember fidgeted more. "My dad just mentioned something about it in some of his research, that's all."

Rowan tapped her finger on the table, a wry smile pulling

at her lips. "That's not all," she replied. "You're hiding something."

Ember sighed as she rolled her eyes. "Fine, but this stays between us. Deal?"

Rowan nodded eagerly as she folded her hands on the table in front of her. "Scout's honor." She grinned.

Ember bit her bottom lip and nodded. "My dad has this journal he used to record a bunch of his research and findings in." She quickly dug through her bag and pulled the journal out, setting it on the table in front of her. "He wrote about something called *The Book of Shadows*." She gently flipped the book open, turning to the page she found the night before. "From what he says, it's supposed to be an ancient book that gives whoever has it power over all magical creatures. It looks like it actually gives them the ability to use other types of magic, to steal it. It might be a stretch, but it sounds a lot like the prophecy Professor Walsh was talking about." She chewed on her bottom lip, her mind running a mile a minute.

"And?" Rowan asked as she leaned forward in her chair.

"And what?" Ember replied, rhythmically tapping on the table.

"There's more, I can see it in your eyes," Rowan replied. "What else did he write?"

Ember sighed as she shifted in her chair. "I don't know if it's connected, but he has a list of names. I didn't recognize a lot of them, but there were a couple I did. Ellingboe was one of them…" She chewed on her lip, wondering if she should tell her everything. Had she already given up too much?

"Hey," Rowan said softly, almost like she could read her mind. "You can trust me."

Ember nodded with a small smile. "Like I said, Ellingboe is on there… but so is Vargr. Look here," she said as she motioned to the corner of one of the pages. "It has a star by it."

"It would make sense," Rowan replied, narrowing her eyes

thoughtfully. "The age lines up with everything I've heard about the prophecy. Where did your dad get all of this?" she asked, as her eyes continued to scan the page.

Ember shrugged. "I don't know. He grew up on the island. Maybe he heard something or knew about something he didn't write down."

Rowan's face lit up as she skimmed the pages. "You know what this means, right?" she asked with a grin, her eyes hungry.

"That we should mind our business?" Ember said hopefully.

"It means we have to find the book before anyone else does. Before they can fulfill the prophecy themselves. We have to stop them."

Ember furrowed her brow. "How are we supposed to do that?"

Rowan sighed as she took another bite of her muffin. "There has to be information somewhere. Your dad didn't write anything else about it?" She reached for the journal on the table, but Ember quickly snapped it closed, hugging it close to her chest.

"No, he didn't," Ember whispered, gently laying it back down.

Rowan nodded as she leaned back in her chair. "Well, there has to be information somewhere," she replied. "You don't just create a book filled with dark magic and then not tell anyone about it."

Ember pressed her fingers on the bridge of her nose and wrinkled her forehead in frustration.

"Ya know," Rowan said as she took a bite of her muffin, "we could always check the library at school. Maybe we'll get lucky."

Ember sighed as she smiled. "Yeah, maybe."

The girls finished their tea and quickly made their way to the Echopoint. Ember slipped off her sweater as they began to walk the path to the ward, the sun beating down on them now, warming them up substantially. The girls walked silently, both deep in thought. Even through the silence, they somehow missed the sound of bells jingling behind them until a voice broke at their sides.

"The Fae have been loud this morning," Odette said dreamily as she walked up beside Ember, bouncing with each step. "They've been whispering your name a lot more, Ember Lothbrok."

Ember squinted at the girl and then back to Rowan, who was doing her best to hold in her laughter. Before she could respond, the sound of heavy footfalls distracted her. She whipped her head around to see Killian and Fen running up behind them, shoving each other in the process.

"Mornin', Starshine!" Killian shouted as he stumbled toward her. Breathing heavily, he pressed his hands to his knees.

"Mum said you left early. I figured you'd already be at school," Fen said through deep breaths.

"I must say," Killian replied as he straightened himself again and turned to Ember, "I'm feeling a little hurt that I wasn't invited to breakfast." He shot her a wink as he brushed the hair out of his eyes and shoved his hands carelessly in his pockets.

Ember rolled her eyes at the boys as she turned to walk toward the school, pushing aside the anxiety that built in her any time Killian was nearby.

"We don't enjoy a side of mischief with our tea, sorry," Rowan retorted as she flipped her hair over her shoulder, linking arms with Ember, who briefly looked over her shoulder and laughed in his direction.

"That's a pity." Killian winked. "Tea is served best with a little mischief."

MORNING CLASSES SEEMED to drag all day—the same classes as the day before, but Ember's brain refused to retain any new information. Her mind constantly wandered back to her father's journal, and she found herself pulling it out to flip through it briefly and examine the writing. She had read his words countless times. The stories comforted her as a scared child and kept her connected to a part of her life she feared would slip away completely.

Reading through it now was different, though. They weren't fairytales her father had conjured up to put her to sleep at night. It wasn't a book of bedtime stories but more of a field guide. It was filled with facts and research, and his love for the island was evident through the fondness in which he wrote. Her heart always ached when she thought about never knowing more about her parents, never having a deeper understanding of them, but now she had this. It was like meeting him for the first time, like she was learning about a part of him she never knew existed.

When their study period finally came, Ember and Rowan made their way quickly toward the large library. They settled into a desk at the back of the room and dropped their bags on their chairs.

"So, what are we looking for exactly?" Ember asked as they started combing through the tall shelves.

"Anything to do with the history of the island I think is the best place to start," Rowan replied.

"History?" Ember asked as she raised her brow. What did history have to do with a book about dark magic?

"Well, it is an ancient book," Rowan quipped. "Surely, there's something tucked away in a history book somewhere that talks about it."

"You do realize how many books that is… right?" Ember replied with a laugh, piling tomes of every size in her arms.

"Do you have any better ideas?"

Ember shrugged as she ran her fingers along the spines of

the books, pulling more into her arms. The girls went back to their table and started flipping through the piles, sitting in silence for what felt like hours, poring over every word of the texts. She read through the island's history, the history of her people, and felt small puzzle pieces begin to shift further into place. Her heart fluttered as she scanned the pages and finally began to feel like she had found where she belonged. She was ten pages deep into a book about the history of the forest that surrounded the school when Rowan patted her hand.

"Look at this!" she whispered with a squeal. "It talks about Merrow and how they've been on the island since before it was ever settled. They helped the Vala settle Sigurvik and worked with them to teach them about the island and all of its wildlife."

Ember took the book from her hands and then pulled her father's journal from her bag.

"I think I remember my dad writing about them," she replied as she flipped through the pages, landing on the one she was looking for and reading the text aloud. "'The Merrow are ancient beings that have lived around Ellesmere since the beginning of time. Their magic is powerful and unlike anything I've ever witnessed, different from our own. They are wise and cautious beings, content to live a life away from others and amongst themselves, and are very wary of Vala.'" Ember chewed on the inside of her cheek as she squinted at the page. "We could talk to one," she said thoughtfully. "If they've been around that long, they're bound to know something about the book."

"The only problem is I don't know any Merrow," Rowan said, propping her elbow on the table and laying her head on her palm. "The one we had was let go a few years ago when Mum decided we didn't need one anymore."

"I met one before term started," Ember replied thoughtfully, "but she works for the Vargrs. I'd be afraid word would get back to Killian if we talked to her."

"Probably not our safest option." Rowan sighed, blowing stray strands of hair out of her face.

Ember furrowed her brow as she pored over the open book, her finger landing in the middle of the page as her eyes lit up. "Look," she said, as she turned the book toward Rowan. "This talks about a Clann that lived in a cove on the west side of the island. Maybe they're still there."

Rowan shrugged as she leaned back in her seat. "They could also be long gone by now. These books are old, and who knows how accurate the information is."

Ember sighed heavily as she crossed her arms over her chest. "Do you have a better idea?"

Rowan nodded her head with a lopsided grin. "I mean, it's worth a shot."

"The west end of the island could take days to search, though. We have to narrow it down more than that," Ember replied with frustration. She twiddled her fingers as she wracked her brain. There had to be something else. Something she missed.

"Asteria might know something," Rowan replied with a shrug.

"The barista from Hidden Moon?" Ember asked in confusion.

"Yeah, she's Fae. They've been around as long as the Merrow, if not longer. I'm sure she's heard something. She's like…" Rowan mouthed some numbers as she counted on her fingers a few times. "A few hundred years old at this point, give or take."

Ember felt her jaw drop. "She's a fairy?"

"Well, of course she is." Rowan laughed. "Most people don't just walk around with wings on their backs."

Ember's eyes widened as she sucked in a breath. "How long do the Fae live?" she whispered.

Rowan let out a quiet laugh as she shrugged nonchalantly. "Long enough, I suppose."

Ember shook her head with a grin as she closed her books, sticking them quickly in her bag. At this point, she shouldn't be surprised. The island was bubbling with magic, of course there were Fae running a tea room in Sigurvik. The girls made their way out of the library and into the busy corridor. Students were chattering loudly while they walked to their next class, and with the newfound confidence she seemed to have, Ember allowed herself to get lost in the sea of children as she made her way down the hall.

As she moved through the crowd, she briefly noticed shaggy, white blond hair out of the corner of her eye. Killian was leaned up against an alcove, angrily whispering at someone. She narrowed her eyes as they landed on Oryn Ellingboe whispering back, shoving his finger in Killian's chest. Fen was nowhere in sight thankfully, and Killian kept looking over his shoulder, presumably making sure no one was watching him with the raven haired boy.

Ember edged closer, trying to catch pieces of their conversation. What on earth he had to talk to Oryn about, she had no idea. They didn't speak during classes, didn't so much as look in each other's direction unless Oryn was sneering. Ember was almost able to catch what they were saying, when a foot fell on top of hers. She let out a pained yelp, and her eyes met Veda's staring back at her.

"Mind your own business, worm," she sneered, eyes boring holes into hers.

Ember hurried in the opposite direction, determined to put as much distance between her and the intimidating girl as possible. She walked quickly down the hall, weaving her way between the students when she heard heavy footfalls behind her.

"What could you possibly have to study during the first week of school," a voice sounded from beside her. "That could keep you in the library for all of our study period? I was hoping you would join me in the café for some coffee."

Ember looked up at Killian as he matched her stride. "We have a café?" she asked, walking briskly down the winding hall.

"Sure." He shrugged. "It's technically off limits for first years, but what Moran doesn't know won't hurt her."

Ember narrowed her eyes. He looked as calm and put together as ever with one hand shoved in his pocket and the other wrapped around the strap of his bag. His clothes were clean and neatly pressed, likely thanks to Maren, just like they always were. He casually flipped the hair from in front of his eyes as a lopsided grin played at the corner of his mouth.

He wasn't the type to be acquainted with people like the Ellingboes. Where they were abrasive and cold, he was warm and inviting. A little cocky, sure, but he had a kindness to him that couldn't be missed.

Which was why the realization of who his family was had been so incredibly shocking. Even if they were as dark as everyone seemed to believe, that didn't mean Killian was destined to follow in their footsteps.

Right?

"You do know you don't have to be studying to read, right?" she quipped.

"Oh, of course," he replied. "I just don't know why anyone would bother, is all. I'd much rather be lying on the lawn in what's left of the summer sun."

Ember kept her eyes glued in front of her, determined not to look at the boy gleefully prancing beside her. Rowan had disappeared, probably thinking the red head was still right behind her. She made her way into her next class, sitting at a desk in the middle of the room. Killian took his normal seat behind her as Fen came running into the room out of breath.

"This giant tree will be the death of me," he said as he worked to slow his breathing.

Rowan laughed as she sat beside Ember. "If you weren't

so busy sneaking food from the kitchen, you probably wouldn't have to run."

Fen narrowed his eyes as he stuffed the half-eaten sandwich back in his pocket and shot her a rude gesture.

Ember smirked and flipped her textbook open as her mind raced, thinking back to the library and the minor altercation she witnessed outside of it. She felt a pang of guilt as she looked over her shoulder at Fen. She knew she needed to talk to him, about what she had seen and the suspicions they had, but she didn't know how. How did you tell someone their best friend might be at the center of a dark legend? How did you break that kind of news? Her heart pounded as she tried to brush the thoughts away. As far as she knew, there wasn't even anything to tell yet. They didn't even know if the book was real, let alone the whole legend. There was no need to worry him over something that might not be true. She would worry about that after they talked to the Clann. They needed solid answers before they ran around starting rumors that could hurt the people close to her.

She turned toward Rowan to ask when they should talk to Asteria and felt her friend nudge her arm with her elbow.

"We can go this weekend," she whispered. "We'll meet back at Hidden Moon and talk to Asteria. If she doesn't know anything, maybe she can point us in the direction of someone who does."

Ember nodded back at the girl. "It's better than nothing, I suppose. After we figure something out that's a little more definitive, I think I need to talk to Fen."

Rowan cut her eye to the boys laughing behind them. "We'll cross that bridge when we get to it. We don't want word getting back to the wrong people."

"The wrong people? What people?" Ember asked, as she raised her brow.

Rowan shrugged. "Anyone who might also be looking for the book. Better safe than sorry. Do you trust your brother?"

Ember winced. "Foster brother," she corrected under her breath, "and I don't know. Maybe. Maybe he could help." She shrugged as she bit the inside of her cheek.

The truth was, she didn't trust anyone. But she wanted to. She would give anything to have the blind faith in people that Fen seemed to have. But what good had trust and promises ever done for her? Her parents had promised her forever, and as it turned out, forever wasn't as long as she thought.

CHAPTER 9
THE EDGE OF THE FOREST

E mber quickly threw her hair in a braid as the sun peeked through her bedroom window. Her mind was already racing as she rehearsed all of the questions in her head that she and Rowan had spent the week meticulously planning. She stared at herself in the mirror, grimacing at the lavender eyes that stared back as she rummaged through the small drawer on her dresser and grabbed the contact case from the bottom. She quickly put them in, blinking a few times until green eyes stared back. Taking a shaky breath, she pulled her bag over her shoulder and made her way through the hall and down the steps.

"Good morning, love. You're up early." Eira's chipper voice sounded as her feet hit the landing. Ember jumped at the sound, assuming that most of the house would still be asleep when she left.

"Oh, good morning, Mrs. Kitt," she said, as she made her way into the kitchen. "I didn't think you would be up yet."

"The farm wakes up well before the sun does, and I have a tendency to rise with it," Eira said as she pulled the singing kettle from the stove. "I just made some breakfast, are you hungry?"

"Oh, no," Ember replied, slightly ashamed that she was lying to the woman. "Rowan and I had plans to meet early at Hidden Moon. We've got a project we need to work on."

Eira smiled at her, hands wrapped around the warm mug as she took a sip. "I'm glad to see you're finding your place here. I think Fen is meeting Killian in town later. I'm sure he'll go with you if you want to wait on him. He's just out back with—"

"Oh, no!" Ember squeaked, quickly lowering her voice when she saw the puzzled look flash across Eira's face. The last thing she needed was Fen and Killian hovering around today. "I mean, no thank you, ma'am. We want to get an early start."

Eira nodded with a small smile. She walked forward, hesitating briefly before giving Ember a small hug. Ember stiffened as she felt her whole body recoil in response. She stopped expecting hugs, or any sort of physical affection, when she was six. At this point, she wasn't even sure what to do with it.

"Be safe, and send a Helio if you need anything," the woman whispered before letting her go. Ember gave her a small smile as she nodded and walked toward the closet at the back of the stairs. She touched the rune on the bronze doorknob and watched the tree above the door begin to glow. She swung open the door and took a deep breath as she stepped over the threshold and into the already bustling terminal.

She walked slowly to the tea room, watching the shopkeepers sweep their stoops and wave at the men and women heading to work. She shuffled her feet along the cobblestone, breathing in the scent of fresh bread coming off the cool breeze from the bakery ahead of her. Her stomach growled as she picked up the pace, regretting for the second time that week that she turned down a home cooked breakfast at the Kitts'.

Pushing open the door to the small shop, bell jingling, she walked over the threshold. Rowan waved at her from a back table, two teas sitting in front of her alongside two breakfast rolls. Ember's mouth watered as she sat down at the table, doing her best not to devour the savory roll in a single bite.

"Figured we needed sustenance if we're going to explore the whole west side of the island today," Rowan said as she took a bite.

Ember groaned as she furrowed her brow. "Hopefully not the whole west side."

Rowan nodded. "Fingers crossed Asteria can help us narrow it down a bit."

The girls quickly finished their breakfast before heading back up to the counter where the young Fae was busy staging a fresh batch of muffins on a sparkling stand. Her body swayed along with the soft music coming from the speakers, and Ember could see the delicate wings on her back flit back and forth lightly as the ends of them brushed the floor. She brushed her hands against the sides of her pants as she took a step back to admire her work, flinging a lock of hair over her shoulder.

"Comin' back for seconds already?" she said to the girls, her back still turned away from them.

"Not exactly." Rowan hesitated. "We were actually hoping you could help us find someone. Or... I guess, technically, a group of someones."

Asteria turned around and leaned against the counter, a mischievous grin spreading across her face.

"A group of someones, eh? I can probably help you with 'someones,' now 'somethings' might be a bit tricky," she said with a wink. "Requires a little more planning."

Ember shifted her weight back and forth, gently tapping her thigh with her fingers. Something about her made the hair on the back of Ember's neck stand up straight. The Fae's amber eyes sparkled as she looked the girls up and down, golds and yellows swirling together. They mesmerized Ember, and it took her a few minutes to pull herself out of the trance-like state she had found herself in.

"We're looking for Merrow…" Rowan said hesitantly, weighing her words carefully.

"Knock on almost any door on the island, and you're bound to find one eventually." She shrugged with a smile. "I'd think you of all people would know that, Rowan O'Rourke."

"Actually," Ember began, plucking up every ounce of courage she could muster, "we're looking for a Clann…" She took a deep breath, pausing to still the quaking in her voice. "There's supposed to be a Clann of Merrow that have lived around the island for ages… We need to talk to them."

"Ah, I see," Asteria said, as she went back behind the counter, busying herself with wiping away stray crumbs. "You're lookin' for the Clann of Loch Lurgan then."

Ember and Rowan both exchanged confused glances. Honestly, they weren't sure what they were looking for, but even a whisper of information was better than what they had so far. Rowan shrugged at Ember as she turned back toward the counter.

"I suppose we are," she stated frankly. "Is there any way you could point us in the right direction?"

"I can." She nodded with a smile. "For a price, of course."

Ember looked at Rowan with even more confusion as the girl beside her sighed and pulled a small bag out of her pocket, presumably filled with coins. The bag jingled as she flipped it between her hands, eyes locked on the Fae in front of her. The two stared in silence as Ember looked back and forth between them, eyebrows cocked in confusion at their staring contest. Rowan broke the silence with a small laugh as she tossed the bag to Asteria, who quickly stuffed it in the pocket of her apron.

"The first thing you need to know," she began, "is that the Clann are a very proud group, more so even than my people. Once upon a time, they shared this land with us, trading fish with our people and learning to hunt on the island. We lived in harmony, but they don't trust easily. When Vala settled on Ellesmere, they cheated and stole and drove the Clann to the water, causing a deep-seated hatred in them for all humans. Their hatred has only grown as the Vala have. Claiming this land as their own when they are merely guests we are *allowing* to live."

Ember cleared her throat as she narrowed her eyes in thought. "But why do they still hate us? That was hundreds of years ago. We didn't drive them off the island, our parents didn't drive them off the island, so what reason do they have to hate us now?"

Asteria cut her eyes at the girl, crimson spreading through the amber. The playfulness had been replaced by a building fire, one that made Ember take a few steps back, just to be on the safe side.

"Your people have done nothing to fix it, either," Asteria replied, resentment in her once song-like voice. "But that is their story to tell, not mine. Assuming they give you the chance to speak with them." Asteria cocked her head to one side, eyes staying on Ember's, and it was like she could see straight through her. A smile returned to her face, her mouth curving up at one side. "Something tells me you won't have much of a problem with that, Ember Lothbrok."

Ember let out a breath. Why did everyone seem to know more about her than she did herself? And what was with all these damn riddles?

Asteria looked back to Rowan, breaking the hypnosis she had over Ember as she continued. "There's an Echopoint at the end of town, an ash tree that will take you to the road leading to Heksheim. Walk down the road, and veer to the left, past the wards. Walk through the Dark Forest, staying to the edge, and follow it until you hear the waves break on the rocks. You should find the cove on the other side of the tree line."

Ember felt her heart thrum steadily in her throat. Weren't they supposed to stay away from the Dark Forest? Wasn't that the first rule they had all been given when they started school? What Fen had explicitly warned her against when he took her flying? Her stomach turned as she thought back to what Professor Moran had told them that first morning.

"Our magic is powerful, but I cannot protect you if you willingly seek out danger."

In her defense, she didn't have to seek out misfortune. It had a tendency to find her.

Something didn't feel right.

"We appreciate your time, Asteria," Rowan replied. She tugged at Ember's arm, shaking her from her thoughts.

"Oh, oh yes than—" But before Ember could finish her sentence, Rowan slapped her hand directly across her mouth. Ember glanced at her, narrowing her eyes as she cocked her head to the side. Rowan shook her head and mouthed "*shut up*" before she turned back to the Fae, who was doing her best not to burst out in laughter.

"We appreciate your time, Asteria, have a lovely day." And without removing her hand from Ember's mouth, she pushed the girl quickly toward the door. As they stepped over the threshold, they heard Asteria call out to them.

"And, girls, don't forget," she said as she laid her palms on the counter and stared intensely, "stay on the edge of the forest. Do not, under any circumstance, venture into its depths. No amount of Vala magic will protect you from what lives in its shadows."

The door clicked behind them, and Rowan immediately dropped her hand and wiped it on her pants as she took a deep breath.

"What the bloody hell was that for?" Ember hissed as she wiped her mouth with the back of her hand.

Rowan rolled her eyes as she grabbed her by the elbow

and pulled her down the street. "That was me saving you from a very large headache in the future," she replied with a laugh.

Ember furrowed her brow as she shuffled her feet on the cobblestone, kicking up dust with each step. "What are you talking about?" she demanded, in a tone that very much resembled that of an angry toddler.

Rowan whirled around and clutched her elbow. "One rule for dealing with the Fae," she stated, "and arguably the most important rule, is to never ever thank them."

Ember scrunched her nose. "Never thank them?"

"No. Thanking a faerie for anything implies that you owe them something. And that can get very dangerous very fast."

"Owe them something?"

"Yeah, ya know, like a cheeseburger... or your first born." Rowan shrugged.

Ember groaned as she let out a breath. Would she ever know everything about living on a magical island, or was she just supposed to wing it for the rest of her life? Her books never covered half of this. She adjusted her bag with a sigh as the two made their way down the street.

The sun beat down on them as they made their way to the edge of town, the bright rays banishing the rest of the cold that had settled in her bones earlier that morning. She breathed in the fresh air, something that was in short supply in Galway. The smell of the wildflowers mixed with the ocean salt and blew through the breeze that whipped stray hairs across Ember's face.

"It's right up here!" Rowan called as she took long strides, leaving Ember almost jogging to catch up.

The tree stood tall, branches reaching in every direction like it was trying to touch the rays of sun that beat down on its leaves. The trunk of the tree was wide, easily over three feet in width. At the base of the trunk, Ember could make out the distinct carving of a rune, the glow behind it pulsing lightly, making the tree seem alive, like it was taking intentional breaths. The girls placed their hands on the rune as the light behind it grew stronger, then Ember felt the familiar tug in her stomach and found herself spinning through starlight, landing by a smaller tree on the side of the road that led to Heksheim.

"Do you ever get used to the spinning?" Ember asked, as she stood up, brushing the dirt off her pants.

"I don't know if you get used to it so much as you just learn to ignore it," Rowan replied with a shrug.

The girls made their way down the dirt road, listening to birds sing above them. The sky was clear, and the faint feeling of hope settled in Ember's chest. She absentmindedly kicked a pebble in front of her, following Rowan's shadow as it wound down the path. She slowed to a stop when she watched the pebble bounce off the air in front of her and back toward them. The magic rippled as Ember ran her hand over the ward, surges flowing through her fingertips and connecting with the metal disk that hung around her neck. Even outside the wards, she felt safer. Like the ancient magic was reaching toward her. It was an embrace that felt warm and familiar, something she knew she had felt before.

Rowan tugged at her arm, and they turned away from the warmth of the ward, toward the cold that was radiating from the forest.

"Maybe we should go back, tell an adult or something," Ember said quietly.

"Scared, Lothbrok?" Rowan grinned.

"And you're not?" Ember replied with a half laugh.

Rowan shrugged. "There're a lot more dangerous things on this island than the forest."

Ember took a shaky breath and nodded, still not fully convinced this was the best plan, but she couldn't back out now.

"She said left, right?" Rowan asked, as they surveyed the tree line.

"Uh, yeah, yeah, I think so," Ember replied hesitantly. She

briefly let her eyes wander along the edge of the tree line. She felt a sinking feeling in her gut as her stomach did flips, the hairs on the backs of her arms standing on end. Shadows danced behind the trees—the shadows of what, though, she wasn't sure.

Friends? Maybe… Foe? Far more likely.

"Can't we just go around?" Ember asked shakily.

"I doubt it," Rowan sighed. "Asteria said we had to enter the forest, which means the Clann likely has wards up outside of the forest. We won't be able to get in if we don't go through. Plus, it would take way longer."

"What's the point of a ward if you can just walk through the woods to get in it?" Ember asked as she scrunched her forehead.

"The Merrow don't bother themselves with warding against other creatures," she stated frankly. "Their wards are for Vala."

"Then, why not ward the whole thing?"

"Because most Vala in their right mind won't go through the Dark Forest if they don't have to. There are creatures in here far more dangerous than the Clann of Loch Lurgan," Rowan replied as she clenched her fists at her sides.

Somehow, that didn't make Ember feel any better. She shuddered as they edged toward the tree line. Any ounce of courage she might have felt when she woke up that morning was sucked out of her chest when she stepped beneath the shadows of the tall trees. The canopy blocked out nearly all the light from the mid-afternoon sun, enveloping the girls in almost total darkness. A chill shot down Ember's spine as they stepped further in, making sure to keep to the edge of the forest.

"Did she say how far it was?" Ember asked in a hushed tone.

"No, I don't think so," Rowan replied. "Just that we would know we were there when we heard the ocean."

A twig snapped in the distance, breaking the deafening silence, and Ember sucked in a breath as she whipped her head around. "What was that?" she whispered, wide eyed as she peered into the trees.

"Turn around," Rowan hissed as she yanked her arm and pulled her down the path. "If you see something," she instructed, "no, you didn't. And if you hear something, no, you didn't. One of the most important rules about this forest is to mind your own business."

Ember didn't argue.

The further they walked, the more Ember regretted not getting more specific instructions from the young Fae. As the sun rose higher above them, she came to the realization that this could take longer than they thought. Her feet already ached, and her stomach started to growl, signaling that it was well past lunch time. She let her mind briefly wander to the Kitt farm and the filling lunch she knew was being prepared by Mrs. Kitt. She shuffled her feet along the forest floor, her muscles protesting every step.

"You think we can take a break?" she asked without looking up. "My legs are killing me... Rowan?"

She was met with silence, spinning around to see no trace of the girl.

"Rowan?" she said as loudly as she dared, careful not to wake anything sleeping in the darkness ahead of her. Her heartbeat quickened as she looked in the shadows for any sight of the curly-haired girl. She was further from the tree line than she realized, barely able to catch glimpses of the sunlight in the distance. She spun around, her braid flying behind her as she tried to see further into the darkness. It didn't matter how hard she looked, though.

She was alone.

Ember started to turn and head back toward the edge of the forest when she heard a twig snap behind her. She spun to find the source of the noise, only to be met with deafening silence. She grabbed the strap of her bag and held it tightly, plucking up any ounce of courage she could muster, before a bush rustled behind her, followed by heavy thud.

"Rowan?" she whimpered into the darkness, but there was no response.

She had to make a decision—make her way back to the safety of the tree line, in the direction of whatever was creeping behind her, or head deeper into the stillness of the forest. Her body responded before her mind ever had a chance, and she sped away at a sprint as the footsteps behind her grew heavier, chasing her deeper into the heart of the forest.

She could feel her heart beating in her throat as she weaved her way in and out of the trees, dodging low hanging branches that hung in front of her face. Adrenaline pumped through her veins as she listened to the creature behind her, matching her own. She leaped over a root protruding from the ground, narrowly missing hooking her toes on it, and turned her head to check behind her. The sound of the footsteps had faded, causing Ember's sprint to slow. She flipped her head forward again, only to find herself caught in a giant spider web, wrapping itself around her face and outstretched arms.

She let out a loud yelp as she stumbled forward, tripping over a root and tumbling down the bank on the edge of the path. Ember felt her forehead hit a large rock sticking out of the ground, and blood trickled down, over her eye and cheek, the taste of iron overpowering her senses as she ran her tongue along the cut on the inside of her lip. Her vision blurred, stars dancing in front of her eyes as she felt along the gash on her forehead. Blood coated her fingers when she pulled her hand away. Sweat dripped into the cut, and Ember clenched her teeth at the stinging sensation of salt on an open wound.

She sat up on her knees, head still spinning as she tried to push herself to her feet. She dug her fingers into the cold dirt, looking for something—anything—to hold on to, but what she saw by her fingers made her breath catch in her chest.

Paws.

But not just any paws. Large white paws. Ember knew immediately that they were canine. All of a sudden, she couldn't breathe. Every attempt was met with what felt like cotton filling her throat. She inched her fingers back, rocking onto her heels as she hesitantly glanced at the animal in front of her.

A large white wolf stood above her, hovering inches away from her head. She slowly stood up, keeping her head low and movements to a minimum. The animal stood tall, its eyes meeting hers. Amber and gold swirled together like honey in tea. She stood mesmerized as it cocked its head to the side, almost as if it was studying her. As terrifying as his size was, the energy he gave off was anything but. His shoulders were relaxed, feet spread apart, and he was taking slow breaths. He was studying her, but not in the way a predator did his prey. He seemed gentle almost... docile. She felt her breathing slow as her eyes connected to his, and her magic tugged in her chest like the string on a guitar. Her hand moved toward the pristine fur—when a voice sounded from behind her, snapping her out of her trance.

"EMBER! EMBER!" the voice echoed through the trees.

Her head snapped around, following the sound of the voice through the trees. She quickly turned back around, and he was gone. As suddenly as the wolf had appeared, it had disappeared without a sound. Ember swung her body around as Rowan bolted through the trees, almost tripping over the same rock that was still wet with Ember's blood.

"Oh, thank the gods," Rowan said through labored breaths. "I swear to Freyja, I thought you were dead." She collapsed on the forest floor, back leaned up against the trunk of a tree as she rested her elbow on her knees.

"Did you see him?" Ember said as she spun on her heels, eyes searching the shadows for a glimpse of white.

"See who?" Rowan asked as she breathed heavily, wiping sweat from her forehead.

"Not who... the big wolf. He was white and like this tall," she said, as she held her hand to her chin. "You really didn't see anything?" Her head cocked as she slumped her shoulders.

Rowan shook her head with a chuckle. "How hard did you hit your head?"

Ember ran her fingers across her forehead, smearing the blood still dripping from the wound.

"Oh my gods, you're bleeding, Em," Rowan said, as she pushed herself to her feet and rushed toward the girl. She pulled a piece of cloth out of her jeans, shaking away the debris that had gathered in her pockets. Ember winced as she dabbed at the gash, the pain of the fall finally settling in her muscles and her head. All of the adrenaline was wearing off, and the severity of the situation they were in was beginning to set in.

"We need to get back to the edge of the forest," Rowan all but commanded, responding to the fear setting across Ember's face.

Ember nodded as she brushed the rest of the dirt and leaves off of her pant legs, moving up the hill and back on the path she had fallen from. The girls followed the mismatched footprints back to the edge of the tree line, the walk seeming so much shorter than when she was running it before. She carefully noted the singular set of prints in the dirt and recognized them as her worn out sneakers. As they got closer to the point where she was led astray, she slowed down to search the bushes around the path.

No other prints.

She squinted into the darkness as she looked around. Had she made it all up? Was she really running from nothing? She shook her head as she turned back around, following Rowan back to their starting point. The girls stayed in sight of the tree line as they made their way through the forest, Ember checking over her shoulder every few minutes. It felt like ages before Rowan's voice broke through the silence as she brushed away branches hanging in front of them.

"I think we found it," she whispered as they stepped into a clearing, waves crashing against the shore a few yards away.

The water was crystal clear, blues and emeralds swimming together like gemstones as the light beat off them. Ember closed her eyes as the heat from the sun hit her face, warming her pale skin down to her bones. The girls made their way closer, and as they did, two figures rose from the water, seemingly from nowhere. A woman with long hair and pale greenish skin appeared first, her seafoam hair peeking out from the red cape that billowed over her shoulders. Long webbed fingers clutched the cape around her chest as she pulled it tighter, looking almost reverent as she held her head high. Next to her stood a tall man with broad shoulders, the same pale green skin and iridescent hair shining in the sunlight. Their eyes met Ember's, and what she saw briefly took her breath away.

Lavender eyes.

CHAPTER 10
THE CLANN OF LOCH LURGAN

"Come no further," the male's voice boomed from the waterfront. He stood steadfast and tall, squaring his shoulders while looking directly at the girls. Ember's knees began to shake. Every question she had prepared seemed to fly out of her head as she stared back at the magnificent beings in front of her. The sun danced on their iridescent skin, bouncing off the waves lapping at the shore. The man had a hand resting on the female's shoulder, and Ember watched the mutual respect between the two.

"We mean no harm," Rowan said calmly as she raised both her hands. "We just need to talk to the Clann of Loch Lurgan."

The two figures in the water didn't so much as flinch. The woman dropped the hood of her cape, letting her long waves of hair fall across her shoulders. Her face was completely void of emotion; if eyes were truly the windows to the soul, hers had been boarded up a long time ago.

"I am Asherah. This is my husband Kaan," she said pointedly. "We are the Clann's rulers. You may address us. What business do Vala have here?" She stayed unmoving and held her head high, refusing to look the young girls in the eye.

"Respectfully, um, ma'am," Ember stuttered, "we have some questions we think you might be able to answer."

The two beings lowered their gaze slightly, looking directly at Ember.

"And what makes you think we will give you these answers?" the man replied.

"My father," she said, as she slowly moved forward to the edge of the cove, "wrote about your people. He said you have been around since before the Vala ever settled on the island. He spoke very highly about you." She stood tall, but the shaking in her voice betrayed her.

"What are you doing?" Rowan whispered harshly as she grabbed Ember's elbow, pulling her back.

"I'm just talking," she hissed. "What else am I supposed to do?" She yanked her arm away from the girl's grasp and continued toward the water. "He said you used to work side by side with the Vala." She directed back at Kaan.

"Before they stole our land. And our daughters," the man said steadily, eyes narrowed.

Ember hesitated as she inched forward, until she could feel the cold water rolling over the tops of her sneakers. The Merrows' lavender eyes bore holes into her, looking her up and down as she squared her shoulders and took a deep breath.

"Y-your daughters?" she stuttered.

Well, that was new.

"Your leaders kidnapped our children from young ages. They turned them into slaves in the homes of the wealthy. Raising your children, cooking your meals, tending to your animals." Asherah took a deep breath as her eyes narrowed on the girls. "Our people have lived in servitude to yours for hundreds of years. They stole our land, destroyed our homes, raped and murdered our women and children. The sins of your fathers are greater than they will ever teach you at that school. The Vala have no business with the Clann."

Ember staggered back, her center of gravity all of a sudden shaken. She felt like she had been punched in the gut, all the wind knocked out of her body. What reason would the Vala have to enslave an entire race of magical beings? Ember's stomach churned as she thought about the small children being ripped away from their parents and taken to a stranger's home. A lump built in her throat as she thought back to her own childhood, how scared she knew those children had to have been. Having your parents ripped away from you was not a fate she would wish on her worst enemy.

"Why don't you leave?" Ember asked, brow scrunched in thought. "If it's so dangerous here, why stay?"

Kaan narrowed his eyes with a sigh. "This is our ancestral land. My father ruled this cove, and his father before him. Our land is sacred to us, and we will not be chased away or go quietly."

Asherah laid her webbed hand on her husband's shoulder and looked at the girls. "We take precautions where we can, keeping our children close, but that doesn't stop them, not always. They will take what they think is theirs to take, no matter who it hurts."

Rowan huffed like a petulant child. "None of that is our fault."

Ember elbowed her in the ribs, wide-eyed as she pursed her lips.

"Standing by and watching the fire burn is far worse than lighting the match," Kaan said stoically. Rowan narrowed her eyes at the man, obviously not being swayed in where she stood. Ember finally broke the silence, hoping to change the subject and get them back on track. The quicker they could get their answers, the quicker they could go back home.

"We want to know about the legend that talks about your peoples' magic being stolen. We want to help," she said gently. "We're hoping you can tell us more about it."

"There are whispers of a legend..." The man nodded.

"Of a young Vala and the power they are told to hold, but that is something I suspect you already know, Ember Lothbrok."

Ember bit the inside of her lip, drawing blood again from where it had pierced the skin hours before. "We know there's a book. We think... we think we have an idea who the legend could be about and that they need the book. We need to know where to find it." She glanced back at Rowan for support but was met only with raised brows and a puzzled frown.

"Why should we help," Kaan said, turning to face Rowan, "the people who seek to destroy us?"

"You don't have to, of course," Ember replied, barely above a whisper, "but we would consider it a personal favor."

"We stopped giving favors out to your kind a long time ago." Kaan glared.

"Maybe," Ember said hopefully, "we can do something for you in return?"

The couple glanced at each other, a conversation happening between the looks they were giving, then Asherah turned back to them.

"We will give you the information you are looking for. And in return, you will bring our daughter home to us."

Ember and Rowan glanced at each other, confusion and frustration bubbling to the surface. Finding an old book and getting rid of it was one thing, but rescuing a child who was kidnapped by the government and sold into slavery? All of a sudden, she felt every bit of fourteen years old—scared and confused and in desperate need of wise words from her parents. Words she knew she would never get to hear. A dull ache formed in her chest as she swallowed the lump in her throat.

"She is with a family," Asherah said calmly. "The Vargrs. Her name is—"

"Maren," Ember whispered, feeling all of the breath leave her chest. The woman who healed her hand, who spoke to her so kindly, who was so gentle with Killian... was a slave? A slave raised him, made his meals, and cleaned his clothes. All of the puzzle pieces began to fall together, one by one, and Ember had never been more certain of anything in her life.

The legend was about Killian. It had to be.

"How are we supposed to do that?" Rowan asked with a frown.

"This is how we are able to travel between worlds, ours and yours," she said, as she held the edge of the red cloak in her translucent hands. "Without this, we are imprisoned on land. When our daughters are taken, their cloaks are stolen from them, hidden and locked away by the government you so blindly follow. Find her cape and return it to her."

"We t-think," Ember stuttered, "the legend is about one of the boys Maren has been raising. There's a book we think he might be looking for, and we need to find it before he does. We're hoping you know where it is."

"*The Book of Shadows*," Kaan said stoically.

Ember felt hope flutter in her chest. "Yes! Yes, that's it. Can you help us?"

"The book you're looking for," Kaan replied, "is full of very dark magic. If it were to fall into the wrong hands, the consequences would be devastating. And if it were to fall into the right hands, the consequences could be worse."

Ember scrunched her brow as she let out a heavy sigh. What was that supposed to mean? She was getting really tired of all the riddles.

"We have to find it," Rowan said strongly, finally finding her voice. "Before anyone gets hurt."

Kaan slowly nodded his head at the girls. "The book has been passed between members of the First Families for generations. While I don't know who is in possession of it currently, I can only guess that it is with a family who has the same affinity for the dark arts as its creator."

Ember swallowed the lump that was forming in her throat

as she nodded her head. All of the things both Eira and Rowan had told her about the Vargrs came flooding back—their history of being involved in dark magic, her father's suspicion of the family, and the strange interactions with the Ellingboes in the hall. If she decided to continue this search, would she regret what they would find?

And would Fen ever forgive her?

Ember and Rowan thanked the leaders for their help and headed back toward the forest to make their journey to town. Rowan was two steps ahead of her when Ember heard Asherah call her name.

"Ember Lothbrok," she said as the girl turned back around hesitantly. "Bring my daughter home."

Ember nodded with a half smile before she turned around to catch up with Rowan.

As soon as they were safely back in the forest—though safe seemed to be a relative term—Rowan aggressively grabbed Ember's bicep and shoved her into the trunk of a tree. Ember grunted as her head made contact with the rough bark, the wood digging into her scalp through her hair.

"Ow!" she exclaimed as she rubbed the back of her head. "What was that for?"

"What was that back there?" Rowan said angrily as she kept a firm hold on Ember's arm.

"What are you talking about?" Ember replied, prying at the fingers that were leaving red marks on her pale skin.

"What were you saying to them?'

"You were right beside me. You heard the whole thing." Ember's face scrunched in confusion.

"I don't speak Mermish. Where did you learn that?" Rowan narrowed her eyes.

Ember furrowed her brow at the girl, who finally released her arm as she stared back in confusion. "I don't speak Mermish; I don't even know what that is." She narrowed her gaze.

"Well, you sure weren't speakin' English, or any other language I know," Rowan said as she crossed her arms over her chest.

Ember instinctively traced her fingers over the runes on her necklace as she bit the inside of her cheek. The more she learned about the island, the more confused she seemed to become. And the more she learned about herself, the less she felt like she actually knew. Her mind reeled as she traced her toe along the dirt at her feet. This wasn't the time to figure out other mysteries. They needed to focus. They had a job to do. And they had to do it right.

"Maybe it's just a weird magic thing, or something my dad taught me, I don't know." She shrugged.

Rowan stared at her for a few moments before taking a breath and dropping her shoulders. "Yeah, I guess so," she said, shaking her head. "Sorry about that. Is your head alright?"

"I mean, yeah," Ember said with a half smile. "But could we maybe keep the violence to a minimum?"

Rowan shrugged. "Fair enough, I suppose."

The girls laughed quietly as they walked through the forest, momentarily allowing themselves to forget about the daunting task that lay ahead of them. Ember kicked the pebbles at her feet as they talked about school and Rowan's family, wincing a little when she thought about Fen. She didn't understand why it was happening this way, why her foster brother's best friend had to be in the thick of this. She couldn't stand the cocky boy, but she knew Fen would die for him.

And that scared her.

The walk back to the entrance of the forest was quicker than it had been earlier that day, considering Ember didn't get herself lost in the middle of it. The girls walked down the dusty path to the tall ash tree standing a few miles down the road.

"I guess our next step is to figure out where the cape is?" Rowan said, as she hung on one of the lower branches.

"Yeah, I guess so." Ember nodded as she kicked the dirt resting at her feet. "Maybe that will lead us in the right direction to the book. Can't hurt, I guess." Except Ember knew that was a lie. It could hurt.

If they got caught, it would hurt immensely. And not just them.

"We'll talk more at school," Rowan said with a smile. "Mum is probably wondering why I've been gone so long. Helio me if you find anything?"

"Yeah, for sure." Ember nodded with a smile.

Rowan waved a quick goodbye before mumbling, "O'Rourke," under her breath and popping out of sight. Ember sighed deeply as she adjusted the strap of her satchel and ran her fingers over the scratch on her forehead. She was exhausted, and all she wanted to do was climb in bed and sleep away the dull ache that was thumping in her skull. She reached up and grabbed one of the branches swaying above her head.

"Kitt Farm," Ember whispered and felt the tug she had grown all too familiar with. Her feet landed with a heavy thud, kicking up the dirt around her sneakers as she shook her head and allowed her eyes to focus on the gate in front of her. She let out a relieved breath as she pushed it open and made her way up to the welcoming house. The farm was bathed in peach and lavender, and the love that radiated from the weathered wood was almost palpable. The sun was beginning to set behind her, making her very aware of just how long she had been gone. She braced herself for the proverbial storm as she quietly pushed the door open and stepped into the house.

"Ember, is that you?" Eira's voice rang from the kitchen. She could hear her footsteps growing louder as she made her way into the foyer. "I hope you worked up an appetite. Supper should be ready soon, and I have Fen—what on earth!" She dropped the mixing bowl that she had cradled in her arm, sending it crashing to the floor, shattering on contact.

Fen heard the noise and came rushing into the room. "Mum, is everything alright? I heard—bloody hell, Em! What happened?" he almost shouted as he came to a screeching halt.

"Language, Fenrir," Eira scolded as she vanished the mess on the floor.

Ember grimaced as she took a step back. The realization of how she probably looked hit her, and she ran her fingers over the gash on her forehead.

"Oh, I'm fine. Really, it-it's not that bad," she stuttered as she wiped the dirt off her clothes. "You should see the other guy." She shot them a small smile, hoping to lighten the mood, but was only met with a concerned glance from the woman in front of her. Fen let out a small chuckle, resulting in Eira smacking him on the back of the head.

"Come in the kitchen, love, and let's get you cleaned up," Eira said as she ushered the girl into the other room. Ember sat down at the table, feeling guilty about the dirt she was bound to be tracking all over the house. Eira rummaged through a cabinet in the kitchen as Ember shifted nervously in her chair, then carried a small jar of ointment over, running her hand over Ember's forehead, mumbling spells as she went.

"I'm sorry about your bowl," she said softly. "I can replace it for you."

"Nonsense, child," Eira replied. "It's only a bowl. There are far more important things in life." Her warm eyes briefly landed on Ember's and began to grow misty. She ran a hand across the girl's jaw and smiled before quickly breaking away to continue the incantations.

"I could heal that easy," Fen said confidently as he puffed out his chest.

Ember shot him a sideways glance as she rolled her eyes. "I think I'll let your mum take care of it."

Eira rubbed the ointment across Ember's now clean forehead and screwed the lid back on the jar. "Why don't you go run upstairs and get cleaned up," she said sweetly as she pushed away from her chair. "Supper will be on in a few minutes."

Ember nodded and made her way up the steps, her muscles feeling like they were made of lead as she lifted them up each stair. She pushed open the bathroom door and leaned on the sink, allowing it to take all of her weight, temporarily relieving the aching that was pulsing steadily in her calves. She turned on the water as she ran her hands down her shirt, still covered in the dirt and blood from the fall she had taken earlier. It was caked all over her face and arms, a trail of dry blood running from her temples and down her neck. She let the warm water wash over her face as she scrubbed at the memories of the dark woods that were burned behind her eyes.

"So, what really happened?"

Ember turned around quickly to see Fen leaning against the door frame, a small frown forming on his face. "What are you talking about? I was doing homework with Rowan," Ember answered a little too quickly, turning her back to him to hide the guilt that she was sure was written all over her face.

"That's what you told Mum," he said with a lowered voice, "but Killian and I were in Sigurvik earlier, and we never saw you at the Hidden Moon."

Ember felt her pulse begin to race as she searched for an excuse. "You must've missed us then, we were working on our Gladr paper all day," she said as she fidgeted with the damp washcloth in her hand.

"Don't insult me, Ember," he snapped, and she turned to look at him. "We looked for you everywhere, and that cut didn't come from you tripping."

She winced at the sound of her given name. She had hated the silly nickname he had given her, but all of a sudden, hearing her name laced with venom rolling off his tongue made her desperately miss it. She bit her bottom lip, finding the cut with her teeth from earlier in the day, digging into it until she tasted copper in her mouth. She hated lying to him. She hated it more than anything. But she was trying to protect him. She was doing the right thing.

Wasn't she?

"I'm not lying, Fenrir," she bit back, harsher than she intended. "You just missed us. It's not like we sat at Hidden Moon all day."

Fen crossed his arms as he glared at her. The guilt settled in her chest as she did her best to take slow, even breaths. He rolled his eyes as he let out a huff. "Let me know when you've decided you trust me," he replied, sounding more hurt than angry, and spun on his heels toward the steps. Ember let out a shaky breath as soon as he was out of sight.

She needed to finish this, and fast.

DINNER THAT NIGHT was a quiet affair, at least for the two teenagers sitting at the table. Ember took small bites, not daring to make eye contact with the moody boy in front of her. She picked at her food, allowing the peas to roll across her plate like they were playing a game of tag—she still hated peas. She vaguely listened to Maeve giggle about her day, laughing under her breath as she went on about her roll in the mud while she was chasing the donkey. Otto recounted his run in with a very large flounder that gave them a run for his money on the fishing boat that morning, making Eira grimace as he showed the table the nasty cut on his arm where the fishing line got tangled around it. Every now and then, Ember would glance up, catching Fen staring daggers at her. She quickly looked down at her plate as she leaned her elbow on the table, laying her cheek in her palm. Eira looked briefly at the two as she cleared her throat.

"So, how is your project coming along, Ember?" she asked as she took a sip of her drink.

"Oh, um, it's going fine," Ember lied. "We got a good bit done today."

Fen laughed under his breath as he leaned back in his chair and crossed his arms. "What project is that again, Ember?" he said with a smirk as he took a bite of the potatoes on his plate.

Ember glared back at him as she ran her tongue over the rough edges of her teeth. "It's for Gladr," she replied, eyes never leaving his.

"That's weird. I wasn't aware we had a project with Professor Walsh."

"Well, maybe," she hissed, "if you weren't so busy giggling with Killian, you would hear what homework we have due." She threw her braid over her shoulder and crossed her arms, daring him to keep going.

Two could play this game.

His eyes narrowed further as he scrunched his nose. "We don't giggle," he hissed in reply before Eira barked at him from the table."Fenrir James, I thought we talked about that! It might only be your first year, but now is not the time to be goofing off."

"Now, now," Otto said calmly. "It's only first year. The boys will settle down, won't you, Fen?"

Fen nodded with a grin as he shot his mom an apologetic look. She threw her hands in the air in defeat as she stood up from the table and began clearing the dishes. "If I receive even one Helio from your professors about your behavior, so help me," she warned, as she aggressively sent dirty dishes flying toward the sink.

Ember let her eyes fall to her lap, the stoic look on her face now completely gone. She was used to lies. At one point, they completely overwhelmed her life, slithering into the cracks, engulfing any chance of happiness like an uncontrollable flame. Her nails dug into her palm as she bit her lip. She couldn't let this happen here. She couldn't allow it to end the same as all the others.

She had to tell Fen.

CHAPTER 11
SECRETS, LIES, AND
BLOODY LIPS

Ember traced the grain of wood on the desk as Professor Walsh droned on at the front of the room. Galdr was normally her favorite class; learning all of the spells and figuring out how to use the magic that had been desperately trying to escape her body for years felt incredible, but today she couldn't focus. The truth was, she hadn't been able to focus on much of anything lately. The guilt she felt about lying to Fen was nearly overwhelming. It made her feel empty. She didn't know how much longer she could keep something like this to herself, especially with the way he was acting.

He hadn't spoken to her since dinner the weekend before. Ember tried to go into his room a few times to talk to him, to maybe smooth things over, but she was always met with a locked door. He actively avoided her at school, rushing out the door and into the hall before Ember could even pack up her books. Dread coiled itself around her, and she was reminded of all of the locked doors that she thought she had left behind. How long would it be before she found herself back on the ferry, leaving Ellesmere for good?

"Miss Lothbrok?" Professor Walsh said from the front of the room.

She popped her head up from where it was lying on the desk and glanced around the room, all eyes now on her. "I'm sorry, ma'am," she whispered as she straightened her back.

"As I was saying," the professor continued, "today, we will be going over standard locking charms, as well as unlocking. Would anyone like to try to demonstrate the locking charm for the class?"

A small hand shot up in the air. The professor called on Odette to come forward where a padlock lay on the table. The girl walked with a bounce to the middle of the room, feet jingling with each step.

"What do you think those bells are for?" Killian whispered as he leaned forward.

Ember hushed him as Professor Walsh sent them a sharp look, causing Killian to slink back into his seat.

"Whenever you're ready, Miss Quinn."

Odette stood in front of the table with a dreamy smile on her face. She seemed to never stop smiling, Ember had noticed. It was like she was in a perpetual state of bliss, and it was almost enraging. No one was that happy. It was just weird. The white-haired girl hovered her hand over the lock, speaking quietly, almost like wind chimes twinkling in the breeze.

"*Sellar*," she said firmly, and the lock clicked shut. She placed her hand back in front of her, the same smile still on her face as she turned to the professor who stood beaming to the side.

"Very good, Miss Quinn. You've been reading ahead." The professor nodded. "And now the unlocking charm, if you don't mind."

Odette nodded as she turned back to the table, hovering her hand back over the lock as she said, "*Desellar*," and the lock clicked back open. It was almost effortless, like blinking or breathing. It seemed to be second nature. Ember sighed as she laid her hand in her palm. Would it ever be that easy for her? Odette floated back to her seat, and Professor Walsh took her place back at the center of the round stage.

"You will work in pairs for the rest of the class, practicing your locking and unlocking charms. On your desks, you will find a padlock that you and your partner will share." As if she had commanded it, locks appeared on each desk in the room. "Please keep the talk to a minimum. You may begin." The professor made her way to her desk, and the sound of children trying, and failing, to master the simple charms floated across the room.

Ember turned toward the center of the table and began to work on the charm as Rowan impatiently tapped her fingers on the desk.

"So?" she whispered as she leaned on the table.

"So what?" Ember asked as she waved her hand over the lock and whispered the incantation, huffing when it didn't do what she told it to.

"What happened when you got home?" Rowan asked. "Were your folks mad?"

Ember shook her head as the lock under her hand refused to do what she told it. "No, mostly just worried about my head. Fen isn't speaking to me now, though."

Rowan scrunched her nose. "Isn't speaking to you? Why not?"

"He thinks I lied to him about where we were the other day." She sighed. "I mean, I suppose I did, but now he thinks I don't trust him."

Rowan rolled her eyes dramatically. "I always knew he was a whiny little git." She leaned casually back in her chair. "He'll get over it."

"I don't know," Ember replied. "He's pretty upset." She chewed on the bottom of her lip deep in thought. In the back of her mind, she knew his recent attitude wouldn't last forever, but that didn't make it hurt any less. She had been ignored for weeks at a time for far less than this.

Rowan waved her hand, as if to wave the worry out of her mind. "He's a boy, he'll get over it. Did you find anything out about the cape?" Rowan asked as she picked at her nails.

"No." She huffed, pushing the lock across the table to the curly haired girl in frustration.

Rowan sat up straight for a moment, mumbling the incantation under her breath with a wave of her hand as the lock under her palm successfully clicked closed.

"You make it look so easy," Ember grumbled as she snatched the lock away from her friend, repeating the incantation over and over to no avail.

Rowan chuckled. "You need to relax. You can't force it. It's like this, watch." Rowan took a breath and shook out her shoulders. She closed her eyes, hovered her hand over the brass lock, and whispered, *"Desellar."*

Ember watched as the lock clicked open. Her voice sounded like water running over a creek bed. The words were rhythmic and effortless. Ember sighed as she took the lock and tried again. She closed her eyes, took a breath, and waved her hand over the lock. *"Desellar,"* she whispered, and the lock clicked open under her palm. Her heart fluttered as she beamed.

"So, you know her, right?" Rowan asked, as she tapped her fingers on the table.

"Who?" Ember asked, as she furrowed her brow and pushed the lock back across the table.

"The Merrow that works for the Vargrs," Rowan replied.

"I met her once, but I don't see why that matters." Ember shrugged.

"It matters," Rowan continued, "because we need to talk to her. If you've already met, maybe she'll be more comfortable talking to us. We don't have any other leads to find the cape, so it's the next logical step."

"How are we supposed to do that?" Ember laughed. "We can't just walk up to the Vargrs house and knock on the door. 'Hello, my name is Ember, and I need to speak with the help.' They would either become terribly suspicious or laugh us right off the front stoop."

Rowan sighed defeatedly. "I suppose you're right. But we can figure out another way. We really don't have many options right now."

Ember glanced over her shoulders at the boys behind her laughing. Killian was hovering the lock over his head while Fen shot tiny balls of light at it, presumably trying to knock it down. She turned back to the table and worked on the lock now sitting in front of her.

"I mean…" she said hesitantly. "I could try to talk to Fen. He might know something we don't."

"I don't know," Rowan replied. "That seems kinda risky, doesn't it? And he's not even speaking to you right now."

Ember shrugged her shoulders. "I know, but he's Killian's best friend. Maybe he's seen something over there that could help."

Rowan sighed. "I still think we should keep this to ourselves. The less people we have to worry about, the better."

Ember's shoulders dropped. She knew Rowan was right. It was too risky. There was too much of a chance of Killian finding out and ruining their whole plan, or his family finding out and putting Maren in danger. There were too many variables. They needed to keep this as quiet as possible. But keeping this from Fen was becoming a burden she was having a difficult time bearing. His silent treatment was deafening. The glares at the dinner table were becoming too much. And if she was being completely honest with herself, she missed him. Fen was the closest thing to a brother she had ever had, though she would deny it if anyone ever asked, and feeling that slip away scared her.

Class was dismissed, and before Ember had a chance to

pack away her things, Fen was already up and heading toward the door.

"Fen, wait!" she called after him, but he didn't turn around. He rounded the corner and disappeared in the sea of students filling the hall. Ember sighed in defeat as she slipped her book in her bag and slung it over her shoulder. Killian leaned on the desk in front of her, studying her movements as a smile creeped across his face.

"You and your brother get into it then?" he asked with a slight laugh.

"Foster brother," she corrected him, "and I don't see how that's any of your business." She tucked her necklace back inside of her shirt and made her way to the door and into the hallway, Killian hot on her heels the whole way.

"So, you comin' to tryouts tonight?" he said as he strutted down the hall.

"Tryouts for what?" she asked, squinting her eyes at him.

"Rukr tryouts, just figured you'd be there since Fen is going out for the team." He shrugged.

"What's Rukr?" she asked as she slowed her gait to match his.

"Well, I guess you'll have to come tonight and find out," he said with a grin. "Might be a decent apology to Fen too, you supporting him and all."

Ember nodded her head as she allowed herself to get lost in the thoughts weaving a web in her mind. There was a chance that Fen would just continue to ignore her and pretend she wasn't even there if she showed up. There was a chance that it would distract him and he would mess up, making him even more enraged at her than he already was.

But there was also the chance that it could be the bridge she needed to get back in his good graces. An olive branch she could extend to him, and they could forget about this whole mess.

That was all the hope she needed right now.

EMBER BRUSHED through her wet hair, wringing the water out of the ends as she dug through her dresser to find a clean pair of pants. She had rushed through dinner so she could take a shower before going back to school that evening and was heavily regretting not taking her dirty laundry down to Eira the night before. She smelled a couple of her shirts, determining that they weren't really that dirty, and settled on an older t-shirt and pair of jeans. She threw on her clothes and quickly searched the room for her missing shoe, finding it peeking out from under the bed. She slipped her bag over her shoulder and heard the front door close beneath her feet, telling her that Fen was leaving. She took in a deep breath and prayed that what she was doing wasn't going to further screw up their friendship.

She took the stairs two at a time and poked her head in the sitting room where Eira and Otto were both cozied up on the couch. "Um, I'm going to go watch the boys try out tonight. I hope that's alright," she said quietly, realizing that she had never actually asked their permission. She had spent her entire life on her own, even when she wasn't, and having a family that cared where she was was still very hard to get used to.

"Oh, you just missed Fen. He's heading that way now," Eira said with a smile before returning to the book in front of her.

"That's alright," Ember said gently. "I don't mind going by myself."

"Keep those boys in line," Otto said with a grin.

Ember nodded with a sheepish smile and headed out the door into the brisk night air. She walked quickly down the dirt path to the gate, not wanting to be late. Rowan said she would meet her at the Echopoint outside of the school, but she didn't want to make her wait.

"Howeyah, Em!" Rowan greeted her as she dropped to the ground in front of the tree by the school.

"Are we late?" Ember asked as she smoothed a hand over her shirt and shook out her legs, straightening herself back upright from the sudden contact with the ground.

"Nah, we've got like fifteen minutes, so we can still get a good seat if we hurry." Rowan grabbed Ember's arm and dragged her down the path toward the ward. Ember held the strap of her bag as she tried to keep up with Rowan's strides, doing her best not to trip on the dips in the dirt road. The girls walked through the ward and onto the school grounds, quickly veering to the right down a path taking them away from the school. The sound of cheering grew closer, and she picked up her pace, making their way down the winding path to the stadium at the bottom.

The arena was rectangular in shape, surrounded by high bleachers on both sides. On either end of the pitch, there was a large H-shaped goal post. Boys and girls from each team sped around the arena on AirWaves, waving what looked like hockey sticks and passing something back and forth—though Ember couldn't tell what it was.

The girls made their way into the large arena, finding a bleacher to sit on that was high enough to see what was going on. Ember pulled her bag over her head, dropping it at her feet as she settled onto the wooden bench. She could barely make Fen and Killian out on the grass below them, talking excitedly back and forth to each other as they strapped into their boards. Ember smiled at the sight, hoping silently that her presence wouldn't be a distraction to her foster brother. She looked around at the field and scrunched her nose.

"So, how does Rukr work?" she asked as she studied the field, and like an answer to her question, the field below them roared to life. All of the players mounted their boards, the same hovering board Killian had been riding the day he nearly ran her over, and took to the sky.

Two balls of light shot into the air, one red and one blue, and hovered in the open space between the players. One of the older boys, who Ember assumed was the captain, held the blue ball in his hand—or was it hovering? Ember couldn't really tell being so far away. Another player took the red ball and slung it toward him. The captain, who Rowan told her was Flynn Maguire, took off toward one of the open goal posts, weaving in and out of the young boys.

"Basically," Rowan explained, "the whole point is to get the Brazul—that blue ball of fire—through your team's goal post. If you get it over the center bar, that's one point." She pointed to the H-shaped post at the end of the field. "If it goes under the bar, through the goal-mouth, that's two points. You can either hold—erm, I guess hovering it since they don't actually touch them—or they can unstrap a foot from their board and kick it, but that's a little hard, and the other team will be trying to hit you with the Broja, that red ball of fire," she said, as she pointed toward the players.

Ember's head felt like it was spinning as her eyes widened.

Balls of hovering fire? Was this a joke?

"What are the sticks?" she asked as she pointed toward the field. Half of the players from each team had what looked like a hockey stick strapped to their backs. She watched as Fen quickly yanked his over his head and hit the Broja as hard as he could away from Killian, who had just caught the Brazul and was speeding quickly toward the goal post.

"The caman," Rowan said, as she nodded toward Fen. "Half of the players have them. It's their job to protect the players that are trying to score points. Some have been known to aim for shins instead of the Broja, though."

"That's allowed?" Ember gasped as her eyes widened.

"Pretty much anything is allowed," Rowan shrugged. "They learn really fast how to dodge. It's a brutal game, depending on who is playing."

Ember watched as each of the players took turns weaving

in and out of the others, dodging the Broja that was hit their way, and then it was Killian's turn. The way he stood on the board was like watching a dove fly, like he was born to do it. He crouched low, holding one side of the board as he spun in a circle, narrowly dodging the bright red flame that barely missed his head. It looked effortless, like he didn't even have to try.

It was mesmerizing.

Killian flew higher and higher in the air, and his laughter carried through the arena. His head swung around, and for just a moment, his eyes caught Ember's. She felt her heart involuntarily race in her chest as his eyes lit, a goofy grin brightening his rosy cheeks. She sucked in a breath and looked away quickly, searching the air for Fen again.

Now was not the time.

Fen hovered high above the ground, eyes darting back and forth, focusing on the game playing out in front of him. He shot up higher into the air, so high that it made Ember's heart pound in her chest. She could hear Flynn shouting at him from below, but he either couldn't hear him or didn't care. Ember's eyes locked on him as he strapped the caman on his back and crouched low on his board, hovering in one spot for far longer than Ember was comfortable with.

"What are you doing," she mumbled under her breath. His eyes scanned the arena, and like an answer to her question, Killian sped up beside him and tossed the Brazul into his gloved hand. He dove so quickly that Ember let out an audible gasp and clutched the edges of the bench she was sitting on. He spun and weaved his way straight through the other players, and lobbed the Brazul lazily through the goal post. Killian was beside him in an instant, smacking him on the back and giving him a high five as they cheered.

After her heart rate slowed, Ember rolled her eyes and sat back in her seat. This was probably something the boys had been practicing all summer, maybe even all year, of course they would use it to show off during tryouts.

Ember was quickly jolted from her trance when someone came and sat beside the girls. Rowan nudged her in the rib with her elbow and used her head to motion at the woman staring down at the field.

"Maren," Ember said under her breath.

The woman turned to the girls and smiled. "Hello, Miss Lothbrok, Miss. O'Rourke." She nodded.

"What are you doing here?" Ember asked quietly, transfixed on the lilac swirling through the woman's eyes.

Maren pointed toward the field at the blond boy gliding above the ground. "I thought Killian would like having someone here for him, but I see I wasn't the only one with that idea," she said as her eyes twinkled.

"We thought Fen would like that too." Ember nodded. "Ya know, support and all."

"There is nothing quite as incredible," Maren stated, "as the bond between siblings. Even when they aren't getting along." The corners of her mouth a small grin as she kept her gaze focused on the field in front of them.

"Oh, no, we're not siblings," Ember replied. "He's just my foster brother."

"There is a lot more to being a family than sharing the same blood. Familial bonds run much deeper than that." Maren smiled.

"Speaking of families…" Rowan interrupted.

"Rowan, not now," Ember hissed, jabbing her in the ribs. Out of all places, the middle of the school grounds was not the place to talk about stealing from one of the most prominent Vala families on the island.

Rowan mouthed *"what?"* to the red head, completely unaware of her boldness.

"Is there something I can help you girls with?" Maren

asked quietly. Something about the way she never flinched told Ember that she knew more than she was letting on.

Her curiosity got the better of her, and drawing from Rowan's courage, Ember inched closer to the Merrow and lowered her voice. "We were wondering if you could tell us about your cape," Ember said quietly, looking around to ensure no one was listening.

Maren looked at the girls with her eyebrow raised, her expression still as unreadable as ever. Ember took a shallow breath as she met the woman's gaze, trying to decipher the look dancing behind her eyes.

"I'm afraid I don't know what you're talking about," Maren said solemnly.

Ember's shoulders slumped and she let out a sigh, resting her chin in her hands. Of course it wasn't going to be that easy.

"Even if I did, though, I'm afraid it wouldn't matter," Maren continued. "Master Vargr keeps his possessions very closely guarded. Only the family can access what is most important to them."

"What, like blood magic?" Rowan said, brows furrowed as she leaned her elbows on her knees.

Maren nodded as she stared forward, hands still folded calmly in her lap.

"What's blood magic?" Ember asked.

"Real dark stuff," Rowan replied in a hushed tone. "I didn't know people still actually used it."

Maren nodded again, tucking a stray piece of hair behind her ear. The woman didn't show much emotion, but Ember could see the pain on her face. A pain she knew all too well. She missed her family. Ember felt a small fire ignite in her belly. She couldn't do anything about the pain of losing her own parents, but she could figure out a way to give Maren her freedom back. Even if they never found the book, she owed her that much. Just as Ember was about to pry more, she heard heavy footsteps running up the wooden bleachers.

"Just couldn't stay away, could ya?" Killian's cocky voice sounded from below her.

"Bloody hell, Vargr, what did you do to your face?" Rowan exclaimed. Ember turned her face to look at the boy climbing the bleachers, blood pouring from his lip and nose. The smile that lit up his face was stained crimson, and his gray eyes looked like campfire smoke against the sun.

"I think it's safe to say I impressed them," he said with a cocky grin, wiping away the blood that had pooled on his bottom lip.

"I don't know if 'impressed' is the word I would use," Fen said with a laugh, jogging up the steps behind him. His smile turned to confusion when his eyes landed on Ember shifting uncomfortably on the bleacher seat in front of him. "You came," he whispered to her, a small smile cutting at the edge of his mouth. "I didn't think you'd come."

"Wild draics couldn't keep me away." Ember let out a breath as the boy's face lit up, a silent agreement to let bygones be bygones. She was relieved that her plan didn't backfire on her and they could get back to normal. She watched as he nodded in her direction and thought about how simple their communication was becoming. No words were needed, almost like he could read her mind, and she his.

Was this what family felt like? No need to beg for forgiveness or hide away until the storm blew over?

"Here, Killian," Maren said as she pulled a handkerchief out of her small bag. "Let's clean you up." She dabbed at the droplets of blood making their way down his chin and mouth, holding it on his split lip. He winced as the cloth made contact with the wound, screwing up his face in pain.

"Don't be such a baby," Rowan snorted.

"Couldn't you just use the healing spell you used on my hand?" Ember asked.

"I could," Maren replied with a grin, "but sometimes boys need to learn lessons the hard way. Just because you can use magic, doesn't mean you necessarily should."

Rowan and Ember snickered as Killian huffed, spitting little droplets of blood into the air.

"We were going to go grab something to eat from Florin's. You guys wanna come?" Fen said, as he wiped the remaining sweat from his brow.

"That's perfect, I'm starving," Rowan replied.

"Are you coming, Maren?" Ember asked as she picked up her bag and prepared to leave.

"You kids have fun," she said gently. "Killian, don't be late. Your mother won't be happy with either of us if you are."

Killian nodded as Maren stood up and made her way to the steps, waving to the group as she gracefully walked away. Ember furrowed her brow, righteous anger bubbling to the surface. Maren should be with her family, with her parents, not taking care of another family's child—doing their laundry and fixing meals like a servant.

Killian walked up beside her as they made their way down the bleachers, elbowing her in the ribs. "Cheer up, Starshine. It won't leave a scar." He grinned as he ran his tongue across the split skin on his lip. "I'll still be handsome as ever." His teeth shined as he grinned, and Ember felt heat creep up her neck and into her cheeks.

"I don't know if handsome is the word I would use," Ember replied, trying to hide her grin, "but it does make you look a bit more human. I'm glad you're okay."

Killian grinned as he leaned in closer. "Careful, Starshine, start talking like that and people might begin to think you care about me."

Ember rolled her eyes as she gave him a gentle nudge with her elbow. "In your dreams, Vargr." Killian shot her one last grin before he turned, jogging to catch up with Rowan and Fen.

Ember watched as he laughed with Fen, carrying on the way they did when they were together, and his smile began to eclipse the anger she had toward his family. Maybe he wasn't all bad after all. Annoying? Yes, but maybe not bad. He couldn't control what his family did any more than Ember could control losing hers. Maybe they weren't that different after all.

Ember quickened her pace to catch up with the group, and they made their way up the path by the school, laughing and carrying on at the expense of the tall blond leading the pack.

"Ya know, I can heal that for you if you want." Fen said with a grin, slinging his board over his shoulder.

"Over my dead body, Kitt." Killian laughed as he shoved his friend's arm, causing him to trip over his foot and into a bush.

"Can we put a cap on all of the bloodshed, please?" Rowan scolded from behind.

Ember did her best to hold back the laughter threatening to bubble from her throat at her foster brother's expense. She reached her hand out and helped him to his feet, brushing the dirt off his uniform, not that you could really tell a difference with how filthy the boys were.

"Are we okay?" she asked hesitantly, as they continued up the hill.

"Yeah, we're good," he assured her with a smile. "I couldn't stay mad at my sister forever, now could I?"

"Foster sister," she corrected with a small grin, "and I'm glad. Honestly, the silent treatment was getting a bit annoying."

Ember watched the group of friends talking and laughing and felt a pinprick of hope ignite in her chest. Her entire childhood was spent in solitude, her only friends were her books and the stars. She would stay up all night talking to the sky, begging for them to answer. Now all of a sudden, she had a family—or at least, she had a home with a family in it that didn't completely detest her—and she had friends. Friends who didn't laugh at her behind her back or run the other way when they saw her coming.

She had friends who forgave. And for the first time in a long time, she felt like everything might be alright. Like maybe this one might stick.

CHAPTER 12

HAN SOLO AND BIRTHDAY CAKES

E mber sat on the edge of her bed, hand stretched out in front of her as she stared at the hairbrush on her dresser. The sun was barely lighting the horizon, but Ember had already been up for hours, pacing the floor of her room, trying to perfect the spell they had been learning in Galdr the previous week. No matter how hard she tried, she couldn't seem to get it right.

"*Vocar* hairbrush," she said firmly, for the millionth time, but it didn't budge. She let out a huff as she flopped back on her bed, whacking her head on the book she had been reading the night before. She sat up to rub the forming lump, and as she did, a familiar ball of blue light zipped under her door and settled directly in front of her.

"Breakfast, love!" Eira's voice chirped from the orb before it disappeared in a cloud of mist. Ember let out a heavy sigh as she ran her fingers through her fiery red hair. She could already feel the effects of the minimal sleep she had gotten start to wear on her as she dragged her feet toward the dresser. Lavender stared back at her, for only a moment, before she put the green contacts in her eyes. She quickly ran the brush through her hair and headed toward the steps at the end of the hall. She could hear laughter traveling toward her, brushing up against her skin and giving her goosebumps. She walked into the kitchen and was greeted with warm smiles. It still wasn't something she was used to—a family that didn't hide away at the sight of her, a family that might actually love her.

Or at the very least, like her.

Ember took her regular seat at the table, rubbing the sleep from her eyes. She sipped on the tea in her cup, praying that a little caffeine would hide how utterly exhausted she actually was. It wasn't until she set the cup down that she noticed the small package laying on her breakfast plate, wrapped in sage green paper, tied with gold ribbon. She turned the box a few times in her hand before looking at the rest of the table. Was she sitting in the wrong seat? As if on cue, Eira walked into the breakfast nook, floating plates of sausage and eggs in front of her.

"Happy birthday, love," she said with a smile as she gently kissed the girl on the top of the head.

Ember furrowed her brow. Was it already October 23rd? How could she have forgotten? She stared at the small gift in front of her, turning it in her hands as she took in how beautiful it was. It was wrapped with such care and love. Ember almost didn't want to open it. She sat it back on her plate so she could admire it just a little longer, taking in the careful placement of the ribbon and the neatly folded edges. The last birthday gift she had received, she was six years old, and she barely remembered it at all. But this gift, this birthday, would be etched in her mind for the rest of her life. She would make sure of it.

"You didn't have to get me anything, honest." She smiled at Eira. "I would've been happy with a nice breakfast and a relaxing day reading."

"Now, now, I'll have none of that," Eira said as she waved her hand. "We can't celebrate our Fen's birthday and ignore yours. You'll have a proper birthday. I just hope you don't mind sharing the day."

"We have the same birthday?" Ember asked quizzically. Fen's birthday wasn't something she had thought about, and she certainly didn't normally enjoy her own.

"I suppose you do," Eira smiled, a smile that was almost painful to look at. A smile that reminded her so much of her own mother.

"Talking about me?" Fen shouted from the mud room. "My ears are ringing."

Ember smiled as the messy haired boy made his way into the house, stomping the mud off his boots before kicking them off.

"That could be all the hits to the head you've taken," she laughed.

"Touché," he replied thoughtfully. "Happy birthday, Em!" He almost shouted as he took his seat at the table, piling his plate with toast, sausage, and tomatoes. "You gonna open it?"

Ember chuckled as she picked the box back up, running her fingers along the seams of the paper. She quickly unwrapped it, doing her best to keep the beautiful wrapping paper as intact as possible, and slipped the gift from its packaging. In her hand was the most beautiful leather journal she had ever seen with a very familiar rune etched in the center of the cover.

The rune on her necklace.

She swallowed the lump that was forming in her throat as she flipped through the blank pages. It was in pristine condition, not a page missing or a scratch anywhere to be seen; it was brand new, and just for her.

"This is too much," she whispered to the happy couple standing at the table, brushing her hand under her eye to keep the tears from falling.

"Nonsense," Eira said with a sniffle, tears forming at the corner of her own eyes as she smiled. "Every fifteen-year-old deserves a place to record her thoughts and adventures. I remember your father always carrying one with him in school, always writing in it. I think it's only fitting you have one as well."

"It's beautiful," Ember whispered. She ran her fingers along the rune etched in the leather. It was almost identical to the one that stayed tucked in her bag. It was like holding a small piece of him, and for just a moment, she could've sworn she could feel him at that table with her.

"Lucky," Fen mumbled, his mouth full of toast and bacon. "All I got was a new watch."

Otto swatted at the back of his head with a chuckle before taking his seat at the table.

"Did you invite Killian tonight?" Eira asked from the kitchen.

"Oh, yeah," Fen replied. "He's got something going on, so he won't be here."

"What about you, Ember?" Otto directed at her. "You can invite Rowan."

"What's tonight?" Ember asked as she scrunched her brow.

"Your and Fen's birthday dinner, love." Eira smiled as she took her seat at the table. "It's not a proper birthday without a party."

Ember felt her heart flutter with excitement. A party? For her? She hadn't had a party since she was little and never one that she could invite friends to. Would there be a birthday cake? Singing? Music? Her mind began to go a mile a minute, imagination running wild.

"I'll send her a Helio after breakfast." She grinned. She hurried to finish eating, inhaling the remaining strips of bacon and pieces of toast, making sure to put her dishes in the sink when she was finished. She thanked Eira and Otto with a wide grin on her face before running toward the steps and disappearing upstairs to send her friend the message.

172

Ember spent the rest of the morning curled up in the library with a book and her new journal, jotting down the things she had learned about the creatures and beings that inhabited the island, along with the things she had learned from Asherah and Kaan. She felt that since her father had dedicated his life to Zoomancy, there was no better way to honor his life than to dedicate part of her journal to it as well. She settled into the chair and felt her eyes get heavier, slipping in and out of sleep as they fluttered and her head bobbed forward. She was jolted awake moments—or was it hours?— later by Fen knocking on the threshold of the open door.

"Taking a pre-party nap?" he asked with a laugh.

"Just didn't get much sleep last night," Ember yawned, sitting up a little straighter in the chair. "So, no plans with Killian tonight?"

"Nah," he chuckled. "Got somethin' important goin' on with his family, and he couldn't get away."

Ember felt her stomach drop; strange meetings with your blood-magic-obsessed family was never a good thing. The guilt she felt about lying to Fen invaded her mind again. At least if she came clean, that would be one less person to keep things from. At least when he found out about Killian, he wouldn't hate her too.

"I'm gonna go for a ride on Arlo if you want to come," Fen said cheerily.

"Actually, could I talk to you about something?" Ember fidgeted in her seat as she twiddled her thumbs.

His face dropped slightly, noting the seriousness behind her voice. "Sure, what's up?" He took a seat in the chair beside her.

"Y-you were right," Ember stuttered. "About what I was doing with Rowan that day we met in town. We weren't study-ing, not really."

Fen nodded, like he was afraid breathing too hard would scare her away. "Yeah, that's sort of what I figured," he said, treading lightly. "Are you gonna tell me what you were really doing?"

She took a shaky breath and ran her tongue along the healing wound on the inside of her lip. She knew she couldn't tell him everything, not if they wanted to finish what they had started, but he deserved what she could give. "Do you remember that legend Professor Walsh talked about on our first day?" she asked quietly.

"I mean... sort of, I guess. Something about someone stealing someone else's magic... or something like that."

Ember rolled her eyes with a laugh. Of course he wasn't paying attention. She wasn't sure why she expected much else, honestly.

"Yeah, something like that." She laughed. "Anyway... Rowan and I found out about this book, my dad wrote about it in his journal. Long story short, we think maybe the person this legend is about is going to try and find this book to fulfill this twisted prophecy, or whatever."

Fen furrowed his brow deep in thought. Ember gave him a moment to see if that was good enough. Maybe she didn't need to go into any more detail? Maybe that was good enough for him?

Except that would be too easy.

"So," he said after a moment. "You and Rowan were... researching? Is that it? Doesn't seem like a real reason to lie."

"Not really," Ember breathed. "I mean, yes, we were researching, but... there were no books involved. My dad talked about Merrow in his journal, and we found out there is a Clann that has been on the island for a long time—"

"Merrow," he interrupted, "Like Maren?"

"Yes," she said with a slow nod. "Rowan and I.... We went to talk to them."

"Talk to them? I've never seen any others that don't work for a First Family. Where do they live?"

"Um," Ember hesitated, "on the west side of the island...

174

through the Dark Forest..." She braced for the explosion, completely expecting him to either scream or storm off. She stared at the floor while she twiddled her thumbs in her lap.

Was this a mistake?

"You and Rowan went through the Dark Forest... alone?" Fen asked calmly.

Ember nodded, suddenly feeling like cotton was lodged in her throat.

"So, is that where that cut came from? Did something hurt you?" he asked, glancing at her forehead where she knew that wound from her fall was still visible.

"Oh, no, that was just me being clumsy," she lied. "Tripped on a root and fell."

Fen nodded and narrowed his eyes, then gave a small shrug. "So, did you talk to them?" he asked, sounding much more invested than before, like he was listening to a great story.

"Um, yeah, we did. They just had a few... stipulations first."

Fen cocked an eyebrow, confusion washing over his freckled face. Ember explained what Asherah and Kaan had told them about their capes and how the young Merrow were kidnapped at young ages, trapped on land. His mouth fell open when she mentioned that Maren was actually the leader's daughter—a princess. His grip tightened around the arms of the chair, sitting on the edge of his seat and leaning forward, hanging on every word that fell out of her mouth. Instead of the anger she assumed she would see, he almost looked excited. Like he had been searching for an adventure and it was finally being given to him.

"So, Maren's cape is locked up somewhere," he repeated as he paced the room, "and the only ones who can unlock wherever it's locked is someone in the Vargr family? And the book is..."

"We don't actually know where the book is. The only thing

they said was it was with a family who had an affinity for the dark arts. Which sounds like it would be a short list until you really start looking."

"Alright," he said firmly. "So, that leaves us with the cape. It's somewhere in the Vargrs' house, right? Why don't we just ask Killian? He probably knows."

"No!" Ember squeaked, a little more firmly than she intended. "We can't tell him anything. It's for his safety. I know he's your best mate and all, but you have to keep this between us, Fen."

Fen nodded his head in understanding, but that wasn't enough for Ember.

"You have to swear, Fen. Swear to it."

"I swear," he said firmly. "I won't tell anyone."

All of a sudden, the library door was slung open, making the children almost leap out of their seats.

"Ember, do you know where—oh. Fen, there you are, love," Eira said upon entering. "I need the two of you to run to Florin's and pick up the cake for the party tonight. It should be ready in about an hour or so."

"You have your only son running errands on his birth-day?" Fen said, gripping his chest, feigning offense.

Eira rolled her eyes at the dramatics, waving her hand as if to shoo him away. "I don't see Ember complaining. I'd imagine she's just grateful to be having such loving parents that want to throw her a party," she scolded, both hands placed firmly against her hips.

She had no idea.

Ember laughed as she quickly tucked her book and journal into the bag at her feet before flinging it over her shoulder. Eira kissed each of them on the cheek as they walked out the library door and toward the steps. Ember was proud of herself. She was finally able to not physically recoil when someone showed any sort of affection toward her, though she still jumped slightly when the contact was made, as if she had placed a physical barrier around herself that shook violently anytime anyone tried to get near her.

"Can you get Rowan to meet us in town?" Fen asked in a hushed tone as they descended the stairs toward the terminal door.

"Probably, why?" Ember asked with a confused look.

"I'm assuming the two of you haven't figured anything out about getting the cape?" he said, more a statement than a question.

"Yeah…"

"Maybe we can come up with something." He shrugged, as if they were just talking about their Sigils and Runes home-work and not the possibility of breaking and entering. Ember felt a sliver of hope as they crossed the threshold into the terminal that was bustling with magic, like now that she had let Fen in on everything, they actually might stand a chance.

"You told him?" Rowan exclaimed in front of Florin's, loud enough for the entire street to hear.

Ember shushed her before pulling her friend to the side, away from prying eyes and ears. "Will you calm down," Ember snapped, as Rowan crossed her arms over her chest.

"I'm just saying," she replied crossly, "I thought we agreed we shouldn't risk it?"

"What do you think I'm going to do? Tell your mum?" Fen snapped, obviously offended at what she was insinuating. Rowan narrowed her eyes at the boy, not backing down from his gaze.

"I think he can help," Ember interjected, trying to diffuse the situation from escalating any further. "And Odin knows we could use all the help we can get at this point."

"Fine, since you're so brilliant," Rowan snapped, arms still crossed tightly over her chest. "What do we do next?"

"We obviously need to figure out a way into the Vargrs' house," he said, as if it was the only possible answer.

"But what do we do when we get there?" Rowan asked. "Even if we do figure out where the cape is kept, we can't get to it. None of us have Vargr blood."

Ember sat at a table outside of the cafe and began rummaging through her bag. "Maybe my dad wrote something in his journal about blood magic. It's a long shot, but maybe—" She stopped short as she looked in the bottom of her bag, and what caught her eye made her heart skip a beat. She gently grabbed the frayed piece of fabric, running her thumb along the edges and gripped it tightly. Ember lifted the cloth out of her bag, holding it up in front of her face for Rowan and Fen to see. There was a stain on the cloth, still fresh but forgotten in the bottom of her satchel.

Crimson.

"What's that?" Rowan asked, scrunching her nose.

"Blood," Fen whispered, a smile creeping across his freckled face.

"It's the handkerchief Maren used on Killian's lip at tryouts." Ember grinned. "She must've slipped it in my bag when I wasn't looking."

"How does that help us?" Rowan asked skeptically.

"I read about a spell this summer," Fen replied. "Maybe we can use it to unlock whatever the cape is hidden in. It's kind of tricky, but not impossible."

The girls stood wide eyed in front of him, mouths hanging slightly ajar as they stared at the boy.

"You can read?" Rowan asked quietly, sending Ember into a fit of giggle.

Fen narrowed his eyes at the brunette before cutting his eyes toward his foster sister, who closed her mouth tightly, trying to control the laughter that was making her chest shake. "Yes, I can read," he spat. "I'm not an invalid."

"Could've fooled me." Rowan shrugged as she turned

back to Ember and grabbed the small piece of cloth. "How will old blood help us? Doesn't it need to be fresh?"

Fen snatched the handkerchief out of her hand, eliciting a glare from the girl. "It looks like it's under a stasis charm. Technically speaking, it is fresh."

"A what?" Ember asked, as she furrowed her brow.

"A stasis charm," Fen repeated. "It's like…when Han Solo was frozen in carbonite. It keeps whatever is under the spell frozen and in the state that it was when the spell was cast. Since the blood was fresh when Maren cast the spell, it's still fresh now."

Rowan narrowed her eyes in his direction. "Did you just… reference *Star Wars?*"

"*Return of the Jedi* was a cinematic masterpiece," Fen defended as he crossed his arms.

"But out of any example you could come up with, you picked *Star Wars?*" Rowan's grin widened as she laughed, and Fen narrowed his eyes.

"I'm going to check on the cake." Ember laughed as she walked away from her bickering friends, making her way into the bakery in front of her.

The Enchanted Florin was beautiful on the inside. Pink tiles of different shades lined the floor, leading to the most pristine white walls and counters. Tree branches stretched across the ceiling, speckled with the most beautiful cherry blossoms, even though the cold was beginning to settle outside. Ember took a deep breath, breathing in the smell of sweet and savory mixing together in the air, as she heard the door open and close behind her.

"Can't be alone with Fen for even five minutes?" She laughed as she turned around, only to be face to face with a small white-haired girl with a faraway look on her face. "Oh, hi, Odette," she said, a bit of surprise in her voice.

"Hello, Ember," she said sweetly. "Happy birthday."

Ember wrinkled her brow in confusion, "Oh, um, thank

179

you." She grabbed the cake on the counter from the plump woman behind it and smiled at the girl as she made her way toward the door. She was halfway to grabbing the handle when she heard Odette speak to her again.

"For you," the small girl said, as she handed Ember a tiny gift bag that jingled as she moved.

"What's this?" Ember asked skeptically as she opened the paper bag.

"They're bells," she replied sweetly. "Next time you go in the forest, make sure to wear them around your wrists or ankles. I prefer them on my shoes," she said matter-of-factly as she pointed to the brown flats on her feet. "Not as bothersome that way."

Ember's jaw hung slack. "Excuse me?" she said quietly. "Why would I need silver bells in the forest?"

"They keep the Fae away, of course," she replied as she stared right past Ember's head. "Less chance of being chased inward by a beast as well." Her eyes sparkled as she tilted her head, like she could hear all of the thoughts racing through Ember's mind.

"Are you talking about the wolf?" Ember asked, as her heart beat heavily against her ribs.

Odette tilted her head. "I'm afraid I don't know what you're referring to." She smiled, but Ember knew she was lying. She didn't know what Odette knew, but it was much more than she was letting on.

"Oh, um, right... thank you, Odette," Ember stuttered as she swung the door and stepped into the bustling street. She chewed on the inside of her cheek as she balanced the cake in her arms. She couldn't figure Odette out, and the riddles she spoke in drove her crazy, but there was something about her that was soothing, something different in her that Ember couldn't quite place.

"Was that Quinn?" Rowan asked, giggling as she ran toward Ember. "What did she want?"

"Nothing," Ember replied, shaking her head. "Just told me happy birthday."

The trio made their way down the busy street to the terminal where they said their goodbyes. Ember held the package tightly in her arms as she and Fen stood in line, waiting for their terminal door to go home.

"Do you think it'll work?" he asked passively, both of his hands stuffed in his jean pockets.

"Do I think what will work?" Ember questioned.

"The blood magic spell."

Ember took a deep breath as she chewed on the inside of her cheek. "It has to work," she whispered. "It's our only chance."

CHAPTER 13

A DASH OF DRAIC'S BLOOD

E mber stepped into the greenhouse, sunlight bouncing off the glass of the high dome. She breathed in the smell of all the plants that wafted through the air and closed her eyes as the faint sounds of birds singing filled her ears. Aside from Galdr, Herbal Magic was her favorite class. Something about turning simple plants into potions and tonics made her feel like she was capable of anything. Growing, pruning, measuring, and brewing—it was like science. Her father always loved science.

Not to mention, she was pretty bloody good at it.

"Gather 'round, gather 'round!" the voice of Professor Flora boomed from the center of the room.

Ember made her way down the steps to the ground floor and found her place around one of the long tables beside Odette, Rowan, and Fen. Professor Flora was a petite woman, barely over five foot tall. Her short, onyx hair bounced right above her shoulders, and her tan skin shined in the sun coming through the windowpanes. Her almond-shaped honey eyes had a permanent sparkle to them, and they crinkled at the corners as she spoke. She wore gloves and an apron around her waist, a bright yellow canary perched on her shoulder. The greenhouse was not only used to grow various plants, but also doubled as an aviary.

"The yarrow we planted at the beginning of term has bloomed," the professor continued, "and the root is in perfect condition." Students gathered around their pots, looking at the various blooms on the plant, making notes in their field journals. "Today, we are unpotting our yarrow plant and using its root to create a draught. Can anyone tell me what drought you get when you combine mugwort, yarrow root, and a dash of draic's blood?"

Hands shot up in the air, children eagerly bouncing on the balls of their feet. Professor Flora's eyes fell on Ember.

"Miss Lothbrok?" she said, motioning toward the girl.

"Draught of Fortitude," she replied with a smile.

"Yes, yes, very good, and what is this specific draught for?" the professor asked the class.

"It acts as both a blood replenisher and healing agent," Odette sang from the back. "It is to be used in circumstances in which healing with a charm to stop blood flow is not possible or too much blood has already been lost."

"Very good, Miss Quinn." Professor Flora smiled. "And when might a healing charm not work?"

"In cases of cursed wounds," Rowan stated matter-of-factly.

"Perfect, Miss O'Rourke," the professor sang. "Now, everyone should have their yarrow root at their table, and the rest of your ingredients can be found in their places around the green house. I would recommend you send one person at your table to gather supplies, and the others should work on preparing the ingredients. You may begin."

Odette left to find the other various ingredients, leaving the trio to begin preparing the draught to brew. Ember smiled contentedly as she cut the yarrow root, carefully placing it on the gold scale beside her hand to get the measurements exact.

Her hands worked rapidly, making small slices as she bit her lip and steadied her fingers.

"Will you grind the mugwort root?" she said over her shoulder. When she got no response, she checked beside her to find Rowan deep in thought, elbow leaning on the table, chin resting in her palm.

"Earth to Ro," Ember said as she waved her hand in the girl's face.

Rowan nearly knocked the small vials off the table as she jumped. "What?" she asked in a daze.

"Mugwort." Ember pointed at the bowl in the center of the table. "Grind it up. Odette will be back with the draic's blood in a bit."

"What's he doing?" Rowan asked crossly as she nodded toward Fen, who was very busy trying to balance his field guide on his forehead.

"He is currently not messing up my grade," Ember replied as she tossed the yarrow root into the smoking cauldron. "And I'd prefer to keep it that way."

"Have you figured that blood magic spell out yet?" Rowan asked as she tossed a piece of the yarrow root in Fen's direction, smacking him in the face and knocking his book onto the table. "Or have you been too busy playing Rukr in the garden?"

"We practice in the orchards, actually," he said with a scowl. "And as a matter of fact, I think I've just about got it figured out."

"Ahem," Ember cleared her throat and shot a look in his direction.

"Right, *we've* about got it figured out," he corrected himself sheepishly.

"When are we supposed to look for the cape, though?" Ember asked as she stirred her cauldron, smoke billowing from top. "I can imagine skipping school is going to raise alarms for everyone, and a weekend is too risky."

"Samhain is coming up," Fen replied, chewing on the tip of his pen. "We could go during the festival."

"That's brilliant, even for you," Rowan whispered. "The whole town will be at the festival, so we're almost guaranteed not to run into anyone."

"The what?" Ember asked as she wrinkled her brow.

"I think you grew up calling it Huh-low-ween," Fen replied, drawing out the syllables of the name.

"You mean Halloween?"

"Right, right, whatever," Fen dismissed. "The Samhain Festival is October 31st. There's a huge bonfire and music and food, and the whole town comes out to celebrate. I think it used to mark the end of the harvest and the coming dark months, but now it's really just an excuse for the whole town to come together and party all night."

"So what, we just skip the festival?" Ember asked. "Won't that seem fairly suspicious too?"

"We won't skip it," Fen replied. "We'll go for a little while, and then when Mum and Dad are distracted and properly smashed, we'll sneak off, grab the cape, and be back before anyone knows we're missing." Fen smiled smugly, very impressed with his own plan.

"That's a great plan and all," Ember agreed, "but how do we get in to actually find the thing?"

"Dear sister, you greatly underestimate me." Fen grinned, the sun glinting off his pearly white teeth.

Ember rolled her eyes, not bothering to correct him this time. The way he referred to her as his sister just seemed to roll off his tongue, like it was second-nature, not something he had to chew on or think about. It made her overjoyed and uneasy all at the same time, like if she allowed herself to get comfortable, if she allowed herself to think of them as family, everything would come crumbling down on top of her. So, her walls stayed high, reinforced with steel beams and self-preservation.

People couldn't hurt you if you never let them in.

She stiffened, almost knocking the smoking cauldron over completely. Rowan shot her a confused look before turning back to their work.

Fen mumbled, his face suddenly dropping. "I still don't love the idea of sneaking into Killian's house behind his back. Can't we just tell him? He could help."

Ember and Rowan both glanced at each other briefly, eyes widening before turning toward the boy.

"Fen, you swore," Ember whispered seriously. "Besides, if he got caught with us, who knows what his family would do. We're keeping him safe." She softly tapped her fingers on the edge of the table, praying that she sounded more convincing than she felt.

"I guess so." He shrugged.

Ember felt the guilt rise up in her throat as she looked at him, and it tasted like bile. She hated lying, but over the years she had learned it was necessary.

No, I didn't knock the vase over. I'm on the other side of the room.

No, I didn't make the light flicker.

I don't know what happened to the garden. I've been upstairs.

Every lie set her on edge, leaving her unable to speak once it left her lips, but sometimes there was no other way.

"Chin up, Fen," Rowan said with a smile. "We're not going to kill his brother, just a little breaking and entering."

The girls laughed as Odette walked up behind them, a small vial of draic's blood in her hand.

Ember watched as the small girl put her hand out in front of her and yelped as the girl edged nearer to the bubbling cauldron.

"Odette, would you like one of us to do it?" she asked calmly. "It's really hot, and you might burn yourself."

"I can find the cauldron just fine, but thank you, Ember," Odette said with a smile, focusing her energy back to her outstretched hand.

"Um, right," Fen replied. "But you're——"

"Blind?" She tilted her head toward his voice. "Yes, I'm well aware, thank you, Fenrir. I can still find my way around just fine." After pulling her hand back to her body, she swiftly uncorked the vial and poured it directly into the cauldron without spilling a drop.

"But how..." Fen stuttered.

"Vision is highly overrated." Odette almost smirked. "I send out soft pulses of magic to help myself see. It bounces off solid objects and back to me, sort of like——"

"Echo location." Ember smiled.

"That's right," Odette replied. "Like I said, vision is overrated." She shrugged with a smile and turned back toward the table.

It was like seeing the girl in a new light. She wasn't odd, just different. Different didn't necessarily mean bad.

After letting their cauldron simmer for the remainder of the class, each taking turns stirring and giving the others' arms a break, Odette filled an empty vial with the draught and walked it up to the professor. The crimson liquid swirled in the glass as the professor twirled it in her hands, examining the specks of gold and silver the sparkled against the sun.

"Perfect!" Professor Flora exclaimed from the front of the room. "The consistency we're looking for is something close to nectar. Too thin and the ground mugwort won't adhere to the draic's blood, but too thick and it will turn into a gel, which makes the draught ineffective." She held the vial up to the light and tilted it back and forth, making it shimmer as she smiled. "We have some very talented first years in this class."

Fen grinned as he preened under the praise, and Ember's cheeks turned bright red. If there was one thing she knew she was good at, it was succeeding in school. Odette skipped lightly back to their table, helping the trio fill the rest of the vials. Ember quickly stuck hers in her bag for safekeeping before flinging it back over her shoulder and leisurely making her way out of the room.

"So, we agree then?" Rowan whispered. "We'll meet at the festival and go to the Vargrs' from there?"

Fen and Ember nodded in tandem.

"Good," Rowan continued. "Bring the handkerchief, and we'll meet at the fountain in town at midnight."

EMBER LEANED up against the inside of an alcove in the corridor, digging through her bag. She was so focused on the bottom of her bag that she barely noticed the voices drifting into her tiny hiding space. Her ears perked up, and her curiosity got the better of her as she inched closer.

"You have to tell him," the female voice said quietly, barely above a whisper.

"He's going to find out sooner or later," the male voice replied. "This isn't my responsibility."

"He's blood," she spat at him. "It's all of our responsibilities."

Ember held her breath as she leaned against the wall separating her from the voices behind it, pressing her ear to the cold stone to try and hear the words that were floating in her direction. Before she could hear the rest of what was being said, the conversation was cut short, and a shadow entered the alcove alongside hers. Her heart beat in her throat as her eyes shot forward, and she straightened her posture, finding herself staring into the most striking blue eyes.

"I thought I told you to mind your own business, worm," Veda spat at her, steel blue eyes burning holes into her own. "If you're not careful, you might just find yourself on the wrong end of a misfired hex."

Ember felt her throat go dry as she tried to form some sort of witty response in her head, but the only thing she could get out was a quiet, "Sorry," before she hurried in the other direction toward her next class.

"You really should be more careful around them," a voice sounded from behind her. Ember nearly jumped out of skin at the sound and felt her heart in her throat as she turned to look at Rowan. "They might look harmless, but their family has always been a bit off."

"They look anything but harmless," Ember mumbled, as they walked into History of the Gods, chewing on the words she had heard in her hidden corner. She thought back for a moment to when she saw Killian hidden with twins, angry whispers being thrown between them. And then, all of a sudden, she realized something.

"Where's Killian?" she asked Fen, as they took their seats.

He shrugged nonchalantly. "Not feeling well, I think. I'm not sure. He didn't answer my Helio at lunch."

Ember and Rowan glanced at each other, both furrowing their brows. That wasn't like Killian at all.

"Please open your books to page two hundred and fifteen," a voice rang from the front of the room. Professor Orion paced up and down the rows of tables, his hands placed firmly behind his back.

Ember opened her book and placed her hand on the yellowed pages. Light danced off them almost immediately, and a beautiful woman came to life in front of her. Her long blonde hair hung over her shoulders in waves mixed with tangled braids. A beautiful necklace hung around her neck, like something Ember had seen in a dream.

"Freyja," the professor began, "Daughter of Njord and Herta, the god and goddess of earth and sea. One of the founders of the First Families. Who can tell me what she was the goddess of?"

"She was the goddess of love and magic," Rowan said with her hand raised.

"Correct," Professor Orion replied. "And she was also the goddess of—"

"War," Veda's voice echoed from the back of the room, as she tossed her raven hair over her shoulder.

"Correct." The professor nodded. "Love, magic, and war. Freyja and her family were part of the Vanir, said to have lived in Scandinavia, settling with the Vikings of the Aesir and passing their magic along to their children. Many of them were shapeshifters; their energy was very powerful, but Freyja's seemed to be the most powerful of the Vanir. Since she ruled over magic and war, she had the ability to bestow her gifts, as well as take them from others."

"Didn't she have a brother?" Rowan asked with her hand in the air.

"Ah, yes," Professor Orion continued, "a twin brother, Freyr. He was widely known as the god of peace, but he was also an angry god."

"Angry, sir?

"He was a jealous god," the professor continued. "Very jealous of his sister and her magic—and what she chose to do with it. He was also not fond of other magical beings that he viewed as lesser than him, as opposed to his sister's views."

"What does that mean?"

"It means that instead of taking their magic and getting rid of them," Oryn sneered from beside his sister, "she wanted to coexist." The look on his face was of contempt for the goddess, which was laughable, honestly. He was tall, but rather scrawny. A goddess like Freyja could easily snap him like a twig.

Ember furrowed her brow. Killian's family wasn't the only ones who thought the way they did, like any other magical beings were a threat to their very existence. Though, that probably shouldn't come as a shock, especially after the way they talked in Galdr the first day. The Ellingboe twins were as dark as they came, from what she knew about dark Vala anyway. They took every chance they could get to torment and bully, even as fifteen-year-olds. Everyone knew their name, and with that, everyone knew not to get in their way.

Professor Orion cleared his throat. "Freyr did not believe that any beings other than the Vala were worthy of magic. He wanted his twin to use her abilities to take their magic, combining it with their own. But she wouldn't. Her beliefs wouldn't waver. She believed magic was sacred, but it was also something to be shared, instead of hoarded."

The light on the pages of the textbooks in the room lit up, flipping through different scenes. Freyja with her brother, drawings that depicted the ancestors of the First Families with the Vanir, and for a brief moment, it landed on a picture of a rune. Ember felt her breath catch in her throat as she tried to touch the image that floated in front of her, while simultaneously reaching for the pendant that dangled around her neck.

The rune on her pendant.

She traced her finger through the air, running her fingers down the lines and shapes that lit up her skin. It was an arrow pointing straight up with a small line pointing diagonally up at the bottom. In the middle there was an upside-down V pointed up and to the left with a small line coming off the right corner. On the bottom of the floating picture, it read *Strength and Protection.*

"Freyja's rune," Professor Orion began, "is a bind rune that is a combination of *Uruz, Sowilo, and Tiwaz.*" His eyes scanned the classroom. "Can anyone tell me what these runes are for?"

Fen's hand shot up in the air, and the professor nodded in his direction. "*Uruz* is for physical, emotional, and spiritual strength," he replied. "*Sowilo* is for vitality, and *Tiwaz* is for…" He looked at the ceiling as he chewed on his lip, eyes scrunched as he tapped his finger on the desk. "Oh!" He smiled as he looked forward. "*Tiwaz* is for the strength of a spiritual warrior."

"Correct." Professor Orion nodded stoically, continuing his lecture as he paced up and down the aisles between the desks. Ember clutched the metal hanging by her collarbone, tracing those same lines that were carved into the cold disk. As quickly as it was there, it disappeared again, snapping Ember out of her trance.

"Where do you think he actually is?" Rowan asked as she nudged her elbow.

"What?" Ember asked, slowly pulling herself back to reality as she tucked her necklace inside her shirt.

"Killian," Rowan continued. "I highly doubt he's sick."

Ember shrugged. "Maybe just needed a mental health day?"

"Do you think Fen said something?"

"What? No. Absolutely not. He swore," Ember defended, but she wasn't really sure. She was only his foster sister, some stranger who he'd only known for two months. He's known Killian for years. Where did his loyalty actually lie? She shifted in her seat, but there was no going back, trust or not. She made a promise to Asherah, and she was bound and determined to see it through.

CHAPTER 14

ONE CAKE GIVEN, ONE
SOUL SAVED

Ember felt like the afternoon of Samhain dragged on forever. She practiced the blood magic spell in the quiet of the library until she felt like her brain was going to explode, scanning the page of the book Fen had given her and twirling her fingers in the air until they were numb. After a few hours and one splitting headache, she closed her journal and tucked it into her bag. If she didn't know how to do it by now, chances were she would never figure it out. It was complicated and dark—she could feel the magic seeping into her bones and turning her blood cold. It wasn't the warm electricity she felt in the air at Heksheim or in Sigurvik. It was heavy. The weight of it clung to her heart and weighed it down like tar, turning her thoughts dark and mood sour. She would be happy when she never had to look at another dark spell again.

"How goes it?" Fen said as he popped his head in the door. "Got everything ready?"

"Yeah, I think so," Ember replied, rubbing her eyes with the palm of her hands. "Ready as I'll ever be, I guess."

"Meet you downstairs?" he said as he pointed his thumb toward the other end of the hall.

"Yeah," she replied, "I'll see you down there."

Ember leaned her head against the bookcase she was sitting under as she listened to Fen run down the steps. Her knees and back ached from sitting in one place so long, joints and muscles popping and pulling as she eased herself up off the floor. She went through their plan over and over again in her head, doing her best to make sure that everything had been covered. The truth was, she didn't feel ready at all. Her mind felt hazy as she shook her head. She wanted to hide away in her bedroom and forget about the book and the legend and the cape and just be normal for once. But if life had taught her anything so far, it was that normal wasn't in the cards for her, and that was just something she was going to have to come to terms with.

Ember dragged her feet toward her bedroom and began rummaging through her closet for something acceptable to wear. What did one wear to both a Samhain Festival and to break into their foster brother's best friend's house?

The possibilities were truly endless.

She settled on jeans, a nicer long sleeve shirt, and a thin jacket to keep the cold at bay. She threw her long red hair into a quick braid before zipping her jacket up and grabbing her father's journal off the bedside table, quickly stuffing it into her bag beside her own.

Eira stood at the bottom of the steps, zipping up Maeve's jacket and adjusting the hat on her head. The little girl's face lit up as Ember made her way to the bottom of the stairs. "Ember, Ember!" she squealed, as she wriggled out of her mother's grasp, and Eira headed back into the kitchen. "Look at my pumpkin! I grew it all by myself!" She held up a beautiful orange pumpkin, one side much larger than the other with a green stem that twisted more than a pig's tail. The gourd was almost as lopsided as the crooked grin on the little girl cradling it in her arms.

"Wow, Maevie," Ember said with a smile. "That's beautiful. You did such a great job."

"Thank you," Maeve replied sheepishly. "It's for the altar."

"Altar?" Ember mumbled in Fen's direction. Before he could answer, Eira came back into the room with a basket filled with small pumpkins, apples, and squash hanging from the crook of her arm. She ushered the children toward the door behind the stairs while she desperately tried to tame Fen's messy hair.

"Muuuuum," he whined as he swatted her hand away, pushing his glasses up on the bridge of his nose. He ran his fingers through his hair, messing it back up in the process as his mother shot him a disgruntled look.

"I would prefer all of my family to look presentable tonight, not just the girls," she said, as her eyes narrowed on the hair sticking up from the back of his head. "The whole town will be there. You can look put together for one night."

"Go easy on the boy, love," Otto said as he wrapped his arm around his wife's shoulder and gently kissed her on the top of the head. "He'll figure it out one day."

"You could put in a little effort, you know." Ember smirked. "Even if it was just to appease your mum." She slipped quickly into the kitchen to grab an apple from the bowl on the table and dropped it into her bag for later before walking back into the foyer to stand by Fen.

Fen scoffed in her direction, like her statement was the ultimate offense. "Says the girl wearing bags under her eyes like they're the latest accessory. I look dashing as ever, thank you very much."

Ember was certain her eyes couldn't roll any further if she tried.

The tree carved into the door above the closet started glowing, and Otto ushered his family over the threshold and into the terminal on the other side. They made their way through the busy building, saying their hellos to friends that were making their way to the festival, and stepped into the bustling street. The town square was swimming with magic. It ricocheted off the cobblestone and weaved in and out of the celebrating townspeople, vibrating in the air against the words being sung by the men and women dancing by the fire.

"Ember, love," Eira said as they stepped into the square. "Take this basket to the altar for me. I need to go speak with Bjorn. Fen, Maeve, go show her the way, please."

Ember followed Fen through the maze of bodies dancing on the street, a tiny Maeve clutching her arm as the amber of the fire bounced off her porcelain skin. It wasn't fully dark yet, the sky still bathed in pumpkin, lavender, and apricot, washing the bodies around her in a brilliant golden glow. The colors swirled and swayed along with the music as the setting sun cast shadows on the rainbow of buildings around her. Maeve laid her pumpkin on the large altar amongst the piles of harvest food and candles, smiling happily as she wiped her hands clean and admired her hard work. Ember sat the basket down that had been hanging from the crook of her arm, as a soft voice echoed from behind the children.

"Blessed Samhain, Miss Lothbrok, Mr. Kitt," Professor Walsh said sweetly behind them. Her smile seemed out of place, like being out of a classroom filled with talkative teenagers somehow gave her the ability to relax her shoulders and the muscles in her jaw.

"May the road rise up to meet you, Professor." Fen nodded to the woman.

Ember furrowed her brow at her foster brother.

"Samhain blessing." He shrugged nonchalantly.

"Are you enjoying your first Samhain Festival, Miss Loth-brok?" the professor asked.

"Oh, yes, ma'am. It's lovely." Ember smiled. "But… what exactly is the altar for?"

"Samhain marks the end of harvest," she stated, "and the

beginning of winter. The veil between our world and Valhalla is thinnest this evening, and the altar is a way for us to honor our dead."

Ember felt a lump forming in her throat as she nodded at the woman. She dug through her bag, finding a small apple she had saved as a snack for later. Apples were her father's favorite. She vividly remembered him lounging in his favorite chair at night, feet kicked up on the coffee table as the fire painted pictures on his freckled face, a bright green apple hanging out of his mouth. Ember laid the apple on the altar among the piles of fruits and vegetables, quickly wiping the moisture away that was building underneath her eyes.

"Your parents would be very proud of you, Miss Lothbrok," Professor Walsh whispered as she gently patted the girl's shoulder.

Ember smiled up at the woman and gave her a small nod before she walked away, leaving the children standing in the light of the fading sun.

"I'm gonna go find Killian," Fen said quietly. "Meet you at the fountain at midnight?"

Ember gave him a quiet nod as she turned to find Maeve, who was staring at the table piled high with treats. Ember's mouth began to water. "Maevie," she said, getting the young girl's attention, "wanna grab something to eat?"

Maeve nodded with vigor before grabbing Ember's hand and pulling her toward the table. The girls each got a bottle of moon cider and one soul cake.

"One cake given, one soul saved," Maeve sang, as she bit into the crumpet-like biscuit.

Ember took a bite of her own, savoring the tastes of dried fruit and spices mingling together on her tongue. It tasted heavenly, sending long forgotten memories rushing back to her with every bite. Ember laughed under her breath as two small girls ran up to them yelling Maeve's name, interrupting her reminiscing. The small girl looked up at Ember, as if she was asking permission to run off and play. Ember gave her a small nod, and the giggling girls ran off into the dark.

She walked around the square, watching people dance and laugh, getting belligerently drunk with friends and family as she drank her cider and breathed in the magic bleeding from the air and into her lungs. She slowly made her way toward the fountain and smiled as she closed her eyes. For just a few minutes, she was going to pretend she was a normal fifteen-year-old without a long night of breaking and entering ahead of her.

HOURS TICKED BY, and Ember spent most of them anxiously staring at the clock at the center of town hall. The hands seemed to move slower than usual, each minute crawling into the next. Ember watched as people drank and danced, their shadows mixing with the light coming off the fire and swimming together on the pavement. The clock ticked closer to midnight, and Ember started making her way toward the fountain. Luckily, most of the town was around the giant bonfire, leaving a clear path between Ember and the fountain. Unfortunately for her, though, that didn't stop the anxiety that was slowly building in her chest.

"You ready?" a voice said quietly behind her, the volume muted by the sound of rushing water.

"As I'll ever be," Ember replied as she turned to Rowan. The girls sat on the edge of the fountain in silence as they waited for Fen. After several agonizing minutes of silently running through their plan in her head, Ember heard the familiar footfall of her foster brother come up behind them.

"What… are you wearing?" Rowan asked through a fit of laughter.

Ember turned to look at Fen, who had appeared out of

the shadows in black pants, a black long-sleeve shirt, and a black cap pulled over his head.

"What?" he asked, genuinely confused. "I'm just trying to be discreet,"

"I think you missed discretion by a few miles." Ember laughed. "Besides, at this point, I think we could announce our plan to the whole festival and no one would remember in the morning."

The trio made their way through the crowd to the other side of town, doing their best to stay far away from any family or friends that might ask questions.

"Should we take the terminal?" Ember asked as she stopped briefly in front of the building.

"Not unless one of you happens to have a Vargr rune handy," Rowan said sarcastically. "The spell only works to let someone with a familial rune associated with the house through the door."

"How does it work for me, then?" Ember asked as she furrowed her brow. She didn't have the Kitts' rune on her necklace, but she could travel through Yggdrasil Terminal as often as she wanted.

"It has something to do with Mum and Dad being your legal guardians." Fen shrugged. "Some sort of loophole."

Ember nodded as she chewed on her lip.

"There's an Echopoint down the road," Fen said, smiling softly at her. "We'll take that to the manor."

Ember nodded before scrunching her face at the boy. "Manor?" she said quietly, more a statement than a question.

Of course he lived in a manor.

They made their way down the dark road toward the Echopoint. The noise from the festival had all but faded into silence, and Ember struggled to catch her breath as she suddenly felt suffocated by the darkness. They made their way to the tall ash tree, and each grabbed onto a branch as Fen whispered, "*Vargr Manor.*" Ember felt the familiar tug as she spun, her stomach spinning as well, and landed on a cobble-stone road outside of a tall, wrought iron gate. The dead leaves of autumn crunched under her feet as she followed Fen toward the towering fence. She wrapped her hands around the metal, feeling the cold permeate through her fingertips and into her bones. A shiver ran down her spine as they stepped through the gate and up the path toward the dark building.

"How are we supposed to get in?" Ember whispered, as Fen jiggled the door handle.

"*Desellar*," Rowan whispered, her hand stretched toward the door. Ember watched as the magic lit up the lock and immediately vanished. Nothing.

"They probably have wards set," Fen said as he chewed his lip. "Let me try something." The boy squatted down on one knee, so his eye was directly in line with the lock on the brass handle. He mumbled under his breath as his fingers twisted in front of the lock. In a few seconds, Ember heard a soft click, and Fen stood up and turned the doorknob, easing it open. He smirked back at the girls as he nudged the door open the rest of the way and pushed his glasses up on his nose, allowing them to walk in first. "Piece of cake." He shrugged with a grin and flipped his hair out of his eyes.

"So, now you're a ward breaker?" Rowan scoffed. "Have a bit too much time on your hands, don't you?"

"Where did you learn that?" Ember laughed.

"You're not the only one who reads, Em," he said with a smirk still stretching across his face. They stepped into the empty foyer, the white marble bathed in the moonlight coming through the tall windows. Ember looked around at all of the intricate details; it reminded her of a palace fit for royals. Funny, though, Killian didn't act like much of a prince. She ran her fingers along the swirls on the oak banister, feeling the grain of the wood beneath her fingertips.

"Okay, stick to the plan," Rowan said, as they gathered in the middle of the open foyer, "I'll take the east wing, Fen will take the second floor, and Ember, you stick in the west wing. Send a Helio if you find anything. And stay quiet. Just because they aren't home, doesn't mean no one is listening."

Ember and Fen nodded silently, and the group went their separate ways, wandering into the dark and decrepit maze that was the Vargr Manor. Ember's footsteps echoed off the ivory tile as she made her way down the hall, looking in all of the rooms and closets on her way. The darkness hung in the air around her, stealing all of the warmth and leaving her shivering. She zipped her jacket further and rubbed her hands together, begging the friction to warm her fingers. She held her open hand in front of her and quietly whispered, *"Lux,"* under her breath. A small ball of white light appeared and hovered directly above her palm. It floated in front of her as she crept down the hallway, lighting the path and bringing a little bit of warmth to the dismal home.

She found herself wandering into a large open study. The wood panel floor creaked under her feet as she creeped through the shadows, inching her way to the bookshelves on the far right of the room. Her footsteps softened as she walked over a black and red rug, and a chill ran up her spine as she watched the crimson bleed into the darkness on the tapestry. She ran her fingers over the intricate etchings carved into the mahogany, breathing in the smell of the ancient tomes lining the shelves, and then she felt her finger run over a notch in the wood that didn't quite match.

"Huh," she breathed, as she continued to trace the coil-like shape, pushing a little harder. All of a sudden, there was a soft click, and the shelf beside her swung outward, revealing the entrance to a dark room beyond the threshold. "Honestly." She laughed as she rolled her eyes and slid into the dark room. The walls were lined with pictures of ancient Vikings covered in armor, dripping with blood. Their piercing eyes followed her as she explored, watching her every move like predators on the prowl. Ember shuddered and turned her head, running her eyes over the ancient books lining the shelf that clung to the stone wall of the room. She got down on her hands and knees, knocking on stones and pushing her ear to them to listen for anything hollow. Crates cluttered the floor, and her knee bumped a small box with etchings on the top as she moved near the corner. She huffed as she shoved it out of her way and stood back up, dusting off the knees of her pants. She dug the heel of her palm into her eyes and grimaced as she sighed.

As she turned her head, one of the pictures caught her eye, and she grimaced as it stared back at her. It was a picture she recognized from her textbook—Freyr.

Ember ran her fingers along the edges of the frame as her skin crawled, feeling for a way to move it, but it wouldn't budge. It was like it was cemented to the wall. Part of her thought to keep looking, but something kept her there, staring into the eyes of the lost god. She knew the cape was behind it; She didn't know how, but she *knew*. It was almost like she could hear it screaming at her from behind the pristine prison, something that vibrated deep in her bones. She dug through her bag and found the handkerchief under her journal. She gently grabbed it and pulled it out, running her fingers along the crimson stains that had sunk deep into the fabric. She laid it open in her palm and began the spell she had practiced from the shadows of her bedroom.

As she chanted, red ropes of magic rose from the center of the blood stain and wrapped around her fingers, down to her wrist. She felt it tighten against her skin like a glove, completely enveloping her arm down to the tips of her fingers. She took a deep breath as she reached her hand toward the picture frame, laying it gently on the gold designs that ran up the side. After a few moments of mumbling the ritual she now knew by heart, she heard an almost silent click, and she wrapped her fingers around the edge and tugged it open. The only thing lying on the inside was a small red cape. Her heart beat wildly in her chest, fingers trembling as she slipped the handkerchief back in her bag and grabbed the red fabric from its hiding place. The cape looked like it was made of satin and rose petals woven together with starlight. It twinkled in the light of the floating orb in front of her, giving it an almost otherworldly essence.

Ember snapped herself out of her trance and quietly whispered, "*Avisodor,*" summoning the small ball of blue light she had become so familiar with.

"Come to the study," she whispered before the ball went whizzing past her in search of Fen and Rowan. After a few minutes, Ember heard the other two come running in, the thump of their feet echoing off the walls around her.

"Ember," Fen whispered hoarsely from the other room before popping his head inside the tiny chamber she was standing in.

"What is this place?" Rowan asked, spinning around to get a good look.

"Some sort of secret room," Ember replied with a shrug of her shoulders. "I found the cape behind this picture."

"Freyr," Rowan whispered as she rolled her eyes. "Why am I not surprised?"

"What are you talking about?" Ember replied as she quickly stuffed the cape into her open satchel.

"Freyr hated all magical beings that weren't Vala," she replied, pointing at the portrait that had swung back into its place. "What better place to hide a Merrow cape than behind the god who hated them the most."

Ember felt a chill run up her spine as she spun the gold ring on her finger. "Let's get out of here," she whispered.

They made their way out of the small room, into the dark study. Ember carefully closed the bookshelf, making sure everything was in its place before she turned to follow the other two out the door. Before she could take another step, she heard the gentle thump of footsteps above her head. She froze in place, listening as the disembodied steps made their way toward the stairs.

The stairs that were right by their exit.

Ember's heart began to thump in her chest so hard that she thought it might break free and flutter away without her.

"Is there another way out?" Rowan asked, almost aggressively as she stared at Fen.

"Um, yeah… yeah, I think so. I think there's a door in the kitchen."

The trio ran as silently as possible toward the kitchen, weaving in and out of the maze of hallways twisting through the manor. Ember tripped on her feet, tumbling to the floor and catching her jacket on a small nail sticking out of the banister beside her as the other two ran past a set of steps. She pulled on the sleeve of her jacket as quietly as possible, begging the fabric to rip free of the silver nail. All of a sudden, she froze, hearing the footsteps coming rapidly down above her, growing louder the closer they got to the bottom of the steps Ember was currently attached to.

"Go! I'll catch up!" she whispered. Fen looked hesitantly between her and their path leading to the door before Rowan grabbed his arm and pulled him out of sight.

Ember yanked one last time as hard as she could, finally pulling herself free, and quickly slipped into the open room beside her just as the footsteps hit the floor in front of her. She tried to steady her breath, doing her best not to give away her position to whoever was lurking in the dark. Everyone was at the festival, right? Fen was supposed to make sure of that before he met them at the fountain. He wouldn't have missed an important detail like that. Had Killian slipped away and come home while they were in the study?

After the footsteps faded, she eased her way out of her hiding space and quietly tiptoed through the dark halls. Her footsteps sounded like canons ricocheting off the pristine tile, echoing off the walls that felt like they were closing in on her.

She could see the back door and began picking up her pace. Right as she entered the kitchen and was ready to bolt for the door, a soft voice echoed behind her, making her blood run cold.

"Miss Lothbrok."

Ember turned on her heels, staring into calm lavender eyes. "Maren," she sighed in relief. "I didn't know you'd be here." She was still out of breath, the adrenaline having all but sucked it out of her chest.

"I had a feeling we would be having visitors this evening." She smiled. "I hope you found what you were looking for."

Ember let out a relieved sigh and laughed quietly. She dug through her bag, gently pulling out the red cape and held it in her hand, slowly handing it to Maren.

"I made a promise to your mum," she said quietly, "and I always keep my promises."

The Merrow's face never changed; her eyes just wandered down to the fabric hanging from Ember's pale fingers. She could've sworn she saw her eyes glisten, but her face remained calm and neutral. Ember slipped the cape into her webbed fingers, feeling the material slip softly over her skin like water through her fingertips. Maren slipped the cape over her shoulders and transformed before Ember's eyes. Fins grew from her temples, stretching down the sides of her high cheekbones, making her look more fish than woman.

"You are a kind Vala, Ember Lothbrok. I owe you a life debt."

Ember smiled as she took a deep breath, feeling relief wash over her like a tsunami. She turned to grab the brass doorknob in front of her, but Maren stopped her.

"Ember," she said quietly, "be careful who you trust. Salt and sugar both look the same. Good luck."

Ember gave her a quick nod as she chewed on the inside of her cheek. She turned and slung the door open, stepping into the icy rain. She ran as fast as her legs would take her toward the Echopoint at the end of the long driveway, where Rowan was standing with arms crossed over her chest, tapping her foot, and Fen pacing anxiously back and forth.

"Oh, thank the gods," Fen breathed as he ran toward her and wrapped her in a hug. "I'm so sorry. I shouldn't have left."

Ember felt her body stiffen at the embrace. "It's fine. It was only Maren. I gave her the cape."

"Did she say anything?" Rowan asked, stepping away from the tree she was leaning against.

"Um… no. She just thanked me, that's all," she replied, eyes darting between Fen and Rowan.

Rowan's eyebrows raised slightly, and she gave a small nod.

The trio decided that they'd had enough adventure for the night and not return to the festival. Ember was ready to collapse in her bed and sleep for an eternity. Rowan waved goodbye, and Fen and Ember headed back to their home. As they headed up the dark drive, guilt settled in her stomach as she thought about the lies that were beginning to pile up, one by one like boulders being stacked on top of one another, creating a wall she wasn't sure she would ever be able to tear down. The moonlight lit up the roof of the house, a house she was slowly becoming comfortable in, and her heart ached.

How long would it be before she was packing her suitcase again, making her way to another house that would never be home? She let out a heavy sigh as she shook the thoughts from her head. Doing the right thing was what was important here, even if that meant she lost everything.

CHAPTER 15
A WAY WITH WILD THINGS

"Em? Hello? Earth to Ember?"

Ember jerked her head up from where it was resting on her palm. The lack of sleep she had gotten between Samhain and the following Monday was borderline disrespectful, and she was paying for it dearly at the lunch table that afternoon. The hall was crowded as students milled about, eating lunch and preparing for their afternoon classes, and all Ember wanted was to go back to sleep.

"Huh?" she said as she rubbed her eyes a few times, like maybe she could force the sleepiness out of them.

"I asked if you'd finished the Herbal Magic homework yet," Rowan said between bites of her crisps. "I can't remember how long a Moon Milk has to brew."

"Oh, yeah, sure," Ember mumbled as she reached in her bag and tossed the paper to her friend. Fen leaned over Rowan's shoulder and pulled out his own paper, quickly scribbling on the page. Homework was the furthest thing from her mind as she sipped the warm tea clutched in her hands, but warm Moon Milk and some dreamless sleep didn't sound half bad.

Ember heard the door to the hall open and close but

didn't have the energy to look and see who had come in. She pushed her potatoes around on her plate, daydreaming about the warm bed that was waiting for her at home. The days were becoming increasingly colder and rainier, meaning most of her downtime was spent curled up under a blanket in her bed or the library with her books. She felt her head nod as her elbow slipped off the table, jerking it up quickly before it came crashing down on the plate in front of her. She felt someone come up behind her, making the hairs on the back of her neck prickle and the pendant around her neck hum. Ember looked up to see Rowan's mouth hanging open, and Fen's face screwed up in confusion.

"What the bloody hell happened to you?" Fen gaped as his fork clanked against his plate.

Ember turned around, and her breath caught in her throat. Killian stood a few inches behind her, hands stuffed in his pockets. The smug look Ember had grown so accustomed to had vanished, replaced with hollow, blackened eyes filled with defeat. It was like all of the happiness had been sucked out of him. It made Ember's blood run cold.

Killian shrugged his shoulders as he took his seat, resting his elbow on the table as he studied the grains of wood winding up and down past the plates and cups. Afternoon sun shone in the windows behind him, carving his harsh features. Ember studied the purple and blue welts lining his jaw. There was still an outline of fingers wrapping around his neck, the indigo and violet mixed with green running down his collarbone. His charcoal eyes were rimmed with red, all of the smoke that gave him so much life had vanished, like the fire had been permanently extinguished.

"Killian, what happened?" Fen repeated, a little quieter this time.

"I'm fine," Killian whispered, eyes still glued to the table in front of him.

Rowan furrowed her brow. "I don't know that I would call

that 'fine,'" she replied, gesturing to the wounds on his face and neck.

Killian glanced around the room, like he was taking inventory of how many listening ears there were before meeting the eyes around the table.

"My dad got mad, that's all," he replied, shifting in his seat.

"Your dad... did that?" Ember breathed, as a chill ran down her spine.

Killian nodded his head and winced, like the mere memory of the hands wrapped around his throat made him hurt all over again. "Mum and Dad got home after the festival, and Maren wasn't there," he whispered. "They thought she was upstairs asleep, but when she never came down and made breakfast or afternoon tea, Mum went up to check on her. She was gone. Dad said someone had to have released her, and that it only could've been someone in our family. Mum and Rafe were with him at the festival, so the only other option was me."

Ember felt her throat go bone dry as her heart thumped in her chest.

"You weren't at the festival?" Rowan asked with a raised brow.

Killian shook his head.

"Where were you?" Fen prodded.

"I just left for a few minutes." He shrugged in reply.

"Why?" Rowan pushed further. She cut her eyes at Ember quickly, but Ember's eyes were still glued to Killian's.

"Does it matter?" he snapped, his face growing angrier. "I didn't let her go!" His knuckles turned white as he clenched his fist on top of the table.

Ember chewed on the inside of her cheek as she inched a little away from the fury radiating off him.

"We believe you, mate," Fen reassured him as he shifted nervously in his seat. "I'm sure it's just a misunderstanding."

"Do you know who did it?" Ember asked in a hushed tone, trying her best not to sound as worried as she felt.

"I don't know," he replied angrily, "but when I figure it out, I'm going to kill them."

His tone was even and steady, and it made a shiver run down Ember's spine. Rowan stared at her with wide eyes, silently pleading with her to change the subject, but Ember couldn't think of anything else to say. She stared at the bruises that ran up and down his jaw and collarbone. Green and purple, old and new, mingling together on his freckled skin. This wasn't the first time his father had done this, that much was obvious, but he buried it all underneath smugness and sarcasm. It was like the mask he bore every day had slipped, and she could finally see the broken boy underneath.

This time, though, it was a direct reaction to what Ember, Fen, and Rowan had done. This was their fault, and the reality of that realization was jarring. Their little quest had gotten him hurt, and they barely had anything to show for it. They had no other leads about the book, no clue where they needed to look next. Someone had to know something.

Maybe...

She stood up quickly, almost knocking her chair out from under her as she tried to steady herself.

"Where are you going?" Rowan asked as she started to stand.

"I just need to talk to Professor Bjorn," she replied, trying to steady her voice. "Just about some homework. Catch you guys later?" She didn't wait for a reply before she turned on her heels and headed toward the door, leaving her confused friends sitting at the table.

Ember steadied herself against the railing as she made her way up the stairs toward Professor Bjorn's office. She could feel bile rising in her throat as pictures of Killian's bruised face and neck ran through her mind. Part of her wanted to feel bad for him—she had been on the wrong end of angry parental figures before, and it wasn't anything she would wish on her worst enemy—but something wasn't right. She knew he wasn't at his house that night, that much was a fact, but where did he sneak away to? Ember always assumed the book was something they would have plenty of time to find, but what if he already knew? What if he was looking for it? She suddenly felt like the walls were closing in on her, like any minute it would all come crashing down.

"Professor?" she said as she walked into the classroom. It was empty, other than the birds that perched in the trees jutting out from the walls. Ember scanned the room as her heart beat in her throat. Professor Bjorn popped his head out of the door at the top of the spiral staircase in the corner of the room and smiled.

"Ah, Miss Lothbrok, come in, come in." He smiled as he opened the door wide.

Ember slowly made her way up the spiraling stairs and into the small office. It was cozy, a plush rug spanned most of the hardwood floor, warm colors swirling together through the fibers. The crimson and gold mixed together with peach and magenta, the light from the fireplace bouncing off them like a sunset at her feet. Cages floated in the air, as if they were being held by an invisible string pinned to the ceiling, and tanks lined the rounded walls.

It was like she had stepped into a living museum. She walked slowly to one of the floating cages and ran her fingers down the cold metal. It looked like there was a bright green leaf laying at the bottom, like it had just been plucked from a tree outside. Ember stared intently as she watched the leaf move up and down slowly, almost like it was breathing. All of a sudden, a small head popped out of the leaf, and Ember sucked in a breath as her eyes widened. The animal uncurled itself, stretching its wings and letting out a yawn before it walked to the bars of the cage and let out a small coo, rubbing its head against the shining metal. Ember reached her finger through to pet its nose, and she could've sworn it smiled back at her.

"You seem to have a way with wild things," the professor smiled from his desk. "Irish Green Noses don't normally take to people so quickly."

Ember smiled as she turned toward the desk, seeing a ball of fur laying on top of it. It looked like a small fox with tiny antlers poking out of the top of its head. It purred as Professor Bjorn scratched behind its ears, flicking its tail back and forth.

"What can I do for you, Miss Lothbrok?" he asked, as he motioned to the comfy chair in front of his desk.

Ember breathed deep as she took a seat, the anxiety returning to her chest and sinking like a rock into her stomach. "I have a question, and I wasn't sure who else to ask," she said hesitantly, running her fingers up and down the fabric on the arm of the chair.

"I'm happy to answer any of your questions," he replied. "Having trouble with school?"

"Oh, no, school's fine. I'm really enjoying Herbal Magic especially." She smiled. "Actually, I was wondering if I could ask you about a book."

"Of course. Do you need suggestions? I have a library full." He pointed to the shelf behind him.

Ember smiled at the stacks of old tomes that lined the mahogany shelves and took a deep breath. "Actually, no," she replied slowly. "I had a question about a certain book... It's called *The Book of Shadows*."

She held her breath as Professor Bjorn took the monocle off his eye and stared intently at her. His usual joking grin had vanished and was replaced with a sternness that made Ember's stomach twist into knots.

"Where did you hear about that?" he whispered hoarsely. Without taking his eyes off the girl, he lifted his right hand, flipped it, and waved it in front of him.

Ember jumped as the office door snapped closed behind

her, and her grip tightened around the arm of the chair. "Um..." she stuttered. "My dad mentioned something about it in one of his journals. I was just wondering if you could tell me about it. He didn't give many specifics." Ember fought back the urge to fidget at the lie.

"What has you interested in a book like that?" he asked as his eyes narrowed on her, making Ember shift nervously in her seat.

"Just curious." She shrugged, doing her best to mask the anxiety growing in her stomach. The last thing she needed was adults asking questions.

The professor rested his elbows on the desk in front of him, holding his giant paws together and leaning his chin against them. "Not much is known about the book," he said thoughtfully. "The lore surrounding it says that it was created by one of the gods who settled with our ancestors, a god full of greed who needed to harness all magic for himself."

"Freyr?" Ember asked quietly as she tugged on the pendant hanging from her neck.

"Possibly," he replied. "No one knows for sure. Some legends say it was lost thousands of years ago, dropped in the depths of the sea at the birth of the island. And good riddance, if you ask me."

"Some legends?" Ember asked as she furrowed her brow. "Are there others?"

"That's the thing about legends." Professor Bjorn almost laughed. "They're not black and white. They're a hundred shades of gray muddled together. Truth and lie mixed to form a story worth telling around the campfire. Don't put much stock in legend, as they're rarely what they seem."

"Are there any legends that talk about where the book is now?" she asked as she fidgeted in her chair. "If it was real, that is."

Professor Bjorn tilted his head as he examined her, fingers thumping on the desk in front of him. "Most of the legends talk about it being passed down to different families, most who had an affinity for dark magic." He leaned back in his chair, crossing his burly paws over his chest. "No one family was ever mentioned, I'm afraid. Is there a reason you're so interested in this?" He cocked an eyebrow as he crossed his leg over his knee.

Ember bit her lip. "No, just curious," she replied as she forced a smile, trying desperately to sound more convincing than she felt. "Just trying to learn a little more about the things my dad was studying."

"Of course," Professor Bjorn nodded as he furrowed his brow. "I'm sorry I couldn't be of more help. Your father liked to keep some of his research to himself, and I'm afraid this is one of those things."

Ember took a breath and nodded, eyes focused on her lap. It wasn't the answer she was looking for, but it seemed to be the only one she was going to get from him. She gave a small smile and stood up, slinging her bag over her shoulder. "Thank you, Professor," she said, and turned toward the door to leave.

"Miss Lothbrok," the professor said quietly, "legend or not, you would do well to stay far away from the book."

Ember swallowed the lump forming in her throat as she grabbed the strap of her bag a little tighter.

"Being curious about the legend is one thing, but searching out dark magic is another entirely. Things are not always what they appear."

She nodded her head slowly before slipping out the door and walking quickly down the spiraling steps and out of the classroom. Frustration rose like bile in her throat as she weaved in and out of students mingling in the halls, eyes fixed in front of her. She shook her head as she blew out a breath. Of course, it wouldn't have been that easy. Even if Professor Bjorn did know something about *The Book of Shadows*, why would he tell anyone about it, let alone a fifteen-year-old student? Her heart thundered in her chest as she walked, the masses of people mixed together in her vision as she zoned out, creating swirls of maroon jumpers and khaki pants. Her breath caught in her throat as turned a corner and ran head on into smoky gray eyes.

"Runnin' late, Starshine?" Killian said with a half smile, not quite his usual chipper self.

"Just going to class," she replied as she swallowed heavily.

Killian nodded as he averted his eyes to the ground, scuffing the toe of his shoe against the rough floor.

"How's your, um, face?" she asked, as she pointed to her chin, mirroring the spot where the purple and blue was blooming on his skin.

"I've had worse." He shrugged. "You get used to it."

Ember looked anywhere but up at the sullen boy, searching the halls for some way out of this conversation. She cut her eyes toward him briefly, and something about the way the different shades of gray and silver swirled together made her pause, pulling her into them and briefly sucking the breath from her lungs. She shook her head lightly, knocking away the odd thoughts that were floating through her mind.

"I, uh, didn't know you had a brother," she stuttered, barely above a whisper.

"I've got two," he half laughed, eyes still stuck to the ground.

"Does your dad—"

"Hit them too?" he interrupted. "Nah, just me. Rafe is a couple of years older, the Vargr heir and perfect son." He rolled his eyes and scoffed, like the mere thought of his older brother was a joke with a terrible punchline. "Leif is the golden child. Mummy's perfect baby." His face screwed up as he talked about his younger brother, disgust and jealousy mixing together in his eyes as he wrinkled his nose. "I, however, am neither," he scoffed. "They've tried so hard to turn me into them, into something noble and pure and as

disgusting as they are. But I'm not them, and I never will be."
Killian rubbed his hand under his eyes and stuffed his hands
in his pockets. He was angry, but Ember wasn't sure if the
anger was more for his perfect family, or for himself for not
fitting into the ancient mold that they all adhered to.

"You didn't deserve that, you know," Ember whispered.

"I know," he replied. "I told you I didn't do anything."

"But even if you did, you didn't deserve that. Doesn't
matter what you did. You don't deserve what he does to you.
He could've killed you."

Killian scoffed. "There are fates far worse than death."

Ember lifted her eyes and was met with campfire smoke
staring back at her. Killian's eyes were rimmed red and misty,
like he was holding back any tears that dared fall down his
porcelain cheeks. He nodded before lifting his head and
looking around them. All of a sudden, Ember noticed how
empty the halls were. All of the students had made their way
to their next class, and it was just her and Killian standing in
the corridor, inches away from each other. Ember waited for
her heart rate to quicken, but it never came. The anxiety that
normally came with being around him was replaced with
something that felt like…

Ember closed her eyes and shook her head.

"Walk you to class?" Killian said with a half smile.

"Oh, no, I'm fine. I can get there myself."

"Come on, Starshine." He smirked as he grabbed her bag
and slung it over his shoulder. "I don't bite."

"No, ABSOLUTELY NOT," Ember exclaimed as she walked in
step with Fen and Rowan out the door and through the
grounds of the school. "We are not going back." She adjusted
the strap of her bag and flipped her braid off her shoulder
with a huff.

"Do you have a better idea?" Rowan retorted, eyebrow cocked as she stared at her friend.

"I mean... no." Ember chewed on her lip. She sighed as she ran a hand down her face. The truth was, she didn't have any ideas at all. She had no clue what she was doing. She kicked a pebble at her feet and let out an exasperated breath.

"Maybe they can help, Em." Fen shrugged as he kicked a rock down the dusty path toward the Echopoint. "It's not like we're doing very well on our own. Part of the deal with releasing Maren was them helping us find the book. We have to go talk to them for that to happen. We're at a dead end."

Ember threw her head back in a dramatic sigh. The very last thing she wanted to do was trek back into the Dark Forest to talk to the Clann, but she couldn't see any way around it. She still had a scar from the tumble she took, and she wasn't looking to add any more to her collection. But Fen was right—they had no more leads. If anything, they were further from figuring out where the book was than they had ever been before. The trio had saved Maren, and now it was time for the Clann to hold up their end of the bargain.

And time felt like it was slowly closing in on them.

It didn't feel like Killian knew about the prophecy, or that it was about him, but it was obvious his father did with the way he reacted to someone breaking into their hidden study. It was only a matter of time before it all came to a head and all hell broke loose. She looked at Fen as he carelessly brushed the hair out of his eyes.

He would be crushed. This was just as much about saving Killian as it was stopping his family, and in turn, saving Fen from losing his best mate to this stupid legend. The weight of that realization was crushing.

"Okay, fine," she huffed. "But we stay together, and we get in and out as fast as we can."

Supper that evening felt like it lasted forever.

Ember and Fen didn't dare make eye contact, with each other or anyone else. They answered any questions directed at them with *mm-hmm*'s or vague nods, eating as quickly as possible without drawing unnecessary attention. Ember swallowed the last chip on her plate before wiping her hands on her pants.

"I've got some homework I need to finish. Supper was wonderful, Mrs. Kitt," she said as she shot a glance toward Fen, who was still shoveling fish and chips into his mouth, barely breathing in between bites. "Don't you have homework too, Fen?" she said with raised eyebrows.

"What homework?" he asked, mouth still full.

Ember kicked his shin from under the table and glared at him.

"Ow!" he yelped, rubbing the top of his shin.

"The project we have to finish *tonight*," Ember hissed.

"Oh. Right, that homework," he replied as he cleared his throat and wiped his face with his napkin. "Thanks for supper, Mum." The two stood up and quickly walked their dishes into the kitchen and dropped them in the sink, something Eira insisted her children do without magic. Fen kissed his mother on the cheek before following behind Ember toward the steps.

"Anything I can help with?" Eira asked.

"No!" they both said in unison, a little louder than necessary.

Eira and Otto exchanged a confused glance before looking back toward the children.

"It's just going to be a long night," Ember said gently. "Wouldn't want to take up your whole evening helping us with homework."

"We're here if you need us." Eira smiled fondly.

Ember and Fen sped up the steps, down the hall, and quickly into Fen's bedroom, locking the door behind them. Fen went straight to his desk while Ember sat on his bed and began working out their plan to get out of the house unnoticed and to the Echopoint, jotting down little notes here and there in her journal. After half an hour, she glanced sideways at Fen to see him leaning back in his chair and playing on his phone.

"Ow," he hissed as he stuck his thumb in his mouth, "stupid thing."

"Are you okay?" Ember asked as she furrowed her brow, leaning forward on the bed.

"I'm fine, just hexed my finger a bit."

She raised her brow as she looked at the phone in his hand, residual sparks still lightly bouncing off it.

"Why do you have that anyway?" she asked.

"Have what?"

"The phone. What's the point? You can just send a Helio if you need to contact someone."

Fen grinned. "Infused magic," he said as he pressed a few buttons. "I want to infuse magic into the technology and use them together."

"Why?" she asked in confusion.

"Why not? Casting a spell to wash the dishes is all well and good, but what if you could do more?" He shifted his weight toward her and started clicking more buttons on his phone. "What if you could cast a spell that acts like a timer to wash the dishes at the same time every night? Or send out automatic Helios from your phone by using a certain word? Magic is wonderful, but nothing great ever happened by standing still."

"That sounds really cool, Fen." Ember smiled. She stretched out on his bed as he fiddled at the computer and picked up the book she was working on. "But maybe don't try to hex the phone."

"I didn't try to hex it," he replied. "I was trying to charm it." He stuffed the phone in his pocket, grimacing as he pulled out a cloth to wrap around his red thumb. "I've been developing magical apps all summer. The apps are finished, but it's the magic that keeps giving me trouble,"

"What kind of app?" Ember asked as she furrowed her brow, glancing over at him again.

"This specific one is an undetectable tracking app," he replied as he pulled a small notebook out of his back pocket. "Most tracking charms leave a small trace of magic if you know what to look for, like a signature from the sender sort of. This app sends out the tracking charm, but it doesn't leave the small trace of magic, and coordinates are sent directly to your phone." He pressed a few buttons as residual sparks flew from the phone again, then he stuffed it back in his pocket with a huff. "At least, it will when I'm done."

"That feels illegal," she replied as she crossed her arms.

Fen shrugged. "What Chief Thornsten doesn't know won't hurt him,"

Ember laughed as she rolled her eyes at his disregard for authority. She watched as he opened a small notebook and began reading from it, twiddling the pendant on his necklace in his fingers. "I always thought mine was one of a kind," she said as she glanced down at his necklace, simultaneously tracing the etchings on her own.

"It sort of is," Fen mumbled, glancing up from his notebook. "The Vegvisir, the pendant, is the same, but the etchings are different on everyone's." He slipped the leather off his neck as he held out his hand to take Ember's.

Ember hesitated, gripping the disc a little tighter. He gave her a soft smile as she slipped the leather cord into his hand, letting her fingers linger briefly over the frayed fabric.

"See this here?" he said as he pointed to the etching in the middle of the disc, an arrow pointing up with a half diamond at the bottom pointed up and to the left. "This is your familial rune. Every family's rune looks different, and the smaller ones around the outer ring vary some too." He pointed at the smaller etchings on the edge of the disc. "But they all do the same thing. It's connected to the familial bond that forms when you enter into a family of Vala blood."

"Bond?" Ember asked, face screwed up as she stared at the tiny etches.

Fen nodded his head, holding the necklaces at eye level so the sunlight bounced off the metal.

"Think of it... kind of like a magical cord. A familial bond binds you to your family, and the magic of your ancestors. The magic is in your blood, but the bond strengthens it, and the familial rune on your necklace gives you the ability to focus it. It's like a wand, but not as annoying. You can still perform magic without the pendant, it just becomes more erratic."

Ember nodded her head slowly as she squinted her eyes at the shapes. "How long have you had yours?"

"You get them the summer before first year normally, wearing one before then makes accidental magic more frequent. Did Thea give you yours before you got here?"

Ember's brow furrowed as she thought back to what her father had said as thunder and lightning crashed around her.

"*Keep this on! It must NEVER come off, Ember. Promise me!*"

Why would he make her promise something like that? The whole reason her other foster families had been so afraid of her was because of the erratic magic that had been building since she was a preschooler. Why would he set her up for failure? Why would he make her promise something when he knew what would happen, what it would cause? An unfamiliar feeling toward her parents built in the pit of Ember's stomach as she twirled the pendant through her fingers.

Resentment.

All of the heartbreak, all of the brokenness could have been prevented if they had just told her the truth.

"I've had it since I was six years old. It was my father's," she whispered.

"That's so cool," Fen said as he slipped his necklace back

over his head. "I wanted Papa's, but he keeps it locked in a safe in his study. You get your familial runes tattooed after you come of age, so it's not like he actually needs the thing now." He let out a huff as he rolled his eyes. "We got mine from the blacksmith in town this summer. I've been practicing basic electromagic spells, but I can't seem to get the magic part right. It's a third-year class, so maybe I'll have it down by then."

Ember chuckled, breathing a sigh of relief that Fen hadn't noticed the emotional wave that was threatening to drown her.

He pushed away from his desk, stretching his arms over his head. "I'm going to get a snack, you want anything?"

She shook her head with a half smile. "I'm good," she replied softly. Fen smiled as he slipped out and closed the door with a quiet click. Ember let out a heavy sigh as she laid against the pillow and took her necklace back off, letting the cold metal settle on her fingers. She bit her lip, a bad habit she gained on her seventh birthday to help keep her emotions in check when she felt like she might explode, and she thought back to what Fen had said. Anger built in her chest as she gripped the necklace a little tighter, tiny sparks of magic cutting into her palms. She gasped as she felt it cut through her skin and watched as crimson trickled out of her closed hand and onto the bed. She closed her eyes, willing herself to slow her breathing as she wiped the stray tears from her face.

She knew better than to wonder. She knew better than to be angry. Anger wouldn't bring them back. Piecing together the broken puzzle that was her family wouldn't put her back together again. She had learned to live with the broken pieces a long time ago. And no amount of anger or grief would ever make her whole again.

One last tear slid down her cheek as she closed her eyes and held her necklace against her heart and tilted her head to the heavens. "I'm going to be okay, Papa."

She quickly wiped the tears from her face, just in time for Fen to walk back into the room, stuffing his face full of potato chips. Ember laughed as she rolled her eyes, then laid on her stomach and began to read, but then it hit her all at once, how comfortable she was becoming. She was having a harder time remembering the days where her evenings were spent locked in her room eating dinner and losing herself in books, hiding from the inevitable downfall that was happening around her. Her evenings now were spent curled up with a book in the sitting room, in front of a roaring fire while Maeve giggled on the floor with her toys. Supper was eaten every night around a table filled with laughter and stories instead of deafening silence. Every room she sat in was filled to the brim with love, and not the kind of love she was used to. Not the kind that came with conditions. Not the kind of love she had to beg for or the kind that seemed to slip through her fingers like sand. This was different. This was real.

This felt like home.

Fen's floor was flooded with tangerine and magenta as the sun set outside the bedroom window. Ember leaned against the door, listening to the sounds of the family making their way to bed for the night. She focused on her breathing, willing her heart to slow down as it beat rapidly in her throat.

"And you're positive we can do this?" she whispered, head leaning against the wall.

"Absolutely," Fen reassured. "I can't tell you how many times I've gone for midnight rides on Arlo. They'll never even know we left."

Somehow, that didn't make her feel any better.

After they were sure the rest of the family was sound asleep, Ember and Fen silently made their way down the hall, steps creaking loudly under their feet. In the silence of the night surrounding them, it sounded like a herd of elephants stampeding through the farmhouse. Ember held her breath as they tiptoed across the foyer and out the front door. The night air immediately hit her skin and sent chills down her spine as they walked quickly down the drive toward the Echopoint.

"Took you long enough!" Rowan huffed as they landed with a thud in front of her.

Ember's legs wobbled as she wiped the dirt from her pants and squinted up at her friend. "Fen spent a solid thirty minutes we didn't have deciding on an outfit," she snorted, as she adjusted her bag over her shoulder.

"My black jacket is in the wash. It's not my fault!"

"Maybe next time you'll remember to bring down your dirty clothes when Mum asks for them." She laughed before stopping short and clearing her throat. "I mean, your mum… Mrs. Kitt…"

Slip of the tongue. That's all.

"So, are we gonna spend all night discussing Fen's poor time management, or can we get goin'?" Rowan interjected sarcastically.

The trio set off silently down the path, allowing the waning moon to be their guide. The November wind bit at Ember's cheeks as leaves crunched under her feet. Stealth wasn't her specialty. She was probably the least sneaky person in Ireland. Which was why the idea of running around a magical island in the middle of the night while her foster parents thought she was asleep was making her sick to her stomach.

"You alright?" Rowan whispered beside her. The wind caught in her curls, making them whip around her head and into her face.

"Just cold," she replied with a faint smile.

It wasn't entirely a lie—she really was freezing.

"When are we supposed to learn warming charms?" Fen whined from the other side of Ember. His face was half buried in the royal blue hood on his head, and his hands were stuffed into the pockets on the front of his jacket. The tip of his nose and both his cheeks were already red from the wind, and his lips were a light shade of blue. Ember could see his teeth chattering underneath his chapped lips.

"Second or third year, I think," Rowan replied as she tied her hair behind her head.

"That's bloody stupid," Fen grumbled as he shoved his glasses up his nose.

"They used to teach it to first years," Rowan said, "but my brother knew someone who caught himself on fire in his year, so I think they have good reason to hold off."

"I guess." Fen shrugged.

"Why don't you have a permanent warming charm on your jacket?" Rowan asked through squinted eyes.

Fen rolled his eyes. "Mum doesn't think magic is the answer to everything."

"We're here," Ember interrupted quietly. The trio stopped at the end of the dirt road, looking up at the towering trees in front of them. If they kept walking straight, they would walk into the safety of the grounds of Heksheim. Protective wards would surround them, keeping them far away from the dangers that lurked beyond the dark tree line.

But safety wasn't what they were here for.

"Why did it have to be the Dark Forest," Fen groaned as he stared into the dark trees. "Why couldn't it have been a relaxing meadow? Or a serene pond?"

Ember didn't answer, instead she grabbed her foster brother's hand and squeezed gently, pulling him toward the forest. Each of them whispered, *"Lux,"* and three balls of light floated into the air above their palms. They edged in slowly, the lights in front of them barely piercing the darkness as the shadows seemed to swallow them whole. The forest was eerily quiet, the wind didn't even dare enter. The light of the moon pierced through the canopy above them, casting shapes on the dirt at their feet. They walked silently, staying as close to the tree line as possible. Every few minutes, Ember glanced over her shoulder, squinting her eyes into the shadows behind her.

She half expected to see ghostly white fur out of the corner of her eye, but there was nothing there, only her shadow playing on the tall oaks. She thought about Odette's bells, just for a moment, but thought again as she watched Fen walk ahead of her. The last thing she wanted to do was attract any attention to them. What did Odette know anyway?

Their path narrowed as they wound their way through the trees and under low hanging branches. Briars hung on Ember's jacket sleeve, scratching her arms underneath the thin fabric. Just when she thought they were going to have to walk single file across the brittle twigs, the path widened, and Ember could hear the faint crashing of waves against the shore.

"Finally," breathed Fen as they stepped into the clearing.

The wind instantly hit Ember on the side of her face, sending shivers back down her neck and spine. They edged through the darkness, following the small white spheres floating a few feet in front of them until they heard a voice break with the waves against the shore.

"Ember Lothbrok," Maren's voice said calmly. "The forest is a dangerous place to wander, especially at night."

"We needed to speak to you," Ember replied, searching for the courage she had when they had left the house earlier that evening.

"You seem to be missing one," Maren said as she tilted her head, eying the two teenagers standing behind Ember.

"Oh, um… it's just the three of us," Ember replied as she shifted her weight. "We need to talk to you about a book."

"*The Book of Shadows?*" Maren asked, more a statement than a question.

"Yes…" She hesitated.

"You know about the book?" Fen said loudly, definitely not fully understanding what was lurking in the woods behind them.

Ember shushed him and he closed his mouth tight.

"I do," Maren laughed. "The island has many secrets you will never learn about in school."

"We need to know where to find it," Rowan continued, "and we were wondering if you knew."

Maren paused for what seemed like an eternity, staring intensely at the children. They looked at each other, trying to determine if they had said something wrong or offensive—could you offend a Merrow without knowing?—when Maren spoke again.

"This is a very dangerous thing you're looking for," she said with a serious tone. "It's not something children should be playing with."

"We're hardly children," Rowan scoffed as she rolled her eyes. "We're fifteen, for Odin's sake."

"We understand the dangers," Ember continued, "but we have to find it. It's very important." She held her breath, bracing herself for the inevitable scolding they probably deserved, but instead, Maren's face softened, and she opened her palm, motioning for them to move closer. She twirled her hand above her open palm and whispered incantations Ember had never heard under her breath. All of a sudden, a glowing rune appeared in the air, floating above her iridescent skin.

"This is the binding rune that marks *The Book of Shadows*. It serves as a lock, protecting the book from those who might have the wrong intentions. But locks can be broken, whether intentions are good or not."

Ember screwed her face up, trying to place where she had seen it before. As quick as it was there, it was gone again, vanishing into mist in the air.

"That's it?" Fen whined. "We walked through a bleedin' forest in the middle of the night for a rune?"

"Fen," Ember hissed, "she's just trying to help." But as badly as Ember wanted to scold him, she was feeling equally as frustrated. After a trek through the cold, risking punishment and possible dismemberment from whatever lurked in the trees, they still weren't any closer than they had been earlier that evening.

"I truly wish I could be of more help," Maren said sympathetically. "But what you're searching for was not meant to be found."

Ember smiled softly at the woman and sighed. Nothing in her life had ever been easy. It made sense that this wouldn't be, either. The trio thanked Maren and turned to walk back into the forest when Ember felt cool hands on her forearm.

"Ember," Maren said quietly, in almost a melodic whisper, "everything is not always what it seems." And she let go, turning swiftly toward the water and disappearing beneath the waves.

She was getting really sick of the riddles.

EMBER'S LEGS felt like lead as she quietly walked up the front porch of the Kitt home. The old wood creaked beneath her feet and sounded as loud as cymbals in the quiet air around them. Fen led the way, opening the door slowly, allowing just enough room for them to slip into the warmth of the foyer. They tiptoed toward the steps, and just as they were about to make a break for it, they heard the distinct sound of someone clearing their throat in the sitting room. They both looked at each other with wide eyes, and Ember's blood ran cold.

"It's a bit late to be out adventuring, isn't it?" Otto's gruff voice sounded from his chair in front of the fireplace. He stroked his thick beard with one hand, holding a pipe in the other.

Ember swallowed the lump that was quickly forming in her throat and followed Fen into the other room.

"I wanted to let Ember ride Arlo," Fen said quietly. "It wasn't her fault."

Otto stared at them both, his face stoic and unmoving.

Ember felt her heart skip a beat, and mentally began to prepare herself to pack her suitcase as soon as she went upstairs. *This is it. It was over before anything ever really started.*

"Your stealth needs work," Otto said with a small smile, as his eyes traveled between the two. "If you're going to sneak around, try not to be so obvious about it. Your mum is asleep, best be quiet when you go up the stairs." And then he picked up the book that was laying in his lap and continued to read.

Fen grabbed Ember's arm and tugged her toward the steps as her mouth hung open. As she turned to leave, she could've sworn she saw a small smirk play across Otto's face.

"You didn't have to do that," she whispered to Fen.

"Do what?" he replied.

"Lie for me," she mumbled. "I can own my mistakes."

"I was trying to keep at least one of us out of trouble," Fen replied with a shrug. "Besides, you would do the same for me."

Warmth spread through her as she looked at this boy, the one who tried to step in front of a proverbial bullet for her. When had anyone ever done anything like that for her?

"Thank you, Fen." She smiled before slipping into her room and quietly closing the door.

She collapsed on her bed and felt her legs ache in reply, the adrenaline of the night finally wearing off, unease beginning to wash over her. She had spent the last nine years taking care of herself, and the idea that some boy she hardly knew was hellbent on saving her from trouble was almost laughable. She didn't need to be saved. She had done just fine on her own so far, and she definitely didn't need a foster brother, who would probably be gone in a year's time, to do the saving.

Now was not the time to get comfortable.

CHAPTER 16

BREAKFAST ROLLS AND BIND RUNES

E mber leaned against the round table of the great hall, nursing a hot cup of tea and a splitting headache. Her notebook lay open in front of her, homework still untouched. She dug her fingers into her temple, desperately trying to force the ache behind her eyes to ease as she stared at the open textbook. She had never forgotten about her homework, let alone turned in her work late, and the stress of finishing it before class was eating away at her.

"Did you figure out number ten?" Rowan asked from across the table, pointing at the page with her pen.

"I haven't even started number one yet," Ember winced as she closed her eyes. After their adventure through the woods the night before, she had only gotten a couple of hours of sleep, and she was feeling every one of those lost hours that morning, deeply regretting not putting an invigorating drought in her tea. Fen, on the other hand, was as chipper as always. Apparently, he wasn't fazed by their trek, and he drank his tea while pouring over a last-minute Herbal Magic paper that was due that afternoon.

"I just don't get it." Rowan sighed as she flung herself

back in her seat, tossing her pen to the table. "I can't remember which rune goes in the second box. This is hopeless."

"I think it's *Othala*," Fen replied, mouth half full of a breakfast roll. "Like this." He reached over and drew a complicated rune on her blank paper, dropping pieces of biscuit as he wrote.

"Runes and breakfast rolls don't mix well, Fenrir," Rowan scolded as she wiped the crumbs off the edge of the table. "Where's your other half, anyway? Go dribble your breakfast all over his homework."

Fen shrugged. "Probably taking his time getting out of bed, the lazy git."

Ember lifted her head from where it was resting on the table and squinted into the light that was pouring through the large windows of the hall. Killian was a lot of things, but late wasn't typically one of them, especially if it meant he wouldn't be able to cause chaos before classes in the morning. The more she thought about it, the more she realized they were seeing less and less of him these days. She rarely saw him in the hall between classes, and even when she did, he was always whispering in alcoves with the Ellingboe twins. His smile had faded, and dark rings lived under his eyes like he could never get enough sleep. The thought of what could be causing him this much physical stress made Ember's stomach turn.

She took a long sip of her tea, pushing away the anxiety that was threatening to invade her chest, and tried to sit up a little straighter. Her headache was just a dull thud now, and her eyes were focusing better on everything going on around her. Students were pouring over forgotten papers, sharing answers to homework with each other and laughing loudly as they ran in and out of the door. She briefly let herself wonder how that felt—to be completely carefree, no worries about whether or not you would have a home at the end of the day eating away at you. It was something she hadn't felt since she was very small, and she was having a harder time remembering how it felt at all. Even watching Maeve and Fen together sent pangs of jealousy and heartache shooting through her chest. They didn't understand loss. They didn't know how it felt to lose something and know you would never get it back. They never had to fight to get out of bed in the morning because the weight of another day alone was far too heavy. They didn't grieve, not like she had to. Not every day. Maybe not ever.

Her eyes wandered across the table and to the paper still sitting in front of Rowan, crumbs still littering the papers around her. She watched her friend draw different runes and sigils, erasing and rewriting, when all of a sudden it was like a light bulb went off in her head.

"Box..." she mumbled to herself, heart thudding in her chest.

"Box?" Fen asked, raising his eyebrow slightly.

"What were you saying about a box?" Ember asked as she straightened her spine and leaned toward her friends.

"I couldn't remember what rune went in box two," Rowan replied. "Why?"

Ember bolted upright, almost knocking her half drank cup of tea over in the process. Fen and Rowan glanced at each other, confusion and concern clouding both of their faces.

"The box!" Ember squealed, pulling her journal and a pen out of her bag. She opened to a blank page and began furiously scribbling as if her life depended on it. Fen reached his hand across the table to grab her arm, but she pulled away, eyes darting back and forth across the quickly-filling parchment.

"Em, are you okay?" he asked quietly.

"Brilliant! It's on the box!" she squealed in reply, smiling from ear to ear.

"We're going to need a little more to go on," Rowan replied as she closed her book, brow furrowed.

"The rune! The rune is on the box! I knew I had seen it somewhere!"

Rowan and Fen looked at each other, mouths slightly open and more confused than ever.

"I think we missed a few chapters," Fen mumbled across the table. "Care to fill us in?"

Ember stopped writing and looked up at the two perplexed faces across the table. She laid her book in the middle and pointed to what she had written.

"This is the bind rune Maren showed us last night, the one she said is connected to the book." She pointed at the carelessly drawn lines in the middle of the page. "I knew I had seen it somewhere. I just couldn't place it."

Fen and Rowan stared at her as if she had grown seven heads. Ember rolled her eyes and let out a sigh.

"While I was searching for the cape in the hidden room at the Vargrs', I saw a small box. I remember thinking it looked awful out of place just lying there, but I had completely forgotten about it. On the top of the box, this rune was etched into the wood. The book has to be in the box!" She took in a deep breath, like she had forgotten to breathe during her rant, and she closed her book loudly with a snap.

"So, the book is back at Killian's?" Fen asked hesitantly.

"Yes! It has to be. It's the exact rune that Maren showed us last night. She said it acted like a lock, like protection for the book."

"How are we supposed to get it?" he asked as he crossed his arms.

"She said all locks can be broken, so I'm sure there's a way to break a bind rune. I'll just have to take a look in the library and—"

"No," he interrupted. "How are we supposed to get it out of the house?"

"We break in again, of course." Rowan grinned, as if it was the most obvious answer in the world.

"Absolutely not." He huffed. "We are not breaking back into Killian's house."

"Then, what do you propose we do?" Rowan asked.

"I don't know," he replied, "but we can't break back in. We can't."

"Fen," Ember said softly, "I don't really see any other options."

"We CAN'T," he almost shouted. "You saw what they did to him over losing Maren! Imagine what would happen if something related to the dark arts went missing. They would blame him for it again, imagine what they would do! We can't do that to him. I know finding the book is important, but he's my best mate." His face softened as Ember grabbed his hand and squeezed. Fen wasn't going to be swayed, and now was not the time to argue.

"You're right. We'll figure something else out," she said with a small smile.

Rowan threw her hands up in the air and let out a dramatic sigh. "I can't wait to hear this," she huffed.

"Maybe we could just talk to Killian." Fen shrugged. "Maybe he could help us figure it out."

"No," Rowan and Ember blurted out at the same time. If there was one thing they definitely didn't need, it was Killian ending up in the middle of their treasure hunt.

"You promised, Fen," Ember whispered. "This has to stay between us."

Fen nodded his head and let out a defeated sigh. Ember squeezed his hand once more before letting it go and reaching for the pendant around her neck.

"Well, when you think of something, let me know." Rowan grumbled before turning her attention back to her neglected homework.

"We'll figure it out," Ember assured her.

"I have to go talk to Professor Orion. See you guys in class?" Fen asked as he stood from his seat and brushed the crumbs from his pants. Ember nodded with a smile, and he took off toward the door.

"So, what do you propose we do?" Rowan asked as she tapped her finger on the table.

Ember let out a heavy sigh and rubbed the bridge of her nose. She didn't want to lie to Fen any more than she already was. She didn't want to lie to anyone. But their only hope in ending all of this was lying in a box inside a hidden room in the Vargr Manor. There was no other option. "We have to get back into the Vargrs' and get the book."

"But you told Fen—"

"I know what I told Fen," she snapped, "but we're running out of options. They're bound to figure out sooner or later that someone is looking for their book, especially since the book is where the cape was. We have to take care of it before they decide to move it."

"What about Killian?" Rowan asked skeptically.

"Killian is the last person I'm worried about," Ember sighed. That wasn't entirely true. She was very worried about Killian. She was worried about how his father would react if he saw the book was missing, worried that they were putting him in even more danger now, but mostly, she was worried about Fen. She was worried about Fen losing his best mate. She had enough experience with loss to determine that she could never let that happen. She could never let him feel what she did every day.

It wasn't an option.

Ember and Rowan spent the rest of the day whispering together and devising their plan, while doing their best not to let Fen hear any of their scheming. Lucky for them, Killian showed up halfway through Zoomancy, serving as a wonderful distraction for her oblivious foster brother. He sat at the empty chair beside Fen, and quickly laid his head down on the desk without saying a word.

"Mate," Fen whispered, "where have you been?"

Killian lifted his head and laid his chin against the palm of his hand with his elbow leaning on the table. "Had a late night," he said with a shrug. "Did I miss anything?"

"He's just been reviewing for the test next week," Fen said with a wave of his hand. "Hey, have you had a chance to practice those barrel rolls yet? I keep missing the second turn."

"Not really." Killian shrugged. "Been kinda busy." He stared at the table in front of him, tracing the grains of wood with his fingertip. He was a shadow of himself. All the mischief and joy were gone, replaced by a perpetual frown.

"We can work on it this weekend then," Fen replied. "You can come over on Saturday, and we can go to the orchard and—"

"I can't," Killian interjected. "We're going off the island for the weekend."

"Off the island? Why?" Fen frowned.

Killian shrugged again. "Dad has to meet with someone in Dublin and says it can't wait. We won't be back till Sunday evening."

Ember's ears perked up, and then she felt Rowan's elbow jam into her ribs. The girls looked at each other with wide eyes, a small smile dancing across Rowan's face. The Vargrs were leaving the island for the weekend. The house would be completely empty. This was the perfect chance to sneak in undetected.

This could be their *only* chance.

CLASS WAS DISMISSED, and Rowan and Ember hurried into the hall, getting lost in the sea of students heading to their next class.

"Think you can get away on Saturday?" Rowan whispered as they made their way down the hall.

"I don't think I should try and sneak out again," Ember replied, remembering being reprimanded by Otto the night before. "Maybe we could go during the day?"

"You don't think anyone will catch us?"

"Not if we're careful." Ember shrugged. "They don't have neighbors, so we shouldn't get caught by anyone."

"Right, so we'll meet at the Echopoint outside of town after breakfast Saturday?"

Ember gave a quick nod in agreement, right as Fen and Killian walked up behind them.

"What are we doing Saturday?" Fen asked loudly.

"*We're* not doing anything," Rowan said with an eye roll.

"Just gonna spend the day in Sigurvik. Maybe go shopping or something." Ember smiled.

Killian and Fen gave each other a confused look before shrugging and walking away.

"Girls are weird, mate," Killian mumbled to his friend as they walked out of view.

"Saturday, then?" Ember turned to her friend.

"Saturday," Rowan agreed.

Ember nodded as they began to walk down the hall, and guilt started to sink in her stomach like a stone. She was doing this for Fen, for his friendship with Killian, for the "greater good," but something about lying to him didn't sit quite right with her.

All of a sudden, none of this felt very good.

CHAPTER 17

BREAKING AND ENTERING

E mber exited the Yggdrasil Terminal and weaved in
and out of the bustling Saturday morning crowd.
They had all weekend to get in the Vargrs', but she
hurried down the cobblestone path anyway. She splashed
through the puddles left from the rain the night before,
soaking the bottom of her jeans and shoes. The sun was
beginning to rise higher in the sky, drying the old stone on the
streets, but the evidence was still there and seeping into her
clothes. The feeling of wet socks against her feet made her
skin crawl, but she had to focus. She zipped her jacket up
further and stuffed her hands in her pockets, keeping her head
down, and focused on getting to Rowan so they could find the
book.

"I was wondering if you were going to be able to get
away." Rowan laughed as Ember hurried toward her.

She leaned against the Echopoint and picked at her nails,
looking more like they were about to go run to the shops
rather than sneak into the house of a family of dark Vala—
again. Ember was jealous of how levelheaded the girl was,
nothing at all seemed to phase her or knock her off course.
She wasn't guarded or closed off, not the way Ember was. She

didn't have walls built so high that it would take a wrecking ball to even begin cracking away at the foundation.

"I think the Kitts have a busy day today, so they didn't seem to notice." Ember shrugged.

It wasn't entirely untrue. The family did seem very busy that morning. They talked over their plans during breakfast, Eira naming off tasks on the list she needed Otto to complete. Maeve had very big plans that consisted of wrestling as many of the animals on the farm as possible, and probably snacking her way through what remained of the fall garden. They had asked if Ember had any plans for the day, and she told them she was going into town with Rowan. None of them batted an eye or inquired further. They simply smiled and told her to Helio if she needed anything, to be home in time for supper.

Their unwavering trust made Ember sick with guilt.

Lying to Fen was bad enough. She seemed to live with a perpetual pit in her stomach, praying to whatever god was listening that it would be worth it in the end. Lying to the Kitts made her feel a whole new level of guilt, though. Constantly teetering between truth and lie, she felt like she was going to topple over the edge at any moment. She had spent her entire life not answering to anyone, doing what she needed to in order to survive. All of a sudden, there were people who cared for her, who only wanted what was best for her, and she was lying to them. What would they do if they found out?

If there was anything Ember had learned since her parents' death, it was that all love had an expiration date. This was no exception.

"Why do you call them that?" Rowan asked, breaking Ember out of her trance.

"Call them what?"

"The Kitts," Rowan replied.

Ember furrowed her brow. "That's their name, isn't it?"

"Well, yeah," Rowan shrugged. "But they're your family now, right? Why not call them that?"

"They're not my family," Ember said sternly, eyes glued to the ground. "My family is dead, and a foster placement won't change that."

Rowan took that as her sign to shut up. The girls grabbed ahold of the branches on the Echopoint and found themselves twirling through space before landing with a thud on the wet ground. Even in the light of day, the manor looked almost eerie. Shadows danced across the ground, moving back and forth like they had a mind of their own. Ember's eyes flashed upwards, to a light on in one of the top rooms, presumably a bedroom. Her heart dropped into her stomach as she grabbed Rowan's arm.

"What's that?" she whispered, like the flickering light had ears and could hear their conversation.

Rowan laughed. "It's probably just an extra security measure."

"Is it magic?" Ember asked as she squinted toward the window.

"Not at all," Rowan laughed. "Did your parents never leave lights on when you went on holiday to deter breaking and entering?"

"I don't remember." Ember shrugged. She actually couldn't remember ever going on holiday before. She had probably been on a few with her parents, but she was so young that most of those memories were hazy at best. Definitely never with any of her previous foster families. She was lucky enough to be taken to the zoo, let alone a weekend long trip. Ember shook her head.

Rowan jiggled the doorknob, and it quickly flew open, beckoning the girls inside. Both girls look warily at one another, and Ember's brow furrowed.

"It's not locked," she whispered.

Rowan shrugged. "Maybe they forgot?"

Somehow, Ember didn't think that was the answer.

The girls creeped into the house, keeping their voices low even though they knew they were alone. Better safe than sorry, right? The floorboards creaked under Ember's wet sneakers, and she left damp footprints behind her, a metaphorical trail of breadcrumbs for anyone who happened upon them. The halls were dark, and their light footsteps echoed off the tall ceilings above them. Ember could feel her heartbeat in her ears as they creeped lightly across the polished floors.

"I think it was this way," she said in a hushed voice as they weaved their way through narrow halls, wiggling locked doors and running their hands over expensive pictures hanging from the walls. It all looked the same—immaculate art hanging from pristine walls, all ancient as far as Ember could tell, intricate designs in the crown moldings, and very expensive furniture. It was so hard for Ember to picture Killian growing up here. His wild, mischievous personality just didn't seem to fit the mold of aristocratic-Northmen-descendant. But there he was, on the wall with the rest of his family, finely tailored suits, perfectly styled blond hair, and gunmetal eyes. Maybe there was more she didn't know about him, things she couldn't see from behind the picture she had painted of him.

Maybe he was more than what she thought.

Before Ember knew it, they were standing in the same study she had found the last time she was here. Dread rolled in her stomach as she inched into the room, a cold chill running down her spine. The sun shined through the window, lighting up the books lining the walls. She skimmed the bookshelf, looking for the familiar notch in the mahogany. Her finger found the small coil, and she pushed gently until she heard a quiet click. The shelf swung open, revealing the cold, dark hallway she hoped she never had to see again. She took a shaky breath and looked back at Rowan, who gave her a slight nod.

"After you." Rowan half laughed, a hint of fear on her tongue.

The girls made their way through the tunnel and into the small room at the back. Ember felt like any warmth that was present in the manor had been sucked out, and the cold threatened to sink into her bones. She wrapped her jacket tighter around her and began quickly searching for the small box she had seen before.

"Do you think they used blood magic on the box too?" Rowan whispered as she searched the other side of the room, turning over chairs and opening old trunks.

"I don't think so," Ember mumbled as she knocked against the stone wall, searching for something hollow. "The Clann said the book didn't have an owner; it was passed down to different families over time. As far as I can tell, the book doesn't belong to the Vargrs, they just have it right now." But the truth was, Ember wasn't entirely sure… about any of this. Six months ago, she had spent her days locked away in her room with her books, reading about magical places, exciting adventures, and strange creatures. Now, it was like she was living in one of her books, except she couldn't skip to the end and see how the story played out. There was no guaranteed happy ending on the last page. The lack of control over her life was unnerving.

"Look at this, Em," Rowan called excitedly from the other side of the room, eyes lit up. Ember rushed across the carpet and knelt down beside her friend, her eyes immediately landing on the small box in Rowan's hands. Her friend was bouncing on her knees with excitement as they crouched on the stone floor, and Ember's heart soared as she stared down at the box. It was old, that much she was sure of. The rune Maren had shown them was carved into the top of the wood, along with several small runes around it. The most perplexing part of the box, though, was that it didn't have hinges. There was no obvious way to open it, no locking mechanism or creases where the top and bottom connected, or a latch of any sort.

"Try and open it," Ember whispered. Rowan pulled and tugged with all her might. She even tried knocking it gently against the stone wall beside her, but it didn't budge. Ember half expected it to electrocute them or throw some sort of hex, but it made no indication that it was magical at all; just a small solid wood box, nothing special about it outwardly at all.

"It's a bleedin' fortress," Rowan mumbled as she tossed the box in front of her and sat on the floor, huffing as she crossed her arms over her chest.

"Should we just take it with us?" Ember asked as she chewed the inside of her cheek. "We can figure out how to open it later."

"No, that won't work," Rowan sighed. "A family like the Vargrs almost definitely has a locating charm on all of their possessions. They'd catch us before we even got back to the Echopoint."

"Won't they have one on the book too?" Ember asked as she furrowed her brow.

"Not likely," Rowan replied as she shook her head. "The charm is probably only on the box, so it won't translate to whatever is in the box unless they put a separate charm on the contents. Which seems highly unlikely since it doesn't seem like it opens." She huffed again as she turned the box a few more times in her hand.

Ember didn't even really know why she was surprised. From everything she had gathered so far, the Vargrs were one of the most powerful of the First Families, not to mention one of the richest. They wouldn't leave something like going out of town and possibly being robbed up to chance. Ember sighed as she picked the small box up and turned it over in her hands, feeling the roughness of the wood under the pads of her fingers. She slowly traced the carving on the top of the box and felt the familiar feeling of magic thrum through her veins, and all of a sudden, the rune started to glow. Not much, not even enough the Rowan seemed to notice, but enough to make Ember's breath catch in her chest.

She traced her fingers along the rune again, feeling the magic inside of her push and pull like the tide, and the glowing intensified. She traced again and again, back and forth, and watched the glow grow brighter and brighter. She could hear what sounded like singing echoing in her skull, but not in a language she had heard before.

Aptr til beginningrinn.

She glanced over at Rowan, who was sitting rigid on the floor, mouth hanging open and eyes wide as saucers.

"What did you do?" she whispered, eyes never leaving the scarlet glow radiating from the ancient carving.

"I don't know," Ember replied. "I just touched it, that's all. What is that song?"

"What song?" Rowan asked, brow furrowed in confusion.

"You don't hear that?" Ember asked, as she pointed a finger in the air, trying to point to where she felt like the ethereal voices were coming from.

"Em, no one's singing," Rowan said quietly.

I'm going crazy. I've lost my mind and have officially gone mad.

Her hand moved on top of the rune, and she laid her palm flat against the top of the box. She didn't know why, but she repeated the words that were being chanted in her head.

"Aptr til beginningrinn."

And as if that was the magic spell it was waiting for, Ember heard a very quiet, airy whirring, like tiny magical mechanisms were working together inside of the box, and then the lid popped open. Inside, on top of a velvet pillow, was a gothic style book, probably the oldest book Ember had ever seen. The leather was a deep onyx, broken and split in places from aging over the years, but something stuck out to Ember, something that didn't quite make sense.

The binding of this book, this book that is supposed to be

thousands of years old, looked like it has never been opened. Other than the fraying leather, nothing hinted that this book had ever been touched, let alone opened and read. The thought sent a shiver down her spine as she gently picked it up and set the box down at her feet. The lid to the box closed immediately, locking back in place.

"Well, no going back now," Rowan mumbled, urgently pushing herself off the ground. "Give me the book, and we can look at it later."

"I'll just put it in my bag, that way we don't accidentally drop it," Ember replied as she hastily stuffed it in the bag slung over her shoulder, not missing the way Rowan's brow pinched together as she nodded.

The girls put the box back where they found it and hurried back through the dark hallway, quickly closing the bookcase behind them. They creeped quietly through the twisting halls, hastily making their way to the large front door. Ember moved her hand to hold the strap of her bag when her elbow bumped into something in the dark beside her. For a moment, it was like she was watching herself in slow motion. Her head whipped around, and she watched the vase she had nudged with her elbow plummet toward the ivory tile at her feet. The fall seemed to last for ages, but Ember couldn't make her hands move. Listening to it shatter against the floor was deafening, but what happened next made her blood run cold.

Both the girls' heads shot toward the steps in front of them as they listened to the sound of a slamming door and heavy, fast footfalls heading toward the landing. Their eyes locked for a split second before they bolted toward the door, not bothering to close it as they sprinted into the pouring rain. Water streamed down Ember's face and stung her skin as she ran as fast as she could down the long drive. Mud splattered against her jeans, but all she could focus on was reaching the Echopoint and not turning around to see who was chasing them. The footsteps behind them drew closer as they slapped against the wet pavement, making Ember's heart race faster in her throat. She pushed harder as the Echopoint came into view, and her and Rowan both threw themselves at one of the low hanging branches. Ember felt herself be ripped through space and starlight, the momentum from her sprint driving the spinning, and she landed with a hard thud in the mud, her head hitting the ground below her. Adrenaline continued to pump through her veins as she stood up too quickly, looking over her arms and shaking her legs.

Nothing's broken. That's good at least.

She did her best to wipe the mud off her pants and ran her hands over the top of her head. She felt warmth on her fingers and pulled her hand away to see it stained crimson. Her heart sank as she realized she had struck her head on a rock when she landed, and the evidence was now trickling down her face.

"We need to go. NOW," Rowan said forcefully, as she grabbed Ember's arm and pulled her toward the Dark Forest looming in the distance. Ember glanced back down the road, toward Sigurvik, and sucked in a breath.

"Shouldn't we go home?" she breathed, but before Rowan could reply, they heard the familiar pop from the Echopoint and someone running not far behind them. They slipped into the tree line and huddled behind a large oak. Ember sucked in air as she braced her hands on her knees. She peaked out from behind the tree, trying to catch a glimpse of whoever was chasing them, but the rain obscured her vision, and the throbbing in her head was making her dizzy.

"There's no time. We need to split up," Rowan panted. "Knock them off course a little. Give me the book." She held her hand out expectantly, eyes wide.

Ember furrowed her brow as rain ran down her temples. She reached in her bag, fingers running along the unbroken spine of the leather tome. "Why?" she asked hesitantly, but before Rowan could reply, the footfalls grew closer. Ember sucked in a breath as she grabbed the strap of her bag.

"Never mind," Rowan breathed as she shook her head. "You go that way, and I'll go this way. Meet back here when the coast is clear."

Ember nodded, and they took off in opposite directions. She immediately regretted the decision as she descended into the darkness of the forest. Her head throbbed as blood mixed with rainwater trailed down her forehead and into her eyes. She squinted as she ran, head still spinning and disoriented from her fall, trying to force her eyes to focus in the dark that was threatening to swallow her whole. Her shoes were caked in mud, and it became harder for her to run as swiftly as she needed to. She weaved her way in and out of the forest, climbing over fallen trees and leaping over rocks.

She sucked in a breath as the ground shifted underneath her, slipping through the sludge, and she searched desperately for somewhere to hide from whoever was coming up quickly behind her. She turned to check behind her, just for a moment, and immediately found herself tumbling headfirst down a steep embankment.

Again.

She felt her body fold into a tree at the bottom, the wet bark digging into her skin. Her ears rang and vision blurred as she turned herself over, trying to push herself out of the mud. She reached forward to find something to pull herself up with when her hand met something that didn't quite fit. What she was expecting was wet mud, rocks, or a rough tree root, but what she got was soft...

Her fingers wrapped around fur, and the fur itself was attached to a giant paw. She quickly let go and moved her body back as fast as she could, making her head spin so fast she thought she was going to be sick. She craned her neck toward the giant animal in front of her and forced her eyes to focus. What she saw when they finally did made her wish she had kept her eyes closed.

Staring back at her were the same amber eyes she had seen the last time she had tumbled headfirst through the forest. She felt like she couldn't catch her breath, though whether that was the fear or a possible broken rib, she was unsure. The wolf tilted his head almost like he was studying her or deciding how many bites it would take to eat her. Ember felt like the gold in his eyes was burning holes in her skull. He slowly started moving toward her, and she edged back at the same speed, still leaning away, against the ground. Her back hit something solid when she realized he had her cornered against the side of a steep hill.

She was trapped.

He inched closer until his long snout was centimeters away from her face. His breath was hot against her freezing skin, and it sent a chill down her spine. She closed her eyes tight and focused on controlling her breathing as he sniffed where she knew blood was running down her face.

Great.

She took a deep breath and was hit with a familiar scent she couldn't quite place. It was like a new book, mixed with fresh cut grass and campfire smoke. She held her breath as he rubbed his muzzle up against the side of her head and prayed that whatever he did would be quick and painless. She opened her eyes, and for a brief moment, she could've sworn the amber and gold in his eyes sparkled. She squinted up at the animal, and something about the way he looked at her felt off. His eyes didn't feel entirely animal. They almost felt... human. Suddenly, the trees around her seemed to shake, and a voice came echoing through the leaves.

"*ENCENDAIR!*" Rowan shouted from above her. Fire licked at the wolf's paws, scorching his pristine fur, and he let out a deep growl that made Ember's heart clench. To her surprise, he took a step in front of her, creating a barrier between her and her friend, and snarled. Ember furrowed her brow as she watched him dig his paws into the mud and brace his legs.

He was trying to protect her.

Fire hit the ground in front of him again as Rowan fired another hex, and he turned his head to stare into Ember's eyes again before he turned tail and ran in the other direction, leaving Ember panting for breath and staring into the space he had been standing in moments before.

"Em! Are you okay?" Rowan called as she made her way down the steep embankment to her friend.

"I'm fine," Ember said as she stood to her feet, "but I think I dislocated my shoulder." Pain shot across her body like fire as the adrenaline started to wear off. She held her arm against her chest as pain radiated from her shoulder every time she took a breath. She was covered in giant gashes and bruises, and her mind reeled with what possible excuse she could give the Kitts this time.

Ember listened quietly for a moment, searching for any signs of the person who had been chasing them, but there were none, not even footprints in the mud. Ember shuddered, realizing they had all but vanished, and somehow, that didn't make Ember feel any better.

"Let's go this way. I think there's a clearing up ahead," Rowan whispered, as she grabbed her hand and headed further into the forest. They walked for a few minutes before they came upon the clearing Rowan had mentioned. It was a near perfect circle, several acres wide, completely devoid of trees. Even in the cold of November, the grass was vibrant and green and wildflowers were scattered about. A beautiful pond was in the middle, water rippling in the breeze.

"What is this place?" Ember breathed as she scanned the large meadow. It was stunning, completely untouched by the bitter autumn that surrounded their island. She stepped further, and the breeze felt warm against her skin, but the most notable part was the rain. Or really, the lack thereof. Even though it was still pouring as they walked through the forest, the sky was completely clear above this specific spot, like it was enchanted to do just that. The thought of who—or what—had that kind of power sent a shiver down Ember's spine.

"Let's get rid of this book so we can get out of here," she said in a hushed tone, wrapping her jacket around her body despite how warm she was now.

The girls walked into the clearing and found a large rock by the side of the pond. Ember gently set the book down on it and walked backwards, not taking her eyes off it for even a moment.

"Do you know how to destroy it?" she asked Rowan, who was standing beside her rubbing her forehead.

"Yeah, I've got a few ideas, I think," she said with a smirk. She took a few steps back and raised her hand, the curse on the tip of her lips and ready to fly off them, when they heard the sounds of branches snapping in the distance. Both the girls froze, then quickly spun around. The footsteps grew louder, and Ember could see the shape of a person running as fast as they could, right toward the opening of the clearing. Her heart rate sped up as she tried to quickly decide what to do. Running didn't seem like a good option—they would only end up further in the forest, and it was very likely they wouldn't be able to find their way out. Her defensive spells weren't great, but it was all she had right now. She darted back to the rock and quickly stuffed the book in her bag, bracing herself for the worst when the shadow broke through the tree line and into the clearing.

"EMBER!" shouted the figure, as it ran as fast as it could toward the two girls.

Ember squinted her eyes, recognizing her foster brother immediately, and let out a relieved sigh, but was immediately flooded with confusion and dread.

Oh, great.

"Fen?" she breathed. "What on earth are you doing here?"

"How did you find us here?" Rowan asked.

Fen ran up to the girls and almost collapsed when he reached them. He bent over, clutching his knees as he took in long, deep breaths. He had obviously been running for a while, maybe even all the way from home, and he was soaked head to toe in rain and mud.

"I... thought... you... were... in... trouble," he said as he choked down air.

"How did you find us?" Rowan said through narrowed eyes. He straightened himself up, finally getting a good look at his foster sister.

"What the bloody hell happened to you?" he nearly screamed.

Ember bit her bottom lip, trying to quickly come up with an excuse for her current battered state. "I just tripped, that's all." She shrugged. Fen's eyes bore holes into her, and she knew immediately he wasn't buying it.

"What on earth are you even doing out here?" he asked as he squinted his eyes at the girls.

Ember panicked. This wasn't a question she was prepared to answer. What possible explanation could she give that would be good enough? She couldn't tell him the truth—he would be devastated. But what possible reason could she give as to why they were romping through the Dark Forest alone on a Saturday afternoon?

"You didn't answer me," Rowan hissed. "How did you find us?"

Fen gave both of them a confused look. "Killian told me he thought you might be in trouble. He said he saw you running toward the forest, and he came and got me."

Killian saw them. Killian had been in the house. Killian knew they were in the house. *Killian knew.* But he didn't tell

Fen. Ember felt a cold chill run over her whole body. Something wasn't right.

"I'm fine, Fen, really. We're fine," she reassured him with a half smile. "Let's just go home." She slipped her bag over her shoulder and winced when she felt the strap press against it. The pain all over her body became very apparent as she walked toward him. She knew she had to look a mess. Her shirt and pants were ripped, and she could feel fresh blood on the side of her head and face. She was also fairly positive she had dislocated her shoulder and possibly twisted her ankle. Fen's face didn't help the hollow feeling in her chest, either.

He looked at her with such sympathy, just like she always dreamed an older brother would. He had no idea the monumental secret she had hidden away from him in her satchel. She gripped the strap tighter and looked quickly toward Rowan, who gave her a silent nod. They would have to finish what they started later, and until then, Ember had to keep the book safe and hidden.

Great. More lying.

"Mum will get you fixed up," Fen said reassuringly, as they walked toward the edge of the clearing. "You really oughta be more careful. Me and Killian won't always be around to protect you."

Ember huffed at the irony. Killian's family was the reason they even had to be sneaking around in the first place. He might seem nice enough now, but she feared what he would turn into eventually. Something as dark and deadly as the magic in the book she had swinging beside her battered hip.

FEN AND EMBER finally made it back to the house and walked quietly in the back door. Ember hesitated as she stepped up to the threshold, fear rolling like a ball in the pit of her stomach. Fen gave her a smile as he reached out his hand, and she took a breath and walked through the door. Eira was standing at the sink, busying herself with prepping dinner, when she spotted the pair. She dropped the plate she was holding, sending it crashing to the floor with a loud bang as she took in Ember and her various injuries.

"What on earth!" Her voice pierced the air as she rushed toward her. She ushered Ember over to the table situated in the corner of the kitchen and immediately began looking her over head to toe.

"I just fell. Really, I'm okay. I promise." Ember tried to smile, wincing when Eira placed her hand on her dislocated shoulder.

"Fine my a—" Fen mumbled, but quickly shut his mouth when his mother sent a dish rag flying his way.

Eira brought out her tonics, potions, and salves and quickly began applying them to the bruises and cuts. Ember drank a light green potion that tasted like watermelon and lemonade and made her mouth tingle. She felt the pain fade away from her limbs and made a mental note to ask about brewing pain potions during Herbal Magic. Eira ran her hands over her shoulder and ankle, mumbling spells and leaving a small trail of silver light along her injuries. Ember sucked in a breath as she watched the silver soak into her skin, and the injuries faded away. After finishing, Eira clasped her hands together and gave her one last once-over.

"That should do it." She smiled as Ember moved her arm back and forth, finally feeling no pain in her shoulder. "Now, what on earth were you doing to have caused that much damage?"

Ember shot Fen a panicked look—a silent plea to her foster brother to not divulge where he had found her and Rowan. "I just slipped in the mud." She smiled shyly, praying that it was a believable enough excuse.

"Em has about as much grace as a baby deer." Fen smirked.

Ember let out a relieved breath.

"Well, you really need to be more careful, love. I'm going to have to stock up on pain potions between you three at this point."

"Where did you learn all of that?" Ember asked, trying to divert the conversation in any other direction. "Do they teach healing at school?"

"Heavens, no." Eira chuckled as she began putting the bottles in their respective cabinets. "I went to university after graduating and studied under a very prominent healer. Though I only used my education for a few years after graduation, it's proved to be very valuable knowledge in motherhood as well. Now, go get some rest, and I'll send a Helio when dinner is ready."

"Thank you, Mrs. Kitt," Ember said as she stood to leave.

"No need to thank me, dear. That's what mothers are for."

Tears pricked at the corners of Ember's eyes, and she quickly wiped them away. She slowly made her way up the steps toward her bedroom at the end of the hall. Her legs felt heavy from all the running, and all she wanted to do was collapse in her bed and sleep the rest of the afternoon away. Guilt filled her chest as she heard Maeve enter the kitchen and laugh with her mother. This family had shown her more kindness than she had ever felt. Otto and Eira seemed to love her just as much as they did Fen and Maeve, and that knowledge made her heart ache.

Ember sat on the edge of her bed, pulling her bag over her shoulder and dropping it at her feet. *The Book of Shadows* slid out, and Ember reached down to grab it. She twirled it around in her hands and tossed it onto her bed with a sigh. It made the air in her room feel heavier, darker, and Ember silently wished that she had handed it over to Rowan when she had the chance. She hopped off her bed, getting on her hands and knees and crawling underneath. She shoved the book into the far corner against the wall and quickly pushed her way back out. Climbing back onto the bed and dropping her head in her hands with a heavy sigh, she felt her walls building just a little higher.

They would find out about her lies eventually, there was no doubt about it, and they would send her off to her next family. She would be moved around until she aged out of the system, and then she would be on her own. Though, that didn't sound much different than what she had been doing since she was six anyway.

No amount of love or magic could stop the inevitable. But then again, that was what the walls were for, and that was why she kept them.

CHAPTER 18
THE ROBIN AND THE WREN

Christmas had always been Ember's least favorite holiday after losing her parents. For a long time, she felt like there was nothing left to celebrate, like all of the joy of the season had been stripped away and all she was left with were hollow memories. Most years, she would get socks or sweaters from her foster families, practical things that served a purpose, not necessarily to bring her any happiness. After she had turned seven, she had come to expect that the holidays would never be the way she remembered them, filled with a warm home and singing holiday songs, and she had come to terms with it.

The halls at Heksheim were abuzz after their last class of the day, all the children chirping about how they were going to spend their winter break. Ember felt almost relieved that she wasn't going to have to force a smile through another Christmas season. She walked slowly through the corridors, admiring all of the decorations. Garland hung from the ceilings wrapped in bells and dried fruit, and candles adorned every window. Ember stopped briefly, running her hands down two wooden birds, a wren and a robin, and let out a happy sigh.

"When we plant a tree, we are encouraging the earth to breathe," Torin Lothbrok *whispered to his daughter, as they searched the snowy forest for the perfect Christmas tree. Ember's eyes lit up as they fell upon the most beautiful evergreen she had ever seen. Branches stretched outwards for the sun that was streaming in through the snow-covered canopy from every direction. It looked like something out of a storybook, and Ember felt like the princess.*

"This one, Papa!" she squealed as she ran toward the tree, which easily stood four times taller than her. She stood on her tiptoes to brush the branches with her ungloved hand. Snow fell on her nose and cheeks as two birds landed on the branches, staring thoughtfully back at the little girl.

"A wren, and a robin." He winked. "I think they agree that this is our tree, Starshine."

"Any plans for winter break?" Rowan asked in a chipper voice. She came up behind her, linking Ember's arm in hers as they made their way through the bustling crowd of students.

"Just going to catch up on some reading, I think," Ember replied with a smile. "Does your family do anything special for Christm—er, um, Yule?"

Rowan laughed under her breath and shrugged. "Nothing special. Mum wants to go to London to visit some friends— boring socialites, if you ask me—but it helps her get through the season, so I grin and bear it."

"Will your dad and brother be going?" Ember asked.

Rowan's face fell slightly. "No," she mumbled. "Just Mum and me."

Ember nodded as she adjusted the strap of her bag over her shoulder.

"Hey, why don't you let me hang on to the book over the break?" Rowan asked as they rounded a corner. "Someone is less likely to stumble across it if it's at my house."

Ember shook her head. "I think moving it around is too risky," she replied. "Besides, it's under my bed, and I can't imagine anyone will go snooping under there. We'll move it when we figure out how to get rid of it."

"Get rid of it?" Rowan asked, as she furrowed her brow. "I thought we were just getting it out of the Vargrs' house. How are we supposed to get rid of it?"

"I don't know." Ember shrugged. "But it seems like the next step, right? It can't just stay under my bed for all of eternity. If we destroy it, we don't have to worry about anyone else finding it."

Rowan took a breath as her shoulder sagged. "Yeah, I suppose you're right. We'll talk more after break."

"Hey, Em! You ready to go?" Fen's voice rang from the other end of the hall. He came running up behind them, excitement written all over his face, with Killian close at his heels.

"Yeah, sure. Are you walking Killian home or something?" Ember laughed at the two who seemed to be attached at the hip as they walked out of the school and onto the grounds. Ember noticed a medium sized suitcase that carelessly swung from Killian's hand.

"Didn't your brother tell you?" Killian smirked. "Mum and Dad are going to Scotland for the holidays, so I'll be spending Yule with you."

"You're not spending Yule with your family?" Rowan asked as she arched a brow and crossed her arms over her chest.

Killian shrugged. "They gave me the option, so I decided to stay. Scotland sounds miserable during the winter."

Ember felt her stomach drop.

Great.

"He's not my brother," she mumbled, but no one seemed to notice.

THE FARMHOUSE WAS a flurry of activity when the trio stepped into the foyer. Ember was immediately hit with the heavenly scent of orange, ginger, and cinnamon that wafted from every inch of the house. Eira could be heard from the kitchen, singing along to whatever holiday song was playing on the radio. Her voice sounded like a million songbirds, and it sent pangs of nostalgia shooting through Ember's chest. She spotted Maeve perched on her father's shoulders, hanging strings of dried fruit and beautiful decorations in the sitting room.

"Ember! Ember!" the small girl squealed as she scurried down from her father's shoulders and ran toward the teenagers. "We're going to decorate the Yule tree after supper tonight!"

"Yule tree?" Ember asked with a puzzled look on her face. "What's a Yule tree?"

"I think you know it as a 'Christmas tree,'" Killian replied with a smirk. "You do know what a Christmas tree is, don't you?"

Ember cut her eyes in his direction. "Of course I know what a Christmas tree is, you prat," she hissed under her breath. A wide grin spread across Killian's face as he picked up his bag and followed Fen up the steps and toward his room. Ember felt if she rolled her eyes any harder, they would come straight out the back of her head.

"Oh, good, you're home!" Eira chirped as she wiped her hand on the dish rag hanging from her waist. "Come in the kitchen, love. I'm about to start the gingersnaps."

Ember dropped her bag in an empty chair and quickly washed her hands before making her way to the table.

"Did you celebrate Yule with your parents?" Eira asked as she whisked flour into the bowl standing on the counter. Her voice was light and airy, like her only worry in the world was pulling the cookies out of the oven in time. Though, Ember was pretty sure Mrs. Kitt had a charm for making sure her cookies were baked perfectly.

"No." Ember shook her head as she grabbed eggs out of

the basket on the counter. "This will be my first Yule and winter solstice, actually. We always celebrated Christmas when I was little."

"We will never replace your mum and dad," Eira said softly, brushing her thumb across Ember's chin. "But I hope your first Yule will ease some of the aching I know this season must hold."

Ember nodded with a smile as she swallowed the lump that was quickly forming in her throat. Now was not the time for a walk down memory lane.

Maeve ate her dinner that evening quicker than Ember had ever seen her eat before. She shoveled potatoes in her mouth like her life depended on it, and drank her cider in two gulps.

"Maevie, it's not going anywhere." Fen laughed as he sipped his drink next to Killian.

"We have to decorate the tree!" she squealed, mouth still full of her last bite of supper. "We won't have anywhere for presents if we don't put up the tree!"

Eira leaned over with a laugh and kissed the top of her daughter's head. "Why don't you run upstairs and get the last box of decorations? I'm sure we'll be ready by the time you come down."

Maeve shoved her chair away from the table and took off toward the stairs before turning on her heels and looking back. "But, Mummy, I can't carry it by myself," she pouted. "I need help."

Ember laughed to herself and ate the last bite off her plate. "I'll come help you, Maevie. I'm finished."

Maeve squealed with excitement and shot up the stairs.

"Need a hand, Starshine? Those boxes can get heavy." Killian grinned as he leaned back in his chair.

Ember rolled her eyes as she pushed away from the table. "I think I can handle it." As much as Ember had grown to love eating together with her foster family at night, she was more than happy to get away from Killian and Fen for a few minutes. Most of the evening had been spent with them either goofing off, accidentally pulling down decorations Otto had put up, or setting a batch of cookies on fire.

Ember and Maeve wandered down to the sitting room twenty minutes later, arms piled high with boxes filled to the brim with decorations. Otto was setting up the Yule tree in the corner of the room, right in front of the giant windows, and it was the most spectacular sight Ember had ever seen. It stood nine feet tall and still didn't brush the top of the ceiling. The branches were a deep emerald that radiated warmth through the entire room. Ember breathed in the smell of evergreen, briefly allowing her mind to wander back to her last Christmas with her family.

"Never seen an evergreen before, Starshine?" Killian's voice echoed from behind Ember, quickly pulling her back to reality.

She cut her eyes at him and started to say something smart back, but decided against it. Nothing was going to ruin her very first Yule, not even Killian Vargr and his sarcasm. She made her way across the room and sat down beside Maeve and Eira on the floor, where they were busying themselves with stringing popcorn and cranberries on long pieces of twine.

"Leave some for the tree, Maevie!" Fen laughed from across the room, right as his little sister popped another piece of popcorn in her mouth with a mischievous grin. Her tiny fingers worked at warp speed stringing the decorations and very carefully snacking when her mum wasn't looking. Fen and Killian worked on wrapping lights around the large tree while Otto supervised, chuckling under his breath as the boys bickered back and forth.

"Weave them in and out of the branches, Killian," Fen huffed. "What are you doing?"

"The white lights need to be on the inside of the limbs, and the colored ones on the outside," Killian argued back.

"Why on earth would I do that?"

"Because it's *aesthetically pleasing*, Fenrir."

Ember's heart fluttered as she watched the family, and she was quite sure that the joy that spun through the air could've heated the entire house if it needed it.

After the boys agreed on placement for the lights, and popcorn and ornaments were hung beside dried fruit and cinnamon sticks, the tree was decorated, lights were lit, and boxes were being shuffled out of the room. Eira did a quick search through each box, double checking their contents, and let out a small, airy laugh as she reached the last one.

"Seems the boys forgot a couple." She smiled. "Ember, would you like to do the honors?"

"Ah, these are special," Otto whispered as he gripped her shoulder lightly, "and arguably the most important. But don't tell Maevie I said that."

Ember giggled as she reached for the ornaments and let out a small gasp when Eira placed them in her hands. There, in her palm, lay a tiny wren and a tiny robin. It was like the world stopped moving, just for a moment. Her heart beat a little faster, and if she concentrated really hard, she was certain she could hear the crunch of snow behind her, the playful voice of a man she was trying so desperately not to forget. Ember cleared her throat, determined not to get emotional over two glass birds with ribbons attached, and walked carefully over to the tree.

She placed them right above her head, both side by side, and quickly wiped away the moisture that was building in her eyes. Otto placed his hand on her shoulder and gave it a gentle squeeze as she reached up to brush her hand over the small glass birds.

"Do you know the story of the robin and the wren?" he asked softly.

Ember shook her head, eyes never leaving the ornaments that adorned the tree.

"At midwinter, the Holly King—the wren—is at his weakest." He pointed to the small bird on the right, and Ember watched as they both came to life, fluffing their wings and tilting their heads to and fro. "The Oak King—the robin—has been resting since his midsummer defeat and comes to challenge the Holly King to yet another battle. At the Winter Solstice, the Holly King is defeated."

"Defeated?" Ember asked quietly. "You mean he dies? Why does he have to die?" she asked, as she furrowed her brow.

"The Holly King must die," Otto said softly, "so the Oak King can bring back the sun."

"He shouldn't have to die," Ember mumbled. "That's a silly story."

"Aye, you're right," Otto laughed gruffly. "He shouldn't have to die. But the Holly King makes a great sacrifice for us every Winter Solstice. He gave his life, so we can grow food and rest in warmth for half the year. Imagine if he didn't? Imagine if he knew what would happen, and chose to stay put, just because he thought we needed him more? Imagine the life we would miss."

Ember chewed on her bottom lip thoughtfully. No one should have to make sacrifices like that for the greater good. Not even in a silly children's story.

"That shouldn't have to happen," she huffed.

"Sometimes we don't understand why things happen the way they do," Eira said gently. "Everything happens—"

"Please don't say 'everything happens for a reason,'" Ember whispered as she closed her eyes. She had heard it a million times since the day she was pulled out of the water when she was six years old, and it was the one thing she knew to be a bold-faced lie.

"It doesn't." Eira nodded. "Sad things happen to us, and a

lot of times, there is no rhyme or reason for it." She gently brushed the stray hair from Ember's eyes as she shifted her weight toward her. "Some of those things will be awful. Some of those things will rip the breath from your lungs and make you wonder if it's worth it to come up for air, but come up for air you must." Ember felt the woman's light grip on her shoulder and choked down a sob. "Some days, breathing will come easy, and other days, you will feel like you've been thrown into a hurricane with bricks as life preservers. Everything happens the way it's going to happen, but how you respond to it will be what sets you apart." Eira brushed her hands along the glass birds and smiled as they nuzzled her fingers. "You can hide behind walls longing for winter, or you can lay in the sun and ride the waves of grief as they come. The choice is ultimately yours. Unfair things happen, sad things happen, but that doesn't mean we have to live there."

EMBER WAS up before the sun, doing everything in her power to not leap down the steps like she was a giddy four-year-old again. She had gone shopping the week leading up to Yule, with the help of Eira and Otto, and was overly excited to give everyone their gifts. After pacing across the bedroom floor for a solid twenty minutes, she threw herself back onto her bed, trying anything to settle the excitement that was threatening to burst through her chest. After not even five minutes of pointless meditation, she heard the soft thumps of feet padding down the hall toward her bedroom.

She wasn't sure what exactly she was expecting, but it definitely wasn't an enthusiastic Fen, still dressed in his festive pajamas, barreling through the door like the house was on fire. His face was set in a wide grin, and he was practically bouncing off the walls with excitement.

"Happy Yule, Ember!" he yelled from the door. "Mum is

starting breakfast, and Dad made coffee!" And with that he was gone, shooting down the hall like lightning. Ember laughed to herself as she pushed off the bed and made her way to the closet on the other side of the room. She pulled out five presents that were neatly wrapped in plain brown paper with string tied in a bow in the middle. She wasn't sure how gift giving worked for Yule, but she knew she had to give them something. She had to try to show them how grateful she was, even if she didn't have much to give.

The smell of bacon, eggs, and fried potatoes hit her as made her way down the stairs, and her mouth instantly began to water. Laughter rang from the kitchen as Maeve squealed in excitement.

"But, Mum, I don't *want* to eat! I want to go see what Odin left under the tree!" the child whined from the other room. If Ember closed her eyes really tight, for just a moment, she was four years old again, sneaking down the stairs before the sun woke up to see what Santa had left her.

"Maevie, Odin didn't—" Fen began, as Ember walked into the kitchen with a laugh, right as Eira smacked him on the back of the head. Ember sucked in a breath as she watched her foster sister narrow her eyes at her older brother. Killian fell into a fit of giggles at the table as Maeve stood wide eyed in front of her parents. Her look of confusion quickly turned to anger as she spun around to her brother.

"He didn't what?" she hissed, arms crossed tightly over her chest.

Fen glanced over toward his parents and cleared his throat. "I mean... Odin didn't forget you," he stuttered. "Of course there are presents under the tree. Um, Mum, do you need more coffee? Let me get that for you."

Ember sipped her coffee as Maeve rushed the rest of the family to finish their breakfast. Everyone decided coffee or tea was more than enough, except for Killian who "needs a proper breakfast to start his day on the right foot, thank you very much." They made their way to the sitting room, and Maeve immediately dove into the pile of toys with her name on it. Her favorite gift, by far, was the small magic-operated draic sitting in front of the tree with a giant bow on its head. It hovered three feet off the ground, and she spent the majority of the morning zipping through the large farmhouse. Ember settled into the large chair by the fireplace and sipped on the warm coffee as she watched the Yule log burn. Despite being a guest for the holiday, Killian had a pile of presents waiting under the tree for him as well, and he tore into them almost as fast as Maeve had.

The whole room felt like it was swimming with magic. It electrified the air, accompanied with the joy and laughter that was bouncing off the walls. Eira summoned another cup of coffee from the kitchen, content to sit curled up on the couch under her knit blanket sipping the mug. Otto charmed Maeve's toy draic to fly higher than it was supposed to, and her giggles bounced off the walls as she flew across the high ceilings of the farmhouse.

"You haven't opened any of your gifts yet, Ember," Maeve said as she zipped back into the living room in front of the tree.

Ember hadn't noticed the pile of gifts under the tree, neatly wrapped in green paper. Her heart fluttered; she wasn't expecting anything, maybe socks at most, but considering the number of gifts she had waiting for her, she was willing to bet it was more than just socks.

"Honestly, I don't need anything," she whispered.

"It's quite bad manners to deny a gift, Starshine." Killian winked.

Ember rolled her eyes as she unwrapped the paper and found boxes of candy, new books, a shining pack of gold self-filling pens, and a sweater that she couldn't wait to wrap herself up in. She smiled as she slipped the sweater over her head, wrapping her arms across her chest as the soft wool brushed against her skin. Even Killian had gotten her a new book, *The History of Ellesmere Island*, which made her slightly uncomfortable, considering she didn't even think to buy him anything. He smiled widely as she flipped the book open and read the first few pages, obviously feeling accomplished in his gift-finding expedition.

Everything inside of her felt jumbled up. Every fact she had about Killian Vargr and his family pointed to darkness. Every branch of their family tree was littered with corruption. So, why should he end up any different? Even still, something didn't sit right, but Ember figured this wasn't the time nor the place to figure out what that was.

"Hmmm, it seems we're missing a present, dear," Otto said to his wife with a smug grin. Before anyone could question him, he slipped out of the room and into the kitchen. Ember heard the backdoor that led to the barn close with a click and wondered what kind of present they could be storing outside. Fen and Killian busied themselves with a new card game, and Maeve was speaking softly to her toys when Otto made his way back in the room. He carried a medium sized box with no wrapping paper on it, only a small bow. Maeve's face lit up when she saw her father and ran toward him with arms stretched out to receive the gift.

"Ah, ah, ah," he said as he shook his head. "This is Ember's."

"Mine?" Ember squeaked as she stiffened, eyes wide. "But you've already given me so much. Really, I can't accept anything else."

"You can, and you will," Eira said sternly with a smile. "Every young Vala needs one to grow up beside, and we thought it was only fitting that you received yours during your first Yule."

"One what?" Ember asked, as she stood and took the box from Otto's outstretched hands. All of a sudden, the box started to move. Ember almost dropped it before she gripped it a little tighter and sat down gently in her seat. The box was fairly heavy, and she quickly ran through every possibility of what it could be in her mind. Had she inadvertently asked for something? Did she need something for school? Were they preparing her for a career in masonry and giving her her first set of bricks? She shook her head and focused back on the box in her lap, watching it gently move every few seconds.

No, definitely not bricks.

She felt the weight of all of the eyes in the room on her as she opened the top of the box, half expecting something to jump out and latch onto her, but nothing moved. As soon as she got the box fully opened, she gingerly peered over the edge. She let out a small gasp and her mouth nearly fell to the floor. Maeve ran beside her and squealed in excitement, but Ember could barely hear her.

Sitting in the box, staring up at her with big, lavender eyes, was the tiniest draic she had ever seen.

Lavender eyes.

She hesitated briefly before lifting the small animal out of the box and laying her gently on her lap. She couldn't have been any bigger than a kitten and curled up into a little ball on the tops of Ember's thighs. She ran her hand over the tiny animal's back, and her sage and coral fur felt like velvet under her fingers. She had little horns poking out of the top of her head, and she rubbed them against Ember as she purred and clicked in her sleep under the weight of her steady hand. Ember felt her magic vibrate in her veins, and an invisible cord wrapped around her wrist and stretched out to the creature in her lap. The draic lifted her head and locked eyes with her for a moment before nuzzling further into her lap.

"This is too much," Ember whispered. "Really, you didn't have to do this."

"Nonsense," Eira dismissed with a wave. "Every young Vala needs a familiar. I saw this little one in Beast and Burden last week, and I just knew she was yours, almost like she told me herself."

Ember's eyes locked with the draic, and she could've sworn she saw her nod. She quickly swallowed the lump that was quickly building in her throat and tried to blink away the tears forming in the corners of her eyes.

"What are you gonna name her?" Maeve all but squealed, as she kneeled beside Ember's chair.

Ember thought back to stargazing with her father and the way he pointed out each and every constellation and astrological sign that was in the sky. Her heart fluttered as the draic nestled itself into her lap, and she smiled. "Maia," she whispered, running her hand along her velvet fur.

"Like the star in Taurus?" Killian asked quietly from the corner, casually leaning against the wall.

"You know constellations?" Ember asked with her brow furrowed.

"Read it in a book somewhere." He shrugged nonchalantly.

Ember arched her eyebrow. "You read?" she asked, stifling back laughter. Fen, on the other hand, didn't even bother to try and hold back his howling.

Killian winked. "I'm quite the enigma, Starshine."

Ember spent the rest of the afternoon helping Eira prepare for the Winter Solstice party they were hosting later that evening while Maia cozied herself up on a chair in the kitchen, eating bits of food that Ember handed her from the cutting board. The table was filled with a beautiful roast pig, various root vegetables, spiced crab apples, stuffing, and delicious looking sun shaped pastries that made Ember's mouth water. Maeve stood on her tiptoes on a stool as she stirred the warm, spiced drink that was simmering on the stove.

"What's that?" Ember asked, as she closed her eyes and allowed the smell of clove and cinnamon to wash over her.

"Wassail," Killian responded from behind her, stuffing a

pastry in his mouth. "Traditional Yule drink. Though, I don't think this one will have as much… kick as I would like."

He shot her a wink right as Eira walked into the kitchen and swatted at his hand. "If you boys don't stop, there won't be anything left for the guests."

"Your pastries are the best on the island." He grinned. "I just can't help myself, Mum."

Eira rolled her eyes with a laugh. "Go help Fen with the chores, and stay away from the sweets." Killian kissed her cheek and left the room, quickly plucking one more pastry from the table as he went. He was close to Eira and Otto, maybe even closer than he was with his own parents, and Eira did what she did best and made sure he felt right at home. It made Ember's heart swell and ache all at once.

Ember briefly marveled at the woman standing in front of her. Her brown hair sparkled in the sunlight that was streaming through the window as she flitted about the kitchen. She was exactly like she had always remembered her own mum—the picture of grace and joy. She thought about how comfortable Killian seemed to be in their home and secretly longed to feel that—like she was part of something. Killian wasn't her son, but he so effortlessly called her "Mum," the woman obviously had a habit of picking up strays. For just a moment, she let a sliver of hope in. Ember's chest was filled with more joy than she had felt in a long time.

Maybe this one will stick.

BY THE TIME the sun started falling, the house was packed with friends and family talking and laughing as they ate and drank. Children ran through the rooms, laughing and carrying on, leaving a trail of giggles in their wake. Ember clutched a warm mug of wassail in her hands as she sat beside Fen and Killian, Maia perched on her shoulder stealing nibbles of food, drinking in the joy that was permeating every inch of the large farmhouse.

"I bet we could sneak out the back and go for a ride through the orchards," Fen whispered. "My board is out back. They'll never know we left."

"First of all," Ember replied, "I don't even know how to ride your silly hoverboards—"

"Excuse me," Killian interjected with his hand on his chest. "Those aren't silly little hoverboards. They are charmed hoverboards. There's more magic in my AirWave than you have in your left pinkie."

Ember narrowed her eyes at him, as Maia let out a high-pitched growl. "And second of all, we can't sneak out of the party your parents have thrown with half the island present. I think you will live for one evening keeping your feet on the ground."

Both the boys let out a huff and crossed their arms, pouting like petulant toddlers. Ember breathed a small laugh as she stood from her seat.

"Can I trust you two alone while I go and get more wassail?" she asked with a condescending smirk.

"Yes, Mum," Fen hissed. "We don't need to be babysat."

Ember laughed as she made her way into the dining room, seeing both of the boys slip out the back door and into the creeping darkness. All of the food on the table was still the perfect temperature from the stasis charm Eira had set on it several hours before. She refilled her mug and inhaled the sweet notes of apple, orange, pineapple, cinnamon, and clove. The warm cider coated her throat, and she could feel the magic in it slowly seeping into her veins.

"I see you've made yourself at home," a kind voice rang from behind her.

Ember spun on her heels to see a familiar woman with long brown hair and emerald green eyes staring back at her.

271

"Thea!" she half shouted before regaining her composure. "I didn't know you would be here."

"The Kitts invited me," she replied, nodding to the sitting room where Otto and Eira were chatting happily with friends. "How has your transition been? I want to hear everything." Her eyes twinkled as they sat in a couple of chairs that were pushed up against the wall. She crossed one leg over the other sipping on her drink as she grinned,

"It's been great." Ember smiled as she shook her head. "Definitely not as bad as the Holloways."

Thea laughed as she threw her head back. "I can imagine the bar was set pretty low to begin with."

Ember grinned as she nodded. "Getting used to such an... affectionate family was difficult, but it's getting easier."

Thea gave her a sympathetic grin and squeezed her hand. "And school?" she continued. "How are you liking Heksheim? Anything exciting happening?" She leaned forward, resting her elbows on her knees as she smiled. She was reminiscent of a gossiping schoolgirl, and something about her smile made all of Ember's worries melt away.

"It's wonderful," Ember grinned. "Lots of studying and reading, nothing too exciting."

Not a complete lie.

"Well, you seem to be settling in quite wonderfully." Thea smiled as she patted Maia's nose. The baby draic cooed and clicked as she nuzzled into her hand. "I hope the transition hasn't been too difficult."

"I'm taking it one day at a time." Ember smiled back. She hesitantly traced the etchings on her pendant as she chewed on her bottom lip. "Thea, can I ask you a question?"

"Of course, love," Thea said, as she leaned back in her chair. "Ask away."

"If wearing this makes accidental magic more frequent for younger Vala," she began, as she held the necklace at her collarbone, "why would my father tell me to always keep it on?

He must've known what would happen. It's the reason no one wanted me. It's the reason I never found a home." She bit the bottom of her lip as she choked back tears, hesitantly glancing up at Thea who was smiling kindly back at her.

"You did have a home," she whispered, "and he did what he had to do to make sure you returned to it."

Ember nodded and quickly wiped away the tear sliding down her cheek. "I just wish finding my way back didn't have to be so hard," she whispered as her chest shook. Thea wrapped her in a hug, and she didn't have the energy to fight it. She sunk into the woman's comforting embrace and hugged her back. "Thank you for finding me." She smiled as she pulled away, wiping the tears off of her cheek.

Thea smiled as she squeezed her shoulder and winked. "You would've found your way back eventually. I just sped up the process." She gave Ember one more hug and stood from her chair, patting Maia on the head one last time. "Now if you'll excuse me, I see a few friends I need to say hello to. Come find me if you need me?"

Ember smiled with a nod, and Thea squeezed her shoulder before walking back into the crowd to mingle. Ember stood up from her chair and turned the corner into the sitting room to see if Fen and Killian had made their way back inside when she ran head on into what she instinctively thought was a giant bear.

Well, she wasn't entirely wrong.

"Professor Bjorn," she gasped as she baptized herself in the wassail that overflowed from her mug. "I'm so sorry. I didn't see you there."

"Not a problem," the professor chuckled. "Here, let me fix that." Before Ember could argue, Professor Bjorn waved his hand in front of her, and her soaked jumper was immediately dry and warm. Ember's jaw hung slack. No matter how much time she spent here, casual magic never became any less incredible.

"Thank you, sir," she said softly. "I didn't realize you would be here. Do you know the Kitts?" She knew the answer already, but she wanted to hear it from him.

"Ah, yes," he replied gruffly. "Went to Heksheim with both Otto and Eira. They've been doing these parties since we graduated, though everyone seems to need a lot less sober up potion the next day." Professor Bjorn's eyes twinkled as he talked, and for a brief moment, he reminded her of her father.

"And my dad?" she asked, before she could convince herself not to. "Did he ever come?"

"Your dad was the life of all of our parties," the professor laughed. "Never would miss a chance to be the center of attention. One year, we had far too much whiskey, and he wanted to go outside and——" Professor Bjorn stopped short. Ember's eyes were as wide as saucers as he cleared his throat. "Your dad never missed the chance to have fun. He really was a great mate."

Ember's chest felt hollow as she imagined her dad as a teenager running around the island with his friends without a care in the world. If he had known what was going to happen, would he have stayed? Could their life have been like this the whole time? She chewed on the side of her lip as she mulled over an emotion she hadn't felt toward her parents in a long time.

Anger.

She could've—should've—had a childhood filled with magic and happiness. She could've grown up with Rowan and Fen on the island, spending her days exploring the beaches with her parents. Instead, she was stuck with foster families who couldn't care less about her or even worse, families that were scared of her. What did she ever do to deserve this? A hollow childhood spent searching for the missing pieces of who she was supposed to be.

"I hope you've thought about what we talked about last,"

Professor Bjorn said quietly. "I know you're searching for answers, but you won't find them in that book."

Ember furrowed her brow.

Answers? She didn't want answers. She had stopped searching for answers a long time ago. She just wanted her brother to be safe.

Foster brother. Right.

"Of course, Professor." She smiled. "I'll leave it alone."

Professor Bjorn nodded and headed back toward Otto and Eira, who were busy entertaining their many friends. Ember carefully slipped out the back door and into the yard. The brisk December wind blew softly, sending goosebumps up her arms. She breathed in the faint smell of salt in the air, a smell that seemed to permeate the entire island, mixed with the smoke rising from the chimney. Killian and Fen's laughter carried to the back door, and she could barely make out the shape of them flying through the orchard. For the first time in forever, peace trumped every other emotion that was swirling through her chest.

Maybe this one will stick.

CHAPTER 19

HOW TO DESTROY ITEMS INFUSED WITH DARK MAGIC 101

E mber spent a large majority of her winter holiday curled up with her new books in the library of the farmhouse, with a hot cup of tea by her side. Maia made herself comfortable in her lap and dozed on and off as Ember absentmindedly rubbed the back of her head. The boys could be heard faintly in the orchard, laughing and carrying on as they spent their days in the cold sun. When the noise from Killian and Fen grew louder, Maia popped her head up and scampered toward the window, resting on the windowsill to look outside. She purred and clicked as her tiny claws tapped against the glass and looked back at Ember.

"I suppose we should go get some fresh air." Ember laughed as she closed her book and set it on the table next to her. Maia clicked and purred some more as she scurried back to the chair and up onto the redhead's shoulder.

Despite the sun beating down on her, Ember shivered as she stepped outside into the cold winter air. In the distance, she could see the boys flying back and forth through the trees of the orchard, laughing without a care in the world. She felt the heaviness in her chest bear down on her. Even with Killian all but moving in during winter break, Yule had done a wonderful job of distracting her from the book that lay hidden under her bed, but with the holidays behind her, the looming weight of what she still had to do was beginning to wear on her. Couple that with the continuous lie she had to carry on with Fen, and she felt like she might implode at any minute.

"Finally make your way out of your burrow, Starshine?" Killian taunted from three feet in the air.

"At least I'm learning something instead of wasting all of my time on a stupid hoverboard," she sneered. If Killian was offended, he didn't show it. His calm composure grated on Ember's every nerve like nothing she had ever experienced. Nothing seemed to faze him. With every stab she made, he just smiled more, like his sole purpose in life was to torment her to the point of exhaustion.

"Hey, Em!" Fen shouted from behind him. "Come ride with us!"

"Absolutely not," Ember replied, shaking her head so furiously that Maia almost fell off her shoulder.

"Come on, Starshine." Killian smirked. "Live a little, why don't ya."

"That's exactly my point," she replied crossly. "I want to continue living. I don't have a death wish today."

Killian rolled his eyes dramatically. "You're not going to die. Stop being a baby, and just get on the board." He motioned toward Fen, who was all but ready to jump out of his skin with anticipation.

Ember narrowed her eyes but decided quickly that she would never hear the end of this from either of them if she didn't try. Secretly, though, she had always wondered what flying felt like.

This was simply to shut them up, nothing more.

"Fine," she huffed. "But just for a minute. And I am not doing those dumb flips you keep doing."

Fen's face lit up as he hopped off his board and ran toward her. Maia leaped off her shoulder and quickly curled herself in a ball under one of the apple trees, watching intently as Ember steadied herself on the death trap.

"These straps will keep you from slipping off," Fen said as he buckled the leather tightly around Ember's feet and ankles. "Keep your weight mostly on your back leg, and use your arms for balance."

Ember nodded gently, afraid that any sudden movement might send her toppling over.

"The board won't flip up unless you actively do it. It's charmed to stay upright unless the rider performs the correct movements to flip it. To go, shift your weight briefly to the front. To slow down or stop, lean backwards. To turn, just shift your weight on your right or left leg. Got it?"

"Uh... yeah, yeah, I think so." She nodded. Fen let go of the board, and it gently hovered about three feet in the air. She stiffened, arms stretched out to either side to balance herself as she took slow, steady breaths. Ember felt her heart beating in her throat as the low buzzing began to drown out Killian's fit of giggles. She took a deep breath, shifted her weight forward, and zipped upwards into the air.

She snapped her eyes shut and felt all of the breath had been completely sucked out of her lungs as she flew through the trees of the orchard. Her arms instinctively went out as she steadied herself on the board, doing her best to keep herself right-side-up despite Fen's assurance that she wouldn't actually topple to her death. After she managed to shift the board to fly straight, she slowly opened her eyes and gasped quietly as she took in the view around her.

It was stunning. The grass below her pulled and swayed in the breeze like an emerald ocean rippling in the wind. The grin on Ember's face widened as she spotted Fen and Killian underneath her, jumping up and down waving furiously.

"Brilliant," she whispered, as she closed her eyes, drinking in the sensation of the wind against her face. She slowed the pace of the board and used her newfound bravery to unstrap her feet from their straps, straddling the board, both feet dangling to the sides as she wrapped her fingers around the edges at the front. She could stay up here forever, completely content with the idea of remaining in the air for the rest of her life. It was like every worry she had stayed on the ground, and for just a moment, she felt free.

Free from grief. Free from the book. Free from doubt. Free from the future, a future that still felt so out of reach.

Free from herself.

"Enjoying the fresh air, Starshine?" Killian chirped from beside her.

Well, that was nice while it lasted.

Killian coasted through the air next to her, stopping abruptly to unstrap his feet and sit on his board as it hovered above the trees.

"Have you made it your mission in life to make me as miserable as possible?" Ember sneered as she shifted her weight to steady herself.

"You figured me out." Killian smirked. "I wake up every morning and think, 'What can I do to ruin Ember's life today?'"

She was certain her eyes couldn't roll back any further if she tried.

"What do you want, Killian?"

"Your brother wanted me to make sure you were okay. Couldn't see much from the ground."

"Foster brother," she mumbled, "and I'm fine. I don't need a babysitter."

"Of course you don't," he drawled. "Tell me, isn't it exhausting acting like you have it together all the time?"

"I've never pretended to have it all together," she hissed. "Isn't it exhausting pretending like you're Odin's gift to earth?"

"Oh, Starshine." He smirked as he ran his fingers through his messy silver hair. "If there's one thing I don't do, it's pretend to be something I'm not. Like you on this board, for instance."

"What's that supposed to mean?" Ember snapped as she narrowed her eyes.

"I only mean balancing and going two kilometers per hour is great and all, but you're not a true AirWave rider until you've bested a veteran in a race."

Somehow, Ember's eyes rolled further back than they ever had before.

"Shove off, Killian," she huffed as she stood back up and strapped her feet in. "I've got better things to do than further feed your inflated ego."

"Oh, Starshine." He grinned. "You have quite a lot to learn about me."

Before she could reply, he strapped himself back on the board and put his hand on his hips, narrowing his eyes toward the horizon. A small smirk played across his face as he looked down at Ember and raised his brow.

"Come on." He thrusted his chin toward the horizon. "One race to the coast and back, then I'll leave you alone."

"You're insufferable, you know that, right?"

Killian shrugged. "Some say insufferable. I like to say charming."

Ember stood on her board and strapped her feet back in, steadying herself as she took a breath. "If I do this, then will you leave me alone?"

"Probably not." He grinned. "But it's worth a shot, isn't it?"

Before Ember could argue, he sped away in the other direction, and she let out a huff before leaning forward on her board after him. The wind bit at her cheeks as she sped through the air, a blur of white and black weaving in and out of her line of sight.

"Killian!" she yelled, but he didn't answer. The blur of white moved further away, further toward the shore that was becoming clearer in her vision. She narrowed her eyes and plucked up every ounce of courage she could muster before leaning forward on the board and tearing after him. She curled her freezing fingers around the edge of the AirWave and crouched lower as she approached him. By the time she sped past him, she could feel the salt from the waves licking at her eyelashes and the water coating her hands. Leaning back gently, she slowed to a stop and turned toward the boy with a huge grin.

"You were saying?" She smirked as she swept auburn strands from in front of her eyes.

Killian slowed down beside her and let out a huff as he crossed his arms. "It's seems you've bested me." He shrugged. "I guess we know who to expect at tryouts next year."

Ember narrowed her eyes in his direction. "You let me win. Why did you let me win?"

"Seemed like you needed a win." He unstrapped his feet and straddled the board, motioning for her to do the same.

Ember breathed a laugh as she sat down, feeling the waves brush the tips of her trainers. "I suppose you're right." She smiled, leaning back on her hands and feeling the sun warm her nose. "But you don't have to go so easy on me."

Killian shrugged as he rested his elbow on his bent knee. "Seeing you smile again is a win in my book."

Ember felt her cheeks flush as she fidgeted on her board. Of all of the versions of Killian Vargr that lived in her head, charming wasn't one of them. Annoying? Maybe. But charming? She was seeing a whole new side of the cocky boy, and she didn't know what to do with it. Her stomach fluttered involuntarily as she shook her head.

"Best be getting back. Wouldn't want to worry Fen," she said as she stood back up. She steadied herself on the board and reached down to strap her shoes back in, but her right foot slipped and sent her crashing into the waves below.

The water felt like a robe of ice draped over her already

freezing skin, and the salt burned her lungs as she fought the current to reach the surface. She felt her magic tug at her chest, pulsing like it was sending out a distress signal as she frantically swam in the direction of the tugging at her sternum. All of a sudden, large hands wrapped around her arm and yanked her toward the surface and out of the water. She gasped for breath as she clung to the edge of the AirWave she was now draped over and coughed up the remaining water that had settled in her lungs.

"Honestly, Starshine, if my presence is that bothersome, you can just tell me." Killian half laughed as he sucked in air, but worry was etched all over his porcelain skin.

Despite her best effort, Ember laughed and rolled over, sitting herself back up as she wrung the water out of her hair. She rubbed at the spot on her chest where she had felt the tug of her magic and shook her head. "And you're still going to sit there and tell me I won fair and square?" She smirked.

Killian hopped gracefully back to his board and strapped his feet back in before holding out his hand to help her up. He smirked as she steadied herself, and she could feel his eyes boring holes into her as she found her balance again.

"Like I said, Starshine, I was the real winner, in every sense of the word."

Before she could respond, he was gone, flying back toward the orchard where Fen waited for them. Ember made her way back to the rows of trees and lowered the nose of the board slowly until she reached the ground. Fen helped her unstrap her feet, and she hopped off the salt-soaked board.

Back to reality.

Fen's face dropped as his eyes met hers. "You're soaked." He turned to Killian and pointed a finger. "What the bloody hell did you do, Vargr?"

Killian lifted both hands in defense and laughed. "She fancied a swim, and who am I to deny her such simple pleasures?"

Ember rolled her eyes as Fen turned back to her and assessed her for any permanent wounds. "I'm fine, Fen, really. Just a little wet."

He let out a small laugh and nodded. "So, did you love it?" he all but squealed.

"It was great," she replied with a smile, but guilt began creeping into her chest again as he stared at her expectantly. It was getting harder and harder to meet his gaze. Every time she looked at him, every time he smiled without a care in the world, the heaviness of her lies settled deeper into her chest. He cared for her. He thought of her just like he did Maeve, like a sister, and she was keeping a secret from him that could potentially upend every life on the island. She didn't know how much longer she could keep up this act.

"Are you okay, Em?" he asked as he furrowed his brow.

"I'm fine." She shrugged with a half-hearted smile. His brow furrowed further in disbelief. "Really, Fen, I'm fine, just need to change into some dry clothes."

She handed the board back to him, and Maia jumped on her shoulder, nuzzling into her neck. Rowan was due back to the island tonight, and if she was quick, they could meet in town tomorrow. Her thoughts drifted back to the book lying under her bed. She had no idea what they were going to do with the book, but maybe they could figure it out together.

ROWAN AGREED to meet the next morning, a few days before the end of their winter break, which was how Ember found herself standing outside of The Bookwyrm before the sun had even fully filled the sky.

"Why does December have to be so bloody cold," she mumbled to herself as she rubbed her hands together and blew into her palms. The day they learned warming charms couldn't come fast enough because, quite frankly, this weather was for the birds.

"Miss me?" Rowan chirped as she skipped up to the front of the store.

"I still can't believe you left me alone with those two eejits for an entire month," Ember huffed.

"Come on now, it couldn't have been that bad." Rowan laughed as she opened the door to the quaint bookshop.

"I was going to have to force feed them both sleeping droughts if I had to listen to one more conversation about the difference between the Airwave and the Solar Rider."

The bell at the top of the door let out a quiet ding as they stepped inside, and they were immediately greeted by the quiet shop owner at the front of the store.

"Good morning, Miss Lothbrok, Miss O'Rourke. Can I help you find something?"

"No thanks, Nessa." Rowan smiled. "Just got some homework to finish up."

Nessa smiled at the girls as they made their way to the back of the store, weaving in and out of the tall cases packed to the brim with every magical book imaginable. They headed to the section named *Charms, Hexes, and Jinxes* and dropped their bags at the nearest table.

"Why can't we just give the book to the Kitts or Professor Bjorn?" Ember asked as she followed her friend through the aisles. "I bet they would know what to do with it."

"If we give it to an adult, that still leaves room for the Vargrs or Ellingboes to get their hands on it," Rowan replied as she pulled a book from the shelf and looked it over before shaking her head and putting it back in place. "And that could put them in danger. Plus, they would know we took it, and we would be in a world of trouble. It's best to just take care of it ourselves, save the island the trouble of someone else getting their hands on it."

"I'm just ready for it to be gone," Ember sighed as she

shook her head. "It makes my room feel so... gloomy." She shuddered as she thought back to the darkness that seemed to radiate from under her bed as she took a breath.

"Why don't I just keep it at my place for a bit?" Rowan asked as she ran her fingers along the spine of the books piled across the shelves. "We can switch back in a couple of weeks, mix it up a little."

Ember shook her head with a laugh. "It's fine, really. Best to just keep it hidden away for now till we figure out what to do."

Rowan sighed as she crossed her arms. "Couldn't we have just looked through our Galdr textbook?" she asked quietly, as her eyes scanned the spines of the books, trying to decide which one to start with.

"They don't bother to teach first years warming charms, so do you really think there's going to be a section entitled *How to Destroy Items Infused with Dark Magic 101?*"

Rowan shrugged. "I suppose," she sighed.

They spent the better half of the morning combing through all of the texts they could get through, everything from harmless jinxes to the darkest curses the small shop had to offer.

"What about this one?" Ember asked, pointing to the image that was projected over the page.

"That would take at least six months to prepare, see?" Rowan said as she ran her finger over the hovering image, making it scroll to the next section. "You have to brew reducing potion to pair with the incantation. Do you want to keep the book under your bed for the next six months?"

Ember sighed as she shook her head in reply.

"I also have no idea where we would get"—Rowan squinted at the bottom of the image—"one quarter inch of vampire fang."

Ember shuddered and flipped the pages of the book. There had to be something else. Anything else. "How are these not illegal?" she asked as she flipped through a much darker book, filled with curses that made her blood run cold.

"Chief Thornsten has outlawed a lot of them," Rowan replied without looking up. "Like that one." She pointed to a particularly gruesome picture of a man laid out on the ground with hundreds with deep gashes and puncture wounds littering his body, blood pouring from all of them. "Cast that particular curse, and the Guard would be on you before the last syllable fell off your tongue."

"The Guard?" Ember squinted.

Rowan nodded as she leaned her face on her hand. "Vala police."

"This is hopeless," Ember huffed as she slammed the book closed and laid her head on her arms on the table.

"We don't even know that the book can be destroyed," Rowan mumbled. "Maybe we should just focus on finding somewhere to hide it, out of sight out of mind."

"That completely defeats the purpose of stealing it in the first place," Ember replied crossly as she furrowed her brow. "If we weren't going to try and get rid of it permanently, we could've just left it for the Vargrs."

"I'm just trying to look at the bigger picture, Em," Rowan huffed. "You can't destroy dark magic. It just isn't possible."

"Anything is possible. We're just not looking in the right places." Ember shook her head as she sat up straight and grabbed another book from their pile. "Go see if we can order one. Maybe there's some obscure book about spells we haven't thought about."

Rowan rolled her eyes as she stood up. "So bossy," she laughed. "Yeah, I'll go ask Nessa." She walked away from the table.

Ember stood up with a sigh and started gathering all of the books on the table and putting them on their respective shelves. "Ow!" she mumbled, as her hip slammed into the corner of the table, sending one of the texts falling open on the floor with a dull thud. Ember rubbed her hip, assuming there was already a purple bruise forming underneath her jeans, and bent over to pick up the book that was splayed open on the ground. The pages were yellowed and worn, and the spine looked like it had been cracked several hundred times. She couldn't remember when she had pulled this specific text from the shelves, and she knew she hadn't seen Rowan carry it over. Had it been there when they arrived? Ember couldn't remember what state the table was even in when they had quickly dropped their bags and ran to the shelves, but she was almost certain it had been entirely empty.

She shrugged and picked the book up, turning it over a few times in her hands.

Wildlings of Ellesmere Island
by T.L.

SHE TURNED it over again to read the back when a small piece of paper fluttered to the floor from inside the pages. Ember hesitated before bending over to pick it up. It was a small picture, roughly the size of a business card. Her thumb brushed the edge of the tiny image, and it immediately sprung to life. The image, now more like a video, danced above the small piece of paper the same way her textbooks did. But that wasn't what caused Ember's breath to hitch in her chest.

Floating in front of her, inches from her face, were her parents dancing on the beach. They couldn't have been older than twenty, and Ember was sure she had never seen them more in love than in that very moment. She sucked in her breath, begging the tears not to run down her cheeks as she watched them sway back and forth, the waves lapping against their heels. Her mother's long brown hair blew in the breeze, and her smile could've lit up a thousand different ballrooms at once. Her father's messy hair fell in his eyes and freckles covered his face, a small detail she had almost completely forgotten about him. If she focused really hard, she could almost hear his barking laughter echoing around her. They were close enough to touch, but still a million years away.

Grief washed over her like a tsunami.

She brushed her thumb over the piece of paper again, banishing the image back inside, and quickly stuffed it in her bag, along with the book that had been holding it. She wiped the moisture from her cheeks and took a deep, shaky breath before slowly making her way back to the front of the store.

"I put in an order for another book, so it should be here tomorrow," Rowan chirped, as Ember walked up behind her. "It's ridiculous that they can't just summon the book we need, if you ask me. The island is so far behind with magical technology. Ready to go?"

Ember nodded her head silently, trying to conjure up some semblance of a smile so she didn't alarm her friend. She had more questions now than ever before, and doubt slowly began creeping into her head, threatening to swallow her whole.

But in her bag, nestled between books, she had a puzzle piece. A small picture that held the memory of her parents and who they were before. Before they left the island. Before responsibility and adulthood fully engulfed them. Before her. Before they were taken away a thousand years too soon. A tiny piece to the puzzle that she had been trying to complete for years, a living memory of their magical lives. Warmth pushed its way into her chest, and a tiny flicker of hope ignited inside her.

Tonight, this was enough.

CHAPTER 20
WILDLINGS OF ELLESMERE ISLAND

W hy Ember had volunteered to go pick up Rowan's order from The Bookwyrm, she had no idea. At the time, it had seemed like a perfectly acceptable thought. She could pick up the book and maybe ask Nessa about the one she had found on the floor the day before. But when she woke up that morning to a Helio from Rowan, letting her know the order was ready, she began to deeply regret her life choices. The sun was barely rising on the horizon, and it was all she could do to open her eyes fully.

She had spent the entire night before combing through her father's journal, looking for any clue as to how they could permanently get rid of the book. She couldn't believe what Rowan said, that it couldn't be destroyed. There had to be a way. She scoured the Kitts' library, reading through every line twice to make sure she didn't miss anything, and came up empty every time. Before she realized it, the clock by her bed read four in the morning, and she could see the beginning of the sun creeping over the horizon out her window.

Her head pounded as she made her way down the steps a few hours later. She never fared well when she didn't get enough sleep, and today didn't seem to be any different. Otto was at his usual seat, sipping his coffee and reading the morning paper while Eira bustled around the kitchen getting breakfast ready. Ember's tea was already sitting at the table in front of the chair that at some point had become hers, and she slumped into the seat. She nursed the warm drink, praying desperately that it would alleviate the pressure that was steadily building behind her eyes.

"Good morning, love," Eira chirped softly. "Put some pepper up potion in your tea, I hope you don't mind." Ember watched the gold potion swirl together with the amber in the tea and silently thanked the gods for Eira Kitt.

"Rough night, Em?" Fen said as he stomped his muddy boots on the mat outside of the mudroom door.

"What?"

"Heard you up all night going in and out of the library. Figured you were getting a jump start on homework or something."

"Oh, right, yeah." Ember nodded. "Time just got away from me, I suppose."

Ember spent the rest of breakfast picking at the sausage and tomatoes on her plate, counting down the minutes till she knew The Bookwyrm would be open. The voices around her droned in and out, and she was unable to focus on anything other than the tasks at hand:

1. Pick up the book Rowan had ordered.
2. Come back home and take a long nap.
3. Make it to Fen's Rukr game later that evening.

She took another sip of her tea as she rubbed her eyes and yawned.

Ugh. The game.

She might just have to settle for several pepper up potions and an early bedtime tonight. She sipped her tea and grimaced as Fen scraped his fork across his plate. It sounded like nails on a chalkboard rattling through her head, sending the steady throbbing deeper behind her eyes. Honestly, did all boys have to be so loud?

"Any plans for today, Ember?" Otto asked as he glanced over the top of his paper.

"I have to run into town and pick up a book for Rowan," she replied, taking a small bite of her breakfast.

"You'll be at the game tonight, right?" Fen asked as he finished off the last of the tomatoes on his plate.

"Wouldn't miss it." Ember smiled. And it was true. Not only because she felt like she owed Fen the support, due to all the lying she was having to do recently, but she was beginning to fall in love with Rukr. After her afternoon of flying with Killian, she had spent what little free time she had doing what she did best—researching every aspect of the game that she could find. The different charms that were used were fascinating, and she found herself wanting to know more and more about it. She even secretly priced out a board for herself, just to ride around the island, but if Killian ever asked, she would deny it until her dying breath.

"Do you need Fen to go with you?" Eira asked from the kitchen.

"Oh, no," Ember replied quickly. "It shouldn't take me long. Thank you for breakfast, Mrs. Kitt."

Ember pushed her chair under the table and carried her dishes to the sink, relishing in the silence that followed her into the empty room. She leaned her elbow against the sink, and stared out at chickens pecking away on the brown grass. Her lies were stifling, piling on top of one another and threatening to swallow her whole. Loneliness had begun to creep in like a shadow, filling all of the cracks and crevices and pushing her further from the wholeness she so desperately yearned for. But walls meant safety, and safety was her top priority right now, even if she stood behind them alone.

What an odd feeling, to feel so alone in a house so full of love.

Ember was really getting sick of the cold.

The wind bit at her cheeks as she stepped out the door of the terminal, and she silently cursed at Rowan under her breath. Not only was she sleep deprived and still nursing a migraine, but now she was freezing.

Brilliant.

The Saturday morning crowd was already starting to flood the streets. Excited chatter filled the air as everyone prepared to get their shopping done. Fishermen headed to the docks, mums chased their toddlers down the cobblestones, and charmed brooms swept the stoops of opening shops. The Bookwyrm finally came into view, and Ember quickened her pace, desperate for the warmth waiting on the other side of the crimson door. The door opened with a quiet ding as she slipped inside, shaking the cold from her hand and fingers.

"Miss Lothbrok, what a pleasure to see you again." Nessa beamed from the front of the store, carefully levitating a book to the top of the shelf in front of her. She almost shined in the sunlight coming through the window, gold and amber hues swirling through her skin. She tucked a strand of platinum hair behind her pointed ear and gave Ember a bright smile.

"Good morning, Nessa." Ember smiled. "I'm picking up a book Rowan ordered. She's busy this morning."

"Oh, of course!" Nessa chirped as she scurried toward the front of the store and began rummaging behind the counter. "Ah, yes." She grunted as she lifted the tome to the top of the counter. "Arrived just a few minutes before you did."

"Thanks, Nessa," Ember said as she lifted the book into her arms. She twirled it in her hands as the gold lettering glittered in the streams of early morning light pouring through the windows.

The Bloodlord's Grimoire of Dark Magic

EMBER SHUDDERED as she slipped it into her bag; something told her this wouldn't be a light read. She waved to Nessa and turned to walk back into the biting December wind. Her hand reached the doorknob before she paused, biting her lip, and turned to face the girl behind the counter.

"Did you put that book on our table the other day?" Ember blurted.

Nessa glanced around at the full shelves. "You're going to have to be a bit more specific I'm afraid," she laughed.

"The, um, the book, um…" she mumbled as she rummaged through her bag. She pulled the worn book out and held it up to read the title. *"Wildlings of Ellesmere Island."*

"Oh, yes, *that* book," Nessa smirked as she leaned against the counter. "Seemed like something you might fancy."

Ember swallowed the lump that was building in her throat. "Did you know him? My dad?"

"I did." She nodded. "Torin was kind to my people; he treated us as equals. I owe him quite a few life debts."

"Your people?" Ember asked hesitantly.

Nessa gestured to her pointed ears, now flicking back and forth, and giggled. "Elf."

"Oh, right, of course," Ember stuttered. "And he wrote this?" she asked, though she already knew the answer, his name adorned on the cover.

"He did." Nessa nodded as she smiled. "He was always writing in that journal of his, so I can't say I was shocked when he wrote a few books of his own." She laughed to herself as she continued sorting through stock of books on the counter, placing some on carts to her right to wheel through the store.

"You said he helped you?" Ember asked as she dropped

the book back in her bag and leaned against the counter. "What did he help you with?" She was suddenly hungry for information, craving any crumb she could get.

"My parents died when I was a child," she breathed. A sympathetic smile tugged at her mouth. "They worked in town, owned a small clock shop, and after they passed, I wasn't welcome back in Elfheim."

"Elfheim?" Ember asked as she furrowed her brow.

Nessa nodded. "There are two gates in the Dark Forest, one that leads to the Fae territory, and one that leads to Elfheim." She flipped a few books over and quickly read the backs before sticking them in the pile to her right and leaned her arms against the counter. "The Fae typically come and go as they please. Several have shops in town or conduct business here. Chief Thornsten keeps a close eye on them, but for the most part, they have their freedoms." She took a breath as she tapped her fingers on the counter in front of her. "Elves are very guarded. They rarely leave Elfheim, they keep their families and businesses far away from the Vala, and they shun anyone who chooses to walk away from their beliefs."

"So, your family was shunned for having a business in town?" Ember asked as she chewed on her lip. "And they wouldn't even let you come home after you lost your parents? You were only a child; you couldn't control the decision they made."

Nessa shrugged as she sighed. "They took it very personally. When the Vala settled on Ellesmere, they didn't just take the Fae's land or enslave the Merrow, they took our land too. They slaughtered our people, so now, they stay hidden and banish anyone who might feel differently." Nessa shook her head as she took a breath, and Ember felt like she was going to be sick.

This island that she had fallen in love with, this place that was beginning to feel more like home than Galway ever did, was not only brimming with magic...

It was covered in blood.

"I'm so sorry," was all Ember could think to say. "Losing your parents is hard, but having nowhere to go makes it even worse." She swallowed the lump building in her throat as she thought about her own childhood and how familiar she was with that kind of grief.

"Your father took me in." Nessa smiled as she tucked a stray piece of hair behind her pointed ear. "He let me stay in his spare room, taught me to read and write, even helped me open this shop and move into the apartment upstairs after he married your mum." Nessa looked around the bookshop, her eyes glistening with unshed tears as she turned back to Ember. "Your father was a good man, and I wish I could repay him for the kindness he showed to me."

Ember's heart ached as her breath hitched in her throat. She didn't think it was possible to miss her parents any more than she already did, but hearing stories about their lives on the island sent her plummeting into the depths of grief all over again every time. She took a shuddering breath as she adjusted the strap on her shoulder and gave Nessa a weak smile. "I should probably be getting back home," she said as she turned to head back to the door. "Thank you for the books." She smiled. "Thank you for everything."

Ember rummaged through her bag, pulling *The Bloodlord's Grimoire of Dark Magic* out, and clutched it tightly against her chest. She was almost completely over the threshold when she heard Nessa call after her.

"Miss Lothbrok?" she said in a kind voice. "I do hope you find what you're looking for."

Ember gave her a small nod and a smile, then slipped out the door into the busy street. She walked quickly in the direction of the terminal, flipping the book around in her hands and flipping through the first few pages, desperate to find a way to distract herself from the cold sinking into her bones. She tucked her head down, trying to walk a straight line while she dug through her bag to check and make sure the small picture was there from yesterday, when all of a sudden, she ran into someone twice her size, landing with a hard thud on the cobblestones. She shook her head as she gripped at the ground to stand back up. Above her was a tall man in a dark suit... with very familiar platinum hair.

"Oh, um, I'm so sorry, Mr...." She stuttered.

"Vargr," he said dryly, reaching down to pick up the book that had fallen from her arms.

Vargr. Great. Of course he is.

"Right, um..." She swallowed. "Mr. Vargr. I'm so sorry. I didn't see you there."

His steel gray eyes bore into hers, like he could read every terrified thought that flitted through her mind. His face was perfectly chiseled, much like Killian's, and the suit jacket he wore stretched around his broad shoulders. He was the picture of aristocratic elegance.

It made Ember nauseous.

He twirled the book in his hand, taking note of the title, as well as the small piece of tape with Ember's name written neatly on the front.

"Lothbrok," he sneered. "You must be the Kitts' newest stray."

Ember winced. No niceties from him, apparently. She bit the inside of her cheek as she felt the hollowness in her chest grow. Was that what people thought of her? That she was just some pitiful orphan? She bit down harder and tasted copper on her tongue. "Ember," she said firmly. "My name is Ember."

If he had heard her, he didn't let on.

"I'm sorry for running into you, Mr. Vargr," she continued. "Thank you." She reached her hand out, waiting for him to give the book back to her, but instead, he continued to twirl it in his hand, studying the cover like there was going to be a test.

"What does a young Vala, such as yourself, need a book like this for?" he drawled, cutting his eyes at her.

"It's for school," she replied, as she furrowed her brow. "Some extra studying material."

"So much like your father," he sneered. "Always sticking his nose where it didn't belong."

Something told Ember that wasn't supposed to be a compliment. Gray eyes met hers again as he straightened his arm, handing the book back to her.

"I would watch yourself, Miss Lothbrok," he hissed under his breath. "You are playing a very dangerous game without so much as a glimpse into the rule book. If you're not careful, you might meet the same sticky end as him."

Ember snatched the book out of his hand and took off toward the terminal, refusing to stop until she was safely in the building. She gasped for breath as she ran inside, tears stinging her eyes as she searched for the door that would take her home. She barreled through the waiting door and slammed it shut behind her. Without checking to see if anyone was home, she hurled herself up the steps, down the hall, and into her bedroom, locking the door behind her. She curled into a ball on her bed, doing her best to silence the sobbing gasps that escaped her mouth.

She couldn't do this anymore. This had to end. She couldn't walk around any longer lying to Fen and his family and jumping at the sight of men in town. It had grown too big, too fast, and she couldn't do anything to stop it.

They had to find a way to destroy this book.

EMBER SLEPT for the remainder of the afternoon and probably would have slept even longer if she hadn't already promised Fen she would be at his game. After deciding she had stared at the ceiling long enough, she heaved her legs over the side of her bed and walked toward the mirror hanging on her wall. Her eyes were still red, but not nearly as puffy, and the panic attack that had threatened to consume her had all but disappeared while she slept, leaving only small pangs of guilt flitting through her chest. She quickly brushed through her hair and threw it into a braid, securing it on the end with a maroon ribbon before putting her contacts back in. She put on her warmest coat, hoping someone at the stadium would know a warming charm, and set off down the steps.

"Oh, good, you're up," Eira said with a smile as she rounded the corner with a basket of clean laundry on her hip. "Are you feeling better?"

"Much better, thank you." Ember smiled. "Is Fen still here?"

"He had to head to the game early," Eira replied, shaking her head. "Can I make you a quick bite before you go?"

"Oh, no," Ember mumbled. "Not really hungry." She was worried her appetite was permanently gone after her run in with Mr. Vargr that morning. She found herself unable to focus on anything. She had one thing on her mind—get to the game and talk to Rowan. Nothing else mattered right now.

Eira stared at her intently for a moment, like she was trying to read between the lines of the vague answers Ember was clinging to. "Is everything alright, love?" she asked quietly.

"Just fine," Ember said with a forced smile.

Eira nodded with a raised eyebrow. "Well, if there's anything you need to talk about, you can always come to me," she said quietly.

"T-thank you," Ember stuttered.

"No thanks needed," Eira smiled. "That's what family is for."

Ember nodded as she bit the inside of her cheek.

Family.

THE CROWD WAS FILING onto the school grounds when Ember dropped from the Echopoint. Everyone was wearing their team colors, decked out in navy and yellow, as well as maroon and silver. The air was filled with laughter as friends walked arm in arm down the winding path toward the stadium, chattering on about life and school and their predictions on the game.

"You made it!" Rowan's voice sounded out from her seat, as Ember made her way up the mountain of stairs in the stands. She was out of breath by the time she made it to the seat Rowan had saved for her and sat down with a huff. "Everything alright?" Rowan asked as she narrowed her eyes.

Ember started to reply, but just as she was about to divulge everything that had transpired over the morning, the whole stadium erupted into a cacophony of applause and cheers as the two teams made their way onto the field. The crowd roared as the players shot into the air, screaming cheers that mixed in the air around them. Ember tried to focus on the players flying through the air, searching for Fen in the sea of maroon and navy. As her eyes cut across the field, he caught a glimpse of white zipping through the air.

Killian.

"Did you hear me?"

Ember's head snapped around to Rowan. "What?"

"Did you get the book?"

"Oh, right, yeah." She nodded as she reached into the bag at her feet.

"Perfect." Rowan grinned as she started flipping through the pages. "Did you get a chance to look through it?"

"Oh, no, not yet. Busy morning." Ember shook her head as she stared onto the field, neither paying attention nor really caring about what was happening or what was eliciting the boos coming from the crowd.

"Okay, give it up," Rowan said, as she snapped the book shut.

"Give what up?" Ember replied.

"Whatever you've got running around in your head that's making you so mopey." She said it playfully, but Ember could hear the concern in her voice.

"Oh, um, I had a bit of a run in with Mr. Vargr this morning," Ember said quietly, twiddling her thumbs in her lap.

"Killian's *dad*, Mr. Vargr?" Rowan asked, as she raised her brow. "What happened?"

Ember shook her head. Did anything actually happen? Or had her anxiety concocted some insane story in her head that had her convinced her life was in danger?

"Nothing really," she mumbled. "But he saw the book. It fell out of my arms when I ran into him."

"Wait, you actually ran into him?" She laughed.

Ember lifted up her hand in reply, showing her the gash running toward her wrist.

"I'm sure it was nothing," Rowan said as she patted her friend's leg. "He's an adult. They don't notice most things, even when they're right under their noses."

"Maybe." Ember shrugged as she watched Fen fly in front of them, swinging his caman in the air and whacking one of the balls, sending it flying toward their opponents, another team within the school. Her heart sank as she thought about his unwavering trust in her, and bile rose in her throat. "But we need to get rid of this book. I don't know how much longer I can keep lying."

Rowan nodded. "I'll take this home and start looking it over." She shoved the book quickly into her backpack that was lying beside her. "I can swing by and get the..." She lowered her voice as she flitted her eyes around and whispered, "*The Book of Shadows*, if you want to switch out."

Ember rolled her eyes. "I really think we need to leave it

where it is. Let's just focus on finding out if we can destroy it. We'll worry about moving it when we have a plan."

Rowan nodded with a sigh.

Ember leaned back on the wooden bleacher and stuffed her hands in her coat pockets. For the first time in a long time, she wished she was back in Galway, closed up in a bedroom with only her books for company. It was lonely, but lonely was all she had ever known. After having a taste of what family felt like, just to feel it slip away from her, she wished she could go back to the ignorance she'd had before.

This was her chance to salvage the relationships she was desperately clinging to. Her chance to create a normal life.

This had to work.

CHAPTER 21
IRISH WEREWOLVES AND BROKEN PROMISES

"**O**h no. Oh no, no, no, no, no," Fen mumbled as he shuffled the papers around in his hand and began digging furiously through his backpack.

"What are you going on about?" Ember turned around in her seat. It was their first day back after winter break, and Fen was somehow already behind in class. Being back at Heksheim raised her spirits a few degrees, though the looming knowledge of the book under her bed and what she still had to figure out sat in the back of her mind, like a kettle threatening to boil over.

"My paper on the Chimera," Fen huffed. "I swear I put it in my bag last night. Did you grab it?"

"You know"—she smirked—"if you focused a little more on school and a little less on flying, you might be a bit more prepared."

"Where's your better half, Fenrir?" Rowan asked as she slid into the seat beside Ember. "Think he got lost in that giant mansion of his getting ready this morning?" The girls giggled to themselves as the door at the top of the spiral staircase closed, and Professor Bjorn made his way toward the front of the room.

"Welcome back, class!" his voice boomed. "I trust you all had a relaxing holiday. Please have your paper on the Chimera out on your desk so I can collect them."

Papers rustled as students pulled their homework out of their bags and laid them quickly on the desks in front of them. Fen groaned audibly and laid his head on his desk instead. All at once, every paper flew up and toward the front of the room, landing in a neat pile on Professor Bjorn's desk. He quickly ran his eyes over the stack of papers before turning back to address the class.

"For anyone who might still be stuck in a holiday rut..." His eyes flitted to Fen. "Bring your paper tomorrow and it won't count against your final grade." He turned and traced the air, while the board behind him lit up. "Now, please turn to page two hundred and fifteen."

Ember laughed as she heard Fen let out a quiet breath of relief as they opened their textbooks. Right as she was about to turn the page, the classroom door flew open, and each head turned to see who had decided to enter the room so dramatically. Ember whipped her head around, just in time to see Killian slink into the room and take his seat silently beside Fen.

All of the arrogance and conceit was missing from his stony eyes, replaced by an emptiness Ember didn't recognize in him. His normally perfect silver hair was a mess on his head, and she could see a purple and blue bruise starting to bloom on his angular chin. His cheeks were hollow, and the shadows under his eyes became shockingly prominent against his porcelain skin. His clothes were disheveled and dirty, looking almost like he had slept in them the night before, and he smelled like a mixture of sweat and something Ember couldn't quite place. Whiskey?

No, certainly not.

He fixed his eyes to his desk, not looking up or around,

even after Fen prodded him for answers about where he had been.

"Glad you could join us, Mr. Vargr," Professor Bjorn said with a confused look. "As I was saying, class, please turn to page two hundred and fifteen."

Books opened and pages were shuffled as Ember turned back down to her already opened textbook, eying the page curiously. She laid her hand briefly on the page, and it sprang to life. Her breath caught in her chest momentarily as she stared at the large animal in front of her.

"Irish werewolves," the professor announced from the front of the room, conjuring the image of a large gray wolf beside him. The image startled Ember. The way it turned its head, looking around the room, like it was intently watching its prey, made him look almost alive. His eyes flitted about the room, and his ears flicked back and forth. Something about him made Ember uneasy, like she had seen him before. The hairs on the back of her neck stood up as her eyes met the glowing form, and a shiver ran down her spine.

"Now," Professor Bjorn continued, "who can tell me about the Irish werewolf?"

Odette Quinn's hand flew up the air. "A werewolf is a man who has been bitten by another werewolf. He turns once a month during the full moon."

"Aye, that would be correct for their British brethren," Professor Bjorn said with a smirk, "but that is not the case for the Irish werewolf." The projection of the wolf beside him began to stalk the aisles of the room slowly, eyes moving up and down the rows of students. "The Irish werewolf cannot be turned. He simply is."

"He simply is? So, it's a wolf?" Fen asked.

"No," the professor replied. "Not a wolf."

"How do they become werewolves?" one of the students asked from the back of the room.

"As you all know," he began, "a British werewolf is turned

by being bitten by another while it is in wolf form during a full moon. An Irish werewolf is a magical genetic trait, something that is passed down to them through their family tree. He isn't infected by lycanthropy, and he can't infect others."

"So, it's a Transmutant?" Rowan asked with a raised brow.

"Of sorts." The professor nodded. "Irish werewolves are more shapeshifters than anything. They are the guardians of children, wounded men, and lost persons. According to some legend, the Irish werewolves were even recruited by kings and chiefs during times of war, though that last bit is debatable by scholars. It is said that they come from Ossory, or modern-day Kilkenny, and have spread across Ireland since."

"Guardians?" Ember asked. "So, they're good?"

"Aye, they are." The professor smirked. "Though they are mighty protective. Getting on the wrong side of a werewolf is a bad idea, no matter what continent you're on."

"So, how do you tell the difference? Between an Irish werewolf and just a regular wolf?"

"The biggest difference between a werewolf and a real wolf is their eyes," he said, as the wolf rounded a corner. "An Irish werewolf has amber eyes with a distinct human likeness to them."

Ember felt her breath catch in her throat. Memories of the white wolf from the forest flooded her mind as the gray spectral strutted toward her. Memories of amber swirling with gold lingering on her, eyes that felt so human she could've sworn the animal was merely just wearing a costume. She shuddered as she remembered the way he had just stood there, unmoving as she dripped with blood at his feet. He hadn't flinched, hadn't moved a muscle when he could have killed her, ripped her to shreds without another thought. But it was just a wolf. Of course it was just a wolf.

Right?

The image of the gray wolf stalked toward her, amber

eyes locked with hers, and then it vanished. Ember jumped when she heard the professor's voice boom across the room, pulling her out of her daydream and back to reality.

"Before class tomorrow, I'll expect you all to finish this chapter and list out all of the differences between English werewolves, Irish werewolves, and natural wolves. Class dismissed."

Chairs scraped against the floor as children hurried toward their next class. The room quickly emptied as Ember stuffed her textbook into her bag, and she turned to talk to Fen and Killian. Before she could get a word out, Killian had flown from his chair and walked toward the door, not saying a word to anyone.

"What's wrong with him?" Rowan scoffed as she slung her bag across her back.

"He hasn't said a word since he got here." Fen shrugged. "Wouldn't even look at me after he sat down."

The trio made their way through the hall and into Galdr where Professor Walsh stood waiting in the middle of the wooden stage. Ember turned to head toward their normal seats and saw Killian already sitting, hands clasped together on top of the table and looking straight ahead. They took their seats, and Ember could hear Fen whispering quietly to his friend.

"Everything alright, mate?" he asked under his breath, but Killian didn't reply. He kept his eyes to the front of the class and didn't flinch when Fen sighed heavily, slamming his textbook onto the desk.

"That will be quite enough of that, Mr. Kitt," the professor said sternly.

Fen mumbled an apology and sank down a little further in his seat.

"You'll have no need for those actually," she said as she pointed to the books littered across the desks. "Today will be a practical lesson. Up on your feet."

Chairs scratched the stone floor as students stood up. As soon as every student was standing, Professor Walsh flicked her wrist, and the desks and chairs immediately vanished. The wooden stage she stood on flattened to the floor, leaving the room completely open. Lines appeared across the ground, dividing the room in half.

"I will pair you up," she sounded. "One of you will go to the left side of the room, and the other to the right. Mr. Vargr, you and Miss Lothbrok will be partners today."

Ember's face fell. Of all people, why Killian? She begrudgingly went to stand by him, his face still steadfast and trained toward the middle of the room.

"So," Ember muttered, "left or right?" She stood there a moment, waiting for him to reply, but his jaw didn't even twitch. "Right then," she huffed. "I'll take the left, I suppose."

Students filed to either side of the room, standing parallel to their partners on the other side. Professor Walsh walked up and down the middle, speaking loud enough for all of them to hear clearly.

"Today, we're working on shielding spells," she announced. "It is arguably the most useful spell to have in your arsenal. Every Vala is only as good as their strongest spell, and this one must be one of your strongest." She stopped her pacing in the middle of the room. "You will take turns practicing your shielding spells while your partner works to disarm your magic. You will work to disarm only. I won't be having any bloodshed today. Mr. Maguire, come to the center of the room please."

Ember watched as Flynn Maguire walked slowly toward the professor, hands visibly shaking. He stood six feet from her, hands crossed in front of his waist while he waited on instruction.

"Mr. Maguire, if you will, do your best to disarm me." She wasn't quite sure, but Ember was certain she had seen a playful smirk play at the corner of Professor Walsh's mouth.

307

Flynn held out his hand and let out a quiet, *"Detenair,"* and a stream of purple light shot across the room toward the waiting professor.

As quick as she blinked, Professor Walsh lifted her arm straight in front of her, fist closed, and then opened it quickly shouting, *"Protejer."* All of a sudden, blue light streamed from her hand, creating a wall of rippling light in. The disarming spell bounced off the shield, dissipating in the air around her in a shower of light. Gasps rang out around the room as the professor lowered her arm and turned back to the wide-eyed students. "You may begin," she announced and walked to the back of the room toward her desk.

Ember turned to face Killian, his eyes fixed on the window hanging above her head. Spells were being thrown around them, students attempting to disarm their opponents, but Killian never moved. Too far away to ask him if he would prefer to disarm or defend, and seeing as he had yet to move, she decided to make the decision for him.

"Detenair," she shouted, and the stream of purple light shot across the room, straight toward Killian and his disheveled shirt.

His hand shot up in a closed fist, and he quietly mumbled, *"Protejer,"* under his breath, meeting her eyes for only a moment before they flitted past her head again. He quickly shot the disarming spell back at her before she was ready, and she found herself flat on her back, her dominant hand tingling, like someone had pressed pause on the magic in her briefly. She sat up with a grunt, narrowing her eyes toward him and shot her spell back at him, which he quickly blocked and immediately sent one to her. She winced as she felt a sting on her arm and looked down to see a tiny stream of blood trickling down her elbow.

"You will disarm only, Mr. Vargr. Do not make me say it again," Professor Walsh snapped at him, but if he heard her,

Ember couldn't tell. His gaze stayed fixed to that same spot above her head, unmoving.

They did this dance for what felt like hours before Professor Walsh dismissed the class for lunch. Ember walked past Killian, toward Fen and Rowan waiting at the other side of the room. She flung her bag over her shoulder when a hand appeared in front of her with a small cloth.

"Sorry 'bout that," Killian mumbled, still not looking her in the eye. Without saying anything else, he turned and headed into the corridor.

"This is getting ridiculous," Rowan said as she rolled her eyes. "Why does he have to be so dramatic?"

"Are you alright, Em?" Fen asked as he inspected her arm.

She pressed the cloth to her skin and gave him a small smile. "I'm fine," she replied. "Just a small scratch, it's nothing."

THE TRIO MADE their way through the crowded hall and down to the dining hall, which was already packed with students eagerly eating their lunch. They found their seats at their normal table and were all equally as shocked to see Killian already there, stuffing his face with shepherd's pie.

"How kind of you to grace us with your presence, Lord Vargr," Rowan said in a mocking tone as she sat in the chair opposite of him. "Whatever have we done to deserve the pleasure?"

"Shove off, Rowan," Fen grumbled as he sat beside his friend.

"Come off it, Killian," she pushed. "What's your deal? You can't just sit there and ignore us all day."

"It's nothing," he mumbled, startling Fen slightly.

"Doesn't seem like nothing," Rowan prodded. "If you ask me, it seems like a whole lotta somethin'."

Killian let out a deep sigh and ran his fingers through his already disheveled hair, the first bit of real emotion he had shown since he walked into Zoomancy that morning.

"You can talk to us, mate," Fen said quietly as he nudged his friend's elbow.

"Just got into it with my dad last night," Killian mumbled into his food.

"He give you that?" Rowan asked stoically, pointing to the bruise blooming on his chin.

Killian nodded, running his fingers briefly over the purple and blue.

"What pissed him off this time?" Fen asked as he narrowed his eyes.

Killian let out another sigh. "They came home from holiday a few days ago. When I got home last night, Dad was in his study. He came out ranting and raving about being robbed, tearing the whole house apart lookin' for whatever he'd lost. Being as I was the only one still on the island while they were away, I guess he assumed I had come home to steal it." He stabbed his fork hard into his food. "Messed me up real good while he interrogated me about it. It doesn't even make sense. Why would I go over to the house while they're away just to steal some bleedin' book from his study?"

Bloody hell.

Fen's glare cut into her like daggers as he turned toward Ember, and she felt like all of the breath had been sucked from her chest. The book was gone because she and Rowan had taken it, something Fen had told them not to do for this very reason. And now his best friend was sitting in front of him, innocent of the charges his father had thrust upon him, battered and bruised. The weight of his gaze was tangible, like the metal from the fork that was digging into her fingers. She shot him an apologetic look, but he cut his gaze away from her. His eyes were cold and unmoving, but she watched his throat bob, like he was choking down tears.

All of a sudden, she wasn't very hungry.

Lunch was mostly silent between the four. Fen refused to look at Ember or Rowan, keeping his eyes locked on the food on his plate that he kept moving around with his spoon. The weight of what they had done sat heavy on Ember's chest like a sack of bricks as she struggled to breathe. She had never been so thankful when lunch was over and they could go to their next class. At least sitting quietly in there wouldn't feel nearly this terrible. She hurried up the steps with Rowan by her side whispering into her ear.

"Let me take the book, seriously," she hissed as they rounded a corner. "Your brother is going to be a jerk about it, and it'll be easier if it's just out of your house." The girls rounded another corner and walked briskly toward the door of their class. "I can just take it to my house and then we can—"

"Stop!" Ember hissed as she grabbed her friend's arm. "We're not moving the damn book, so will you just drop it?" Her heart was beating in her throat, and her voice shook as she talked. She was angry at herself, scared of losing Fen, and she was taking it out on Rowan now. Even with that knowledge in the back of her mind, she couldn't stop the harsh words from rolling off her tongue. "You think you know what's best because you've lived here longer than me, but you *don't*, Rowan. Everything is falling apart, and the last thing I need is for something to happen to that book, then this would all be for nothing." Her chest shuddered as she bit her lip. "Just leave it alone, for Odin's sake. You're not helping."

Rowan narrowed her eyes and sucked in a breath. She yanked her arm out of her friend's grip and shoved past her, flinging the classroom door open with a thud as she walked through. Ember ran her hand down her face and sighed as she tried to slow her breath.

"Ro, wait, I'm sorry," she said as she walked toward the door. She was about to step over the threshold into History of the Gods when she felt fingers wrap around her arm and yank her to the side.

"What did you do?" Fen hissed as he all but pinned her against the wall.

"We had to, Fen," she whispered. "We had to get the book. We didn't have a choice!" While she believed the words she said, she knew in her bones it didn't matter.

"You made a promise, Ember!"

She winced when she heard her given name roll off his tongue, like it was some sort of slur coming out of her foster brother's mouth.

"You gave me your word, and you lied to me! Now, look what happened!" Anger and fear mixed together in his eyes, and Ember felt like she would crumble under the weight of his gaze.

"We didn't have a choice," she pleaded, softening her tone. "You have to understand, I wouldn't have done it if I thought there was any other way."

"You always have a choice," he hissed, "but no matter what the consequence, you never betray your family." His words felt like knives repeatedly being driven into her chest.

She couldn't think. She couldn't breathe. All she wanted to do was turn back time and never go after that bloody book that was ruining everything.

He straightened his back and stepped away from her. "Pride," he spat. "It will cost you everything and leave you with nothing." Without waiting for a reply, he turned around and walked into the room, leaving her leaning against the wall as the hallway emptied, hands trembling against her side.

There was fire in his voice. Like everyone else, she learned that fire burned, but she never expected it to feel so cold.

CHAPTER 22
A THIEF IN THE NIGHT

E mber felt like she was suffocating. Now that Fen knew what she had done, there was no hiding from it. It was out in the open on display, and his silence on the matter was deafening. Rowan wasn't speaking to her after their fight in the hall, and the walls she had built were threatening to close in on her, taking any semblance of hope she had with them. To make matters worse, Fen wasn't being subtle about any of it in the least. He wore a perpetual sneer these days, and anyone with eyes could see that it was directed toward Ember.

Supper that evening was no different. Ember sat in her seat, picking at the potatoes and ham on her plate, trying to listen to Maeve go on about her adventures in the pasture that morning. She forced laughter and eye contact, doing her best to act normal, but Fen made no such effort. His eyes were glued to his plate, and a permanent frown painted his mouth. Eira's voice was light and cheerful, but her eyes told a different story.

"Fenrir," Eira said calmly. "How are you doing with balancing school and Rukr?"

"Fine," he grumbled with a shrug.

"And your grades aren't slipping?"

"Guess not," he replied, eyes still stuck to the table.

Ember saw Eira's eyes narrow for a moment and then she turned to look at her.

"So, Ember," she asked. "How are your classes going? I know Professor Orion has a tendency to assign mountains of homework."

Ember gave a weak smile. "It's going fine. Fen is great about helping me with the things I don't quite understand." She gave him a sideways glance, hoping this invisible olive branch would be enough.

It wasn't.

"Well, that's very thoughtful of you, Fen. Family has to stick together," Eira said as her eyes flitted between the two teenagers.

Fen scoffed, shrugged his shoulders, and mumbled something unintelligible, and that was apparently the last straw.

Supper was over, and everyone took their plates to the sink. Maeve ran off to play, and Otto took his usual seat in the living room with his book. Ember turned to head upstairs, content with locking herself away in her room for the foreseeable future, but Eira stopped her.

"Sit," she said sternly at the two teenagers and pointed back to the kitchen table. They took seats opposite of each other, Fen still refusing to look her in the eye. Ember twiddled her thumbs on the table, preparing herself for the lecture she knew was coming.

"Now, does someone want to tell me what exactly is going on?" Eira asked as she took the seat at the head of the table.

Neither of the teenagers spoke; they just kept their eyes trained down. Ember bit the inside of her cheek, waiting for Fen to expose her and everything she had done. Waiting for him to give the Kitt matriarch any reason at all to throw her out of their home and never look back.

"It's nothing, Mum," he mumbled in reply.

"It doesn't seem like nothing," she replied. "Nothing doesn't cause family to act the way you two have been acting."

"What is that phrase?" Fen snapped. "I have the right to remain silent?"

Ember rolled her eyes and mumbled, "You have the *right* to remain silent, what you lack is the *capacity*."

Fen narrowed his eyes at her, the first time their eyes had met in days, and his gaze cut like glass.

"That will be quite enough of that," Eira scolded. "What has gotten into the two of you?"

Fen glared at Ember for a moment longer before turning his head back toward the table. "Nothing, Mum."

"You are family," Eira scolded the teenagers, "and family doesn't treat each other like this."

Ember felt her heart sink, and anger began to take the place of the guilt that was festering in her chest.

"My family is *dead*," she whispered. "This is not my home, and I do not have a family." She looked up briefly, and after seeing Fen's face, she immediately regretted her words, but there was no going back now.

Fen looked like he had been punched square in the chest. His face dropped, and his eyes widened, tears glistening in the corners. He cleared his throat and narrowed his eyes, apparently determined to not show any emotion whatsoever.

"Ember," Eira said softly, "you will always have a home here."

"My home was in Galway," she snapped, unable to stop herself. "My home was a cottage on the edge of town with my mum and dad. My family. I won't be here long enough to ever call this place home."

Ember expected Eira to raise her voice or scold her for acting like a petulant toddler, but instead, her voice was kind, soft, and steady. She wasn't angry, though she probably should be.

"Oh, love." She smiled sadly. "Home is so much more

than where you were born or the building you happen to live in. Home is…" She paused, trying to think of the words that were obviously heavy on her heart. "Home is running through a garden filled with vegetables that you planted the summer before. Home is muddy feet galloping across a freshly scrubbed kitchen floor with beams of sunlight piercing through the window." She laughed quietly to herself as she glanced into the kitchen. "Home is hushed laughter under the glow of a full moon, far past your bedtime. Home is family. And sometimes…" She glanced back at the teenagers, her face becoming serious. "Home has to be fought for. But I'll let you in on a little secret." She leaned on the table and gave them a soft smile. "Sometimes, the most important things in the world require a little bit of a fight."

Ember felt like the floor was going to fall out from under her feet at any second. She wanted to reach across the table and apologize to Fen. Apologize for breaking his trust and driving this wedge between them, but her body wouldn't move. Because while she was so busy building the walls that the Kitts were trying so desperately to tear down, Fen was constructing some of his own. Brick by brick, forged from every lie that came out of Ember's mouth. Every time she tiptoed around him, every time she twisted the truth. This was her fault, her own doing, and she couldn't really blame him for the betrayal in his eyes.

She would lose them, just like she lost everyone. She accepted that the night she snuck into the manor and stole that godsforsaken book.

"I have some homework to do. Thank you for supper, Mrs. Kitt," she whispered as she pushed her chair out and hurried toward the steps. She couldn't change what had already happened, but she could fix it. She could fix all of it. She just had to get rid of the book. If she could get rid of it for good, that would fix everything.

Right?

After quietly locking her bedroom door, Ember slid under her bed and snatched *The Book of Shadows* from the corner she had stuffed it in, pulling it back out with her. It felt like darkness seeped from its unopened pages as she held it in her hands, and her mood began to turn sour. She shook her head as she laid it down and rummaged through her bag, pulling out her dad's journal as well as her own. With her arms piled high and Maia on her shoulder, she snuck across the hall into the library, locking the door behind her. She sat in the comfy chair she had grown so accustomed to and laid all the books out in front of her. Maia hopped into her lap, curling herself into a tight ball on her thigh as she ran her fingers over her father's older journal and felt a steady lump growing in her throat.

"I'm trying, Papa," she whispered. "I don't know how to do this without you, but I'm trying." She opened the leather cover and began reading through the pages, jotting down notes in her own journal as she went.

She spent the rest of the night reading through almost every book in the library. She cross-referenced things she read with notes and research she had put in her own journal, as well as her father's. Her frustration grew as the moon creeped up in the sky, casting an otherworldly glow on the rug below her feet. How could she have learned so much, but still somehow managed to not learn anything at all? Not anything of importance, at least. She sighed in frustration as she pinched the bridge of the nose, feeling a headache threatening to break through.

Deciding that everyone was probably asleep and she had earned a break, she laid Maia's sleeping form on the rug, stuffed *The Book of Shadows* under a pile of other books, wrapped a blanket around her shoulders, and quietly creeped down the steps for a glass of water and something for her head.

Did Vala use acetaminophen?

The whole house was dark; the only thing lighting her way across the cold floor was the light from the moon shining through the windows. She stepped lightly into the kitchen and made her way to the sink, filling up a glass of water and gulping it down like her insides were on fire. The grass outside of the window swayed in the midnight breeze, like water rippling across a giant lake. The stars were bright, brighter than she had seen in a long time, and she was pulled back to nights with her father, standing under the moon and drinking them in.

Stars didn't look the same anymore. Not without him. They left a bitter taste in her mouth.

After washing her glass and putting it away, she quietly creeped back up the steps and made her way down the long hall to the library. She stopped in her tracks and her breath caught in her chest as she heard the window in her bedroom scratch against the wood, and the distinct sound of footsteps creaking across the worn floorboards. Ember's heart beat rapidly in her throat as she inched closer, listening to the thuds that sounded as her belongings hit the floor on the other side of the door. She reached for the door handle as she stepped on a very creaky board and held her breath as the movement from her room stopped, followed by quick footsteps and then silence. Ember threw her bedroom door open, and her throat went dry as she looked around the room.

Everything had been torn from her shelves. Books lay open on the floor where they were dropped, her clothes were scattered across her dresser, hanging carelessly out of their drawers. Her closet door was wide open, and all of its contents were thrown outside of it in piles, and her bedroom window was wide open.

The breeze from the open window sent a chill down Ember's spine as she quickly walked over and slammed it shut, peering out into the darkness to try and catch a glimpse of the intruder. She took a shaky breath as she flicked the lock and closed her eyes. Whoever was there was long gone. She turned around to start picking up her things off the floor when her eyes landed on her bed.

Everything that was under her bed was now lying beside it. Empty bags, her old suitcase, clothes she had kicked under when she was too busy to pick them up—everything was open like it had been rifled through. Ember's heart beat rapidly as she thought about *The Book of Shadows* that was tucked away in the locked library with Maia. Had someone come looking for it? Her stomach dropped. Even if they weren't looking for the book specifically, they had come dangerously close to finding it.

She quickly ran across the hall, unlocked the door, startling Maia awake, and yanked up both journals and *The Book of Shadows*. She found an empty box in the corner and slipped the dark tome inside of it, snapping the lock shut and stuffing it in a corner she was praying no one would look in. She checked that the large windows and the door to the hallway was locked, then took a shuddering breath as she climbed back into the oversized chair. She wrapped herself up in the blanket and clutched her father's journal to her chest as her eyes finally grew heavy and dread settled deep in her stomach. Fen knew what she had done. Someone had broken into her room and almost found the book. She had snapped at Rowan, and now they weren't speaking. The walls felt like they were slowly closing in on her, and it was stifling.

She was running out of time.

CHAPTER 23

THE BEST LAID PLANS OFTEN GO AWRY

E mber squinted her eyes as light poured through the
library window. Her head was throbbing again,
which seemed to be more normal than she would like
these days. She straightened herself up in the chair, and Maia
purred and clicked under her arm as she rubbed her eyes,
willing the aching behind them to stop. What time was it? The
sun was high in the sky, and the house was eerily quiet for a
weekday morning. She hurried herself across the hall and
quickly threw on clean school clothes, making sure Maia was
content for the day before stuffing the spell book in her bag
and making her way quickly to the kitchen.

Fen was nowhere to be seen, which Ember didn't mind at
all. His negative presence was becoming overwhelming. She
was almost looking forward to having a meal without his attitude looming over her. But the absence of her foster brother
wasn't what puzzled her this morning. It was the absence of
everyone else, and it left a sinking feeling in her stomach.

The kitchen was empty, no breakfast was cooking or tea
boiling. Maeve couldn't be heard giggling from the table, and
Eira wasn't standing by the stove humming to herself. It was

unnerving. Her stomach did a flip as she walked through the house, checking for signs of the family, but there were none.

She really needed to get a watch.

"Oh, good, you're up, love," Eira said as she came in through the back door. "I was starting to worry. Your tea is on the table if you'd like some."

Ember furrowed her brow and glanced at the steaming mug on the table. It obviously had a stasis charm on it. How long had she slept?

"Where is everyone?" Ember asked as she walked to the table to grab the mug.

"Maeve is just outside taking care of the hens. Fen left early for school this morning."

"This morning?" she choked. "What time is it?"

"Almost noon," Eira replied. "I already called the dean. It seemed like you needed a lie in."

Ember chewed on the inside of her lip. Even after everything she had said last night, the horrible way she had talked to Eira, she still made the choice to look out for her and put her best interest first, even if that meant missing school. Her heart simultaneously swelled and ached.

"Thank you, Mrs. Kitt," she said quietly. "I think I'll go try and make the last half of the day. I don't want to get behind with Professor Orion."

Eira smiled. "I think that's a fine idea." And before Ember could turn to leave, Eira walked up to her and kissed her gently on the head. "Have a good day, love."

EMBER QUIETLY SLIPPED into her seat in History of the Gods beside Rowan and pulled out her textbook, waiting for the rest of the students to file into the near empty room. Her friend's eyes were trained down at the table, studying the grains of wood, and she didn't so much as glance up. Ember sighed as she twiddled her thumbs on the table.

"Ro, can we talk?" she whispered, but Rowan didn't reply. Her jaw tensed as she tapped her finger on the table.

"Rowan, please," Ember whispered as she reached over and grabbed her friend's hand. "I'm sorry I snapped at you. I was just stressed about Fen. Please talk to me."

Rowan's face fell as she glanced at Ember, and a small smile pulled at the corner of her lips.

"Forgive me?" Ember asked as she squeezed her hand.

"I suppose so," Rowan breathed with a smile, as she relaxed in her seat. "So, any luck with your brother?"

Ember stiffened. "Foster brother," she murmured. "He still isn't speaking to me, can't say I blame him, though."

"He's being a prat," Rowan said as she rolled her eyes before giving Ember a reassuring smile. "He'll come around, just give it time. Let him sleep on it for a few nights."

Sleep.

Ember's head popped up as she remembered what had happened the night before. She flexed her hands a few times as she glanced around the room. "I completely forgot. Something happened last night," she whispered as she leaned toward her friend, resting her elbows on the desk.

"Oooh, gossip," Rowan grinned. "Do tell."

Ember shook her head with a laugh, but before she could continue, the classroom door opened and students began pouring in, Killian and Fen taking their seats behind the girls.

Rowan huffed as the room was flooded with students, and Professor Orion made his way to the front of the room, shuffling papers as he sat at his desk.

"We'll go down by the waterfall during our free period," she whispered. "We can talk there."

Ember's brow furrowed. "Waterfall?"

The encounter with her foster brother in class was just as uncomfortable as Ember thought it would be. Fen didn't so much as look up when he walked in the room and took his seat behind them.

"You couldn't even bother to wake her up?" Rowan snapped at him as they sat down.

His eyes briefly flitted up at her, stone cold and closed off. "Do I look like her keeper?"

Ember rolled her eyes as she turned in her seat. He really was dead set on holding this grudge forever, it seemed.

Class seemed to last forever as Ember sat at her desk and spun her pen around her finger, not bothering to try and soak in any of the information that Professor Orion was rapidly firing at them. Her mind was focused on one thing and one thing only—fixing what she had broken with Fen. As soon as class was dismissed, Rowan grabbed Ember's elbow and dragged her quickly out of the classroom and toward the winding steps. They slipped quietly out the large front doors and onto the frost-covered grounds.

January was one of the colder months of the year, and today was no exception. The wind bit into Ember's cheeks as she walked, leaving them red and stinging. They rounded the grounds, walking through groves of apple trees and clover-covered lawns, making their way to a corner that Ember had never seen before. At the edge of the grounds where the wards met the Dark Forest was the most extraordinary waterfall Ember had ever seen. The water was crystal clear, and it looked like a pool of moonlight. Bright flowers bloomed all around it, despite the bitter cold in the air, and an ancient magnolia tree sat just on the edge.

"I would love to say I'm shocked," Ember mumbled, "but honestly, I'm not sure much could surprise me anymore."

"Ellesmere has that effect on you," Rowan laughed. The girls rounded the pool at the bottom of the waterfall, making their way underneath the giant tree.

"Are we even allowed back here?" Ember asked.

Rowan shrugged. "My brother told me about it. He found

it during his second year, and I don't think many others know about it."

"What is this place?"

"I've only ever heard stories." She lowered her voice. "Stories about places like this. Mountains that you can't see the top of, waterfalls that seem to come from nowhere, streams with no beginning and no end. They're supposed to be portals for the Fae. Dryads live and work on the grounds at Heksheim, so I suppose that would make sense."

Oh, yes. Perfect sense.

"So, spill," Rowan said as they made themselves comfortable in the clover surrounding the tree. "What happened last night?"

Ember took a shaky breath and looked around to make sure no one was lurking. "Someone broke in last night."

Rowan's eyes went wide. "Someone broke in?" she whispered as she shifted her weight forward. "What did they take? What did your parents say?"

"I didn't tell them," Ember replied as she shook her head. "And that's the part that scares me—nothing was taken. They tore my room apart, but they didn't take anything." She wrung her hands in her lap as her heart beat in her throat. "They pulled everything out of my closets and dresser, knocked things off shelves, and pulled everything out from under my bed."

Rowan stiffened as she sucked in a breath. "The book was under your bed."

Ember nodded as she shifted uncomfortably.

"Well?" Rowan prodded. "Did they get it?"

Ember shook her head. "No, thank the gods," she breathed. "I had moved it a few hours prior, and I wasn't even in my room when it happened." She shivered as she wrapped one arm around the other, scraping her nails across her skin.

"Do you think they were looking for the book?" Rowan asked as she furrowed her brow.

Ember closed her eyes as she shook her head. "I don't know," she breathed. "But either way, they almost had it last night, whoever they were." A chill ran down her spine. "I think we need to hurry and figure something out. I don't want to put the Kitts in danger if someone really is after the book."

"And you're still opposed to me keeping the book at my house?" Rowan asked as she gave her a playful grin.

"I think this would be the worst possible time to move the book," Ember laughed. "Especially if someone knows I have it. They could be watching and someone could get hurt. Better to not risk it."

Rowan sighed as she nodded. "Yeah, I suppose you're right."

Ember chewed on her lip. "Have you gotten anywhere in the grimoire?" she asked as she twirled the end of her braid.

"Lucky for you, your best friend is a genius." Rowan grinned. "I think I found a spell that will work to destroy it for good, if that's still what we want to do."

"Of course it is." Ember nodded as she furrowed her brow. "Are you sure it'll work?"

Rowan leaned back on her elbows as she smirked. "I'm pretty positive it will work perfectly." She grinned. "Shall we go tonight?"

"Tonight?" Ember stuttered, heart pounding in her chest. The last thing she wanted to do was spend all night trekking around the island, especially after not getting much sleep the night before. She took a breath as she closed her eyes, pinching the bridge of her nose. She needed to fix things with Fen, and the first step in doing that was getting the book out of her house and destroyed once and for all.

Sleep could wait.

Rowan nodded as she stood up, lending a hand to help Ember off the ground. "It's as good a night as any. The sooner the better, if you ask me."

Ember bit her lip and nodded. They might as well do it

tonight. But all of a sudden, a strange sense of anxiety was creeping into her stomach. She pushed it aside and slung her back over her shoulder. "Tonight it is, then."

SUPPER THAT EVENING WAS SILENT. Or at least, Ember was silent. She couldn't bring herself to meet anyone's eyes, not even as they prodded her with questions. All she answered with were *mm-hmm*'s and nods. The shorter the answer, the better. Fen's eye's cut into her like daggers anytime he happened to glance her way, and it was all she could do to swallow the small bites of food she was taking.

Her secret ate away at her, consuming her from the inside out. She felt her walls growing steadily by the hour, but she was powerless to stop them. It was like she had traveled back in time, like she was surrounded by people she knew deep down didn't really want her. She was their stray, like Mr. Vargr had so eloquently put it. She wasn't their daughter. She wasn't their sister. She wasn't their family. So, why bother? What good would polite conversation actually do? Why bother keeping up with the charade when the ending was always the same?

She had a family. A happy family. And then she didn't. At six years old, in the middle of a thunderstorm, her entire world had been flipped upside down. Her happily ever after had been permanently snatched away from her, leaving only broken puzzle pieces for her to look back on. Her parents were living, breathing royalty in her eyes. A prince and princess. But in that moment, as her father's limp, bloody body was pulled off the jagged rocks, and her mum's was washed further out to sea, she realized that 'until death do us part' was not a promise, but a curse.

"I think I'll head to bed early," she whispered as she

cleared away her plate and left the room, not bothering to wait for a response from anyone.

She laid in bed until she heard the last door click shut, then waited a few minutes more for good measure. She had one chance. One chance to get rid of the book and move on with her life. If she was caught, if she didn't succeed, she might not have another opportunity. She snuck across the hall into the library and pulled the small box out from the corner she had stuck it in. She unlocked it quietly and quickly slipped the book in her bag. The familiar sense of dread creeped in as her fingers lingered over the spine before she quickly flipped her bag closed and made her way back into her room. The way it weighed her bag down felt unnatural, like it held so much more than paper and ink. She pulled on a heavy coat, laced up her shoes, and gently hoisted Maia up on her shoulder, running her hand down her long snout.

"We have to be quiet, little one," she whispered, as the draic buried herself into her coat.

The old floorboards creaked under her feet as she tiptoed down the hall. It wasn't loud, but in her ears, it was like a thousand cannons being shot off. She winced as one board let out a low groan and quickly pulled her foot up. She made it to the top step and was preparing to take them two at a time and bolt straight out the front door when a tiny voice alerted her to the presence of someone else in the hall.

"'Ember?" Maeve's sleepy voice said from the door of her bedroom as she rubbed her eyes. "Where are you going?"

Ember sucked in her breath. "We're just going to get some air," she said softly as she turned to face the little girl standing barefoot in the hall.

"It's so cold, though," Maeve replied, rubbing her eye with the back of her hand.

Ember shrugged. "A little cold never bothered me much. You should be in bed, though."

"Can you tuck me in?" Maeve asked as she pouted out her bottom lip. "I had a bad dream."

Ember bit the inside of her cheek as she let out a sigh. She was not the mothering type. She hardly remembered her own mum these days, and she never had much of an example after that. She forced a smile and did her best to do what she thought Eira would have done.

"Of course, little love," she cooed as she led the girl back into her room, tucking her tightly under the covers.

"Thank you, Ember," Maeve said sleepily as she wrapped her arms around her neck and squeezed. "I love you."

Ember stiffened under her embrace as her bottom lip quivered, stiffly returning the hug before the little girl laid back down.

Maeve drifted back to sleep almost instantly, and Ember stood over her for a moment, watching the shadows cast from the moonlight dance over her face, choking back the lump that was building in her throat.

Would she still love her if she couldn't fix the mess she'd made? Would any of them still love her if they found out what she had done?

Would Fen ever forgive her?

By the time she made it out the front door, she was already shivering, though whether it was from the cold or the anticipation of what was to come, she had no idea. The trek to the Echopoint felt longer than normal, and by the time she reached it, her shoulder and calves were aching. She landed with a thud on the side of the dirt road leading to Heksheim and found Rowan already waiting for her.

"I was starting to think you had changed your mind." She smirked as she leaned against the tree. "Can't say I would blame you, though. Our last few treks through the forest haven't been without injury."

Ember shuddered as she remembered the way blood ran down her hand and face. It was something she had no desire to experience again and was bound and determined to walk out of the forest without bruises this time. Maia shifted her weight on Ember's shoulder, nuzzling her snout in her chin.

"Stay up there, little one," she whispered.

The girls followed the familiar path to the opening of the forest that they had come to know so well. Somehow, tonight, it seemed darker than normal. They both cast a quiet, *"Lux,"* and made their way through the winding path, ducking under low hanging branches and inching down steep hills, clinging to rocks so they didn't slide through the wet earth. Their light did very little to brighten the forest, so they kept their eyes ahead. Ember heard a tree branch snap behind her and quickly spun around to look. Just as quick as she had turned her head, Rowan yanked her arm and turned her forward again, shaking her head as Ember nodded.

If you see something, no, you didn't. If you hear something, no, you didn't.

The girls continued their hike in silence, and Ember did her best to ignore the sounds of life in the trees around her. Just when she was certain she couldn't make her legs move any further, the forest opened up to a gorgeous meadow, and she was met with a warm, welcoming breeze.

Maia stretched her head up as she clicked and purred, then jumped off Ember's shoulder to run through the soft grass. Ember giggled as she watched her familiar chase the fireflies that lit up the meadow. For the second time, it was like she had stepped directly into a storybook, and she was immediately flooded with peace.

The girls found a small rock toward the middle of the field and made their way over to it. Rowan kicked it a few times while she turned her head from side to side, using some sort of mental calculator to make sure it was a decent enough altar for their proverbial sacrifice.

"This should work." She smirked as she wiped her hands together. "You brought the book, yeah?"

Ember nodded and reached into her bag, pulling the heavy tome out and clutching it in her sweaty palms.

"Set it right there, and we'll stand back here," Rowan said as she pointed six feet in front of the rock. Ember walked slowly forward, scared that any sudden movement would jolt the book to life, and laid it gently on the boulder in front of her. She was still shaking, and it wasn't from the cold this time.

"And to think," Rowan laughed, "we almost didn't get the chance to do this since you left your bedroom window open."

Ember laughed as she stood back up, wiping her hands one her jeans, but her smile quickly fell as her breath caught in her throat. "I never told you how they got in the house," she whispered.

But that was as far as she got.

It all happened in a split second, but felt like it was happening in slow motion.

Her necklace vibrated against her collarbone, and searing pain shot through her entire body, like her blood was boiling underneath her skin. The breath had been completely sucked from her lungs, leaving her gasping for air. Her head landed on a rock with a sickening crack, and stars floated through her vision. The side of her face and both arms throbbed. The taste and smell of copper filled her throat, pouring from her lip. Maia landed on top of her body, crying for her, but Ember's ears felt like there were a million bells ringing in them. The last thing she saw was a large white wolf standing at the edge of the forest. Stars twinkled around him as the world faded around her.

And then it all went black.

CHAPTER 24

YOUR WINGS ARE MADE OF SCALES, MY DEAR

"Just one more, Papa! Just one, please!" The tiny redhead squealed as her father spun her through the air and threw her toward the sky, a fit of giggle erupting from her lungs. The summer breeze blew through her tangled hair as their shadows danced under the light of the full moon, the grass rippling beneath their feet. Ember snuggled herself into her father's chest, feeling the weight of his arms wrapped around her. "Just one more time, Papa," she whispered.

"I think that's all we have time for today, Starshine." His bright green eyes met hers, lavender flecked with amber and ash. "I have to go."

Ember wrapped her arms tighter around his chest, afraid if she let go he might slip out of her fingers. "I want to go with you," she whispered, tears threatening to fall from her eyes. "I can't do this without you."

"You're stronger than you give yourself credit for, kiddo," he laughed gruffly.

"I don't feel strong."

"You're a dragon trying to be a fairy." He smiled, tilting her chin upwards. "Your wings are made of scales, my dear."

Ember tightened her grip around his waist as he rubbed the top of her head. She needed more time, just a little more time. "I want to go with you."

"Not yet. It's not time. I have to go," he said as he broke their hug, taking a step back. *"I love you."*

"Forever?" she asked softly.

"And always, Starshine." He smiled. *"You need to go. You need to wake up."*

Ember furrowed her brow at him. *Wake up?*

"Wake up, Starshine. Wake up."

Ember's eyes fluttered open, and she felt a steady throbbing on the back of her head. She ran her tongue over her lip, feeling the deep gash and tasting copper, and she flexed her fingers. It was at that moment that she realized a few things were wrong.

First, her magic felt off. She could feel it, but it was far away, like she was trying to swim toward it through a riptide, but it kept getting yanked further out to sea. Next, Maia was on her chest, but she wasn't sleeping. She was standing as tall as her tiny legs would allow, back arched and teeth barred like she was standing in between Ember and certain death. And finally, as she flexed and pulled at her hand and arms, she realized she couldn't move.

Her hands and feet were bound together.

"Gods, finally," a voice cut through the air. "I didn't think you were ever going to wake up."

"Rowan?" Ember coughed. "What happened? Get me out of these things." Ember tugged a few more times at the invisible restraints, feeling them tighten with each pull.

"Afraid I can't do that," Rowan replied. "You know, you've really given me a run for my money, Lothbrok."

Ember pushed herself up to a sitting position, blinking away the stars swirling in her vision. Rowan was a few feet in front of her, sitting cross legged on a rock, twirling the book in her hand. "What are you doing?" Ember whispered, trying desperately to understand what had happened, what she had missed.

"What I should have done the night we got this bloody

thing," she snapped in reply, "but your pitiful excuse for a brother interrupted us instead. All you had to do was give me the book, Ember." She rolled her eyes. "You just had to give me the bloody book and none of this had to happen. I asked for it over and over again. I even tried to get in your room to find it," she huffed, as she slammed her hand on her knee and her voice grew louder. "But you had to make this difficult. You had to turn me into the villain."

"That was you," Ember breathed. "You broke into my room. Why?" She felt like cotton was lodged in her throat, and she couldn't get air to her lungs no matter how hard she tried.

"I needed it, Ember!" she almost shouted. "I needed this bloody book, and you just wouldn't let me have it!"

"Needed it for what?" Ember asked as she furrowed her brow. "We were supposed to be working together."

"He promised if I got close to you and found the book, he would help me," Rowan said, as she raked her fingers through her hair. "He said he would make them pay for what they did."

"You're not making any sense, Rowan," Ember said as she tugged at the restraints around her wrists. "Make who pay for what?"

"Every damned magical creature on this godsforsaken island!" she shouted. "Every being that feels like they're worthy of magic, every creature that wants to be equal to us. If we should have to pay for the sins of our fathers, so should they." Her chest was rising and falling rapidly, and there was fire in her eyes, a fire Ember didn't recognize. "You know," Rowan continued, "I really did believe the legend was about Killian in the beginning. All of the pieces fit. He's the right age, he comes from the right family, and he seemed to be the only option." She stood up from the ground and began pacing back and forth, twirling the book in her hands. "And then you showed up."

Ember cut her eyes at her, confusion and pain muddying her thoughts. "What's that got to do with anything?"

"You were so desperate to find this thing." She tossed the book in the air. "So, I thought, sure, free help is never a bad thing, and then I heard you speaking Mermish, and that was when I realized it."

Ember felt a chill run down her spine as she tried to scoot back, not that it was doing much good.

"The legend was never after about Killian." Rowan grinned almost manically. "It was about *you*."

Ember was certain if she had been standing, she definitely would have passed out again. The world felt like it was spinning a million miles an hour, and she was suddenly struggling to breathe. Her heart thundered heavily against her ribs as she tried to suck in air. That was impossible. It wasn't about her. It couldn't be. Because if it was that meant...

I am destined for darkness.

Rage and fear mixed together in her chest, and she felt like she was going to be sick. Maybe she was dreaming? Maybe she had fallen and hit her head too hard, and this was just some terrifying nightmare playing inside of her brain. She squeezed her eyes shut, praying that when she opened them again, everything would be back to normal.

It wasn't.

"There are parts of the legend most people don't know about." Rowan laughed. "Having the ability to speak to creatures in their own tongue is one of them. I must say, I was a bit shocked when I realized it. I mean, you're not exactly the face I pictured when I thought about destruction of non-Vala magic." She made a displeased face. "But you'll do, I suppose."

"Who is telling you all of this?" Ember asked as her lip trembled. "Who are you helping?"

Rowan beamed, "Father, of course."

Ember furrowed her brow. "Your father?"

"*The* Father," Rowan replied. "You didn't think I was doing this on my own, did you?"

Ember closed her eyes and tried to breathe, desperately trying to make sense of any of this. "Why are you doing this?" she whispered, as she choked on the lump building in her throat.

"Because he promised me a family again," Rowan replied steadily.

"You have a family, Ro," Ember replied as she shook her head, squinting.

"I don't," Rowan hissed as she shook her head. "Not anymore. Not really."

"Why does he need this book so bad?" Ember asked.

"It's the only way to fix our island," Rowan breathed as she shook her head. "*The Book of Shadows* will give us our power back over all of the magical creatures that live here. We can finally get rid of them for good and take back the island." She furrowed her brow as her jaw tensed. "They will finally pay for the way they've wronged us."

"Wronged us?" Ember scoffed as she pinched her brow together. "How on earth have they *wronged* us? You were there when Kaan and Asherah told us about what happened to their children. You helped me set Maren free, for Odin's sake! How on earth can you justify what he—*Father*—is going to do to them? This was their land first."

"They're not as innocent as you think, Lothbrok," Rowan hissed. "They deserve everything that's coming to them."

"So, now what?" Ember asked as she struggled to hold back tears. "You just take the book and leave me here to die?"

"I'll take the book back to Father," she said, "but I want you to come with me."

"Come *with* you?" Ember asked as she furrowed her brow. "Why would I do that?"

"He can help you." Rowan almost smiled, like she truly believed the words she was saying. "He can help you understand who you are, and he can give you a family again. This is your fate, whether you like it or not. It's in your blood. You can't change who you are."

"I will not hurt other people." Ember scoffed as she shook her head.

Rowan scrunched her nose and rolled her eyes. "They aren't *people*, they are *creatures*. They aren't worthy of magic, and deep down, you know that to be true. Your destiny is to destroy them, and you can't run away from it."

Ember felt her blood boil as she clenched her fists, struggling against the restraints at her wrists. "I will not help you," she hissed.

The truth of the matter was, Ember never thought of herself as brave. She didn't want to be a martyr. She didn't want to sacrifice herself for the 'greater good.' Out of all of the feelings bubbling in her chest, not one of them was courage. At that moment, she was just a terrified, fifteen-year-old, wishing desperately that she had just stayed in her room that night.

"Come with me," Rowan whispered with a smile. "You can learn magic you never dreamed possible. You can have a home, a real home. Please, Em."

"I'm not going anywhere," Ember hissed as she blinked away the tears filling her vision. "Just leave! You won't convince me."

Rowan hung her head with a sigh. "I'm sorry it had to be like this," she whispered.

Ember closed her eyes tight as she bit her cheek and clenched her fists. The bitter taste of betrayal rose like bile in the back of her throat, muddying her thoughts and sending her head spinning. Suddenly, the air broke around her with a blood curdling scream, and Ember wondered if she was dead. But after a few seconds, she realized the scream wasn't coming from her.

It was coming from Rowan.

Her eyes flew open to see a great white wolf flying through the air and landing directly on Rowan's chest. The animal bared its teeth and let out a deep growl as it dug its claws into the earth. The hair on the back of its neck bristled, and its ears laid back on its head. Ember felt her heartbeat pick up as she tried to scoot further back, away from the beast, when she heard a loud roar sound from the sky. The wolf turned his head, only for a moment, to look in the direction of the noise. Rowan took her chance and shot a blue light at his chest, knocking him back. Ember spun her head around to see Arlo land behind her, and Fen slid quickly off his back.

"EMBER!" he shouted as he barreled toward her, narrowly dodging a stream of light coming from Rowan's hand.

"I'm okay," she shouted. "Get the book!"

Fen gave her a quick nod, then tore off toward Rowan, who was throwing hexes back and forth as the wolf dodged them. The wolf charged at her but was stopped short when Rowan sent a curse through the air. It ripped across his ivory fur, staining it crimson, and he fell limp to the ground. Fen was two feet from the book when a purple light hit him square in the chest, sending him flying.

"Fen!" Ember shouted as she tugged harder at the magic wrapped around her wrists and ankles, as if that would make a difference. Rowan whipped her head around, a maniacal grin sliding across her face, and made her way toward Ember, her arm stretched out in front of her. Ember held her breath, bracing herself for what was to come, like a rabbit caught in a snare.

"Leave my sister alone! *Detenair!*" Fen screamed and hurled a jet of light at Rowan, knocking her face first into the dirt. Fen and the wolf ran toward the book, but Rowan was faster. She jumped to her feet, practically flying through air, and snatched the book off the ground. Starlight spun around her and then she was gone, and the book with her.

Ember took in deep breaths as she looked around, waiting for her to pop up somewhere else, but they were alone. Her heart beat heavily against her ribcage, and she was once again aware of how terribly her whole body hurt. Fen turned around and ran back toward Ember, snatching her pendant off the ground and kneeling on the dirt next to her.

"Em, are you okay?" He breathed heavily, but his words were lost in the ringing in her ears. Her head started spinning again, and Fen sounded like he was a thousand miles away. Her vision began to blur as he called out her name, the white wolf walking up beside him, but she couldn't answer. She felt his arms wrap around her shoulders, and the world went dark again.

CHAPTER 25
FATE IS FICKLE

The dark was fading when Ember opened her eyes, streams of golden sunlight breaking through the air around her, and it took her a while to realize she was laying in her bed. Maia was curled up on top of her pillow, right above her head, sleeping soundly, one paw protectively on her hair. Ember looked around and breathed a heavy sigh of relief when she saw Fen curled up beside her, snoring in her ear, and Killian at the foot of the bed, legs draped over the side. She took a ragged breath as she closed her eyes.

She was home. She was safe. It was over.

She noticed a glass of water sitting on the table by her bed and realized just how dry her throat was. She tried to sit up and reach for the cup, but every muscle in her body felt like it was on fire. She looked down to see her arms covered in bruises, and her head was still gently pounding behind her eyes, just enough to be annoying. She let out a small gasp when she lifted her arm and felt pain shoot through her shoulder like a bolt of lightning. This was all it took to wake both Killian and Fen from their sleep.

"I wouldn't do that, if I were you." Killian yawned. "You dislocated your shoulder, so you'll be sore for a few days."

"Oh, thank gods," Fen breathed as he sat up in bed, rubbing the sleep from his eyes. "How are you feeling?"

"Like I got caught under a stampede of unicorns." She laughed weakly as she rubbed her burning shoulder.

"If you wanted a near-death experience, all you had to do was ask, Starshine." Killian grinned as he propped himself on his elbow, his platinum hair falling in front of his eyes. "Also, your sheets are quite uncomfortable. What's the thread count?"

Ember rolled her eyes with a small grin. "You didn't have to sleep in my bed. I'm really okay."

Fen shook his head. "You'll be lucky if I don't move my bed in here after yesterday. I'm not letting you out of my sight again." There was a fire in his eyes that Ember didn't quite recognize, and she felt her magic thrum in her veins, as if it was reaching out for something she couldn't quite pinpoint.

"Unfortunately, you're stuck with us, Starshine." Killian smirked. Before Ember could argue, her bedroom door creaked open, and Eira waltzed in.

"Oh, good, you're up," she chirped as she walked over to the bed. "You gave us a right scare, love." She sat on the edge of the bed and laid a potion vial on the table beside her. "How is your head?"

"It's been better." Ember smiled weakly.

Eira uncorked the vial and handed it to her. "Drink this; it will help with the pain." She stood up from the bed and put her hands firmly on her hips. "You know, I should ground all three of you until you graduate." She looked firmly at the teenagers laying on the bed. "But I think the natural consequences of your little adventure far surpass any that I could dole out."

Ember stared wide eyed at both the boys. Had they told her what she had done?

"What on earth were you thinking?" Eira asked, voice mixed with anger and concern.

"It was my fault, Mum," Fen said before Ember could reply. "I talked Ember into going for a night fly on Arlo. She slipped off and hit her head. We should've been more careful, I'm sorry."

"Well, what's done is done," she said softly as she wiped her hands on her dress. "I need all three of you to be more careful. I can't bear the thought of anything happening to you." Tears formed in the corner of her eyes, but she quickly wiped them away and cleared her throat.

"We'll be more careful, Mum," Killian said with a wide grin. "Scout's honor."

Eira rolled her eyes and ruffled his hair. "What I need you two to do," she said, as she pointed to Fen and Killian, "is let Ember get some rest."

"We will, Mum." Fen smiled, and Eira closed the door softly behind her, leaving the teenagers to whisper amongst themselves.

Ember let out a heavy sigh as she dropped her head back to her pillow, going over the events of her "adventure" in her head as she silently thanked whatever gods were listening that she was safely in her bed. Her brow furrowed as a thought quickly flickered through her mind.

"How did you know where I was?" She turned to Fen.

Fen shot a quick glance at Killian before looking back at her. "Killian sent a Helio and said you were in trouble. I rode Arlo and followed the Helio to the meadow." His story was plausible, but he still shifted uncomfortably, not quite meeting her gaze with his.

"Okay…" she thought out loud, "but how did you know where I was?" Now, it was Killian's turn to look anywhere but back at her.

He let out a long sigh as he looked at Fen. "She's going to find out eventually, mate." He shrugged. Fen nodded as he bit his bottom lip. Killian stood up from his spot at the foot of the bed and made his way to the middle of the room.

"Going to find out what?" she asked as she glared back and forth between the boys.

Neither of them answered, and just as Ember was about to ask again, what she saw in the middle of her bedroom made her breath hitch in her chest.

Killian was there, and then he wasn't. Not really, anyway. In a matter of seconds, she watched his hands and feet transform into large paws, and his pale skin turned into pristine white fur. His smoky eyes were replaced with amber, and the reality of what he was hit her like a train barreling straight at her chest.

"You're a—"

"A werewolf, yeah," Fen whispered beside her.

"You knew?" She turned angrily toward him. "You knew, and you went on and on about how my lying to you was such a huge betrayal? You ignored me for weeks."

"This wasn't my secret to tell, Em," he said softly, and she knew he was right. She gave him an apologetic smile and nodded her head. When she looked back to the center of the room, Killian was back in his human form, kicking the toe of his shoe on the floor.

"It was you in the woods, wasn't it?" she asked hesitantly. He nodded his reply, staring sheepishly at the ground. "Why?" she asked quietly. "Why have you been watching me? Why are you always there when I'm in trouble? Why?"

"You're pack." He shrugged. "It's instinct."

"Pack?" she asked quietly, glancing down at her hands to make sure she wasn't growing fur.

"Yeah." He nodded again. "We're connected somehow— me, you, and Fen. I felt it that first day we met in town. I don't know how to explain it." He ran his hand through his platinum hair.

Ember shook her head. This made no sense, but honestly, none of the last twenty-four hours made much sense. She rubbed the side of her head, running her hand along the bruise forming on her jaw, and thought back to the hex that had hit the wolf—or Killian—in the chest in the meadow.

"Do you remember anything when you're..."

"A wolf?" He laughed lightly. "Yeah, I don't lose any time. I'm completely sober, for lack of better words. And anything that happens in wolf form, sticks around afterwards."

Ember raised an eyebrow as he unbuttoned the top half of his shirt, revealing a deep gash running across his pale chest. She let out a gasp when she saw the rest of his skin.

His body was littered with scars, a living tapestry of near misses. Cuts and gashes in various stages of healing ran up and down his arms that were normally hidden under pristine button-down shirts. Bruises bloomed across his shoulder, and Ember wondered what was from last night and what was from another time completely. She turned to look at Fen and noticed for the first time the bruises running across his jaw and arm. Tears welled in her eyes that she didn't bother to hold back as she looked between the two battered boys. They had put their life on the line for her, even after all of her lies.

"I'm so sorry," she whispered as tears cascaded down her cheeks.

"There's nothing to be sorry for," Fen replied calmly. "It's not your fault your best friend turned out to be a raving lunatic."

Ember closed her eyes and sniffed. "No, I'm sorry for everything. I'm sorry for lying to you. Neither of you would have been in that position if I wasn't keeping secrets." She quickly wiped the tears from her eyes, but they were replaced by more just as fast. Her head shot up quickly as she looked around.

"The book," she said hoarsely. "Where's the book?"

Fen bit the bottom of his lip. "It's gone," he whispered. "She took it when she got away."

Ember felt like the walls were closing in on her. "Oh gods," she whispered as she laid her head in her palms. After all that, all that happened, she didn't even have the bloody book?

"I feel like I've been waiting very patiently," Killian chirped, "but someone is going to need to fill me in on exactly what this book is and why it almost caused a bloody assassination in the middle of the forest."

Ember raised her head and looked up at Fen. "You didn't tell him?"

Fen shrugged with a half smile. "Wasn't my secret to tell."

Ember smiled softly at her foster brother as he sat carelessly on her bed, messy hair and bright blue eyes glowing behind his glasses. A pang of guilt shot through her chest again. She had lied to him endlessly, snuck around like a small child trying to steal sweets from the kitchen, and he still showed up for her with no questions asked, desperately loyal to her. He didn't hold a grudge, didn't blame her for nearly dying at the hands of a deranged teenager. He was there when she needed, no questions asked, simply because he….

No. People didn't love her.

She let out a shaky breath. "I suppose I owe you an explanation."

And explain she did. She ran the sheets through her fingertips as she spoke, not having the courage to look either of them in the eyes. She told him about the legend and the information she had found in the journal her father had left her. She told him about the Clann of Loch Lurgan and how she had been the one to free Maren. She let out a pained breath as she told him about *The Book of Shadows* and how she suspected him, how she had snuck into the manor the second night she had found the book and stolen it out of his father's secret study. She laid out every secret she possessed on the rumpled bed sheets between the three of them. By the time she finished, she felt like her lungs were on fire. How could either of them ever forgive her? They had every reason to walk away and never look back. Everything she touched turned to ruin.

"Wow," Killian muttered. "That sure beats my whole werewolf surprise. You'd think if I had a legend written about me, my father would be quick to let me know,"

"Well, that's another thing…" Ember mumbled. "It isn't about you." She took in a deep breath and looked them both in the eye. "Apparently, it's about me."

Fen opened and closed his mouth several times, unable to form the sentences he was looking for. Killian furrowed his brow in deep thought, and Ember thought she was surely going to spontaneously combust if one of them didn't hurry up and say something.

"So, what do we do about it?" Killian asked seriously.

"I don't think there's anything we can do." She sighed. "It was written down before I was even born. You can't change fate,"

Fen chewed the bottom of his lip. "We'll figure something out," he replied as he gave her arm a gentle squeeze. "We won't let you do this alone."

Killian shrugged as he leaned back on the bed. "Fate is fickle."

But despite their gentle words, Ember knew otherwise. As the memory of Rowan's words sank into her chest, she realized just how different she was. Even on an island bubbling with magic at every corner, she still managed to stick out like a sore thumb. Her heart ached for a reality that would never exist for her, a reality where she didn't have to fight for her place in the world. A reality where she was loved because of who she was, not in spite of it.

But that reality was not hers, and she didn't imagine it ever could be.

CHAPTER 26

HISTORY IS WRITTEN BY THE VICTORS

Eira insisted that Ember stay in bed for at least two weeks while all of her wounds healed. As much as she felt like she should protest, she was in no hurry to get back to school. Her only true saving grace was Fen and Killian. They raced home in the afternoons, arms full of her schoolwork, and piled onto her bed to tell her about their day. Their presence never failed to lighten her spirits, but when they inevitably had to go, the darkness began to sink in again.

The longer she stayed in her bed, the more alone she began to feel. Guilt weighed on her consciousness as she relayed the night in the meadow, spurring nightmares as she thrashed in bed. Pictures of what could have happened to Fen and Killian flashed through her mind, a devastating reality had luck not been on their side.

The book Nessa had given her became a permanent fixture in her bed, consuming the words hungrily as she heard her father's voice reading them in her head. The picture of her parents sat in her lap, or laid on the pillow beside Maia, as she watched their memory sway back and forth, oblivious to how bleak their future truly was.

Days bled into weeks, and she found herself closing the

Kitts and Killian out more and more, living behind her locked bedroom door. By the time the days began getting longer and Eira insisted that it was perfectly safe for her to return to school, she was a shell of her former self. Her eyes bore dark circles that no amount of sleep could erase, and her face was painted with a perpetual frown. Her interactions with Fen and his family were few and far between these days, and she preferred to keep it that way.

Because then no one else could get hurt. *She* couldn't get hurt.

She found herself back at Heksheim the next day, walking slowly down the corridors a few paces behind Killian and Fen, who were chattering wildly about the score from the game the night before. Students laughed and joked, making plans for the upcoming Spring Equinox Festival, and a strange sort of hollowness settled in Ember's chest. She took her seat in Zoomancy and glanced briefly at the empty seat beside her. Tears pricked the corners of her eyes as she quickly turned her head away and kept her eyes trained on her desk, studying the way the grains of wood weaved in and out of one another.

"Is this seat taken?" a voice asked from beside her.

Ember looked up to see Odette smiling, one hand on the back of the chair.

"I suppose not." Ember shrugged.

She couldn't recall what the lesson was about, though she wasn't sure that it really even mattered. All she could focus on was making it through each of her classes and going back home to lock herself away in her room. She was simply going through the motions at this point. She reached in her bag to grab the picture of her parents that she had stuck in there that morning, and instead, her fingers met the spine of the book it had lived in. She pulled it out, setting it quietly on her desk in front of her.

The Wildlings of Ellesmere Island.

WHAT SAT in front of her was a culmination of years of research her father had put together, though the more she read it, the less sense it actually made. It seemed to be mostly stories and theory with very little evidence-based facts anywhere in it. It felt like a fairytale, some silly little story someone had made up about things they couldn't explain. One thing did stick out to her, though, one thing that made her throat run dry and her heart race in her chest.

JUST LIKE THE VALA TRAIT, the Wildling trait is a genetic one. No one is quite sure where the anomaly came from or when it appeared, but it has been present on the island since its creation. There seems to be no rhyme or reason as to why a wildling is born, but we do know a few things about them.

1. A wildling is a Vala, born to two Vala parents, and just because one child has the gene does not mean other children in the family will.

2. While they look just like any other Vala, there is one distinct feature that sets them apart: their piercing lavender eyes.

CLASS WAS DISMISSED, and Ember slowly stood up from her seat and made her way to the door, the book still clutched tightly in her arms.

The rest of the day seemed to pass in a blur. Oddly enough, History of the Gods was the only class she was able to pay an ounce of attention in. Odette took the seat beside her again and shot a bright smile her way. Ember tried to return the kind gesture, but she knew her efforts were futile. She couldn't even successfully fake it anymore.

The professor drawled on about Odin and his descendants, and Ember felt her attention slipping as her mind wandered until she heard something that made her chest clench.

"The descendants of Odin, no matter their age, addressed him as Father," he spoke softly. "Though most thought him to be a benevolent leader, his family's ideals more closely mirrored Freyr's. Whether that was his doing, or them straying, no one is quite sure. There isn't much we know about this specific family."

"What about the people who are descendants of his children?" someone asked from the back of the room.

"Ah, now that"—the professor smirked—"is where the story gets murky." He paced back and forth up the aisles between the rows of desks. "When the children of the gods made their way to Ellesmere Island, Odin's children never arrived with them. It is thought that they stayed behind or were lost at sea, but there has always been a rumor that instead of settling with the rest of the Vala, they simply took to the far north end of the island and created their own community past the vastness of the Dark Forest." His eyes twinkled as he spoke, and a chill ran down Ember's spine. "As far as we are aware, there are no living descendants of Odin."

Ember chewed on the bottom of her lip. Could that be the Wildlings in her father's book? Could she be one of the last descendants of Odin and not even know it? It didn't really make sense, but what about any of this made much sense at all? Taking a deep breath, she raised her hand high in the air, every eye looking at her.

"Were they Wildlings, Professor?" she asked as calmly as she could muster.

"Excuse me, Miss Lothbrok?" he asked, dumbfounded.

"Wildlings. Were the lost families Wildlings?"

He straightened his back and cleared his throat. "Wildlings are a myth, Miss Lothbrok," he said sternly. "The lost families were a group of Vala, nothing more."

Ember put her head down as she heard quiet laughter erupt at the back of the room, laughter she recognized to be the Ellingboe twins. She felt her neck and face burn red, and she knew she was a deep shade of crimson by now.

Class was dismissed shortly after, and Ember left the room as quickly as she could before she was pulled into another quiet meeting with one of her professors. Killian and Fen were hot on her heels, and as she rounded a corner, she felt Killian's hand wrap tightly around her arm, pulling her into a nearby alcove.

"What were you going on about in there?" he asked, not angrily, but with concern. She winced as his grip tightened around her arm, and he quickly dropped it.

"Nothing," she muttered. "Just something I read about in a book."

"What's a Wild-thing?" Fen asked as he leaned against the wall beside her.

"Wildling," she corrected, "and it's nothing, really, just something I've been reading about."

"It didn't seem like nothing," Killian prodded.

"It's nothing," she hissed, causing both of the boys to take a step back, looking at each other with confusion. "I'll see you later," she snapped and shoved her way between them, not bothering to look back.

Anytime she let someone in, they got hurt, or were put in serious danger. She wasn't about to make that mistake again. She could figure this out on her own. She had to.

CHAPTER 27
THE LOST FAMILY

E mber resorted to doing what she did best when her
life got hard, and that was to seclude herself entirely
from everything and everyone. She had convinced
herself that it was to protect others, but it was more that it was
to protect herself. To protect herself from more heartache.
More loss. If she didn't let anyone in, then no one could ever
leave, so she kept her walls up, determined to never let them
fall. She locked herself away in her room, researching desperately to find a way to stop the legend, to stop herself from
falling headfirst into it.

She wandered down to breakfast late one morning, quickly
taking her seat at the table amongst the chattering family
members. Ember knew they must have noticed the way she
had pulled away, but if they did, they never said anything. She
was still greeted warmly by Eira every morning, Otto still
kissed her head before he left work and asked her about her
day every evening, even if she only answered with mumbles,
and Maeve still hugged her every night before bed and
showed off all her artwork when she got home from school.
And even though Fen knew she was pulling away, he did
everything possible to pull her back in.

"Sleep well, love?" Eira asked happily from the kitchen as she flipped the bacon in the pan.

"Yes, ma'am," Ember whispered and took a long sip of the tea sitting in front of her.

"Me and Killian were going to go for a ride in the orchard later," Fen said quietly as he pushed the tomatoes around his plate. "Want to come with us?"

"No thanks," she mumbled. "I think I'm going to go into town later."

"Oh, good!" Eira said cheerfully as she entered the breakfast nook. "Fresh air will do you some good, love." She kissed the top of Ember's head and laid her plate of breakfast in front of her. Ember didn't have much of an appetite these days, but she ate a few bites and pushed the rest of her food around on her plate so she didn't hurt Eira's feelings. After clearing her plate, she silently grabbed her bag and headed for the terminal door behind the stairs.

The sun warmed her face as she stepped out of the terminal and onto Waterware Street. Spring was on its way, and it was more than apparent in the way people bustled happily down the cobblestones. Flowers bloomed in front of Bontanica Magica, the smell of hydrangeas and tulips drifting in the breeze. Children chased each other through the street, squealing as they narrowly missed running directly into a fisherman's legs.

Ember wasn't sure what she was looking for or what she planned to accomplish in town, but the one thing she didn't count on was hearing her name being called from down the street.

"Ember Lothbrok?" a young woman said as she walked up to her, wringing her hands together. Her eyes were puffy, like she had spent days crying, and her clothes looked like she had been wearing them for several weeks in a row.

"Um, yes, ma'am. I'm Ember," she replied cautiously, eyes narrowed on the petite woman in front of her.

"It's very good to finally meet you," she said with a small smile. "My name is Nora O'Rourke. I'm Rowan's mother."

Ember was positive the world had started spinning backwards. She sucked in a deep breath and found herself unable to form real sentences. "Oh, um, hello, ma'am."

"I'm glad I ran into you," Nora replied. "I've been to the guard, but they haven't been much help, and I'm not sure who else to turn to."

"Um, I'm sorry, but I don't understand." Ember furrowed her brow. What on earth was she talking about?

"I was wondering if you had heard from Rowan," she said plainly.

Ember flinched, that was quite the loaded question. "Heard from her?" she asked hesitantly.

"Yes, she's been missing for several weeks. I thought she had run off to visit family in London—she's known to leave without telling me—but no one has heard from her."

"The last time we, um, spoke," she stuttered, "she mentioned something about her father. I think she might be with him? Wherever that may be." It wasn't a lie; that was basically what Rowan had told her word for word before she tried to murder her in cold blood.

Maybe she would leave that detail out.

"Her father?" Nora mumbled. "That doesn't make any sense."

"Um, is he not nearby?" Ember pushed further.

"No, sweet girl," she said as her eyes began to glaze over. "Rowan's father is dead."

Well. That was a new development.

"My husband and son died five years ago," she continued. "I'm sorry. I thought you knew."

Ember furrowed her brow further. That didn't make any sense. Why would Rowan mention her father if he wasn't alive? What on earth was she doing? Was this a necromancy thing? This was a necromancy thing, wasn't it?

"Oh, um, maybe I misheard her," she mumbled. "I'm sorry. I don't know where she is." It wasn't a lie. Ember hadn't the foggiest where the murderous git had run off to.

The small woman thanked Ember and walked away in the other direction, leaving the girl swimming in confusion. Anxiety bubbled in her chest as she tried to figure out what this could mean. Was she bringing him back to life? Had she already brought him back to life? Was she completely mental and having visions of her dead father helping her take over the magical world?

The last option seemed the most plausible.

She picked up her pace and hurried back to the terminal doors, determined to get as far away as she could and back to the safety of her bedroom. If she was going to figure out what was going on, she had a lot more research to do, and that wasn't going to happen in the middle of town surrounded by people. She didn't know why, but she had a feeling she didn't have much time left. She needed to get to the bottom of all of this, and fast.

The halls of Heksheim were abuzz the next day with the news of the missing first year. Everyone had a theory, which they readily shared with anyone who would listen. Everything from a Fae kidnapping to running away with a Russian prince was being whispered in the halls, and it set Ember's anxiety on edge. Her free period finally rolled around, and she made a beeline for the library, picking a table in the very back, as far away from everyone else as she could get. She flipped through her father's book and his journal, triple checking to see if he left any clues about what she was or how she was connected to all of this. She didn't even register that other people were in the room until…

"Thought we might find you here," Fen's voice sounded from above her.

She jumped and quickly snapped her book shut, looking up at the boys hovering over her.

"You know..." Killian smirked. "I'm beginning to think you're purposefully avoiding me, Starshine."

"Just have a lot on my mind," she mumbled, rubbing her hands together on the top of the table.

"Anything we can help with?" Fen asked as he sat down on the opposite side of the table, Killian quickly following suit.

She bit the side of her lip. "What do you know about the O'Rourkes?" she asked quietly.

Killian leaned back in his chair. "Her older brother Jamie was in Rafe's year, died the summer before their third year. The whole island was a mess when it happened, him and his dad. It took a while for things to get back to normal."

"How did they die?" she asked, furrowing her brow.

"Rumor is that it was a rogue Fae attack," Fen whispered. "One of the reasons the Fae are only allowed near town if they have a business to run. And even then, Chief Thornsten keeps them on a pretty tight leash."

"B-before you showed up in the meadow," she stuttered, "Rowan mentioned her dad. She said that she was helping him, that what she was doing was part of some plan."

"Well, that doesn't make any sense," Killian scoffed. "Maybe you misheard."

Ember narrowed her eyes at him. "I think I was paying pretty good attention to what was coming out of her mouth," she hissed.

Killian threw his hands up in surrender and leaned back further in his chair.

"But it got me thinking," she continued, "about something Professor Orion mentioned in class the other day. Odin's descendants called him 'Father.' They supposedly disappeared off the face of the earth, but what if they didn't?"

Fen chewed at the cap on his pen. "I'm not following," he said with a raised eyebrow.

Ember sighed. "Their beliefs were less than ideal and caused a lot of turmoil within the Vala community from everything I've read. So, what if they disappeared on purpose? I mean, this island is huge. They very well could have created their own community beyond the edge of the forest, somewhere no one dares go, and have been living there ever since."

Fen sighed as he leaned on the table. "Em, I'm trying here, but what in Odin's name are you talking about?"

"That's exactly my point!" she almost shouted at the confused boys. "Odin. Rowan mentioned her father, but I don't think she was talking about her real father. I think she was talking about the Lost Family."

"You think Rowan O'Rourke… is conspiring with Odin?" Killian looked at her as if she had three heads.

"Not with Odin," Ember huffed as she rolled her eyes. "One of his descendants. Honestly, are you both that daft?"

"So, say you're right," Fen said as he waved his hand. "What are we supposed to do about it?"

"If I'm right," she replied, "it means they have *The Book of Shadows*, and we can get it back."

"I don't know, Em," Fen said as he looked sideways at Killian. "That's an awful lot of dark magic."

Ember saw their faces cloud with worry, and the guilt made its way back into the pit of her stomach. Keeping secrets didn't bode well for her before, but she wasn't going to chance putting them in harm's way again. She knew what she had to do, but she also knew she was going to have to do it alone.

"You're right," she said quietly. "You're right, just forget about it." She closed the book in front of her and ran her fingers along the front of it.

"No, that's not what I mean," Fen said softly. "I just mean maybe we should—"

"I said you're right!" she snapped. "Just drop it, okay?"

"Ember, what's going on?" Killian's brow furrowed in confusion, and she could see the pain in his charcoal eyes. She didn't want to hurt him, either of them, but she knew being close to her would end up hurting him even worse. It was odd when she thought about it, the differences between her and Killian Vargr.

She was running as fast and as far from any form of love that she could, and all he wanted was a family he didn't need to run from.

"Nothing's wrong," she mumbled.

"I'm sorry," he muttered quietly, trying to decipher what her words actually meant. "I just wanted—"

"I'll talk to you guys later." She stood up to walk out of the library, ignoring the loud whispers as the boys called out for her.

She was used to being alone. She could do this alone. Maybe she could fix this. Maybe she could get the book back from Rowan and destroy it once and for all without putting anyone else in danger.

Maybe this would work.

CHAPTER 28

MAYBE THIS ONE WILL STICK

Ember barreled through the door of the Kitt home after school and ran straight up the stairs. She quietly slipped into the library and closed the door, furiously pacing the sun-soaked floor. How hard could it all be, really? As long as she was adequately prepared, she could easily best Rowan in a duel and get the book and find a way to destroy it. That should be no problem. She didn't need Fen. She didn't need Killian. She didn't need help. She was perfectly content to do this on her own.

Maybe if she said it enough, she would actually begin to believe it.

Maia lay curled up in a ball in the big chair by the window, sleeping happily as Ember paced the room. Late afternoon sunlight broke through the window, washing the entire room in warm light. The door creaked open behind her, and Fen and Killian stepped into the quiet room.

"I'm kind of busy," she prompted as she pulled a book from the shelf and sat down in the chair, pulling Maia onto her lap. "Can we do this later?" It was more of a statement than a question, but Fen replied anyway.

"Em, talk to us," he pleaded. "Why are you acting like this?"

"Because I have to fix what I broke, Fen," she replied. "I have to finish what I started."

"Let us help you," Killian said quietly.

"No," she replied. "I have to do this on my own."

Fen all but rolled his eyes at her dramatics and gently kneeled in front of the chair she was sitting in. "Em, we're family," he said quietly. "You don't have to do this alone."

"But I do," she whispered hoarsely. "I won't let either of you put yourselves in danger for me, not ever again." Tears stung her eyes as she took in a shaky breath. "This is my mess. I have to clean it up myself."

"Who told you that?" Killian huffed as he leaned against the wall.

"Excuse me?"

"Who made you think you weren't worthy of a family who would fight for you, beside you?" His words felt like bricks on her chest, the heaviness of them weighing down on her making her struggle to breathe.

"I've been alone my whole life," she whispered. "I am perfectly capable of doing it now."

Fen stood up so quickly it made Ember jump. He stood in front of her, tears welling in the corners of his eyes. "You're in a dark place, and you think you're all alone, but you're not. Do you hear me?" His voice shook as he spoke, and he didn't bother to stop the tears falling down his red cheeks. "We are in that dark place with you. You don't have to do this alone anymore, not as long as we're breathing."

Ember looked between the two boys standing in front of her. She couldn't remember a time in her life where anyone had bothered to make her feel welcome, let alone like she was worth something more than a check from the government every month. She swallowed the emotions welling in her throat and took a shaky breath.

"People don't get a second chance at having a family," she breathed as she shook her head. "I have to stop thinking that I'm the exception,"

"You are our exception," Killian replied with a softness Ember didn't recognize in him.

"Let us in," Fen whispered. "Let us help."

And it was like an avalanche broke through the walls she had so intricately built, and they came crashing down around her. She let out a choked sobbed as she pulled her knees to her chest, soaking the tops of them with tears. Everything she had done to protect herself for the last nine years—all of the safe-guards she had constructed—all shattered, broken and warped at her feet, and she didn't know where to begin to pick up the pieces and put herself back together again. Fen wrapped her in a hug, and without thinking, she squeezed him tightly, gripping his shirt like a life raft in a hurricane. Killian smiled gently down at her, wrinkling his nose as he tilted his head, and that was when it hit her.

She didn't have to fix anything, not alone. They would pick up all of the burnt and shattered pieces with her, taking their fair share of cuts and scrapes without complaint. And she would do the same for them.

Was this what a family felt like?

She nodded with a small smile, taking a breath as she wiped the moisture from her cheeks. "I'll try," she whispered.

"Alright," Killian said as he clapped his hands together. "Enough of the emotional garbage. What's our plan?"

Ember smiled as she walked them through her ideas, and they nodded intently, hanging onto her every word. "I feel like there's something we're missing," Ember said as she mulled over the research laying on the floor between them. "If we're going to do this, we need to do it right. We can't just chase after her without a solid plan." The boys nodded. "I think we need to go back and talk to Kaan and Asherah."

"Again?" Fen whined as he threw himself dramatically on

the floor. "You're going to take me into that bleedin' forest again?"

Killian patted him on the knee with a smirk. "I'll protect you, mate."

Fen swatted at his friend, who promptly swung back, causing both of them to roll across the floor at Ember's feet. Her heart swelled, and for the first time in a long time, she felt like everything was going to be okay, like she was finally seeing the glowing light at the end of the tunnel.

Maybe this one will stick.

The door to the library swung open, and Eira walked in, wiping her hands on the apron around her waist.

"Well, I'm happy to see you've all made up." She smiled. "Killian, dear, are you staying for supper, or are you needed at home?"

"And miss out on your shepherd's pie, Mum? Absolutely not." He beamed as he swung pieces of white hair out of his eyes and pinned Fen to the floor.

"Ember, love, please keep them from killing each other," she laughed, and then quickly closed the door behind her.

After Ember succeeded in pulling the boys apart and making them shake hands, the trio made their way down the steps, following the smell of shepherd's pie and apple pastries floating in front of them. Ember's mouth was already watering by the time she sat down, and it took all of her strength to wait to dig in until everyone was seated.

Maeve enveloped her in a hug, and she picked the small girl up as she wrapped her arms around Ember's neck.

"Mum said you needed some space," Maeve whispered through a toothless grin. "But I thought maybe you needed a hug more."

"Your hugs are magic, Maeve Kitt," Ember whispered as she nuzzled the little girl's nose with her own.

Maeve slid out of her arms and ran into the dining room, climbing up on the table and bouncing on her knees as she waited for her food. Eira floated through the kitchen, finishing supper, humming happily to herself as she summoned a spoon, charming it to scoop out the shepherd's pie and place it on the six waiting plates. Otto walked through the back door, kicking off his boots and sneaking up behind Eira to wrap her in a hug. Their laughter carried through the whole house, filling all of the nooks and crannies with so much love it was almost palpable.

"Coming, Em?" Fen asked as he nodded in the direction of the dining room. Ember nodded with a smile as she followed him in, sitting in the middle of Fen and Killian. Eira summoned the plates to land at each spot on the table, and Otto brought cider from the fridge as they both came to sit down. Laughter carried through the house all through dinner, and Ember took a deep breath, soaking in every second.

She sat in the same seat, in the same room, and with the same people that she had every night for the last eight months, but something felt different. In the last twenty-four hours, something had shifted. The air around her felt lighter, like all of the pressure and loneliness that stifled her lungs had vanished and was replaced with a feeling she didn't quite recognize but devoured just the same. It felt like hope and peace and love all swirled together and washed over her like a tidal wave. She looked around at the family talking and laughing together, and it hit her like a ton of bricks.

She was home.

Supper went like it normally did, but instead of making herself as small as possible, she found herself laughing at Fen's dumb jokes, asking Maeve about her adventures that morning, and carrying on a conversation with Eira and Otto about school. It felt normal, like she had been doing it her whole life, like she had never known a time of loneliness or heartache.

"Have you heard anything about Rowan?" Eira asked calmly as she looked between the three teenagers, catching all of them off guard.

"Oh, um, no," Ember stuttered. "We haven't heard anything."

"I do hope they find her soon. I can't imagine what Nora is going through, especially after losing her oldest." She sniffled as she dabbed a napkin at the corner of her eye. "I don't know what I would do if anything ever happened to any of you." She leaned over and kissed Fen on the cheek as she silently sobbed.

"Ugh, Mum," he groaned as he pulled away and rubbed his cheek violently, making Ember snort into her cider.

"You four have to take care of each other," she said as she looked around the table, including Killian in her words. "Family is all you've got in this world, the only thing that is constant."

Ember felt her heart soar as she looked around the table, and peace settled over her.

I think this one will stick.

CHAPTER 29
A CHOICE TO MAKE

"E mber, we're going to be late for Galdr," Fen whined as she stuffed her books back in her bag and tossed it across her shoulder.

"It'll take five minutes, Fenrir. Stop your griping," she replied as she rolled her eyes. "Besides, Professor Bjorn can help us, and we could use all the help we can get."

"Are you sure we can trust him?" Killian said hesitantly as they made their way up the spiral stairs leading to the professor's office.

"I don't think we have much of a choice." She shrugged. She adjusted the strap of her bag, gripping it a little tighter, and knocked loudly on the wooden door. Without a word from the other side, the door swung open, and they walked slowly inside.

"Ah, Miss Lothbrok, Mr. Kitt, Mr. Vargr." Professor Bjorn nodded in their direction. "To what do I owe this pleasure?" His pen scratched across the parchment in front of him.

"We had a question actually, Professor," Fen stuttered as he stood in the doorway beside Killian. Ember shoved both of the boys inside the room and quietly shut the door behind them.

"I'm afraid I can't give you another extension, Mr. Kitt," the professor replied as he kept his eyes on the papers in front of him. "If I don't have your paper on the unicorn rebellion of 1875 by Friday, I'm afraid I'll have to give you a zero."

"Actually, Professor," Ember replied as she took a deep breath, "we were wondering if we could talk to you about the Lost Family."

Professor Bjorn's pen stopped scratching, and he peered over his monocle at the trio. "I think Professor Orion would be better suited for those questions, don't you?"

"Actually, um," Ember stuttered, "the topic is sort of... sensitive."

For a few seconds, the silence was deafening. He slowly took the monocle off his eye and attached it to his vest, clasping his hands together on the desk in front of him. After a few beats, he motioned to the chair in front of him and quickly conjured two more. The trio sat down silently, glancing at each other. It was one thing to talk amongst each other about what they thought, but it was another entirely to sit in front of their professor and try to remember the monologue they had rehearsed in their heads.

"We were, um," Ember stuttered. "We were just wondering, um, if you—"

"We wanted to know what information you can give us about the Lost Family," Killian all but demanded without even blinking.

Ember straightened her spine, momentarily taken aback by the fierceness dripping from his tongue. Gone was the goofy, sarcastic boy she had watched her brother wrestle in the orchards, momentarily hidden behind an air of aristocratic superiority as he puffed his chest.

"Ah." Professor Bjorn nodded. "I assume you know that there is no definitive proof that they even existed, yes?"

"Yes, Professor." Ember nodded. "But—"

"But we know," Killian interrupted again, "that proof

does not necessarily equal truth, and truth is what we're after."

"Duly noted." Professor Bjorn smirked. "Can I offer you some tea?"

The trio nodded slowly and watched as the professor twirled his hand through the air, conjuring a kettle and four cups. He placed one in front of each of the teenagers and flicked his wrist to send the tea kettle swishing through the air in front of them, gently pouring tea into each waiting mug. Ember sipped quietly as her eyes darted between the two boys and her professor, holding her breath as she waited impatiently.

"Helvig was the family name of the original children of Odin"—he cleared his throat—"allegedly."

Ember sucked in a quiet breath and silently slid forward in her seat, hanging onto every word he said.

"The Helvigs were a powerful family," he continued. "Very powerful. They controlled most of the lives of the First Families. Some say Odin himself told them about Ellesmere Island and gave them the coordinates to get here, along with the wards and repelling charms placed around the island to keep undesirables out."

"If the Helvigs were the ones who decided to settle Ellesmere," Fen asked as he scrunched his face, "why didn't they make it here with the rest of the families?"

"Now that is the question, isn't it?" The professor smirked. "Their values didn't quite align with the rest of the families, even Freyr, who had some questionable beliefs. They believed that the Vala were the only ones worthy of magic. Clann Helvig believed that they were superior. Their beliefs became dangerous. Some say their ship went down a few hundred miles off the coast and were lost at sea. Others say they never even made it onto their ships."

"And what do you say?" Killian asked through narrowed

eyes, lounging in his chair as he sipped his tea, as if this was normal, everyday conversation.

Professor Bjorn let out a gruff laugh and leaned back in his chair, folding his hands over his tweed vest. "There are stories that say the family successfully made it to the island, and instead of settling on the south end here with the rest of the families, they went to the north."

"But that's past the Dark Forest," Fen whispered. "No one goes past the forest."

"Aye," Professor Bjorn nodded. "That would make it the perfect hiding place, wouldn't it?" His face was serious, but Ember could've sworn she saw his eyes twinkle.

"I don't understand," Ember replied. "How could an entire group of people live right on the other side of the island and no one knew? It's impossible."

The professor leaned forward, propping his arms on the edge of the table as a small grin played at the corner of his mouth. "My dear girl," he chuckled, "we live on an island teeming with magic on every corner. I dare say nothing is outside of the realm of possibility."

"Thank you, Professor," Killian said genuinely as he downed the rest of his tea and stood up. "You've really helped a lot."

The trio made their way to the door as Professor Bjorn began cleaning up the cups scattered across his desk. The boys made their way down the spiraling staircase, but Ember stopped at the threshold, gripping the side of the door as she chewed on the bottom of her lip. She whipped her body around, slowly making her way back toward the desk.

"Do you need something else, Miss Lothbrok?" Professor Bjorn asked as he took his seat.

Ember fidgeted with her bag as she shifted her weight back and forth on the balls of her feet. She opened her bag, pulled the tattered book out that she had been carrying around, and laid it on the desk in front of her. "Did my father tell you?" she asked as she pointed to the worn cover. "Did you know about me?"

Professor Bjorn picked up the book and twirled it in his hand, studying the old lettering on the front. His eyes landed back on her, and he let out a small sigh as he sat back down in his chair. "I had a hunch," he breathed as he flipped through the book. "After you were born, your dad dove into his research, learning everything he could about the Wildlings. He wanted to understand about you... he wanted to protect you. Sometimes, I wonder if that put him in more danger."

"So, it's true then," Ember replied. "I'm a—"

"A Wildling," he whispered as a small grin played at the corner of his mouth.

"And the legend?" she asked as she twirled the end of her braid around her finger. "Did you know about that too?"

"I had my suspicions. He never said anything, but after your dad picked up and left the island, they were all but confirmed." His eyes floated from the book up to Ember, moisture gathering in the corners. "I don't know what you remember about your parents, but everything your dad did was to protect you, Ember... Everything."

Ember swallowed the lump that was steadily growing in her throat as she nodded. As usual, she had more questions than she did answers, but she wasn't convinced voicing them was going to do any good. "Thank you, Professor." She did her best to smile. She grabbed the book and stuffed it back in her bag, adjusting the strap back over her shoulder and turned toward the door.

"Miss Lothbrok," Professor Bjorn said as her fingers brushed the cold brass on the doorknob, "I know you have been dealt a hand that most could never endure. Your story has been a hard one, with more sad endings than happy, but you mustn't forget the happy ones. I'm not asking that you be happy that those parts of your story are over, but you must keep reading."

Ember nodded and slipped out the door so he couldn't see the tears slipping down her cheeks. She wiped away the moisture with the back of her hand as she hurried down the spiraling steps and toward the classroom door where Fen and Killian were whispering together on the other side. She brushed past them, grabbing both of their hands and pulling them down the empty corridor.

"Slow down, Starshine," Killian laughed as he pulled her backwards, causing her to trip over her feet. "What's the rush?"

Ember shook her head. "Not here," she whispered and dragged them down the hall, slipping into an empty bathroom and locking the door behind her. Her heart beat rapidly in her throat as she paced back and forth, chewing at her bottom lip and twirling the end of her braid.

"Um, are you okay, Em?" Fen asked as he glanced around the room and shoved his hands in his pockets. Ember didn't reply. Instead, she walked over to the nearest sink, bending forward and looking into the glass. She blinked a few times and took a shaky breath, then quickly slipped the green contacts out of her eyes. Lavender eyes blinked back at her, and she spun around to face the boys before she lost the little bit of courage she had found.

"Bloody hell," Killian mumbled under his breath, smoky eyes as big as saucers.

Ember scuffed the toe of her shoe against the floor as she chewed on the bottom of her lip.

"Your eyes," Fen whispered, "They're—"

"Yeah," she whispered in reply. "It's always kind of freaked people out." She gave a sheepish grin, internally begging them to say something… anything. Worst case scenarios of them running away like every other family flew through her mind as she chewed heavily on her lip, the faint taste of copper running across her tongue.

"Seems bleedin' stupid to be freaked out by someone's

eyes." Killian shrugged. "Almost as stupid as lying about them." His face was serious, but a small smile tugged at the corner of his mouth. That, however, did not stop Ember's heart from falling into her stomach. Of course, he was right. She had been lying since the day she met him—since the day she met both of them—but what choice did she have?

"I spent my whole life alone because I was different," she replied, eyes glued to the floor in front of her. "I wasn't about to give anyone else a reason to whisper about me."

"Who cares what people think," Killian scoffed, as if it was the most pointless argument he had ever heard. "Let them jump to their own conclusions."

Ember breathed a small laugh. "People can be more cruel than I think you realize."

"And those people?" Fen replied seriously. "They can change the narrative, but they can't change the facts. We know who you are, and that's all that matters."

Killian nodded his head, crossing his arms over his chest. "We're pack."

Tears pricked the corners of Ember's eyes as she did her best to keep them from running down her cheeks. She took a shaky breath, stuffing her hands in her pockets as she looked up at the two boys standing in front of her.

Pack. Family.

"No more secrets," Fen said stoically. "At least not with each other."

Killian let out a barking laugh that made Ember's chest feel like it was filled with a thousand stars, the entire cosmos beating in her veins.

"Only secrets from others," he replied, his eyes twinkling with mischief.

"While we're on the topics of secrets," Ember said as she narrowed her eyes, "care to share why you've been lurking in alcoves with the Ellingboe twins, Vargr?"

Killian's cheeks turned crimson as he mumbled something unintelligible under his breath.

"What was that mate?" Fen prodded.

"I said they're my cousins," he huffed. "As I'm sure you're aware, I don't come from the best family." Fen let out a snicker, and Killian quickly elbowed him in the ribs. "They were convinced by my parents to try to get me to join the *family business* when I come of age."

"Family business?" Ember asked with a raised brow.

Killian shook his head. "I've told them no a thousand times, but they won't let up. With my *affliction*, as my father likes to call it, they're all convinced I would be the perfect Dark Artifacts dealer."

Aaahh, so he is a prince. He just doesn't want to be.

"What is a Dark Artifacts dealer?" Ember asked as she crossed her arms and arched her brow, leaning back on the sink behind her.

"It's like the Vala's version of the black market," Fen replied, pushing his glasses up the bridge of his nose. "You can get all sorts of stuff like illegal potions and plants, cursed objects, Illegal spell books, things of that nature."

To both of the boys' surprise, Ember let out a loud laugh. "Honestly," she smiled, "have they even met you?"

Fen smiled as he clapped his friend on the shoulder. "Alright, now no more secrets."

Ember stared at the boys for a while, allowing the heaviness of the secrets they all clung to for so long to fade away with every breath that left her chest. "No more secrets."

"How much further?" Fen groaned as his shoes squished through the mud on the forest floor. Ember laughed as she heard Killian huff, stuffing his hands deeper into his pockets as the glowing light hovered in front of his face, illuminating the path in front of them.

"If you ask again, I'll hex you and leave you for someone else to deal with," he grumbled.

Water dripped from the leaves above them sporadically, the remnants of the rain shower that evening making its presence known as it soaked through Ember's light jacket and fiery curls. Spring was well on its way, the days growing longer and longer, but the cold still bit at her cheeks.

"Play nice," she laughed. "Nobody is hexing anyone tonight." She shot a glance at the boys, who both let out a huff and stuffed their fists deeper into their pockets. She could hear them whispering behind her, and just when she thought she was going to have to break up yet another squabble, the path they were on widened and moonlight bounced off the damp ground below them.

"Finally." Fen sighed as he picked up his pace, bursting into the opening at the edge of the forest. Ember laughed as he sped through the wet grass and his foot caught on a rock hidden in the dark, sending him face first into the mud.

"See," she giggled to Killian. "Hexing him wasn't even necessary."

"He does have a tendency to beat me to it." Killian smirked. Fen heaved himself off the ground, wiping away the wet dirt clinging to his jeans and hoodie, and spun around to sling some snide remark at the pair giggling behind him. Before he was able to get the first syllable out, the water broke behind him, sending him spinning in the other direction.

Three beings made their way out of the water, red cloaks draped over their iridescent skin. They left webbed footprints in the wet sand, and the only noise that could be heard was the sound of waves breaking off the rocks in the distance.

"I thought we might be seeing you soon, Miss Lothbrok." Maren smiled as she slid the red hood from her head. "And I see you took heed to my warning." She nodded toward the boys standing behind Ember, laughing as Killian quickly snapped his mouth closed.

"Yes." Ember smiled. "I just wish you could've been a bit more specific."

"One meets their destiny often on the road they take to avoid it," she replied quietly, eyes twinkling under the moonlight.

Ember nodded. "We were hoping we could talk to you a little bit about something; the Clann seems most likely to know better than anyone else on the island."

"The Lost Family, I suspect?" Kaan stated more than asked from behind Maren. His webbed hands were folded neatly in front of him and his face was unreadable.

"Um, yes, sir," Ember stuttered. "How did you—"

"You are a bright young Vala," Asherah said calmly with a kind smile, "but you still have a lot to learn."

Ember nodded and glanced to her left, immediately noticing that both the boys had backed up several steps, almost hiding behind her. She rolled her eyes as they huddled together, looking anywhere but at the beings in front of them.

"Honestly," she breathed as she rolled her eyes.

Maren beckoned them forward toward a group of rocks at the edge of the shoreline. Ember turned around, grabbing both of the boys by the wrists and dragging them toward the edge of the water. Maren sat in front of them, the picture of elegance and grace with her hands placed gently on her lap.

"There was a family that landed on the north end of the island," she began. "They stayed there, never wandering very far. The Dark Forest kept them hidden, though from what I'm not sure."

"Are they still there?" Fen whispered, squirming slightly on the rock he was perched on.

"I'm not sure." Maren shook her head. "Not even our kind venture to that side of the island. Dark creatures live in the forest, but I'm afraid they don't get much better when you come out on the other side."

"We think…" Ember stuttered. "We think Rowan might be there. Maybe with them, or I guess their descendants. We need to find her."

"She has the book." Maren nodded knowingly. "Are you sure you know what you're getting into?"

"Of course we do." Killian smirked, suddenly finding his courage again. "And what we don't, we'll figure out as we go." He leaned back on the large rock, resting his elbow on the cold surface and began throwing pebbles into the water, like this was any old evening adventure.

Ember rolled her eyes.

Heavily.

"You must be careful," Maren said gravely. "There are things on the north end of the island far more dangerous than Rowan O'Rourke."

The trio nodded solemnly and stood up from the rocks. The boys gave their thanks and said their goodbyes, walking back toward the tree line. Ember stood up, giving Maren a small wave, and turned to follow them before something stopped her. She tightened the grip on the strap of her satchel and turned back around to face the Merrow.

"You knew about me, didn't you?" she asked, voice almost shaking. "You knew the legend was about me. You knew I was a Wildling."

Maren nodded her head. "I did. We've been waiting a long time for you to come home."

"But why?" Ember whispered. "If I am supposed to do all these terrible things—terrible things to your people and so many others—why have you been waiting for me? You would've been better off if I never learned about Ellesmere."

"Just because something is written, doesn't make it so." Maren smiled. "Not every story is true. Sometimes the things that were wicked before become the things that save us, and the things that were good doom us to misery and pain."

"Then, why does everyone believe it?" Ember asked quietly, frustration building in her chest.

"Nothing is set in stone," she said, "but set on a dirt road. If you roll your wagon down the same path enough times, it will be the only path you can take without struggling."

"So, you don't believe that I'll be the downfall of all magical beings?" Ember asked with a forced laugh.

Maren smiled sweetly, running the back of her hand down Ember's freckled cheek. "We believe that fate is fluid, but you have a choice to make, and no one can make it for you."

Ember chewed at the bottom of her lip, searching for the words to say. So many questions reeled through her mind, but she couldn't muster up the courage to voice any of them. She nearly jumped out of her skin when she heard Killian yell.

"Come on, Starshine! Let's get movin'!"

Ember let out a small laugh and turned to face Maren again.

"Thank you," she whispered, grabbing the Merrow's hand. "Thank you for everything."

Maren gave her a small nod and turned to walk back into the water. Ember spun around, walking quickly toward the tree line to catch up with the boys, who were waiting very impatiently.

"Everything alright?" Fen asked as he furrowed his brow.

"Yeah." Ember smiled. "Yeah, I think it will be."

CHAPTER 30
A BEAUTIFUL NIGHT FOR A COUP

T he March sun warmed Ember's face as she leaned back against an apple tree, thumbing through the book she had snagged from the library that morning. She tugged her sweater tighter as a gust of wind whipped through the trees, sending a shiver up her spine and goosebumps down her arms. Killian and Fen's voices carried through the orchard as they sped above the trees, twirling and diving on their boards, seemingly without a care in the world.

Maia nuzzled further into Ember's lap, making small clicks as she ran her hand down her velvet back. Ember knew she should be researching, or gathering her things, or doing anything in the world to prepare for what they would be doing later that evening, but instead, she decided relaxing in the orchard was what she needed.

"That was a foul!" Fen shouted as he and Killian landed on the grass beside her, effectively snapping her out of her trance.

"It wasn't a foul, you prat." Killian laughed. "You're just a sore loser."

Ember laughed as Fen crossed his arms with a huff and planted himself on the grass beside her.

"Em, tell him it was a foul!"

"You know he wouldn't act like this if you would come fly with us." Killian smirked as he sank to the ground gracefully, running his fingers through his shaggy blond hair.

"I'm fairly good at math," she quipped, "and I'm pretty sure three people can't ride on two boards."

"We can if we share." Killian winked.

"We could ask Mum and Dad to get you one!" Fen proclaimed, ignoring his friend. "It's more fun with three anyway."

"Or," she replied sarcastically, "I could sit down here with Maia and read while you two gracefully try to kill each other."

Fen shrugged, ignoring the insult, and reached his hand up in the air, successfully summoning an apple from one of the top branches and taking a satisfying bite out of the side of it. After a moment, a grin broke out across his face, and he summoned two more, handing one to Ember and tossing the other up in the air a few times.

"Wanna play fetch?" he asked Killian, flashing a grin in his direction.

Killian cut his eyes at him, his mouth forming a straight line. "I'm a werewolf, not a dog," he hissed and snatched it out of the air before Fen could try anything funny.

"Are you two done?" Ember breathed a laugh. "Or am I going to have to figure this out myself?" She snapped her book closed and stuffed it in the bag lying next to her knee, jostling Maia awake from her nap.

"Whoa, wait," Fen said as he rapidly scrolled on his phone. "Did you see this?"

"How on earth did you get the island's paper on your phone?" Killian squinted as he yanked it from his friend's hand.

"That's not the point," he replied as he snatched it back. "Chief Thornsten did an interview today, look." He held his screen up for the two teenagers to get a better look. "He's warning everyone to stay clear of the Dark Forest, and they're even adding extra warding around the school." He furrowed his brow as he rapidly scrolled down further on his phone. "It looks like the Fae have been more active and have more guards up around the entrance to their territory, like they're preparing for something."

"Sounds like they know something we don't," Killian mumbled as he leaned against the tree.

"Or maybe we do," Ember whispered as she whipped out her notebook and began flipping quickly through its pages.

"Care to share with the class, Starshine?"

"If they are guarding their territory more than normal, something out of the norm has to be happening," she stated. "And not something on this side of the forest, or we would know about it."

Both boys gave her a confused look which prompted her to sigh and roll her eyes.

"If we know nothing has happened on this side of the forest, then it's only plausible to believe they're preparing for someone else… on the other side."

"The Lost Family?" Fen whispered as he slipped his phone back in his pocket. "But there's no proof they're even still alive."

Ember shrugged. "If proof was all that was needed, the world would tell you I didn't exist, either."

"Okay, so Rowan is on the other side of the forest, either alone or with backup," Kilian sighed. "What do we do?"

"We can't go around it," Fen huffed as he sunk to the ground and rested his head against the tree behind him. "There are too many wards up to prevent that very thing from happening. Honestly, how has no one questioned that before now?"

"We can't go around," Ember agreed as she sat beside Fen, Killian quickly following suit. "So, we have to go through."

"I'm sorry, Starshine." Killian laughed. "But I think you missed the part about the band of Fae lying in wait."

Ember shook her head. "We don't have any other options. Just because she's there now, doesn't mean she will be for long. We have to get that book back. This could be our only chance. We'll just... I don't know, stay as far away from the entrance to their territory as possible."

"Okay, I have a plan," Killian announced as he took another bite from the apple, leaning back on his elbow in the grass.

"Is it a good plan?" Fen squinted.

"...I have *a* plan."

"Well?" Ember asked.

"I think we should go tonight," Killian replied.

"Tonight?"

"Think about it," he said as he sat up. "The whole island will be in town for the Spring Equinox Festival. All we have to do is sneak off to the Echopoint, and no one will even know we're gone."

"No," Fen said as he shook his head. "No. Absolutely not. No. They would find us out in a heartbeat."

"Do you have a better idea?" Killian snapped in reply. Fen glared at him, ready with some witty reply, when Ember laid her hand on his forearm.

"He's right, Fen," she said gently. "We don't have much of a choice. We have to finish this sooner rather than later."

Fen's face softened, and he nodded, not willing to fight his point with her.

"They'll never know, mate," Killian reassured. "We'll be back, unscathed, before the sun rises on the better half of the year." His eyes twinkled in the light breaking through the leaves of the orchard, and Ember was certain if she stared for too long, she would get hopelessly lost in them. She shook her head lightly, banishing the thoughts threatening to distract her from the task at hand.

"Tonight then," she breathed. "We finish this tonight."

"REALLY, FEN? AGAIN?" Ember said as the boy sauntered up to her and Killian. "You're supposed to blend in. People are staring."

Fen stared at them dumbfounded, like he couldn't possibly understand why his outfit, made up of a black jacket, black boots, and black pants, could ever make him stick out while people were running about in bright spring colors.

"You look like an international spy, mate," Killian barked as he leaned against the large fountain. "Planning a coup, are we?"

Fen rolled his eyes as he zipped his jacket and stuffed his hands in his pockets, ignoring the laughter coming from his friend. "Let's just go before anyone sees," he mumbled and trudged toward the Echopoint at the end of town, leaving Ember and Killian a few paces behind him.

"You know…" Killian smirked. "It is a beautiful night for a coup. You could count the stars, it's so clear." He lifted his hand to the sky and began tracing patterns in the air.

Ember breathed a small laugh. "It's quite pointless to count stars."

"Aye." He nodded. "It's also pointless to count freckles, but I know you have twenty-four on your left hand."

Ember felt heat creep up her neck and turned her head to hide the seven shades of crimson she knew were staining her cheeks. Before she could think of a witty reply, she felt his hand grab hold of hers, and she was certain her heart was going to leap straight out of her chest.

"You're scared, aren't you?" he asked, already knowing the answer.

Ember bit the corner of her lip. "I'm not," she mumbled. "Not really anyway."

Killian slowed to a stop, turning his body toward her. "Your brother and I…" he stuttered. "We won't let anything happen to you. I know our friendship has been anything but normal, but I will do everything in my power to protect you. Always."

She looked back at him, lavender eyes meeting gray, and really saw him for the first time. His hair was still a mess, and in the glow of the moonlight, he looked more handsome and more human than she had ever seen him.

"I guess I'm asking you to trust me," he whispered.

Ember swallowed the lump forming in her throat and nodded her head, willing her heart to slow down. "You're awfully dramatic," she replied, trying to laugh off his words.

"And you're the storm I never saw coming." He grinned.

"We haven't got all night!" Fen cried from down the road, waving an arm frantically in the air. Ember let out a laugh as she caught up to him, Killian trailing behind her. The trio grabbed the low hanging branch on the tree and spun quickly through the air, dropping on the wet grass as they landed.

"I'm having many regrets," Fen grunted as he wiped the dust off his pants.

"I told you that outfit was a bad idea last time." Ember shrugged with a laugh, adjusting her satchel back onto her shoulder.

"This outfit is stealthy, for your information," Fen hissed. "It allows me to become one with the shadows. I am the night." He leaped forward over a boulder on the edge of the road, bound and determined to prove that his outfit choice was not in vain. Instead of landing gracefully on the other side, though, the toe of his boot stuck in a crevice in the rock. His foot stayed in place while the rest of his body flung through the air, and he landed with a hard thud on the ground.

"Not the night," Killian laughed, "but most definitely a nightmare."

Fen huffed as he stood back up. "Let's just go."

The trio walked silently down the road toward the edge of the Dark Forest. A light breeze blew through the air, bringing with it the smell of lavender and honeysuckle. All of the warmth from the day was gone, and the cold was starting to seep into Ember's fingers. She stuffed them into her pockets and glanced up at the sky. She drank in the light radiating from the moon and stars, knowing that in a few minutes the darkness surrounding the trees would engulf them entirely. She tugged the strap to her bag a little tighter when clicking sounds came from inside of it. She furrowed her brow as she opened it, and a little velvet head popped out.

"What on earth are you doing here, girl," she said to Maia as the draic jumped out of the bag and scurried up her arm, perching herself on her shoulder like a bird. She nuzzled her snout into the girl's fiery hair, cooing and clicking as if to say hello.

"She's rather attached to you," Killian said as he rubbed Maia's head lightly. "Most draics don't bond well with people."

"It runs in the family." Fen smirked.

Ember let out a small laugh and wondered just how much nature actually trumped nurture.

They reached the edge of the forest, and Ember stopped for a moment, toeing the line between heading forward and running as fast as she could back to her safe, warm bed. She chewed on the bottom of her lip as her heart rate increased, and she felt the familiar feeling of fight or flight kick in, and flight always won. She reached slowly in her bag, pulling out a small silver bell, and looped it around the strap on her bag. It let out a small jingle before going silent, like it was listening to a cue from the environment around it.

"What's that?" Killian asked.

"Silver bell," she mumbled in reply, fidgeting with the string holding the cold metal in place.

"A bell? Are you trying to give away our position?" Fen asked with concern. She didn't look, but she was certain Killian was nodding beside her.

Ember felt her face turn red and quickly untied the string, slipping the bell deep into her bag, placing it between books and papers to muffle any sound that tried to escape. She trained her eyes back on the tree line in front of her and took another shaky breath.

Before she could bolt in the opposite direction, she felt a hand wrap around hers and give her a gentle squeeze. She looked to her right to see Fen giving her a small smile.

"You ready?" he whispered.

She bobbed her head lightly and took a deep breath. "Ready."

Killian whispered, "*Lux,*" beside her, and a small ball of light appeared, floating ahead of him. They made their way under the looming canopy, and Ember tried to keep her feet as silent as possible. The forest was quiet for now, but she knew better than to tempt fate.

"How many dangerous creatures do ya think there are in here?" Fen asked nonchalantly, as he kicked a rock at his feet. "Like fifty?"

"The creatures are the least of our worries." Killian shivered. "We're dangerously close to Fae territory."

"Are you scared, Vargr?" Ember teased, jabbing him in the rib with her elbow.

"Scared? Absolutely not," he quipped. "But even a werewolf isn't stupid enough to get in the way of the Fae."

"Aren't you out here a lot?" Ember asked. "I mean, that's how you found me all those times, isn't it?"

"No," Killian breathed a laugh. "I wasn't already in the forest. I came in looking for you."

Ember furrowed her brow as she thought back to the times she had landed at the wolf's feet, bruised and bloodied and terrified. She remembered how far she had run into the forest, how lost she had felt when she couldn't figure out where she was. Her heart beat steadily in her chest as she remembered the way his eyes looked.

So human, she had thought.

"If you weren't already there," she mumbled, "how did you know where to find me?"

Killian furrowed his brow. "I don't really know," he replied. "It was like there was this invisible string tugging at my chest." He patted his hand over his sternum. "Right here. I could feel it in my veins, like my magic was making me move. I just transformed and followed the pull, and it led me to you."

"I felt it too," Fen whispered.

Ember jumped at the sound of his voice, almost forgetting he was there.

"That night you snuck off with Rowan, I knew something was off. I felt the tugging and honestly thought I was going crazy." He let out a shaky breath, like he was piecing together a puzzle. "I knew something was wrong before Killian even told me. I knew you were in trouble."

Ember felt her stomach form a tight knot as she remembered the way her magic had thrummed in her veins that day in town. The day Killian had, literally, run into her and sent her tumbling to the cobblestones. She remembered the way the invisible chord had tugged toward him, the way the magic felt like electricity in the air.

And they had felt it too.

She was abruptly pulled from her thoughts when she heard a bush rustle in the distance, followed by a dull snap from a twig on the forest floor. She stopped in her tracks, both hands flying beside her at each of the boys.

"Stop," she whispered. "Did you hear that?"

The boys looked at her with furrowed brows, and Killian looked like he wanted to say something along the lines of, "There's nothing there, you're hearing things," but whatever words he planned to say died in his throat when another twig snapped, this time much closer to them.

"Should we run?" Fen whispered. "I feel like we should be running."

But none of them moved. Each set of feet were glued to the ground below them, refusing to budge even an inch. Ember felt like her heart was going to jump straight out of her chest. Her pulse quickened, and despite the cold air around her, beads of sweat dripped from her brow. A shiver ran down her spine when she heard a whisper behind her.

"*Run.*"

The hair on the back of her neck stood up, and she instinctively reached down by her side, taking hold of Killian's hand.

"What did you say?" she whispered.

Killian tore his face away from the brush in front of them and furrowed his brow in confusion. "I didn't say anything…"

Ember swallowed the lump that was forming in her throat and tugged the boy's hand, "We need to move. We can't stand here like sitting ducks."

But before she could take a step further, the brush in front of them rippled ominously, and the bush suddenly moved, walking straight toward them.

But no, the bush wasn't moving. Bushes didn't have feet. They didn't creep through the woods or snap twigs left in their wake. Nevertheless, whatever it was was walking very fast.

And it was headed straight for them.

Before the trio had a chance to bolt in any other direction, the ominous bush stopped abruptly, and slender green hands reached out from the leaves. That was when a lightbulb flashed in Ember's head. It wasn't a bush, of course not. It was a person. Or something resembling a person. Its long slender fingers grasped the brush, what Ember now realized was a hooded cloak covered in leaves and twigs, and flung it off their head. Ember sucked in her breath as tangled black hair fell from under the hood, ivy weaving in and out of the waves. His feet were bare, save the dirt plastered all over them, and his face was unreadable. Ember heard both the boys beside her let out an audible sigh of relief, and her head snapped to the left.

"Thank the gods," Killian breathed as he ran a shaky hand through his hair.

"What is it?"

"Ghillie Dhu," Fen whispered, visibly relaxing at the sight of the being in front of them.

"Ghillie what?" Ember hissed.

"Ghillie Dhu," the being in front of them replied. "This is my forest to protect, and you are dangerously far from home, young ones." His voice was stern but gentle, like they were being scolded for not being home in time for supper.

"We're trying to make it to the other side of the forest," Killian replied confidently. "We aren't here to cause mischief."

"It's not safe for your kind out here, nor over there," he replied. "I urge you to turn around." His voice was low and foreboding, and it seemed to reverberate in Ember's mind.

"We won't linger long." Fen smiled, obviously feeling more calm now. "We'll be in and out, scout's honor." He held two fingers up, giving a confident smile as Killian choked back his laughter.

"See that you do," he replied. "There are far more dangerous things out there than my kind." And without another word, he turned and left, disappearing like a shadow into the trees behind him.

Ember turned around and promptly swatted both boys on the arm.

"What was that?" she hissed. "He could've killed us!" But her scolding fell on deaf ears. Both of the boys were doubled over, trying to stifle their laughter that bounced off the canopy above them.

"It's a Ghillie Dhu, Em," Fen said as he wiped tears from

his eyes. "He might look like a right terror, but he wouldn't harm children."

"He can't harm them," Killian said with a chuckle. "A Ghillie Dhu's only two jobs are to protect the forest, and the children that might wander in it."

"What did he mean by 'his kind?'" Ember asked as she ran her hand over Maia's back, who had finally come out of hiding from the back around her shoulder. "Are there more of him?"

"Lots more," Killian replied. "He's Fae, and this forest is theirs, but he's right. We shouldn't stay long. They aren't all quite so kind. Or protective."

Ember nodded with a heavy sigh. The trio ventured forward silently and only made it a few minutes down the path when they heard rustling in the bushes behind them again.

"For Odin's sake," Killian hissed. "Really, the last thing we need is an overprotective Fae following us around." He whirled around to face the direction of the noise. "We're fine!" he shouted, but he got no reply. Instead, the ground shook beneath their feet, like an earthquake. The trees in front of them seemed to bend to the will of the being walking through them, arching back and forth as the figure emerged.

Except it wasn't a being at all. It was an animal—covered in pitch black fur, bright glowing eyes, and fangs that could easily rip each of them in half with one bite. Ember's breath lodged in her throat as she stumbled back.

It was the biggest dog she had ever seen.

CHAPTER 31

FOLLOW THE STARS

"Bloody hell," Fen mumbled as the dog stepped further into the small clearing, gnashing his teeth as he went.

"What is that," Ember whispered as she reached for Maia, who was back to burrowing herself in the girl's neck.

"Cu Sidhe," Killian hissed, grabbing her free hand in his. With every step the giant dog took, his grip tightened around her fingers. For a brief moment, she was afraid they might break, but she couldn't bring herself to pull away.

"We're too close to the gateway," he continued. "The Cu Sidhe is a protector of the Fae. They will stop at nothing to protect their territory, including disposing of a few unsuspecting Vala children." He stood tall, but it didn't stop his voice from shaking.

"Oh perfect," Fen hissed. "I was beginning to run out of nightmare fuel. Where's that damned Ghillie Dhu when we need him?"

Killian took a slow step in front of Ember, squeezing her hand once more before letting go. "Stay behind me," he whispered, "and whatever you do, do not turn your back on it until Fen tells you to."

Before Ember could reply, his porcelain skin and platinum hair were replaced almost instantly by white fur. He turned his head toward her, golden amber eyes meeting lavender, and gave her a small nod. She felt the pull of an invisible cord stretching, reaching out to the wolf in front of her and the boy beside her, and braced her feet underneath her as it tugged tighter. She felt Fen's hand wrap tightly around hers.

"Don't move until I say so," he whispered, squeezing her hand tighter as he braced himself against the fear that had to be bubbling in his chest. Ember watched as Killian dug his giant paws further into the dirt, and a shiver ran up her spine as she heard a low growl emit from his throat. He turned to Fen, giving him a small nod before focusing his attention back on the giant dog in front of them, who was still slowly stalking toward them.

"On the count of three," Fen whispered, "I want you to run. Run and do not look back."

"Fen, no!" she hissed in reply. "I'm not going without you."

"We'll be right behind you," he assured her, giving her hand another small squeeze, "Just run and don't look back."

Ember nodded hesitantly, doing her best to mask the fear on her face.

"One," he whispered.

She turned her feet outwards.

"Two."

She took a deep shaky breath.

"Three!"

And she bolted. She ran as fast as her legs would carry her, not daring to look back. She could hear Fen's footfalls behind her, and not much further was the heavy thudding of Killian's paws. She ran and ran until she felt like her legs were going to collapse underneath her. She didn't dare look back, even to check that her friends were still there, even for a moment.

But it didn't matter.

Before she could turn around to see if they were out of harm's reach, she was face to face with the wild beast, its hot breath filling her lungs and stinging her eyes. She opened her mouth to cry out, but no sound came. She stared into his glowing eyes, unable to move and completely forgetting how to breathe. Before she had a chance to move, a streak of white came flashing over her, lunging straight for the dog's neck. The animals rolled through the dirt, kicking up dust and snapping twigs on the ground, leaving a trail of splinters in their wake. Ember's breath caught in her throat as she watched them roll through the mud, fangs ripping fur and ruby staining the dirt below them.

"Ember, move!" Fen shouted, running up quickly from behind her. She ducked just in time to see a jet of light soaring over her head as Fen shot a hex at the Cu Sidhe, hitting him between the shoulder blades. The fur on his neck bristled, and he turned his head quickly toward the source of the annoyance, setting his glowing eyes on Fen. A loud growl sounded from his open mouth, and the ground shook under Ember's feet. The dog took off toward Fen, and while Ember's mind reeled, trying to remember any hex she had tucked away in the catalogs in her brain, the wolf shot out from behind him, latching his canines into the dog's throat.

The Cu Sidhe shook furiously, using its weight to try and dislodge the smaller wolf from the skin around his neck. After several attempts, he successfully threw him off, directly into a large tree. He landed on the ground with a deafening yelp. He strained against his body weight, trying to heave himself up from the forest floor, but before he could, the giant dog ran toward him, swinging his paws, and slashed him directly across the chest.

"Killian!" Ember screamed, but he didn't move. She threw every hex, jinx, charm, and curse she could think of toward the animal as it ran at her, tears stinging her eyes and running down her cheeks. Fen came at him from the side, shooting jets of light with precision that Ember had never seen in him before, but it didn't seem to faze the beast. His raven fur was acting like a shield, and every bit of magic they threw his way bounced off him and fizzled to nothingness.

It was hopeless. They weren't powerful enough to stop him, or even slow him down. Her eyes locked with Fen's, and he bolted toward her, grabbing her hand and holding it tightly. She closed her eyes as the beast moved closer, and just when she was certain she could feel the heat from his breath, a voice rang out from behind her, stopping the dog in its tracks.

"*Sios.*"

Ember opened her eyes and saw a girl standing in front of her, running her hand up and down the muzzle of the dog, who was now kneeling on the ground in front of them. But no, it wasn't a girl, it was…

"Nessa!" Ember cried. The elf gave a small smile and then motioned toward the tree on the edge of the clearing.

"'I've got it from here. Go see to him," she said softly.

Ember's eyes shot toward the tree where Killian was now laying on the dirt. His shirt was ripped to shreds, and blood poured from his chest and head. Ember and Fen took off toward him, falling to the ground at his side.

"Killian," she whispered, running her hand through his blood-spattered hair. "Killian, what did you do?"

His eyes fluttered open, locking with hers. "I promised," he gasped for air, "to protect you, and I intend to keep that damn promise."

"We must hurry," Nessa said as she came up quickly behind them. "I've sent him away, but I can't guarantee others that I can't control won't return. The king and queen don't enjoy having their watch dog attacked."

Ember quickly wiped away the tears running down her cheek. "He can't walk. I don't think we can carry him."

Nessa waved her hands in front of her, levitating him and conjuring what looked like a stretcher underneath him.

"We must hurry. Follow me," she whispered, and then she was off.

Ember and Fen ran behind her, weaving in and out of trees and ducking quickly under low hanging branches. The young elf seemed to move like she was flying, one foot barely touching the ground before the other was in the air. It felt like hours before Ember saw the moon peeking through the canopy, the leaves slowly spreading further apart. She took one last breath and held it until they came tumbling out of the forest and into a grassy field. Ember grabbed her knees tightly and sucked in cold air like she hadn't breathed in days. Her throat burned as she tried to hold back the tears that were threatening to spill over.

She lifted her head to see Nessa lowering the stretcher that held Killian to the ground and Fen on his knees beside him. She made her way toward them, hesitant to see the state that her friend was in under the light of the moon. His eyes were open, but just barely, and the bleeding seemed to have slowed down. He gave her a small smile as she sat down, no doubt trying to calm her nerves. Tears pricked at her eyes as he grabbed her hand and squeezed, wincing as he tried to draw in a shallow breath.

"Ya know…" Fen choked a laugh as tears streamed down his dust covered face. "I can heal that for you if you want."

Killian breathed a small laugh. "Over my dead body," he said quietly.

Ember choked back another sob. "You're insane," she whispered. "Why did you do that?"

"There's no hope without risk." He smirked, wincing again as Nessa ran her hand over the gash on his head.

She mumbled to herself as she touched the gash on the back of his head, and then it was gone. "I can take care of your head since you split it open on the tree," Nessa said quietly, "but I'm afraid there's not much I can do about this one." She pointed at the deep, crimson claw marks running across his chest. "Injuries from a Cu Sidhe are cursed. There are some things even my magic can't touch." She stood up, brushing her hands against her pants. "I have to go make sure nothing followed. Stay here. Be safe."

"It's not much further," Ember said under her breath, as she stood up from the ground, brushing the dust off her pants.

"Well, let's go," Killian grunted as he pushed himself up on his elbow, then immediately fell back down on his back, hissing in pain.

"No," Ember replied. "You can't move. You have to stay here." She took a deep breath, searching for any remaining bits of confidence she had left. "I'm going to go on my own. Fen, stay with Killian."

"Are you mad?" Fen yelled as he jumped to his feet. "I'm not stayin' here while you run off to save the bloody island on your own."

She couldn't tell if his voice was laced with fear or anger, or maybe a little bit of both. She grabbed his hand and squeezed it tight. "I'll be okay," she whispered with a small smile. "Helio Maren. Stay with Killian, promise me."

Fen shook his head with a sigh. "I don't make promises I can't keep."

She bit the inside of her lip as she held back the tears that were welling in her eyes and gave him a small nod.

"Don't do anything I wouldn't do, Starshine." Killian smiled weakly.

She turned away quickly to head further into from the forest, away from the safety of her friends—her pack—and toward the unknown. Her chest shook as she walked, letting the tears fall that she had been holding back, giving herself one more moment of weakness to clear her mind. She shoved the memory of Killian injured and Fen distraught to the back of her mind and forced herself to focus. The hills rolled in front of her, each blade of grass rippling silently in the breeze. She had no map, no real way of knowing where she was supposed to go, but in the silence surrounding her, she let a distant memory float through her mind.

"*But, Papa, what if you get lost?*" *the tiny girl asked her father.*

"*Lost?*" *he barked.* "*I could never get lost, not with my little Starshine always calling me home.*" *The little girl let out a squeal as her father swung her through the air, her fiery braid whipping in the wind.* "*Follow the stars, and you'll never be lost.*"

And follow the stars she did.

She felt her magic pull her forward, like it was intertwined with the constellations hanging above her. She walked steadily, barely noticing her feet moving beneath her until she found herself at the bottom of a steep hill overlooking the dark valley. Steps lined the hill, twisting and winding above her, leading up to a large house. She felt her magic tug toward the steps and started the climb. She expected to be out of breath by the time she reached the top, but the adrenaline steadily pumping up her veins gave her stamina she had never experienced before. She reached the top and found herself standing in front of two large doors. From the bottom of the hill, it looked like an average sized house. But from where she stood now, she could see just how wrong she had been.

It was a manor, not unlike the one Killian lived in. At least three stories high, it seemed to reach directly to the heavens, and Ember's blood ran cold as a wave of terror washed over her. She quickly brushed it aside. It would do no good to dwell on what might be. She took a deep breath to steady herself and slowly pushed the large doors open.

Dark wood lined the floor, and each panel seemed to creak under her feet with every step she took. The walls were lined with expensive portraits and paintings, and the vaulted ceiling was littered with cobwebs. If anyone lived here, it was very obvious that they couldn't be bothered to clean. Ember felt a shiver run down her spine as a small breeze blew from somewhere in the drafty house. She made her way through the entryway toward two large double doors. She quietly shoved them open, stepping into the ballroom of the abandoned mansion. She looked around, squinting into the shadows for any sign that someone had been there.

"Oh, finally," a voice echoed from a far corner. "I was beginning to think you weren't going to make it."

She sucked in a breath and froze, unable to move or breathe for what felt like ages. Her entire body went cold as she whipped around, facing the person who had so casually announced their presence moments before. "Rowan."

CHAPTER 32
A CHOICE TO MAKE

"I trust you had no trouble finding the place?" Rowan smirked as she strolled about the room. "GPS sometimes gets turned around up here." She waved her hand in the air with a small laugh that sent a cold chill up Ember's spine.

Her former friend stood tall, looking confidently around the room like she owned the place. Her hair was neat, recently washed and styled, and her clothes looked brand new. She had an air about her that Ember didn't recognize, a confidence that she almost envied, but it annoyed her, nonetheless. Maia scurried down her arm quickly, hiding herself in the satchel that hung over her shoulder.

"Where is it, Rowan?" Ember demanded, feet planted firmly on the floor.

"I'm afraid I don't know what you're referring to?" she replied, feigning innocence.

"You know bloody well what I'm talking about," Ember hissed in reply. "Where's the bleedin' book?" Her patience was growing thinner with every moment, and her concern over getting out without a fight grew larger.

"Now, now, Ember, language," Rowan said calmly. "No

need to get nasty. I have it right here." She strolled toward a table on the other side of the room and gently picked the book up that was laying on top of it. "Can't very well let it out of my sight, now can I?" She flipped the book around in her hand a few times, tracing her fingers over the marks etched along the spine.

The sight of the book made Ember's stomach drop, and memories flooded back to her like a tsunami, threatening to knock her off her feet. Memories of afternoons in the library, of midnight adventures. Memories of laughter and jokes and a friendship she never imagined could be real, let alone possible. She closed her eyes as flashes of the serene clearing in the forest flashed across her vision and sucked in a breath as she remembered the feeling of watching the reality she thought she knew slip away for the second time in her life.

"I trusted you," Ember whispered, letting her mask fall. "You were my friend."

"I wasn't your friend," she quipped. "I needed you in order to find the book. You were a convenient means to an end."

Ember sucked in a breath and winced as she felt like a knife had been plunged through her back. Her chest shook lightly as she tried to remember how to breathe, and she chewed on the inside of her cheek. "Rowan, what are you doing?"

"I'm doing what I have to do," she hissed in reply. "I'm doing what you aren't strong enough to do."

Ember shook her head. "Ro, this isn't strength," she replied softly. "This is weakness."

"I am not weak!" she shouted. Ember felt magic ripple through the air, sparking at the end of Rowan's brown hair. The walls seemed to vibrate around them, threatening to close in and swallow them whole.

Ember took a small step back before bracing herself once

more. "I know about your father and brother," she whispered calmly. "I know what happened to them."

"You don't know anything," Rowan hissed.

"I know it wasn't fair," she replied. "Having them taken away from you like that... Nothing about it was fair. But that doesn't make this right."

Rowan balled her fist, her face contorting in rage, and Ember fought the urge to back up further, the urge to bolt for the door and forget about this crazy plan. Instead, she stood firm, feet planted, not letting her confidence waver. If she began to doubt herself, even for a moment, she knew it would be truly hopeless.

"You don't have to do this," Ember whispered. "It's self-destructive."

"I know," Rowan sneered.

"Do you?"

"Yes."

"Then, why are you doing it?" Ember asked softly.

"Because I want everyone to hurt as bad as I do," Rowan choked, teetering on the edge of emotion. "I want them to know the type of pain I'm going through. I don't want to be the only one who has to hear the monsters in my head, telling me to destroy myself. I want them to feel the torment that comes with living with this, with losing a piece of yourself, because I wasn't given any other option."

Ember looked across the room and watched the facade fall. She wasn't a villain hellbent on destroying the magical world. She wasn't the great monster she had made her out to be in her head. She wasn't evil or vindictive or teetering on the edge of insanity.

She was a child, and she was hurting.

She was a scared, young girl still grieving the loss of her father and brother. She needed someone to blame, she needed something to fill the void that they had left, so she stuffed it full of the only thing that made sense in that moment. Truthfully, it was like looking in a mirror and seeing all of the dark secrets she had only ever whispered to the stars. In that moment, seeing Rowan for who she truly was, she didn't feel anger or betrayal or fear.

She just felt pity.

"You still have a choice," she whispered, voice shaking slightly. "You can still make the right choice."

Rowan shook her head as she scowled. "I didn't get a choice then, so I'm making mine now. They took my brother, they took my father, and now I will take their life force."

Ember swallowed the lump forming in her throat and closed her eyes, letting the realization of what she was going to have to do sink into her heart. She let the heaviness weigh on her and silently let go of any hope she might have had walking in.

There was no room for hope. Not right now.

"You have a choice too, ya know," Rowan said stoically from the other side of the room, turning their conversation back on Ember.

Ember furrowed her brow. "A choice?"

"Aye," Rowan nodded. "You can help."

Without even realizing it, Ember let out a breathy laugh before squinting her eyes in disbelief. "What? You're serious?" she asked. "Help you?"

Rowan nodded her head again. "You can come home." A wry grin worked its way up the corner of her mouth. "Either willingly or not, it doesn't matter to me." She shrugged, flipping her hand over to nonchalantly check her nails. "Father would prefer you made the decision yourself, but I've been given allowance to bring you back by whatever means necessary."

Ember furrowed her brow. "Why on earth would you want me to help you? You can't possibly trust me."

Rowan rolled her eyes and let out a sigh. "Ember, I don't need to trust you. It is your duty to fulfill the prophecy.

Besides…" She tossed the book in her hand gently. "Father needs you to open it."

And that was when the realization hit Ember all at once. That was why Rowan had been so easy to find, why she hadn't just vanished without a trace, disappearing with the book into thin air. She couldn't fulfill the prophecy by herself because the book only answered to one person. Not to her. Not to her father. But to Ember. To a Wildling.

Bloody brilliant.

"What makes you think I would willingly go anywhere with you?" Ember hissed.

"Because you can have a home," Rowan replied. "You can have a family again. A real family. We're more alike than you might think."

Ember's thoughts floated to the Kitts, the way they had loved and protected her so fiercely since the day she arrived, even when she didn't deserve it at times. She thought to Fen, who had put his own life in danger more than once, just to protect her. To bring her home. Her chest filled with warmth as she thought about cold nights in front of the fire, warm tea waiting for her every morning, and her cozy spot in the library where she spent weekends huddled up by the large window. She squared her shoulders, planting her feet firmly on the floor.

"I have a family," Ember replied calmly, gathering strength from every sweet memory she could find. "I would rather die than become everything I have fought against. I'm not like you."

Ember jumped as Rowan let out a roaring laugh. The sound echoed through the empty building, bouncing off the dusty walls and cold tiles. Ember felt her heart racing in her chest, bracing herself for whatever was going to happen next.

"Silly girl," she laughed, "can't you see the truth right in front of you?" She took a slow, methodical step forward, gazing at Ember with a horrifying grin. "This is *his* kingdom," she hissed. "You can either rule with him or burn with the rest of them."

Ember stood as tall as she could muster, wishing desperately for Fen and Killian to be by her side. She felt the familiar feeling of a cord tugging out from the center of her chest, and she wondered briefly if the boys were feeling it too.

"I'd rather burn," she whispered.

Rowan shrugged as if Ember was simply telling her she couldn't come over for supper. "Have it your way, I suppose." She began pacing up and down the length of the vast ballroom, keeping her body strategically facing forward. "As I recall, you're not actually needed alive for the book to work." She grinned. "A cold body works just as well as a warm one." She planted her feet firmly and grinned wildly at the redhead. "One last chance, *Starshine*."

Ember's face was set in a scowl as she raised her hand, feeling her magic steadily thrum through her veins, like it could anticipate what was going to happen next. She took a deep breath, balling up her fists and feeling all of the anger and grief that had built up over the last nine years coming to the surface. Wind whipped around her, and a burst of magic pushed out through her hands, shattering every window in the room. "I don't like nicknames."

CHAPTER 33
A VERY SPECIFIC PROMISE

Jets of light filled the empty ballroom, illuminating it with shades of yellow, red, green, blue, and purple. The sound was deafening as spells bounced off every solid surface—and some not so solid—crackling and erupting as the girls fought to overpower one another. The room was like walking into a stained-glass window as the sparks bent against the shattered glass on the floor, sending light shooting in every direction. The smell of magic rippled through the air, like copper and lavender on her tongue, permeating every surface of the room and Ember thought it must've been a beautiful sight to see.

That was, if it wasn't for the whole dodging-certain-death-thing she was currently doing.

Rowan sent a strong jet of light directly toward Ember's chest, narrowly missing her as the redhead shot her hand in the air, using another spell to act like a shield.

"Been practicing your defensive spells, I see?" Rowan laughed. "Unfortunately, I don't think they're going to do you much good here." She sent off three spells in a row, back-to-back, and Ember had to dive out of the way to escape them. "While you were wasting your days at that pathetic excuse for a school, Father has been teaching me useful magic." She shot two more hexes, catching Ember once in the cheek. "Magic that doesn't require extensive defense."

Ember ran her hand quickly against her jawbone and wiped away the blood that was trailing down her face. She clamped her jaw closed, refusing to give into the taunting Rowan was slinging at her. She knew very well that it would distract her, and distraction was something she could not afford. The cord pulling at her chest tightened, her magic thrumming through it like electricity. The steady pulsing grew stronger, sending sparks rippling across her fingertips. The energy was different somehow. Stronger, but steady. It felt familiar, like a small piece of her that had been missing was finally back, and she was whole again. The smell painted a picture in her mind that she couldn't quite place. Like the trees in the orchard and the pages of a well-loved book.

Maia was alerted to the change in the magic in the air and promptly popped her head from the leather satchel she had been hiding in. Like she had suddenly found brand new courage, she leaped on top of Ember's shoulder and let out a low growl. Rowan grinned at the show, shooting another jet of light toward Ember's chest. She successfully dodged it, but in the same breath, Maia leaped off her shoulder and hurtled herself toward the angry Vala on the other side of the room.

Rowan was quicker, though. She saw the tiny creature coming and sent a quick hex in her direction, hitting her directly in the back. Maia crumpled like a rag doll on the floor, laying completely motionless.

Ember sucked in a breath and forced herself not to cry out, not to show any weakness. "Maia," she breathed. She set her eyes back on Rowan, who was now grinning like a maniac.

"I've always thought draics made terrible guard dogs," she laughed.

Ember felt all of her hope waning. She was in a giant

manor, miles away from home, and completely alone. No one was coming to rescue her. No one could help her. Fen and Killian were miles away, waiting for her to return successfully, and she couldn't even tell them anything was wrong. Her chest felt heavy as she weighed her options. She only had two, as far as she could tell. Either surrender now and pray to the gods that whoever was in charge was merciful, or go down fighting.

She planted her feet firmly on the floor, prepared to fight until she had absolutely nothing left in her, when a loud explosion sounded from the entryway behind her. Rowan's face screwed up in confusion, and Ember quickly turned around to see who—or what—had made the loud noise.

Walking in through the dust floating through the air was Killian and Fen. Killian had more of a limp than a walk, but he still stood tall, looking every bit of an aristocrat walking into the ballroom. Fen glided a few steps in front of him, anger and determination etched on his face. Ember felt the invisible cord tighten further and strum wildly the closer they got, and she felt the familiar comfort of home wash over her.

"Oh, lovely," Rowan drawled, rolling her eyes. "The big bad wolf and his little pet, how charming."

Ember expected some sort of sarcastic quip from Killian, but his mouth was set in a straight line. His eyes narrowed on the girl on the other side of the room, and she could see small sparks bouncing off the palms of his hands. He looked toward Ember, noticing the blood trickling down the side of her face. For a moment, fear flashed across his eyes, but it was immediately replaced with rage. In a matter of moments, the room was filled with bright lights again, and it was all Ember could do to duck out of the way and get to somewhere that wasn't smack in the middle of the proverbial battlefield.

Ember took off toward Fen, planting her feet between him and Killian. Fen threw a wild hex that barely missed the side of Rowan's head, and she retaliated with a curse that hit the archway behind them, shattering it into a million pieces.

"Em, is that blood?" Fen asked as he shot a quick glance at the side of her face.

"No?" she replied.

"That's not a question you're supposed to answer with another question." Fen pushed her gently a few steps behind him and quickly cast, "*Detenair,*" toward Rowan, who blocked it with very little effort. "I thought we agreed to tell each other when we were planning on putting our lives in imminent danger," he quipped as they both quickly ducked behind the shield charm Killian had just cast.

"That is a very specific promise I don't remember making," she replied, a small smirk playing at the corner of her mouth.

He shot a small smile her way, the first genuine smile she had seen from him in so long, and she felt like her heart was simultaneously shattering and mending itself at the same time. For just a moment, he was the fourteen-year-old boy who had greeted her in the kitchen the summer before, all smiles without a care in the world. The boy she tried so desperately to push away. The same boy who refused to let her. Her attention was pulled away when she heard Killian let out a cry and land on the floor, one arm cradling his ribs. Rowan had hit him with what seemed to be a fairly mild hex, but there was already too much damage from the Cu Sidhe. He was still losing blood, the crimson liquid soaking through the makeshift bandage Fen had apparently tried to wrap around his abdomen, and Ember knew he couldn't continue fighting like this.

She threw every hex she could think of in Rowan's direction, trying to distract her from the easy prey on the ground behind her. Her plan was successful, if only for a moment, and Rowan focused her attention back on the redhead flailing wildly in the middle of the room. Ember took steady steps forward with every blow she struck, successfully backing Rowan into a corner of the grand ballroom. She took a breath, thinking that she finally had the upper hand, as Fen showed up beside her.

It only took one second—one measly moment—for all of her hope to be shattered.

The next few seconds seemed to happen in slow motion. Fen shot her a smile, both of them taking their eyes off Rowan for only a moment, and she saw her chance. She shot a single curse at Fen, with perfect precision, and hit him directly in the chest. His eyes grew wide, and his mouth hung open, gasping for air that he couldn't get into his lungs. He reached a hand out for Ember, missing her by centimeters, and then his body hit the floor with a sickening thud. He lay motionless on the cold tile, and Ember felt like she had died alongside him.

"Fen!" she cried as her knees hit the floor beside his limp body. "Fen, no!" She didn't bother to hide the tears streaming down her face as she gasped for air. Her head flew around, lavender eyes locking with Rowan's, and jumped to her feet, turning on the girl in the corner.

"Leave my brother alone!" she choked out as she advanced toward her, but Rowan was quicker. She seemed completely unfazed by the lifeless body only a few yards in front of her as she slung her arm wildly toward Ember. Streams of light flew around her, narrowly missing her limbs, and Ember backpedaled, unable to keep up with the speed at which she was being attacked. She reached the point again where her brother lay on the floor and tripped over his foot. She hit the ground, and her head made a sickening crunch against the tile. Her vision blurred, and black spots flashed in front of her as she tried to focus her eyes.

"Such a pity," Rowan said calmly, standing in front of her, "to waste Vala magic. You could've been so powerful."

Ember threw herself on top of her brother, burying her head in his breathless chest. It was over. She did everything she could, but it wasn't enough. Killian was bleeding to death, Fen wasn't breathing anymore, and she would rather die than live in a world without them in it. It felt pointless. Ember closed her eyes tightly as she heard Rowan utter the curse, the curse she knew was aimed to kill.

"*ASASIENATO!*" she cried, but when Ember looked up, instead of a jet of red light hurtling her way, it was bouncing off a shield of bright blue and going straight back toward Rowan, hitting right above her head. A spell Ember couldn't place was whispered behind her, hitting Rowan in the chest, and Ember watched as she crumpled to the floor.

Ember took a shaky breath and spun her head around to see a familiar face standing behind her. "Maren!" she breathed. "How did you—"

"We don't have time," she said sternly, motioning for the girl to move away from her brother. Ember was reluctant but ultimately gave in and sat back on the floor, hugging her knees as she pulled them to her chest.

"He's dead," she whispered, tears beginning to stream down her face again. "He's dead, and it's all my fault."

Maren shook her head and whispered, "*Aguacura,*" and a small stream of water came down from her hand and swirled around his chest. "Not dead," she whispered. "Just stunned." And then almost immediately, Fen's eyes shot open, and he gasped for air.

Ember launched herself at her brother, sobbing once again into his chest. "I thought I lost you," she cried. "I thought you were gone."

Fen let out a weak laugh. "Can't get rid of me that easy." He propped himself up on his elbow and tried to look around the half-destroyed room. "Is Killian alright?"

Ember's heart dropped as she remembered the blood covered boy in the back of the room. Her head shot up, and she took off across the cracked tile, dropping to her knees beside him. Maren was already there, working on closing the wounds running along his chest, and Ember did her best to stifle her sobs.

He looked lifeless. His skin was pale, and his lips were a shade of gray that could give his eyes a run for their money. His fingers felt like ice as she intertwined them with hers, and they were already beginning to turn blue.

"Can you help him?" she whispered to Maren, as she watched her hands rapidly move across the boy's chest.

"'I can heal the wounds"—she nodded—"but he's lost a lot of blood. I'm afraid there isn't much I can do about that."

At that moment, she felt a small nose nuzzle against her hand.

"Oh, Maia," she whispered, picking the baby draic up and squeezing her to her chest. She looked down and saw that Maia had dragged her bag over to her.

The creature hopped out of her embrace, burrowing into the bag. When she emerged, she had a small vial in her mouth and looked expectantly up at Ember.

Ember let out a small gasp. "Oh, you're so clever," she breathed. She took the vial from Maia's mouth and gave her a quick pat on the head before turning back to Maren, still busily working on the wounds on Killian.

"Draught of Fortitude," she whispered as she shoved it in the Merrow's direction.

"Prop his head up with your elbow," she instructed, "and tip it into his mouth." Ember did as told, cradling his cold head in her arms. "Now, run your fingers down his throat so he swallows it… Yes, yes, just like that, perfect!" Maren smiled.

Almost immediately, color came back to his skin. Within a few seconds, his eyes were fluttering open, campfire smoke staring back into fields of lavender. "Miss me, Starshine?" he said hoarsely.

Ember let out a small laugh as she wiped away the remaining tears pooled at the bottom of her lashes. "You boys will be the death of me," she whispered.

Fen made his way slowly over to the group and sat down beside Killian and Ember, leaning back on one elbow.

No one spoke, save for the quiet healing spells Maren was mumbling over open cuts and bruises, but Ember could feel the steady thrumming of the invisible cord as it reached from her chest and tightened, pulling her toward the boys at either side of her. It felt warm and safe, like something she had been searching for her whole life.

It felt like home.

CHAPTER 34

FOREVER AND ALWAYS

After everyone was properly healed and Maren felt like it was safe for them to travel, the trio collected the book, stowing it safely in Ember's bag, and made their way out of the destroyed manor. Ember hesitated for a moment at the threshold, gripping the side of the door as she chewed on the bottom of her lip.

"Everything alright, Em?" Fen asked as he furrowed his brow. "Does your head still hurt? We can rest a while longer if you need to."

Ember shook her head. "No, it's not that. It's just… It doesn't feel right." She nodded in the direction of the ballroom. "Leaving her here…" She turned her head to look into the room where Rowan's body still lay on the floor. "She has a mum who misses her something terrible," she whispered.

Killian and Fen glanced at each other and nodded. Maren conjured a stretcher, lifting the young girl's body on top of it. "She's only stunned, so it should wear off tomorrow," she whispered. "We can give her a better chance than leaving her here, though." She levitated it out the door, despite the young boys insisting they were capable, and the group made their way down the steep steps and away from the manor.

The walk through the forest was silent, everyone seeming to be lost in their thoughts. She thought back to her first day at Heksheim, how Rowan was so eager to befriend her and seemed to genuinely care, and wondered how she could've been so blind. The wedge Rowan drove between her and her brother, and her and Killian, made her nauseous. Fen must have noticed the way she was staring, because he slowed his gait to walk beside her.

"It wasn't your fault, you know," he said quietly, hands stuffed in his pockets.

"What?" she asked, pulling her head from her self-induced trance.

"Rowan," he said as he nodded toward the stretcher. "It wasn't your fault. None of it."

Ember shrugged. "I should've noticed something was off."

Killian let out a barking laugh from beside her. "How?" he asked. "In case you didn't notice, she had us all fooled. It wasn't just you. Someone lying to you is never your fault."

Ember chewed on the inside of her lip as she fidgeted with the pendant around her neck, tracing the indentions with the pad of her thumb. "The legend is about me," she whispered to everyone and no one.

Fen shrugged. "It's over now. No more dark books, no more plotting friends."

"Is it, though?" she sighed. "I have a feeling it's much bigger than the book." She took in a ragged breath as she traced the cold metal against her collarbone. "Something tells me this is only the beginning."

"So, we burn that bridge when we get to it." Killian smirked from beside her, elbowing her gently in the arm. "But your fate isn't sealed, no matter what some old prophecy says. Not if I have anything to say about it." Something about the way he spoke, the way his brow furrowed and his jawline tensed, told her he wasn't lying.

"Ahem," Fen interjected, "*we*. If you think you're both

411

doing this without me, you've lost your bloody minds. We're family."

Family.

"They'd be proud, ya know." Fen smiled.

"Who?" Ember asked, but she had a feeling she already knew.

"Your mum and dad," he replied. "They'd be really proud…"

Ember smiled, a genuine smile for the first time in what felt like weeks, and dropped the hold on her necklace, reaching to grab her brother's hand instead. "They would be." She nodded. "I just hope *our* mum and dad here are equally as proud and don't ground us for the rest of eternity."

Ember wasn't sure she had ever seen him smile quite so bright. Tears pricked at the corners of his eyes that he didn't bother to swat away, and he squeezed her hand a little tighter.

"Our mum and dad," he whispered with a grin, like he had just received the best Yule gift he could ever imagine.

Killian laughed and reached over to swat his friend on the back of the head. "Quit your blubberin'," he barked. "You got another sister, not a new AirWave."

Ember knew he was joking, but even if she didn't, the huge grin plastered on his face would've been a dead giveaway.

The group made it to the cove where Kaan and Asherah were already waiting for them. They gave Ember a solemn nod as she walked straight toward them, fishing *The Book of Shadows* out of her bag. It felt heavier than she remembered as she gripped it in her sweaty palms. She turned it over in her hands a few times, running her fingers over all of the intricate carvings in the leather, then promptly handed it to the Merrow in front of her.

"Maren said you would know what to do with it," she whispered, arm stretched out. "She said you could take care of it."

Asherah nodded, gently taking the book from Ember's hand and pulling it to her chest.

"Can you destroy it?" Fen asked hesitantly. "We never did figure out the proper way to do it." He shoved his hands in his pockets, waiting patiently.

"I'm afraid not," Asherah replied nonchalantly, looking each of the children in the eye.

Ember furrowed her brow. "But Maren said—"

"That we could take care of it," she interjected, "and we can. But I'm afraid that does not mean we can destroy it."

"You can't?" Killian asked as he crossed his arms over his chest. "Or you won't?"

Asherah looked up at him, arching her brow. "I don't appreciate what you're insinuating, Mr. Vargr."

Killian turned a brilliant shade of crimson as he averted his eyes and stuffed his hands in his pockets. Fen let out a quiet laugh, earning him a swift elbow to the ribs. Ember shot both of them a warning glance before turning her attention back to Asherah.

"There is some magic," she continued, "so powerful, and so dark, that it cannot be destroyed. As much as we would like to believe the world would be a better place without the darkness, that is not always the case. There is a delicate balance between the light and the dark, a fine line that I'm sure you witnessed today." Her eyes fell to the stretcher on the ground behind the group, and Ember felt her chest tighten.

"How many people believe this is right?" Ember whispered, staring at the body of her former friend. "That this darkness is the way our world should be? That we are the only beings worthy of magic?"

"Not everyone," Asherah replied. "Some of us choose love over power." She nodded in Killian and Fen's direction with a small smile. "Indeed, most of us do."

Ember swallowed the lump forming in her throat as tears pricked her eyes. She would never forget how lucky she was to have people who loved her. Not in spite of her differences, but because of them.

"So, while I cannot destroy it indefinitely," Asherah said gracefully, "I can put it somewhere to make sure it never ends up in the wrong hands again." She handed the book to Kaan, who was standing stoically beside her, and he turned around promptly, diving into the waves that barreled toward the shore.

All of a sudden, Ember felt like a giant weight had been lifted off her chest, and she could finally breathe again. "Thank you," she whispered.

"Thank you, Miss Lothbrok," Asherah replied with a small smile. "I'm glad to see you decided to take the road less traveled."

The trio said their goodbyes to Maren, who tried to insist that she follow them at least to the edge of the forest and made their way back home. Their walk through the forest was uneventful, and at one point, Ember was certain she was going to fall asleep standing up. Killian had her lean against him with his arm draped over her shoulder as Fen led the way, guiding them out of the foreboding darkness. They parted ways at the Echopoint, and by the time Fen and Ember reached their house, the moon was just barely beginning to set for the night. They walked up the long drive, watching the sky get soaked in pinks and purples, and Ember drank in the peace that washed over her.

"See," Fen said quietly. "Told you we'd beat the sun."

Despite Maren leaving her at the edge of the forest, Rowan's body was never found. The story that was circulating the island was that she had wandered into the forest at some point and met the same demise that her father and brother

LEGEND OF THE WILDLINGS

had. All of the Kitts, Ember included, attended the memorial that following Saturday.

Mrs. O'Rourke gave a beautiful eulogy, reminiscing on her daughter's childhood and speaking kindly of all of her friends. Eira was a blubbering mess during the whole affair, squeezing each of her children one by one.

"Oh, thank Odin it wasn't one of you," she whispered as she dabbed her eyes. "I just couldn't bear the thought of picking out a casket for any of you and lowering you into the ground."

Ember was certain she had said something else, but she couldn't make out any of the words after the tears started falling again. She glanced around the room and took note that the whole island seemed to be in attendance. Parents and friends, professors and shopkeepers, and not a dry eye was among them. Her eyes met Professor Bjorn's, and he gave her a solemn nod before turning back toward the grieving mother.

After, she followed her family outside and found a tall tree to sit under while the rest of the island mingled, giving their condolences to Mrs. O'Rourke. She took in a shuddering breath as she felt tears run down her face, quickly wiping them away with the back of her hand. Fen and Killian made their way toward her and sat down, and she felt her brother nudge her in the arm with his elbow.

"You're allowed to be sad, ya know," he whispered.

Ember shrugged. "I don't really know why I am," she whispered. "I mean, she tried to kill me. She tried to kill you. I should be thankful, not crying."

"She was your friend," he replied. "You are allowed to grieve that loss, even if it didn't play out the way you imagined it would."

Ember nodded her head, allowing a few more tears to escape before she brushed them off her cheek. She grabbed both the boys' hands and gave them a gentle squeeze. Grief was a fickle thing, but at least she didn't have to ride that wave alone. Not this time.

AFTER A WEEK OR SO, the trio seemed to get back in their regular groove. School was spent with Ember trying to convince the boys that, "Yes, you do have to study for final exams," and Fen and Killian causing mischief at every turn. Ember attended every Rukr game for the rest of the season, cheering on her brother and best friend while her knuckles turned white clutching the bench. Their weekends were spent in the orchard where Ember practiced flying, and they spent lazy afternoons eating apples under the trees while Maia napped in her lap.

Killian became a permanent fixture at the Kitt Farm, spending most of his weekends bunking with Fen and driving Eira up a wall, though Ember caught her smiling ear to ear several times as the boys wrestled in the sitting room. Ember passed her exams with flying colors, both of the boys barely skating by with a passing grade. Much to Ember's annoyance, however, all of the teachers gave them a pass, considering they had just lost a classmate a few weeks prior.

Ember didn't talk to them for two days.

On the last night of school, after supper was cleaned up and all the chores were done, the trio—with permission from Eira and Otto—made the short hike to the shore at the end of their property. They threw blankets on the sand and laid back contently, gazing at the stars above them. Ember let out a heavy sigh, followed by a genuine smile, which had become a surprising habit these days.

"What is it?" Killian asked, rolling over to prop himself up on his elbow.

"Me and my dad used to do this," she said as she motioned to the sky. "We would come out late at night and just stare at the stars. Out of all of the memories I have of him, that one is the most vivid." She let out a breathy laugh. "I was so convinced that I would never be whole again. I tried so long to piece together who I was without them that I almost missed it."

"Missed what?" Fen asked as he sat up.

Ember lifted herself off the blanket, leaning back on both her elbows. "A family." She smiled. "I thought I wasn't worthy, that I had to put myself back together first. I spent so long looking for the missing pieces to a puzzle that was already complete."

Fen let out a small laugh as he grabbed his sister's hand. "I'm afraid you're stuck with us, Em."

"Forever?" she asked.

Killian grabbed her other hand, giving it a gentle squeeze. "And always, Starshine."

THE END

Honduran-American Young Adult author with a penchant for adventure. When Brittney isn't writing about magical schools and sarcastic Norse witches and wizards, she can often be found burrowed in her nest on the couch with her emotional support water bottle, reading Dramione Fan Fiction. Brittney lives in the East Tennessee mountains and spends her days chasing dogs, kids and chickens around their small homestead with her husband. She loves to crochet, explore, and get lost down winding dirt roads. *Legend of the Wildlings* is her first novel- born of her rich Honduran, Norse and Irish ancestry- and she hopes to have the privilege of writing about magical worlds for the rest of her life. If you enjoy reading, writing and incoherent rants, Brittney can be found on both Instagram and TikTok @bbrewerauthor for your entertainment.

Made in the USA
Las Vegas, NV
05 April 2024

88295891R00249